Uncommon Type

Uncommon Type

SOME STORIES

Tom Hanks

PHOTOGRAPHS BY
KEVIN TWOMEY

RANDOM HOUSE
LARGE PRINT

Copyright © 2017 by Clavius Base, Inc.

All rights reserved.
Published in the United States of America by Random House Large Print in association with Alfred A. Knopf, a division of Penguin Random House LLC, New York, and distributed in Canada by Random House of Canada, a division of Penguin Random House Canada Limited, Toronto.

"Alan Bean Plus Four" first appeared in **The New Yorker** on October 24, 2014.

**Cover images by FlamingPumpkin/ iStock/ Getty Images
Cover design by Oliver Munday
Emoji art on pages 19–20 supplied by EmojiOne**

The Library of Congress has established a Cataloging-in-Publication record for this title.

ISBN: 978-0-5255-9050-7

www.randomhouse.com/largeprint

FIRST LARGE PRINT EDITION

Printed in the United States of America

10   9   8   7   6   5   4   3

This Large Print edition published in accord with the standards of the N.A.V.H.

For Rita and all the kids.

Because of Nora.

Contents

———

CONTENTS

Uncommon Type

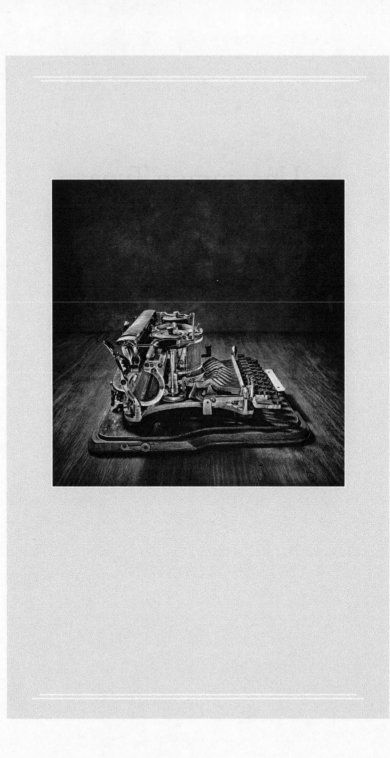

Three Exhausting Weeks

DAY 1

Anna said there was only one place to find a meaningful gift for MDash—the Antique Warehouse, not so much a place for old treasures as a permanent swap meet in what used to be the Lux Theater. Before HBO, Netflix, and the 107 other entertainment outlets bankrupted the Lux, I sat for many hours in that once-splendid cinema palace and watched movies. Now it's stall after stall of what passes for antiques. Anna and I looked into every one of them.

MDash was about to become a naturalized U.S. citizen, which was as big a deal for us as it was for him. Steve Wong's grandparents were naturalized in the forties. My dad had escaped the low-grade thugs that were East European Communists in the 1970s, and, way back when, Anna's ancestors rowed boats across the North Atlantic, seeking to pillage whatever was pillageable in the New World. The Anna family legend is that they found Martha's Vineyard.

Mohammed Dayax-Abdo was soon to be as American as Abdo Pie, so we wanted to get him something vintage, an **objet d'patriotic** that would carry the heritage and humor of his new country. I thought the old Radio Flyer wagon in the second warehouse stall was perfect. "When he has American kids, he'll pass that wagon on to them," I said.

But Anna was not about to purchase the first antique we came across. So we kept on hunting. I bought a forty-eight-star American flag, from the 1940s. The flag would remind MDash that his adoptive nation is never finished building itself—that good citizens have a place somewhere in her fruited plain just as more stars can fit in the blue field above those red and white stripes. Anna approved, but kept searching, seeking a present that would be far more special. She wanted unique, nothing less than one of a kind. After three hours, she decided the Radio Flyer was a good idea after all.

Rain started falling just as we were pulling out of the parking lot in my VW Bus. We had to drive slowly back to my house because my wiper blades are so old they left streaks on the windshield. The storm went on well into the evening, so rather than drive home, Anna hung around, played my mother's old mixtapes (which I'd converted to CDs), cracking up over Mom's eclectic taste, in the segues from the Pretenders to the O'Jays to Taj Mahal.

When Iggy Pop's "Real Wild Child" came on, she asked, "Do you have any music from the last twenty years?"

I made pulled-pork burritos. She drank wine. I drank beer. She started a fire in my Franklin stove, saying she felt like a pioneer woman on the prairie. We sat on my couch as night fell, the only lights being the fire and the audio levels on my sound system bounding from green to orange and, occasionally, red. Distant sheet lightning flashed in the storm miles and miles away.

"You know what?" she said to me. "It's Sunday."

"I do know that," I told her. "I live in the moment."

"I admire that about you. Smart. Caring. Easygoing to the point of sloth."

"You've gone from compliments to insults."

"Change **sloth** to **languorousness**," she said, sipping wine. "Point is I like you."

"I like you, too." I wondered if this conversation was going someplace. "Are you flirting with me?"

"No," Anna said. "I'm propositioning you. Totally different thing. Flirting is fishing. Maybe you hook up, maybe you don't. Propositioning is the first step in closing a deal."

Understand that Anna and I have known each other since high school (St. Anthony Country Day! Go, Crusaders!). We didn't date, but hung out in the same crowd, and liked each other. After a few years of college, and a few more of taking care of my mom, I got my license and pretended to make a living in real estate for a while. One day she walked into my office because she needed to rent a space for her graphics business and I was the only agent she could trust because I once dated a friend of hers and was not a jerk when we broke up.

Anna was still very pretty. She never lost her lean, rope-taut body of a triathlete, which, in fact, she had been. For a day, I showed her some available spaces, none of which she wanted for reasons that made little sense to me. I could tell she was still just as driven, focused, and tightly wound as she had been at SACD. She had too keen an eye for the smallest of details and left no stones unturned, uninspected, unrecorded, or unreplaced if they needed replacing. Adult Anna was exhausting. Adult Anna was no more my type than Teen Anna had been.

Funny, then, that she and I became such solid

friends, much closer than when we were kids. I am one of those lazy-butt loners who can poke my way through a day and never feel a second has been wasted. In fact, as soon as I sold my mom's house and parked the money in investments, I walked away from my fake business and settled into the Best Life Imaginable. Give me a few loads of laundry to do and a hockey game on the NHL channel and I'm good for an entire afternoon. In the time I spend lollygagging over my whites and colors, Anna will drywall her attic, prepare her taxes, make her own fresh pasta, and start up a clothing exchange on the Internet. She sleeps in fits and starts from midnight to dawn and has the energy to go full throttle all day. I sleep dead to the world as long as possible and take a nap every day at 2:30 p.m.

"I am going to kiss you now." Anna did just as she said.

We had never done that, other than those pecks on cheeks that go with brief hugs. That night, she was offering a whole new version of herself, and I tensed up, confused.

"Hey, relax," she whispered. Her arms were around my neck. She smelled damn good and tasted of wine. "It's the Sabbath. A day of rest. This is not going to be **work**."

We kissed again, this time with me a collected and invested participant. My arms went around her and pulled her close. We leaned into each other and loosened up. We found each other's necks and worked our way back to our mouths. I had not kissed a woman like that in close to a year, not since the Evil Girlfriend Mona not only dumped me but stole cash from my billfold (Mona had problems, but kissing? She was fabulous).

"Atta baby," Anna sighed.

"Shabbat shalom," I sighed back. "We should have done that years ago."

"I think we could use some time spent skin on skin," Anna whispered. "Take off your clothes."

I did. When she took off hers, I was a goner.

DAY 2

My Monday morning breakfast was buckwheat pancakes, chorizo sausage, a huge bowl of berries, and **percolated** coffee. Anna opted for some herbal tea I had long ago tucked away in the pantry and a tiny bowl of nuts she chopped up with a cleaver. She counted out eight blueberries to round out her nutritious breakfast. I shouldn't say that neither of us wore clothes as we ate, as it will make us sound like nudists, but the fact is we tumbled out of bed without the slightest inhibitions.

As she was getting dressed for work she told me we were signing up for scuba diving lessons.

"We are?" I asked her.

"Yep. We are going to get certified," she said. "And you need to get some workout clothes. Running shoes and sweats. Go to the Foot Locker in the Arden Mall. Meet me for lunch at my office right after. Bring the wagon and the flag for MDash and we'll wrap them."

"Okay," I said.

"I'll make dinner at my place tonight, we'll watch a documentary, then we are going to do in my bed what we spent last night doing in yours."

"Okay," I repeated.

DAY 3

Anna ended up taking me to Foot Locker, making me try on five different pairs of shoes (we settled on cross-trainers) and four versions of sweatpants and tops (Nike). Then we bought food and drinks for the party Anna wanted to throw for MDash. She said my house was the only place for such a bash.

Around noon, MDash was one of sixteen hundred soon-to-be Americans standing on the floor of the Sports Arena, right hands raised as they swore allegiance to America—new citizens who would preserve, protect, and defend what was now their Constitution as much as it was for the President of the United States. Steve Wong, Anna, and I were in the bleachers, witnessing the naturalization of a sea of immigrants, their skins all the different colors of human nature. The sight was glorious and made the three of us emotional—Anna the most. She wept, her face pressed into my chest.

"It's . . . so . . . beautiful," she kept sobbing. "God . . . I love . . . this country."

MDash's Home Depot co-workers who could get the time off showed up at my place with a lot of cheap American flags, purchased with their employee discounts. Steve Wong set up a karaoke machine and we made MDash sing songs with "America" in the lyrics. "American Woman." "American Girl." "Spirit of America" by the Beach Boys is actually about a car, but we made him sing it anyway. We used the Radio Flyer wagon as an ice chest and six of us planted the forty-eight-star flag like we were the Marines on Iwo Jima, MDash being the guy in the very front.

The party went long, until only the four of us were left watching the moonrise, listening to Old Glory flitter and flap on its pole. I had just opened another beer from the slosh of ice in the wagon when Anna took the can out of my hands.

"Easy, baby," she said. "You're going to need

all your capabilities, just as soon as those two go home."

An hour later, Steve Wong and MDash headed out, the new American citizen singing "A Horse with No Name" (by the band America). As soon as Steve's car was out of the driveway, Anna took my hand, leading me to the backyard. She put cushions down on the soft grass and we lay there, kissing, then, well, you know, putting my capabilities to the test.

DAY 4

Anna runs whenever she can jam a few miles into forty minutes, a habit she was going to force upon me. She took me to one of her routes, an uphill path that loops around Vista Point and back, and told me to get going. She would zip along ahead of me and meet me coming back down, knowing I'd never keep up with her.

My exercise is an option-only affair. Occasionally, I'll ride my old three-speed to Starbucks or play a few rounds of Frisbee golf (I used to belong to a league). This morning I was chuffing up the dirt road, Anna so far ahead I didn't see her, my feet breaking in my new cross-trainers (note to self: move up a half size). My blood was surging up and down my body in unfamiliar fury, so my shoulders and neck tensed up and my head pounded. When Anna came charging down from Vista Point, she was clapping her hands.

"Atta baby!" she called out, passing me. "Good first effort!"

I spun around to follow her. "My thighs are on fire!"

"They are rebelling," she called back over her shoulder. "In time they will submit!"

Anna reorganized my kitchen when I was in the shower. She thought I kept my pans and lids in the wrong cupboards, and why was my flatware drawer so far from the dishwasher? I had no answer. "Let's get going. Can't be late for our first scuba lesson."

The Scuba School smelled of rubber wet suits and the chlorinated pool. We filled out papers and were given workbooks to study, along with the schedule for our classroom sessions, as well as options for the date of our open water certification. Anna pointed to a Sunday four weeks away and reserved our berths on the boat on the spot.

We went to the Viva Verde Salad Cafe for a lunch of salads made of salads with salad on the side, after which I wanted to go home for a nap. But Anna said she needed my help moving some stuff around her house, a chore she had been putting off. This was barely true, almost a lie. She actually wanted me to help her rewallpaper her hallway and home office, which meant I had to move her computer, printer, scanners, and graphic equipment, then do her bidding all afternoon.

I never made it home that evening. We had dinner in—vegetarian lasagna with vegetables on the side—and watched a movie on Netflix about smart women with idiot boyfriends.

"Look, baby," Anna said. "This is about us!" Then she cackled and reached into my pants without so much as kissing me. I either was the luckiest man in the world or was being played for a sucker. After Anna let me reach into her pants as well I still wasn't sure which.

DAY 5

Anna had to work at her office. She employs four no-nonsense women and an intern who is an at-risk girl from high school. Last year she landed a contract for doing the graphics for a textbook publisher, steady work but as boring as wallpapering for a living. I told her I was going home.

"Why?" she asked. "You've got nothing to do today."

"I'm going to get a run in," I said, making that up on the spur of the moment.

"Atta baby," she told me.

I went home and did put on the cross-trainers, then jogged around the neighborhood. Mr. Moore, a retired cop whose house shares my back fence, saw me running by and hollered out, "What the fuck got into you?"

"A woman!" I yelled back, and not only was that true, but I felt good saying it. When a man thinks of a lady and looks forward to telling her that he ran forty minutes, well, partner, he's living in Girlfriend Territory.

Yes. I had a girlfriend. A girlfriend changes a man from the shoes he exercises in right up to how he cuts his hair (which Anna did the very next day, in front of my barber)—alterations I was due. Fooled by the adrenaline of romance, I ran farther than my body could stand.

Anna called just as I had given up on a nap because my calves were as tight as beer cans. She told me to get over to her acupuncturist; she'd call to arrange an immediate treatment.

The East Valley Wellness Oasis is in a minimall/professional building with underground parking. Driving my VW Bus, which has no power steering, around and around those descending circular ramps took physical effort. Figuring out the multiple elevators of the facility taxed my brain. When I finally found office 606-W, I filled in five pages of a Wellness questionnaire, sitting beside a fountain that made more noise from its electric pump than from its cascading water element.

Do you accept the practice of Visualization? Sure, why not? **Are you open to Guided Meditation?** I don't see how it could hurt. **Explain your reasons for seeking treatment. Please be specific.** My girlfriend told me to bring you my tired, my poor, my balled-up leg muscles yearning to be freed.

I handed in my answers and waited. Eventually, a guy in a white lab coat called my name and took me into a treatment room. As I stripped down to my skivvies he read over my paperwork.

"Anna says your legs are bothering you?" he asked. He'd been working on Anna for the last three years.

"Yep," I said. "My calves, among other muscles in revolt."

"According to this," he said, tapping my paperwork, "Anna's your girlfriend."

"A new development," I told him.

"Good luck with that. Lay on your stomach." When he put the needles in me, my whole body tingled and my calves twitched uncontrollably. Before leaving the room, he hit play on an old CD boom box for my guided meditation. I heard a woman's voice tell me to clear my mind and think of a river. I sort of did that for half an hour, wanting to fall asleep, but couldn't because I had needles sticking in me.

Anna was waiting for me at my house, having made us a dinner of leafy plants with seeds and rice the color of dirt. Afterward, she rubbed my legs so hard I winced. Later, she said she had not made love five nights in a row since college, but was going to give it a whirl.

DAY 6

She had set the alarm on her phone for 5:45 a.m. because she had to get a lot done. She made me get up, too, allowed me a single cup of coffee, then made me put on my running clothes.

"My calves still hurt," I told her.

"Only because you are telling yourself they hurt," she said.

"I don't want to run this morning," I complained.

"Tough titties, baby." She threw my sweatpants at me.

The morning was cold and misty. "Perfect for roadwork," she said. She forced me to imitate her twelve-minute stretching routine right there in my driveway, setting a timer on her phone with a tone that **bing**-ed every thirty seconds. There were twenty-four body positions I had to hold, each one stretching some sinew or muscle inside me, each one making me wince, cuss out loud, and get light-headed.

"Atta baby," she said. Then she explained the route we would take around my neighborhood, twice for her, once for me. Mr. Moore was getting his morning paper from his front lawn just as I was running by.

"Was that your woman? Who ran by a minute ago?" he called to me. I was panting so hard I could only nod. "What the fuck she see in you?"

A few minutes later, Anna lapped me, spanking my buttocks as she passed. "Atta baby!"

I was home and in the shower when she joined me. We kissed a lot and touched each other in our wonderful places. She instructed me on how to scrub her back and told me to come to her office at lunch so we could study our scuba workbook. I had yet to read the first few pages, but she had already completed half of it. When she had the time is beyond me.

I spent the afternoon hanging around her office, answering multiple-choice questions about scuba equipment and its uses, scrolling through some real estate listings (I still dabble), and trying to amuse the women who were bent over their graphic work. No dice. All this while Anna took a long conference call with a client in Fort Worth,

Texas, designed new title pages for a series of textbooks, proofread three projects, helped her at-risk intern with her geometry homework, reorganized a supply closet, and completed the second half of the scuba assignments. We had yet to take our first classroom session.

Not that it mattered. We were the only students. We watched videos about the glorious underwater world, then got into the pool. We stood in the shallow end while Vin, our instructor, explained to us every piece of the self-contained underwater breathing apparatus. That took a long time, mostly because Anna had at least five questions for every bit of gear. Finally, Vin had us put the regulators in our mouths, drop to our knees so our heads were submerged, suck in the metallic-tasting pressurized air, and blow out bubbles. The class ended with us taking a water fitness test by swimming ten laps. Anna went to the task like an Olympian and was out of the pool and drying off in a few minutes. I swam a languid breaststroke, finishing a distant second in a race of two.

Afterward, we drove to the East Village Market Mall to meet Steve Wong and MDash at Ye Olde Sweet Shoppe for milkshakes. Anna had a small cup of sugar-free nondairy yogurt with a dusting of real cinnamon. Sitting there, enjoying our treats, Anna tucked her hand in mine, a gesture of affection that did not go unnoticed.

In her bed that night, Anna was going through her pre-sleep iPad scroll when I got a text from Steve Wong.

SWong: U boffing A???

I pinched out my reply.

Moonwalker7: Your bizniz?
SWong: Yes/no?
Moonwalker7: 😁
SWong: U Nsane??????
Moonwalker7: 🛏️🏃🚀🎯🏹‼️🏁😊

Then MDash joined the chain—

FACEOFAMERICA:
Moonwalker7: I was seduced
FACEOFAMERICA: "when cooks fuck the stew burns"
Moonwalker7: who says that? The village shaman?
FACEOFAMERICA: "when coaches fuck the team loses" Vince Lombardi

And so it went. Steve Wong and MDash saw no good coming out of the pairing of Anna and me. Too bad! That very night Anna and I went at it like stew cooks in Green Bay, Wisconsin, hell-bent on pleasure.

😌

DAY 7

"Should we have a chat about our relationship?"

That was **me** asking. I was standing in Anna's kitchenette, wrapped in only a towel after a shower, plunging her Swiss press coffee apparatus for my morning elixir. She had been up for an hour and a half and was already in her running togs. Luckily, my cross-trainers were back at my place, so no marathon training for me.

"Do you **want** to have a chat about our relationship?" she asked, cleaning up the few outstanding coffee grounds that had fallen onto her surgically spotless countertop.

"Are we an **item**?" I asked.

"What do **you** think?" she asked back.

"Do you think of me as your **boyfriend**?"

"Do you think of me as your **girlfriend**?"

"Is either one of us going to make a declarative statement?"

"How should **I** know?"

I sat down and took a sip of coffee that was too strong. "Can I have some milk for this?" I asked.

"Do you think that gunk is good for you?" She handed me a small bottle of nonpreservative almond milk, the kind that has to be used up in only a few days, the kind that is sold as "milk" but is actually liquefied nuts.

"Could you buy real milk so I can have it in my coffee?"

"Why are you so demanding?"

"Is asking for milk a demand?"

She smiled and took my face in her hands. "Do you think you're the man for me?"

She kissed me. I was about to make a declarative statement, but she sat on my lap and undid the towel I was wearing. She didn't get in her morning run.

DAYS 8–14

Being Anna's boyfriend was like training to be a Navy SEAL while working full-time in an Amazon fulfillment center in the Oklahoma Panhandle in tornado season. Something was going on every moment of every day. My 2:30 naps were a thing of the past.

I was exercising regularly, not just the morning

jogs but also swimming in scuba class, doing yoga stretches for what grew into a half hour, and joining Anna in a hot-room spinning class that was so taxing I upchucked. The number of errands we went on was maddening, and they never came from a to-do list or shopping helper app, but were all spur of the moment, ad hoc. Incessant. If unoccupied with work, working out, or working me over in the sack, Anna was making something, looking for something, asking to see what the store had in the back, driving to an estate sale across town, or going to Home Depot to ask Steve Wong about a belt sander for me, as the top of the redwood picnic table in my backyard needed smoothing. Every day—all day—I spent following her orders, which included precise driving instructions.

"Make the next left. Don't get off here. Take Webster Avenue. Why are you turning right **now**? Don't go past the school! It's almost three o'clock! The kids are just getting out!"

She organized a rock-climbing demonstration for Steve Wong, MDash, and me at a newly opened adventure superstore that had a climbing wall as well as an indoor rushing river to demonstrate white-water canoeing and a skydiving chamber—a huge fan that blew straight up a silo with so much force it simulated free fall for helmeted customers. Need I say that in one evening the four of us did all of them? We were there until closing. Steve Wong and MDash felt like he-men after a full day's work wearing those unisex aprons at Home Depot. I was exhausted, having been on Anna's overloaded schedule too long. I **needed** a nap.

We had time for protein snacks at the Energy Stand at the front of the store when Anna left for the restroom.

"What's it like?" MDash asked.

"What's what like?" I said.

"You and Anna. Sitting in a tree. K-I-S-S-I-N-G."

"You holding up?" Steve Wong asked. "You look exhausted."

"Well, I did just go faux skydiving."

MDash threw his uneaten half of a protein bar in the trash. "I used to look at you and think, That guy has figured it all out. He has his sweet little house with a nice backyard, he doesn't work for anyone but his own self. He could throw away his watch because he never **has** to be anywhere. To me, you were the America I hope to live in. Now, you kowtow to a boss lady. Alas."

"Really?" I said. "**Alas?**"

"Tell him that proverb you told me," Steve said.

"Something else the village shaman taught you?" I wondered.

"Actually, the village English teacher," MDash said. "To circle the globe, a ship needs only a sail, a wheel, a compass, and a clock."

"Wise words in a landlocked nation," I said. MDash grew up in the sub-Sahara.

"Anna is the compass," MDash explained. "You are the clock, but you keeping time with her means you've become unwound. Your hands are right only twice a day. We'll never know our longitude."

"Are you sure Anna isn't the sail?" I said. "Why can't I be the wheel and Steve be the compass? I don't follow this analogy."

"Let me put this into a language you can understand," Steve said. "We are like a TV show with diversity casting. African guy, him. Asian guy, me. Mongrel Caucasoid, you. Strong, determined woman, Anna, who would never let a man define her. You and her pairing off is like a story line from season eleven when the network is trying to keep us on the air."

I looked at MDash. "Are you getting this pop culture metaphor?"

"The gist of it. I have cable."

"The four of us," Steve explained, "are a perfect square. You taking to the sheets with Anna is going to misalign our geometry."

"How?"

"She makes things happen in our lives. Look at us. It's nearly midnight and we've been dangling and rowing and parachuting indoors. Stuff I'd never do on a school night. She's our catalyst."

"You've used sailboats, TV shows, geometry, and chemistry to point out why I shouldn't see Anna. And I still don't buy it."

"I predict tears," MDash said. "For you, for Anna, for all of us. Tears shooting out of our eyes."

"Look," I said, pushing away a protein brownie that actually tasted like a brownie. "One of these things is going to happen between me and my girlfriend. Yes, **girlfriend.**" I stole a look at Anna. She was far away chatting with an employee at a counter with a sign over it saying, INVEST IN ADVENTURE! "One. We get married, have kids, and you are their godfathers. Two. We break up in a public display of hurt feelings and recriminations. Both of you will have to choose sides: remain pals with me or go against the established rules of gender and stay friends with the woman. Three. She meets some other guy and dumps me. I become a melancholy loser, and **do not** say that's already what I am. Four. She and I part ways, amicably deciding to be **friends,** as seen on TV. What memories remain are those of pseudo–rock climbing et al. and the finest sex I've had in a lifetime. We can handle any of those fates because we are all big boy grown-ups. And admit it—if Anna wanted to make out with you like she does with me you'd be all for it."

"And **you'd** be the one predicting tears," Steve Wong said.

Just then Anna returned, waving a thick and glossy color brochure, a smile on her face. "Hey, guys!" she said. "We are to go to **Antarctica!**"

DAY 15

"We'll need the correct gear." Anna was dipping a fresh Rainbow Tea Company tea bag into a mug of hot water. She was in her running clothes as I was putting on my cross-trainers. "Long johns. Parkas and shells. Fleece pullovers. Waterproof boots. Walking sticks."

"Gloves," I added. "Hats." The trip to Antarctica was three months, many time zones, and thousands of miles away and Anna was already in Full Planning Mode. "Won't it be summer at the South Pole?" I asked.

"We won't make it to the pole. To the Antarctic Circle maybe, but only if the weather and sea cooperate. Still gonna be a lot of ice and wind."

We went outside to do forty-five minutes of stretches on my front lawn, getting our downward dogs and cobras wet from the morning dew. **Bing.**

The timer went off and I bent over, trying to touch my forehead to my kneecaps. Fat chance.

Anna was able to fold herself up like a card table. "You do realize," she said, "the Apollo astronauts went to Antarctica, to study the volcanoes." Anna knew of my **jones** for all things spaceman related. But she didn't know just how well I knew that stuff.

"They trained in Iceland, young lady. If any astronauts went to the South Pole, it was long after they retired from altering the course of human destiny by cheating death in NASA rocket ships." **Bing**. I tried to reach out and grab my ankles, setting my poor calves afire.

"Going to see penguins and whales and science stations," Anna said. "And B15K."

"What is B15K?"

"An iceberg the size of Manhattan, so large it's tracked via satellite. Broke off from the Ross Ice Shelf in 2003 and is independently moving counterclockwise around Antarctica. If the weather holds, we can book a chopper and land on it!"

Bing. That was the final exercise. She took off running. I tried to keep up with her but no way that was going to happen, not with her all pumped up about B15K.

As I trotted by Mr. Moore's house, he was just getting into his car, a travel mug of coffee in his hand. "That girlfriend of yours ran by a second ago. She was hauling ass."

After showers and a breakfast of avocado on toasted spelt bread, Anna took that belt sander she bought from Steve Wong and started grinding down my picnic table. I joined her with some sandpaper of my own.

"After you take it down to the grain, you'll need to repaint this. Do you have paint?" I did. "You should have this done by tonight. Then come to my place. We'll have dinner and sex." Fine by me, is how I felt. "I have to go to work now." Before leaving she pointed out other wooden objects that needed sanding and paint as well—a bench, the back door to my kitchen, and the old shed where I keep my lawn toys and sports equipment. I spent the rest of the day on the work detail.

I was sweaty, dusty, and splattered with paint when Anna texted me.

AnnaGraphicControl: dinner in 15

I got over to her place in half an hour, but needed a shower before dinner. We ate in the living room—huge bowls of Vietnamese **pho**—watching two episodes of **Our Frozen Earth** on Blu-ray. For over three hours we learned all about the chinstrap penguins and crabeater seals that live only in **guess which part of our planet.**

I fell asleep before we got around to any sex.

DAY 16

Anna had scheduled an early morning scuba class without telling me.

Vin had us in full wet suits—the tanks, the weight belts, everything—sitting on our knees at the bottom of the deep end of the pool. We had to remove every piece of the scuba apparatus, including our masks, hold our breath, then put it all back on again. Afterward, Vin said I was behind in my workbook and had better get cracking.

"Why haven't you finished the workbook?" Anna wanted to know.

"A date with a belt sander took up my time."

Driving home, I felt a chalky tickle in the back of my throat, like I was getting a cold.

"Don't say you are getting a cold," Anna said. "If you tell yourself you are sick, you **allow** yourself to be sick."

Her phone went off and she took the call hands-free; it was one of her clients in Fort Worth. A fellow named Ricardo told jokes about color templates, making Anna laugh as she pulled into my driveway. She stayed in the car to finish that call. I went inside.

"We have to go to Fort Worth," she announced when she finally came into my kitchen. I was making chicken noodle soup from a packet.

"Why?" I asked.

"I have to hand-hold Ricardo through a presentation. That is not soup, by the way, that's a sack full of sodium."

"I'm allowing myself to be sick. Soup will help."

"That shit will kill you."

"I have to go to Fort Worth with you?"

"Why not? You aren't doing anything. We'll stay overnight and see the sights."

"Of Fort Worth?"

"It will be an adventure."

"My nose is running and I feel like a hive of bees are swarming in my head."

"You can make it stop if you stop saying such things," she said.

In response I sneezed, coughed, and blew my nose into a tissue. Anna just shook her head.

DAY 17

Here are the sights I saw in Fort Worth:

The huge airport. Jammed with so many travelers it seemed like the Texan economy had collapsed and the population was fleeing.

Baggage Claim. Under renovation and therefore a place of chaos and borderline fistfights. Anna had checked three suitcases, which were among the last to come shooting down the chute.

A bus. Painted all around in huge letters that said PONYCAR PONYCAR PONYCAR. PonyCar was a new travel option in competition with Uber and the rental companies. Anna had a voucher for a free weekend—why, I don't know. The bus took us to a lot filled with tiny cars also painted with the PonyCar logo. I have no idea where PonyCars are manufactured, but they are clearly designed for small people. The two of us and our luggage had to be squeezed into a vehicle sized to fit the two of us and one-third of our luggage.

The DFW Sun Garden Hotel. Not so much a hotel as a collection of efficiency suites and vending machines meant for business travelers with limited expense accounts. Once we were in our little room, I lay down. Anna changed into professional clothes while she was on her cell phone with Ricardo. She waved goodbye to me and was out the door, trailing her professional rolling bag behind her.

In a fog due to my lousy health, I could not get the TV to work. The cable system had a menu unfamiliar to me. All I could get on screen was the Sun Garden Hotel Channel, which showed the glories and wonders of all the Sun Garden Hotels in the world. New branches were opening soon in Evansville, Indiana; Urbana, Illinois; and Frankfurt, Germany. I could make no sense of the phone system, either. I kept getting the same main voice menu. I was hungry, so I dragged myself down to the "lobby" to shop in the vending machines.

The machines were in a separate little room shared with a small buffet table that held bowls of apples and dispensers of breakfast cereals. I took some of each. One of the vending machines sold pizza by the slice, another offered toiletries, including a few cold remedies. After four tries at getting the machine to accept my crinkled twenty-dollar bill, I bought some capsules, some pills, a few single-dose liquids and something in a small bottle called Boost-Blaster! that bragged of its megadose of antioxidants, enzymes, and whatever good stuff is in Swiss chard and certain fish.

Back up in the room, I made a cocktail of two of every purchase, tearing off the safety foil, figuring out the childproof caps, and chugging down the Boost-Blaster! in one pull.

DAY 18

I woke up with no idea where I was. I heard a shower running. I saw a crack of light from under a door and a stack of textbooks on the nightstand. The bathroom door flew open in a flash of illuminated steam.

"He's alive!" Anna was naked, drying herself off. She had already been out for a run.

"Am I?" My cold was no better. Not at all. The only new feeling I had was wooziness.

"You took all this stuff?" She waved at the small desk littered with the debris left over from my self-medication.

"Still sick," I said in feeble self-defense.

"Saying you are still sick makes you still sick."

"I feel so rotten your logic actually makes sense."

"You missed it, baby. Last night we went out for organic Mexican food. It was Ricardo's birthday. There were about forty of us and a piñata. After, we went to a racetrack and drove miniature hot rods. I called you, texted you, but nothing."

I grabbed my phone. Between 6:00 p.m. and 1:30 in the morning AnnaGraphicControl had called and texted me thirty-three times.

Anna started getting dressed. "You better pack. Gotta check out of here, and then go to Ricardo's office for a meeting. To the airport from there."

Anna piloted the PonyCar to an industrial park somewhere in Fort Worth. I sat in the reception area, feeling horrible, blowing my nose again and again, trying to focus on a book about astronaut Walt Cunningham on my Kobo digital reader, but

I was just too foggy. I played a game on my phone called 101, answering true/false and multiple-choice questions. True or false: President Woodrow Wilson used a typewriter in the White House. True! He hunted and pecked a speech on a Hammond Type-o-Matic, hoping to drum up support for World War I.

After a long sit I needed some air, so I took a slow walk around the industrial park. Every building looked the same and I got lost. I found my way back when, luckily, I spotted a parked Pony-Car that turned out to be ours.

Anna was there, cooling her heels with her clients, waiting for me. "Where were you?"

"Seeing the sights," I said. She introduced me to Ricardo and thirteen other textbook executives. I shook hands with none of them. I had a cold, you see.

Returning the PonyCar was as effortless as promised, but the courtesy bus to the airline terminal took forever to show up. To make our plane, Anna and I had to run through the DFW airport like two characters from a movie that was about either wacky lovers on vacation or federal agents trying to stop a terrorist attack. We did make the plane, but not in time to get seats together. Anna sat up front, I was way in the back. My clogged ears were killing me on departure and hurt even more hours later on descent.

On the way to my house, she stopped at a liquor store for a small bottle of brandy. She had me drink a large shot of the booze, then put me into bed with a pillow tuck and a kiss on my forehead.

DAYS 19 AND 20

I was ill, pure and simple, with bedrest and liquids being the only remedies, as has been the case with colds since the first Neanderthal came down with the sniffles.

Anna, though, had her own ideas. For two days she was on a mission to cure me sooner rather than gradually. She had me sit naked in a chair with my feet in a tub of cold water. She wired up my limbs to something akin to an EKG machine, made me take off any metal I was wearing, which was none, then flipped a switch. I felt nothing.

But in time, the water around my feet turned first murky, then brown, and then began to congeal until the tub looked like the most unappetizing Jell-O mold imaginable. The goop was so thick that pulling my bare feet out was like extracting myself from swamp mud. And the stuff stank!

"That's the bad juju coming out of you," Anna said as she flushed the slop down the toilet.

"Out of my feet?" I asked.

"Yes. It's proven. The bad food you eat, the body poisons and fats. They leach out of your feet."

"Can I go back to bed now?"

"Just until your steam shower."

"I don't have a steam shower."

"You will."

Anna installed a series of plastic curtains in my shower with a portable steam maker set on high. I sat in it on a footstool, sweating, until I was able to polish off three big bottles of weak tea of some kind. This took some time, as the tea tasted like gutter water and a man's bladder can only hold so much gutter water.

An exercise bicycle was delivered. Anna had me ride it every hour and a half for exactly twelve minutes, until I had worked up a sweat to prove I had raised my body temperature.

"This is to cook out the mucus and such," she said.

For three meals in a row she fed me bowls of watery stew with chunks of beets and celery.

She had me do one-hour, slow-stretch sessions from her iPad, but I had to move **exactly** as did the instructor on the video.

She plugged in this thing the size of an electric bar of soap that made a **humming** sound and vibration, a bit of homemade medicine with Russian lettering on the box. She had me lie naked on the floor and rubbed my entire body, both sides, with whatever that thing was. The Commie machine made different sounds over different parts of my body.

"Atta baby!" Anna said. "We're getting to it now!"

Without telling her, I chugged some NyQuil and chewed up a few Sudafeds just before I crawled back into my bed to disappear into the Land of Nod.

DAY 21

I felt better in the morning. My sheets were so damp with my night sweats I could have wrung them out like a chamois.

Anna had left a note taped to my percolator.

Left you sleeping deep and silent. I like you like that. You will no longer be ill if you finish the soup in the refrigerator. Drink it cold in the morning, hot at lunch. Do the exer-bike twice before noon and take an hour for the stretch routine on the link I emailed you. And RE-STEAM, until you've downed three bottles of distilled water! Leach that sodium! A.

I was alone in my house on my own terms, so I immediately ignored Anna's instructions. I had coffee with hot milk. I read an actual print copy of the **Times**—not the online version, which Anna preferred because newsprint paper was a sin against the earth, regardless of my recycling. I treated myself to a nutritious breakfast of eggs with fried slices of **linguica** (a Portuguese sausage), a banana, a strawberry Pop-Tart, papaya juice from a carton, and a large bowl of Cocoa Puffs.

I did not do any stretching. I did not get on the stationary bike nor did I go into the plastic steam stall. I did not open her email link, thus stretched not a whit. Instead, I spent the morning doing laundry—four loads, including the bedsheets. I played my mixtape CDs and sang along. I reveled in obeying not a single one of Anna's commands. I lived the best life imaginable.

Which meant I had answered the question Anna had put to me two weeks earlier: No. I did not think I was the man for her.

When she called to ask how I was, I confessed to ignoring her instructions. I also said that I felt healthy, rested, and like myself and despite how wonderful I thought she was and what a dope I am and **blahditty blah-blah dittity-blah.**

Before I could muster the vocabulary to actually break up with her, Anna did it for me.

"You are not the man for me, baby."

There was not a smidgen of rancor in her voice, neither judgment nor disappointment. She said it straight out of her face in a way I couldn't. "I've known for a while," Anna said, chuckling. "I was wearing you down. Would have destroyed you over time."

"When were you going to let me off your hook?" I asked.

"If you hadn't backed out by Friday morning, we'd have had the Talk then."

"Why Friday morning?"

"Because Friday night I'm going back to Fort Worth. Ricardo is taking me hot-air ballooning."

A bit of my man-pride had me instantly hoping that this Ricardo fellow would not be the man for Anna, either.

———

He wasn't. Anna never told me why.

For the record, I did get my scuba certificate. Anna and I joined Vin and a dozen other divers, offshore in the kelp beds. We breathed underwater, swimming through what looked like a tall forest of sea trees. There's a great picture of Anna and me, on board afterward, our wet-suited arms around each other and big smiles on our cold, wet faces.

We leave for Antarctica next week. Anna arranged a big shopping spree, seeing to it that we have all the necessary gear. She spent extra time with MDash, making sure he was going to have enough layers to stay warm. He's never been to a place cold enough for chinstraps and crabeaters.

"Antarctic Circle, make way," I hollered, modeling my green parka and shell. Anna laughed.

We'll fly to Lima, Peru, then change planes for Punta Arenas, Chile, where we'll board a boat to make the crossing from South America to the old science station at Port Lockroy, our first stop. The seas in the Drake Passage can get pretty rough and tumble, they say. But with a strong sail, a firm wheel, a true compass, and a reliable clock, our ship will journey south, bound for the Antarctic Circle and adventure galore.

Oh, yeah. For B15K, as well.

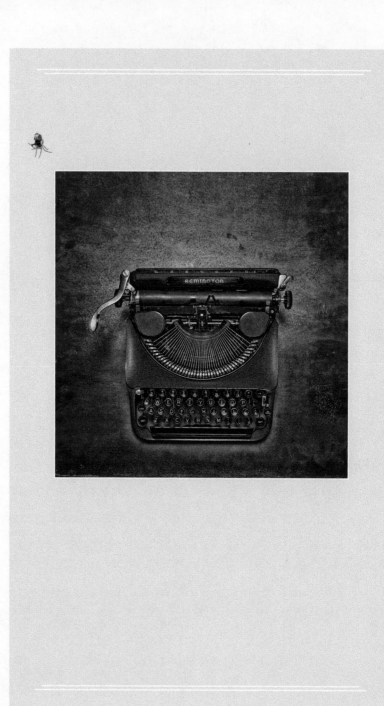

Christmas Eve 1953

---✦---

Virgil Beuell didn't close the shop until nearly dinnertime, when a light snow began falling. The road back home was slick and getting slicker so he drove slowly, wonderfully easy to do in the Plymouth with the PowerFlite automatic transmission. No clutch, no shifting, an engineering marvel. Skidding off the icy road and getting stuck in the snow would be a disaster tonight; in the Plymouth's trunk were all the treasures due in the morning from Santa, kept hidden and undiscovered there since the kids had declared their wishes weeks ago. Those presents had to be under the tree in a few hours, and transferring them from the trunk of a snowbound car to the cab of a tow truck would alter Christmas Eve horribly.

The drive home took longer than usual, sure, but the length of the trip did not bother Virgil. The cold was what he hated. PowerFlite or not, he often cursed the folks at Plymouth, who were unable to build a car with a heater worth a damn. By the time he slowly pulled up to the house and the yellow spread of the headlamps played on the screen of the back porch and there was the **hush** of tires coming to a stop on the gravel drive, he was aching slightly from the cold. Virgil had to be extra careful not to slip on the front walkway, as he had done too many times before, but he still got inside the house as fast as a working man could.

As he stamped the snow off his overshoes and hung up his layers of warm clothing, Virgil's body softened in the warmth pumping up from the cellar through the grates. After buying the house, he self-installed a furnace that was far oversized for the modest home. He put in, too, a beast of a hot-water heater, a commercial unit that never, ever ran out of the liquid heaven that allowed for the kids' baths and his own long showers. The winter fuel bills were worth the comfort, as was the price of two cords of firewood every winter.

A fire was going in the family room. He had taught Davey how to build one by stacking the wood the way he did his toy Lincoln Logs, like a square house around the kindling, never a pyramid. The kid now viewed making the fire as his sacred duty. Come the first frosts of November, the Beuell home was the warmest place for miles and miles.

"Dad!" Davey came running from the kitchen. "Our plan is working **great**. Jill is completely **fooled**."

"Good news, Big Man," Virgil said, giving his boy the secret handshake known in the entire world only by the two of them.

"I told her we'd write the Santa letters after dinner, then lay out some snacks, just like you did with me when I was little." Davey was turning eleven in January.

Jill was setting the kitchen table, her specialty being the straightening of napkins and silverware. "My daddy is home, hooray hooray," the six-year-old said, lining up the last of the spoons.

"He is?" Delores Gomez Beuell asked, standing as she cooked at the stove, baby Connie straddling the nooks of her elbow and hip. Virgil gave each of the women in his life a kiss.

"So he is," Del said, pecking him back, then dishing fried potatoes with onions onto a platter and getting it to the table. Davey brought his father a can of beer from the new, huge Kelvinator and ceremonially levered the two opposing openings in the top with a church key, another sacred duty.

Dinnertime with the Family Beuell was a show. Davey was in and out of his chair—the kid never sat through a meal. Connie squirmed in her mother's lap, content with a spoon she worked around in her mouth or banged on the table. Del cut food for the kids, wiped up spills, placed bits of mashed-up potato into Connie's mouth, and, occasionally, had a bite herself. Virgil ate slowly, never repeating a bite of any one food, but working his fork around his plate in a circle as he enjoyed the theater that was his family.

"I'm telling ya, Santa needs only three cookies." Davey was explaining, for Jill's sake, the facts surrounding the evening's expected visitor. "And he never finishes a whole glass of milk. He's got so much to do. Right, Dad?"

"So I hear." Virgil gave his son a wink that Davey tried to return, but he could only scrunch up the one side of his face to force one eye closed.

"Anyways, everyone leaves him the same snack."

"Everyone?" Jill asked.

"Everyone."

"I can't figure out when he comes. When does he show up?" Jill needed to know.

"Not at all if you don't touch your dinner." Del tapped Jill's plate with her fork and separated some of her potato from her meat. "Bites get Santa here sooner."

"Right when we all go to bed?" Jill asked. "We have to be sleeping, right?"

"Could be anytime between bedtime and when we wake up." Davey had answers for every one of his sister's queries. Since he had figured out the deal with Santa over the summer, Davey had assigned himself the task of keeping his little sister a believer.

"That could be hours. If his milk sits out too long, it'll go bad."

"He can make it cold with just a touch! He just sticks his finger in a glass of warm milk and does a **whooshy** thing and boom. Cold milk."

Jill found that fact amazing. "He must drink a lot of milk."

After dinner Virgil and the kids did KP, Jill standing on a chair over the sink drying the forks and spoons one by one while Del was upstairs putting the baby down and grabbing a short, much-needed nap. Davey opened his father's final can of beer for the night and set it on the telephone table right beside what was called Daddy's Chair in the front room, by the fire. Once Virgil was sitting and sipping, Davey and Jill lay in front of the phonograph and played Christmas records. With the room lights off, the tree threw colored magic onto the walls. Jill found Virgil's lap while her brother played the Rudolph record over and over until they knew all the words and started adding their own.

Had a very shiny nose.

"Like a lightbulb!"

Used to laugh and call him names.

"Hey, Knothead!"

When it came to the line about going down in history, they yelled out, "And arithmetic!"

Del came downstairs, laughing. "What would you goofballs make of 'Joy to the World'?" She took a sip from Virgil's beer before sitting in her corner of the sofa, tapping a cigarette from her leather case with the snap clasp, and lighting it with matches from the ashtray set beside the phone.

"Davey, poke that log a bit, would you?" Virgil said.

Jill perked up. "Lemme poke the fire!"

"After me. And don't worry. Santa's boots are fireproof."

"I know. I know."

After Jill took her turn stabbing the fire, Del sent the kids upstairs to change into their pj's.

Virgil finished his beer, then went to the hall closet to pull out the portable Remington typewriter. Delores had bought the machine brand new for Virgil when he was in the Army hospital on Long Island, New York. He had typed letters to her with his one good hand until the therapists taught him to use what he called five-and-a-half-finger touch typing.

He took the writing machine out of its case on the low coffee table and rolled in two sheets of paper, one on top of the other—always two sheets so as not to damage the platen.

"Leave your messages for St. Nick or Father Christmas or whatever his name is," he told the kids when they came back downstairs smelling of toothpaste and fresh, clean flannel.

Jill wrote hers first, one **clack** at a time, letter by letter, key by key.

> dear santaa clas thank you for coiming again
> and thank you for the nurse kit and my
> Honey Walker I hpoe you give me bothh
> merry chirstmas I love you JILL BEUELL

For his letter Davey insisted on his own separate piece of paper. He told Jill that he didn't want to confuse Santa. Getting the two pages into the typewriter and lined up straight took him a few tries.

12/24/53

Dear Santa Clause. My sister Jill believes
in you and so. Do I. still. You know what I

want for this chrismas and believe me you
have NEVER DISAPPOINTMED ME..!"
Hear is some cold milk of course and 'snack
cakes' thar tar also called cookies. Next year
you have to bring presents for baby Connie beecause she will be old enuogh by then
Okay????? if the milek is warm make it cold
with yuor finger.

David Amos Beuell

Davey left his letter hanging out of the typewriter carriage, posing the machine to face the
fireplace, where Santa was sure to see it.

"You guys should arrange your presents in piles
under the tree. To make things simple come morning," Virgil said. Santa always left the wished-for
presents that were his responsibility unwrapped
on Christmas morning, ready for immediate play,
so Virgil and Del would have time for their morning coffee. The family gifts—from Uncle Gus and
Aunt Ethel, from Uncle Andrew and Aunt Marie,
from Goggy and Pop, from Nana and Leo, from
as far away as Urbana, Illinois, and as close as
Holt's Bend—had been collecting under the tree,
wrapped in colorful paper, for days, growing with
almost every stop at the village post office.

Once twin stacks of gifts labeled DAVEY and JILL had been built up, the kids put the records back in their sleeves and the albums back up on the shelf. Del asked Jill to tune the big cabinet radio to the Christmas Eve Programs, for seasonal music that was not about a deer with a red nose.

Cookies had been baked on December 23. Jill pulled them out of the Kelvinator and arranged them on a plate while Davey poured milk into a tall glass, then they carried the snacks to the coffee table, setting them beside the Remington. From then on it was a waiting game. Davey added another log to the fire as Jill reacquainted herself with her father's lap while the radio played Christmas carols celebrating wise men and holy nights and the birth of Jesus.

Not long after, Virgil carried his sleeping daughter up to her bed, sliding her between the covers, marveling at the softness of his little girl's closed eyes and the lips that were Del's in perfect miniature. In the front room, Davey was on the sofa, leaning close against his mother as she played her fingers in his hair. "She swallowed it hook, line, and sinker," he said.

"You're a good big brother," Del told him.

"Ah, heck. Anyone would do it." Davey was looking into the fire. "When Jill first asked me if Santa was really real, like she was afraid to ask you and wanted it to be a secret between just us, I didn't know what to say."

"How'd you handle it, honey?"

"That's when I came up with the plan. To have an answer for every question she had. How does he make it to every house? He goes superfast and there aren't all that many houses anyway. What about a house with no chimney? He can use the oven or the furnace."

"Touching the milk to make it cold," Del whispered to her son as she brushed hair off the soft skin of his forehead. "So smart. So quick."

"That was cinchy. He's a magic man."

"You'll have to do the same for Connie soon."

"Of course. It's my job now."

Virgil came back downstairs to Daddy's Chair as a carol, in Latin, was crooning out of the mouth of Bing Crosby.

"Dad, how does radio work?" Davey wanted to know.

———

At quarter past ten, Davey went off to bed, announcing this might have been the best Christmas Eve ever.

"Should I put on some coffee?" Delores asked.

"You'd better," Virgil said, following her into

the kitchen, where he stopped her from reaching for the coffee can, wrapped his arms around her, and kissed her. She kissed back, both of them feeling that such a kiss was one of the reasons they were still married. The kiss lasted longer than either of them expected, then they smiled at each other. Del prepared the coffee as Virgil stood next to her at the stove.

"Next year, let's try to get to the Midnight Mass," Delores said. "We are raising godless kids."

"Just Davey." Virgil chuckled. Davey had been born seven months after their wedding day.

"The Midnight Mass is so beautiful."

"Three kids up all hours on Christmas Eve? The drive all the way to St. Mary's? If we'd tried that tonight with the snow?"

"The McElhenys manage."

"Ruth McElheny is as nutty as a can of Planters. Ed doesn't dare cross her."

"Still. The candles. The music. So pretty." Del knew that in years to come they'd make the drive to Midnight Mass. Not because he didn't dare cross her but because he loved to give her what she wanted. But for this Yuletide, there was just his hand over hers in the quiet, warm kitchen of the snowbound house as they sat with their coffee.

Virgil put his overshoes back on and pulled on his heavy coat, cracking open the front door just wide enough for him to slip through. Nearly three inches of snow had collected. Hatless, he went to the Plymouth's trunk to retrieve Santa's bounty. Not wanting to risk a fall on the frozen walk, Virgil made two trips carrying small loads. Closing the trunk, he paused a moment to ponder the final hour of Christmas Eve 1953. A cold night, yes, but Virgil had been colder.

Stepping carefully, he felt the pull of a ghost pain where his lower left leg used to be. He took the five steps to the front door one at a time.

Del laid out the nurse's kit by Jill's stack of treasures. Honey Walker, the walking doll "just like a real little girl," needed batteries. Santa had batteries. Before too long Davey would find his Space Rocket Launch Base, with towers and soldiers and spring launchers that, once Virgil assembled the components, actually flung spaceships into the void. Connie would delight in a new play blanket and a set of blocks direct from the North Pole. When all was laid out and Honey Walker had taken a test stroll, Virgil and Del sat close together on the sofa and kissed some more.

After they'd sat, arms entwined, quiet and still for a while, Del eyed the fire, then rose up. "I'm done in," she confessed. "Try to answer on the first ring, honey. And give him my love."

"I will." Virgil checked his watch. It was almost

11:30. Seven minutes after midnight, the shrill peal of the phone broke the silent night. As instructed, Virgil picked up before the first ring gave way to the second.

"Merry Christmas," he said.

An operator was on the line. "This is a long-distance call for Virginia Beuell from Amos Boling."

"Speaking. Thank you, Operator." As always, the operator had gotten the name wrong.

"Sir, your party is on the line," the operator said, clicking off.

"Thanks, honey," said the caller. "Merry Christmas, Virgin."

Virgil smiled at his nickname. Because of Amos Boling, the whole outfit had come to call him Virgin. "Where the heck are you, Bud?"

"San Diego. I was over across the border yesterday."

"You don't say."

"Lemme tell you something about Mexico, Virgin. The place is loaded with cantinas and cathouses. Nice and hot, too. How deep is the snow up there in Dogpatch?"

"Seen worse. But I'm sitting by a nice fire, so no complaints."

"Delores still burdened with you?"

"Gives her love."

"You are one lucky son of a bitch and that gal could have done better."

"I know that but haven't told her."

Both men chuckled. Amos "Bud" Boling forever joked that when Delores Gomez was taken off the market by Virgil "the Virgin" Beuell, there was no longer any point in getting married. There had been a time, more than thirteen years before, when someone else in the outfit might have come along to snag Delores. Ernie, Clyde, or Bob Clay, or either of the two Johnny Boys would have all taken a run at her had Virgil not met her first. A dance at the Red Cross Center was so chockablock with soldiers, sailors, and airmen that Virgil needed some air and a few moments away from the crowd. He stepped outside for a smoke and found himself lighting a cigarette for a brown-eyed girl named Delores Gomez. By the end of the next morning she and Virgil had danced, laughed, had griddle cakes with lots of coffee, and kissed. Two lives changed forever.

———

In the years since, Bud had not married and Virgil knew he never would. Not landing Delores had nothing to do with it. Virgil had, years before, figured Bud was one of those men, like his father's youngest brother, Uncle Russell. Virgil had been around his uncle rarely, the last time during the long day that was his grandmother's funeral. Uncle Russell had driven from New York City with a friend, a man named Carl, who called Russell "Rusty." After the service, the burial, and a reunion dinner at the house that ended with coffee and pie, Carl and Rusty drove off into the night, headed all the way back to New York City, still wearing their funeral suits. Virgil remembered his father later saying, under his breath, that "women were neither the weakness nor the passion" of his kid brother. Bud Boling had plenty of weaknesses and a few passions, but just as for Uncle Russell, none of them involved women. "So," Virgil said. "How you been, Bud?"

"The same, the same," Bud answered. "Came down here three months ago from a town up north near Sacramento. That's the state capital, you know. Bought a Buick secondhand and drove it down. Nice town. Navy town. Every cabdriver will tell you he was at Pearl Harbor."

"You working at all?"

"Not until someone makes me."

"I know I say this every year, but here it is: I've got room for you at the shop. In fact, I could use you with the way things have been going."

"Doing well, are you?"

"Bud, I've got so many orders I'm working six-day weeks."

"Hell on earth."

"I'm serious, Bud. You come work with me and you'd be set for years."

"I'm already set for years."

"I'll pay you more than you're worth."

"I ain't worth a flat plug nickel, Virgin. You know that."

Virgil laughed. "Then just come by for a visit. In the summer. Hop in that Buick and we'll go fishing."

"You country boys always make a big deal about fishing."

"I'd just like to see you, Bud. Del, too. Little Davey would be over the moon to meet you."

"Maybe next year."

"You say that every Christmas." Virgil kept going. "Come see us, Bud. We'll go to Midnight Mass. We'll say prayers for all the fellows."

"I've already said all the prayers for all the fellows I'm ever going to pray for."

"Aw, come on. Next year will be ten years."

"Ten years?" Bud let the static crackle on the long-distance line. "Ten years for **who**? Ten years for **what**?"

Virgil felt like a fool.

Bob Clay had been killed in Normandy on the same day that Ernie, wounded in his right thigh, had bled out. No one realized his artery had been severed because the pool of blood under Ernie never spread, but was absorbed by the damp ground. Nobody saw it. Attention was not paid as closely as it should have been since there were Germans trying to kill them from somewhere on the other side of a thick hedgerow in the French **bocage**. Mortar rounds coming at them from the unseen enemy kept the outfit pinned down for nearly an hour. Bud and Virgil were in two squads sent to hack through the roots and trees—impossible but for the use of grenades. They flanked the enemy position and killed all of them, but at a cost. Bud's squad leader, Corporal Emery, was cut in two, literally, by a German machine gun. Virgil was unsuccessful giving first aid to Sergeant Castle, who took three rounds in the chest that severed his spine. Burke's head wound was beyond aid, and a fellow named Corcoran lost an arm that was cut clean from his shoulder and he was moved back to an aid station. No one knew if he lived or not.

A week later Johnny Boy disappeared and the other Johnny Boy cracked, and one by one, others in the outfit were lost in ways soldiers are lost. For fifty-eight days, from the seventh of June to early August, the outfit was either fighting or moving toward the fighting. Bud was promoted to corporal and Virgil's teeth began to go rotten from eating nothing but K rations.

On Day 59, the outfit rested at a camp in France—there were cots with blankets and relatively warm showers, hot food, and all the coffee a GI could stomach. Later, a big tent served as a theater where movies where played. Clyde was transferred to Intelligence because he spoke decent French. Every airplane in the sky was either the RAF or the USAAF, and the word was the Germans were on the run, that the worst of the fighting had happened and they'd all be home by Christmas. New guys came in from the replacement depots and had to be drilled and trained. Bud was tough on all of them, and Virgil didn't want to learn any of their names.

In the middle of September the outfit was given new uniforms, rearmed, and loaded into transports for an offensive in Holland. Four of the trucks slammed into each other in the dark of night. Five soldiers were killed, three were so injured they were no good for the war anymore. The trucks were repaired and moving by daylight. Three days later the outfit was surprised by a German attack just before dawn. The command post was blown up, leading to a confused, chaotic battle that had Virgil and Bud fighting the enemy hand to hand. By chance, three tanks, British Cromwells, were close enough to roar in and overpower the German advance. Many of the new guys were killed in what was their first time in combat, and plenty happened that made no sense, no sense at all.

Virgil lost count of the days before he found himself back in France, where he and Bud slept and slept and slept. They walked around huge, ancient cathedrals and played football. Movie stars came to put on shows. There was a cathouse not far from the barracks, a place called Madame Sophia's. While many of the officers had three-day passes in Paris, Bud and Virgil and the other enlisted men drilled and trained more replacements, even in the rain. There was a different movie every night. Then came the coldest December on record, and the Germans roared into Belgium. The outfit was loaded onto trucks, driven hell-bent into the night, and dropped off on a road somewhere between Paris and Berlin. Virgil appreciated the spirit of one driver—a colored fellow—who gave him a pack of Lucky Strikes and a wish for God to look out for him.

The outfit marched on roads and across ice-solid fields, along trails dragged out in the gathered snow, hauling ammo and supplies for themselves as well as for others who were already up ahead in the fighting, which Virgil could see in the distance like Fourth of July fireworks. They fought along with the paratroopers who had taken heavy casualties, moving forward in a show of arms meant to convince the Germans that an entire division was at the ready to take them on. The ruse worked. But lives were lost.

The outfit came under artillery fire in the Belgian woods and some guys were blown apart, vaporized. Then Virgil, Bud, and the outfit were sent marching the other way, through Bastogne proper. They passed a neatly arranged stack of dead soldiers just outside the church, burned-out, useless tanks with their treads thrown off, and a pair of cows eating hay a farmer had stocked. The farmer and the cows seemed oblivious to the Germans, who were trying to retake the port at Antwerp, and to the general hullaballoo. The cold cut them all to the bone. It was inescapable. The cold killed some men in the outfit. Sleep was so rare, some guys went nuts and had to be sent back into Bastogne. The hope was that they could gather themselves so they could return to the cold and the fighting.

A new kid—Something Something, Jr.—had the watch. Virgil was in the hole, under the roof of branches, on top of the pine needles that lined the floor, wrapped in a single GI blanket. Sleep was a joke. He had a few Charms fruit candies left in a roll, so popped two into his mouth. One remained, so he rose up from the frozen-ground floor of the hole and palmed the final square of hard candy into the hand of the new kid.

"Merry fucking Christmas," Virgil whispered.

"Thanks, Virgin."

"Junior, call me Virgin again and I'll crack you one."

"Isn't your name Virgin?"

"Not to fucking new guys."

The hole was at the far left of these woods, two trees in from the edge of the rise, overlooking, in daylight, a Belgian farmer's barren field and, just beyond it, a collection of houses built along a narrow road leading northeast. At night, there was only the void. Somewhere down there were supposed to be the German soldiers. The rest of the outfit was in holes and shelters of their own, spaced off to the right. This was the main line of defense, theoretically. In reality, the idea of an MLD was as laughable as that of a cozy nap. The line was so thin there was no listening post forward of the trees. There was little heavy armor in the rear. The big guns had only a few shells left. There was no kitchen and thus no hot food for miles.

This hole was the seventh Virgil had chipped out of the frozen ground and covered with tree limbs since they had walked through Bastogne. Virgil didn't want to dig any more of them. Moving to another position meant shouldering weapons and gear, carrying it who knew how far or for how long, digging another hole, and building another shelter, working up the sweat that, in the subzero winter, caused a man's uniform to freeze to his back. Frostbite had taken more men off the line than wounds from enemy fire. Some of the freezing guys had been able to get out before the encirclement. Those that hadn't had already lost toes and fingers, some even their feet and hands.

Virgil didn't want to be one of those guys. He kept his one extra pair of socks tied together and draped across the back of his neck under his uniform to hang in his armpits. His body temperature, what was left of it, would dry the socks out some. He hoped he could always have that reserve of semidry socks to avoid frostbite. He also hoped Hitler was going to come walking across the field waving a white hankie to surrender personally to PFC Virgil Beuell. Right after Rita Hayworth dropped by to offer a blow job.

"I sure could use some coffee," Junior whispered.

"Tell you what," Virgil whispered back. "I'll start a warm and toasty fire to percolate us up a couple of pots. I got some cake mixings, too, and we'll make a batch for the whole squad and shut the fuck up, you fucking fucker."

"**Butterfly. Butterfly!**" A sharp whisper came from the dark to the left of the hole, the password for the day.

"**McQueen!**" Virgil hissed in response.

A second later, Sergeant Bud Boling tumbled into the shelter, weaponless. He had been trying to sleep during daylight hours, covered up in a hole of his own. Once it got dark he roamed the front in silence, alone, returning at daylight to report whatever he had seen to the CP before tucking away in his dark hole again.

"Krauts. Twenty-five of them. Who the fuck are you?" Bud meant the new guy, Junior. Before a name could be offered Bud said "never mind" and gave an order. "Gimme your rifle and get to the CP and tell them a Kraut probe is coming on the left."

Junior's eyes went wide. He had yet to be in any combat. As he kicked his way up and out of the hole, Bud repeated "Kraut probe on our left."

And the kid was gone. Bud readied the M1 rifle, tucking spare ammo clips into his jacket.

Virgil lifted the machine gun in one piece, tripod and all, and faced it at the foxholes nine o'clock. "I was right ahead of them, Virgin."

"They see you?"

"No fucking Luger-head ever sees me." The men whispered with the confidence of experienced soldiers, which they were, not like twenty-two-year-old boys, which they also were.

A footfall from the darkness cracked hardened ice.

"Light 'em up," Bud hissed.

PFC Vigil Beuell pulled the trigger of his machine gun, spitting fire into a column of enemy soldiers not three yards in front of him. Bright muzzle flashes and red tracer rounds illuminated the shapes of bodies and the trunks of trees as other American boys took to their weapons. A fury of fighting lit up the woods, and the thin line of defense took on the look of an impenetrable wall. In a flash as well defined as that from a Speed Graphic camera ringside at a prizefight, Virgil saw the helmet of a German soldier explode in a cloud of fine, blood-red mist and soggy clumps of what had been the man's head. The German soldiers spread out quickly and spewed death themselves. Bud raised up just high enough to aim his rifle and squeeze out a full clip into the invading force—eight continuous **BLAMs**—spreading his rounds with a geometric precision until the **pi-cling** of his empty clip flying out of its breach meant his ammo was spent. Instinctively, Bud reloaded and was raised up again when a body came crashing into the shelter through the pine branch roof.

The German was firing as he fell, hitting Virgil in his left knee without Virgil feeling a thing. Another shot made the fingers on Virgil's left hand sting like a hornet's bite.

"Fuck you!" Bud yelled, driving the butt of his M1 across the German's jaw. "Fucker!" he yelled, smashing the German's face twice more. Someone began firing parachute flares that lit up the woods in a harsh limelight, and Bud saw he had broken the nose and smashed the jaw of the German, who lay glassy-eyed and motionless. He spun his rifle around, pointed the muzzle at the middle button on the soldier's uniform, fired two rounds point-blank, and ended the man's life. "One less of you fuckers," he said to the dead enemy soldier.

The small reserve force of American boys was coming forward now; what had started as a probe by the enemy had become a severe and deadly mistake for them. A pursuit was under way as the Germans retreated. Virgil ceased fire and was breaking down his weapon to join the move forward when he realized something was wrong. His hand was sticky and his leg was numb.

"My leg fell asleep!" he yelled. Trying to stand, Virgil fell back, on top of the faceless, lifeless German. He tried to stand again, but his left leg bent the wrong way at the knee and Virgil could not figure out what had happened. Luckily Bud Boling was there to help him up. But rather than getting him on his feet, Bud squatted, pulled Virgil over his shoulders, and lifted him clean off the ground.

That much, Virgil remembered of Christmas Eve 1944. Somewhere between the foxhole and the aid station to the rear, he slipped into the slumber of the unconscious.

————

Virgil felt like a **god damn** fool.

Next year was an anniversary for him because the war ended for PFC Beuell on Christmas Eve 1944. He awoke at an aid station in Bastogne proper, after the American tanks had come and the German advance had collapsed. A few days later, he woke up again at a field hospital in France. Weeks later he became one of thousands of wounded men in hospitals in England. When Germany surrendered and the war was over in Europe, Virgil began to think of himself as one lucky bastard. His left leg was gone, severed above the knee, and three fingers of his left hand were now stumps, wrapped in so many bandages he looked like he was wearing a gauze catcher's mitt. But he still had two thumbs, one good leg, his sight, and his manhood. Compared to many other guys in those hospitals and on the ship home, Virgin felt like he had won the 1945 Irish Sweepstake. All he really wanted back was his wedding band, which had been lost somewhere in those woods in Belgium.

Amos "Bud" Boling stayed in Germany for his full enlistment, which meant the duration of the war plus six months. While Virgil was being treated for his wounds and the deadly infections that came with them, Bud was attacking the Siegfried Line and killing his way into Nazi Germany. Then he breached the Rhine River and later the Elbe, swept south into pockets of enemy country that had seen no signs of the war in the four and a half years it had raged around him.

Bud had never been wounded but he'd seen too many who had been, and too many killed. He had also killed a great many German men and boys. He had ended the lives of German soldiers who had been looking to surrender and survive but instead found Sergeant Bud Boling's merciless eyes. Eighteen German officers were shot dead by his hand, alone or two or three at a time, off the roads and under the cover of trees, behind farmhouse walls or out in open fields. Bud used his .45 sidearm to wring a justice out of the war that made sense only to him. Bud killed one last German in August 1945. He had heard stories about a particular local, a former Nazi Party official who was using the false name of Wolfe. He found the man standing in a line of refugees who were hoping to return to their home cities in different parts of what had been the Third Reich. When Wolfe produced his papers, Bud ordered him out of the line. Behind a low brick wall Bud drew his sidearm and shot Wolfe square through his neck and calmly stood over the former Nazi bigwig as he thrashed about for the last few moments of his life. Bud Boling never talked of any of this. He never talked of the camps he'd seen, either. Virgil never knew any of the specifics. But he suspected. He saw the emptiness, the difference in his friend.

———

"How long you thinking of staying in San Diego, Bud?"

"Maybe a week, maybe a year. May head up to Los Angeles for the New Year and catch that big parade."

"The Rose Parade?"

"Yeah. Supposed to be gorgeous. I'd ask you

where're you headed but I already know. The shop for six days a week."

"I like my work, Bud. Don't know that I could just amble about like you do."

"Virgin, I'd rather punch a cop than a clock."

The men laughed.

"Merry Christmas to you. And you'll be mighty welcome should you amble our way sometime."

"Always good to talk to you, Virgin. Glad you're a happy man. You deserve such blessings."

"Thanks to you, Bud."

"Almost 1954. Can you believe it? There you are with Del and Davey and Jill and, uh, Connie? I get the new one's name right?"

"Connie it is."

"Virgil the Virgin has three kids. I understand the biology but the reality's a fucking mystery . . ."

The men gave each other a round of holiday wishes, repeated goodbyes, and hung up. They would talk again in a year.

Virgil sat in the quiet, watching the fire until one in the morning. Then he pulled up out of Daddy's Chair to bank the flames so that Davey would have embers to start up the Yule logs. He found the plug for the Christmas tree lights and yanked it from the wall socket, using the thumb, forefinger, and knuckle stumps of his left hand.

After almost forgetting, he stopped in front of the plate that held Santa's cookies and ate three of them. He hesitated, then took a bite out of a fourth cookie, put it back on the plate, and drank a few sips of the milk that had gone warm.

In darkness, he found his way to the stairs, climbing one riser at a time, his left shoe matching his right foot. He checked on both of the sleeping kids and Connie in her crib beside Del's side of the bed. Del always laid his pajamas out for him, so once he was out of his trousers and had undone the straps and buckles of his prosthetic leg, he set the thing to rest beside the chair and wriggled into his sleeping clothes.

A short stutter of a hop got him into bed. As he did every night, he found Del's lips and kissed them softly, causing her to purr through her sleep. Virgil pulled the covers over him—the sheet, the two heavy blankets, and the thick quilt. He rested his head on his pillow after the long day and, at last, closed his eyes.

As he did almost every night, he saw the lightning-like image of a soldier's helmet exploding in a cloud of blood-red mist. He saw the soggy clumps of what had been the man's head. Virgil forced himself to think of something else, anything else. He searched his mind for an image and settled on a vision of Bud Boling as a young man, twenty-two years old, standing in the warm sunshine on a California street, part of a great throng of people, all with smiling faces, cheering on a parade of floats covered with roses.

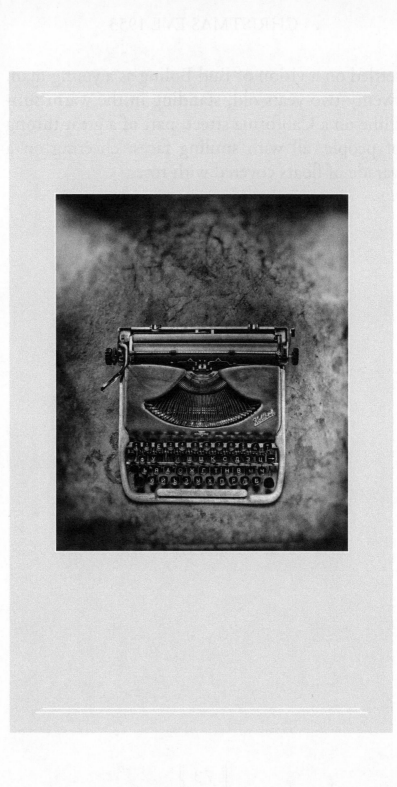

A Junket in the City of Light

What brown fox jumped quickly over dogs that are lazy?

Hey, this writing machine actually works!

What the <u>hell</u> has happened? Who am I <u>today</u>? Still Rory Thorpe, I guess, but who is <u>he</u>?

Last night—just hours ago—I was the guy in a huge movie that everyone was talking about, the guy who made out with a glamorous beauty, a guy with a fine ass. In the capitals of Europe—and America—I was hustled around like a politician, into cars and into ballrooms filled with camera-totin', question-hollerin' reporters. I waved to seas of people, many of whom waved back, even though no one knew who I am, even though I am, in fact, a no one. Although, I have in my possession...certain documents...that reveal Willa Sax's TOP-SECRET CODE NAME (it's Eleanor Flintstone!).

I was 2 Days into taking the City of Paris by storm, with a 3rd to go, and Day 3 was going to have FIREWORKS! I had all my expenses paid. I was wearing free clothes. I could ask for a sandwich whenever I wanted, even though I was kept so busy I didn't have time for much more than a few bites.

But this morning all that is <u>over</u>. I have to be out of my room at checkout time. Too bad. This is a nice hotel. The Nazis stayed here.

A good rule of thumb when traveling in Europe—stay in places with a Nazi past. The place in Rome had been Gestapo headquarters during the war. Big rooms. High ceilings. A beautiful garden. In Berlin, the hotel had been leveled when the Russians clobbered the Nazis who were hiding in it. To rub in their victory, the Commies never bothered to rebuild it or much of anything else in that part of East Berlin. When the wall came down, the hotel went back up and now the joint has a special room just for smoking cigars. In London, the old lady of a grand hotel had been bombed by the Luftwaffe sometime between the Nazi glories of Rome and the ass kicking they took from the Reds a few years later. The Queen has had dinner there twice since 1973.

Finally, this Parisian hotel had been the

headquarters of the German Occupation Staff. They say Hitler had a cup of coffee on one of the balconies before he drove around to take in the sights of his conquered City of Light.

All this has been free of cost for me, including the hotels in L.A. and Chicago and New York, on the studio's dime, because I play Caleb Jackson in **Cassandra Rampart 3: Destiny at Hand**. (Cassandra Rampart a.k.a. Willa Sax a.k.a. Eleanor Flintstone!)

Day 3 of my junket—sorry, my Press Tour— would have been another wild ride of a day. Instead, I have to pack my bags and check out by 1:00 p.m.—I'm sorry, by 13:00 …

TO: RORY THORPE
CC: IRENE BURTON, etc.
FROM: ANNETTE LABOUD
RE: PARIS PRESS SCHEDULE

Welcome to Paris!

We know you must be exhausted, but want you to know how thrilled we all are to be working on the French release of CASSANDRA RAMPART 3: DESTINY AT HAND! Our colleagues in Rome, Berlin, and London tell us the movie has been welcomed with wild enthusiasm … thanks to you! Our tracking numbers are strong, just 3 points off CASSANDRA RAMPART 2: AGENT OF CHANGE and only 10 points off CASSANDRA RAMPART: THE BEGINNING. For a sequel, these are fantastic numbers! It seems audiences are responding to the sexual tension between Cassandra and Caleb.

We all feel France is a good territory for the film, as the Cassandra Rampart universe has a megafollowing on all social media platforms.

As Irene Burton and the Marketing Dept. may have already explained to you, France does not allow the promotion of films via paid spots on television—which is why you may notice a few more on-camera interviews during your stay with us. These interviews are crucial in the French market. You have done <u>so well</u> on the U.S. tour and in Rome/Berlin/London there is no question you are <u>warmed up</u>!

So have fun!

Below is the schedule for the next three days. (Separate schedule for Eleanor Flintstone.)

<u>DAY 1</u>

1:10 (approx)—Arrive Charles de Gaulle Airport from London—Transport to Hotel.

7:10—Grooming in Room 4114.

7:40–8:00—Live appearance on "¡Nosotros Cacauates!" This is the most popular Young Adult morning show in Spain with a strong On-Line presence (4.1 million views). They have come to Paris especially for CR3:DAH.

8:05—Transfer to Media Center on 3rd Floor.

8:15–8:45—Print Media Round Table #1 (approx 16 outlets. List available)

8:50–9:20—Print Media Round Table #2 (approx 16 outlets. List available)

9:25–9:55—Print Media Round Table #3 (approx 16 outlets. List available)

10:00–10:30—Print Media Round Table #4 (approx 16 outlets. List available)

10:35–11:05—Print Media Round Table #5 (approx 16 outlets. List available)

11:10–11:40—Print Media Round Table #6 (approx 16 outlets. List available)

11:45–11:50—Reddit A.M. Session (for U.S.)

BREAK

12:00–13:00—Social Influencers Mini-Interviews (3 to 5 minutes each). The Social Influencers have at least 1.5 million followers. Each will have a specific request for their postings. Some will be very quick; others will be limited to 5 minutes.

13:05–14:00—Photo Shoot on Hotel Roof (Note: Eleanor Flintstone will join you for last 10 minutes.)

14:05–14:45—Lunch/Interview with PARIS MATCH. (Note: A photographer will be present.)

14:50–15:00—Radio interview with TSR-1

15:05–15:15—Radio interview with RTF-3

15:20–15:30—Radio interview with FRT-2

15:40–16:00—Informal Coffee with approved Social Media Outlets (approx 20) with minimum of 3.5 million followers. (List on request)

16:05–16:10—Touch-Ups

16:15–16:45—Live TV remote from Balcony for Belgian TV "PM TODAY." (Note: Eleanor Flintstone will be joining you at 16:30.)

17:00—Proceed by car to Studio du Roi for Air France promotional shoot. This will play on all Air France International flights to support CR3:DAH opening. Shoot will take approx 3 hours.

20:00 (approx)—Proceed by car to Restaurant Le Chat. Dinner hosted by UPIC. (Note: A photographer will be present.)

After dinner you are free to stay or return to hotel.

Rory Thorpe thanked his lucky stars for Irene Burton; those stars had been mighty benevolent over the last two years. He'd been in a movie with none other than Willa Sax—Cassandra Rampart herself! He had money in the bank for the first time in his life! And he was getting a free trip to Europe out of the deal! All he had to do was give some interviews over there! His enthusiasm had Irene Burton mutely laughing her ass off.

Irene was sixty-six years old, had worked in marketing for every one of the six major film studios, and now lived in semiretirement in a beach house in Oxnard—far enough away from Hollywood to avoid the daily stresses of showbiz yet close enough to pop in when she was needed to clean up the occasional PR flameout. Eleven years ago, she escorted a young, talented, and beautiful actress through the press tour for a horrible movie called **Dementia 40,** which did lousy business but is now legendary for introducing audiences to the young, talented, and beautiful Willa Sax. The press called her Willa Sex for a few years—a fitting moniker—but now Willa was Cassandra Rampart, a one-woman industry who had her own line of exercise clothes, a home for orphaned pets, and a foundation that promoted literacy in third world nations. The first two Cassandra Rampart movies had grossed $1.75 billion worldwide. Willa Sax didn't just command $21 million a movie plus profits, she commanded respect.

"Irene," Willa told her on the phone. "You gotta help me."

"S'up, punkin'?" Irene called all her young actors punkin'.

"Rory Thorpe is as dumb as a box of hair."

"Who is Rory Thorpe?"

"The guy in my latest thing. I just saw his EPK." The electronic press kit is a house-controlled interview given to the press as background for a movie. "Most of his answers start with 'Well, um. It's like, you know . . .' We have the junket coming up and I can't go around the world with Doofus McGillicuddy as my costar. He needs to be told what the fuck not to do."

"I can do that."

So Irene did. She took Rory shopping at Fred Segal and Tom Ford for the clothes he'd need—casual-look outfits for interviews and black-tie tuxes for premiere galas. No charge. She took him luggage shopping at T. Anthony for the right trunks and suitcases—at a steep discount the studio covered—so those outfits would be ready to don at a moment's notice. He'd be photographed in two-shots with one of the most beautiful women in the world and needed to look like he rated the position. He'd be answering the same questions a thousand times over, so she drilled into him the talking point memos the studio had provided: **CR3—DAH brings the C. Rampart universe its most compelling & sophisticated film, for she is not just a heroine for our times but a woman for the ages. Please use "woman for the ages" whenever describing Cassandra.**

Irene had perfected her ability to keep her laughter to herself when one of her clients said something really stupid or naïve—in Rory's case, his thinking his first ever trip to Europe was going to be free.

"Oh, punkin'," she told him. "You'll be working your ass off."

The junket began in Los Angeles: three days jammed with interviews, photo shoots, video conferences, Q and A sessions, forums with fan bases, and as many talk show appearances as possible, each needing an hour of preinterviews with the segment producers. Irene saw to it that Rory was well dressed, well groomed, and well versed in what the fuck not to do. And there was the trip to the Comic-Con convention in San Diego. Willa Sax needed a team of bodyguards to keep the fans at bay; many of them were costumed as Cassandra, the former Secret Service agent with computer chips implanted in her brain, formula-enhanced, superstrong sinews, able to communicate subconsciously with the Seven, the extraterrestrials who live among us, aliens who may be good guys, may be bad guys, and who et cetera et cetera et cetera you get the idea. Many Comic-Coners were costumed as the Seven. No one was dressed as Caleb Jackson, pro surfer/software whiz, because no one had seen the movie yet. The fans seemed thrilled at the screening of a twenty-minute teaser of the movie, making it a trending topic for most of the day on both Twitter and Poppit!

Two days later in Chicago, the teaser was screened on the campus of Northwestern University, the alma mater of Willa Sax herself. Her old dorm was renamed in her honor. Irene steered Rory through two days of interviews, a parade, a charity volleyball match, the dropping of the puck at a Blackhawks hockey game, and a screening of the movie to benefit literacy in Africa that was held at the same theater where the gangster John Dillinger had been gunned down.

Four days of junket were held in New York City, starting with a press conference staged in the ballroom of the Waldorf Astoria, attended by 152 media outlets. Rory did not get a question until Willa had talked for thirty minutes, mostly of the challenges of shooting with the new FLIT-cam digital process and the new SPFX system called DIGI-MAX. She was a producer on the film, after all, having optioned the rights to the Cassandra Rampart graphic novel in 2007 for a mere ten thousand dollars.

She laughed off questions about her husband's investment genius and his supposed bedroom prowess. "Guys!" Willa protested. "Bobby is a banker!" Bobby was her husband, and he was worth $1.2 billion. Willa told the press that he really was a regular dude who had to be told to take out the trash.

That led to Rory being asked, "How does it feel for a guy like you to kiss the most beautiful woman in the world?"

"It's a kiss for the ages," he said. Irene smiled, knowing she'd done her work well. The crammed room remained silent, save the clicking of camera shutters. When the press conference ended, Willa was whisked away as more questions were shouted at her. Irene escorted Rory into a smaller ballroom set up with multiple round tables, each crowded with journalists and their microphones. Rory spent twenty minutes at each table, one after another, with no break, answering versions of the same three questions.

What is it like working with Willa Sax?
What is it like kissing Willa Sax?
Is that really your ass in the hurricane scene?

Irene took him to the Media Center on the eighth floor, to sit through a total of fifty-seven television interviews, lasting no more than six minutes each, all held in the same room, Rory seated in the same chair with a one-sheet of the movie behind him. In the poster, Willa was staring off into space, a look of ferocious concentration on her beautiful face, her torso clad in a tight sweater, a rip exposing her shoulder and the top sphere of her left breast. Behind her was a mosaic of images from the movie—an explosion, dark figures running in a tunnel, a massive, cresting wave, and Rory wearing a headset and looking at a computer, serious as all hell. WILLA SAX IS BACK AS CASSANDRA RAMPART was printed in big letters. Rory's name was in the cluttered billing block at the bottom of the poster, in typeface the same size as that of the film's editor. Irene kept him plied with green tea, protein bars, and small bowls of blueberries.

The movie was promoted on **CBS This Morning** the entire week. Every morning at 7:40 and 8:10, Rory reported the national weather in front of a green-screen map. Willa Sax was a guest host with Kelly Ripa on **Live with Kelly**. The two women did Pilates on the air.

The premiere of the film was supposed to take place on one of the piers on the Hudson—special facilities had been constructed with seating for five thousand people, but a predicted thunderstorm put the kibosh on that. Instead, cinema screens all over the city were booked for simultaneous digital projections of the movie. Rory and Irene were delivered to every one of them by SUV—a total of twenty-nine personal appearances. Willa Sax attended only the special screening held at the Museum of Natural History to raise money for its Programs for Young Scientists.

At the end of the nine days of the domestic press junket, Rory was exhausted, talked out, dizzy; he had seen little more than cars and rooms and cameras. Worst of all, the questions had been the same for four-hundred-plus interviews.

What is it like working with Willa Sax?
What is it like kissing Willa Sax?
Is that really your butt in the hurricane scene?

Rory now felt that working with Willa Sax was like eating a peanut butter sandwich on a motorcycle, kissing Willa Sax was like Christmas in July, and the butt in the hurricane was that of a talking horse named Britches.

"Welcome to the big leagues, punkin'," Irene told him. "Tomorrow, Rome."

Willa Sax flew to Italy on a chartered plane, along with her team, her posse, and her handlers. The studio plane took the other five producers, all the executives, and the marketing heads. With no seats available for either Rory or Irene, they flew business class on TraxJet Airways, changing planes in Frankfurt.

Three days of press were held in Rome, each as busy as those in the U.S. On the last night the teaser was shown outside at the Circo Máximo—where the chariot races were held in ancient times. To Rory it looked like just a big field. Scenes from the movie were projected onto a huge tempo-rary screen, but not until after a local soccer team was presented with the trophy they had won in some championship. The crowd was estimated at 21,000. When Rory appeared onstage to wave to the Romans, nothing happened. When Willa appeared to do the same, fistfights broke out as a tide of fans in soccer jerseys rushed the barricades to get to her. The Italian carabinieri got into a melee with the thugs as Willa was hustled into an armored car and whisked away to the airport. The next morning, Rory and Irene took a commercial flight—Air Flugplatz—to Berlin, where another three days of press were on tap.

In Berlin, Rory's body clock was so jet-lagged that he found himself flush with energy at 3:00 a.m., so he went out for a run. Leaving the hotel, he was ignored by the dozens of fervent German Cassandra Rampart fans who'd lingered all night and would continue to do so all morning, hoping for a glimpse of her. He jogged along the dark paths of the Tiergarten, stopping to do push-ups on the steps of a monument to the Russian Army, complete with actual tanks, that crushed Berlin in 1945. At noon the next day he was so tired he felt like a sleepwalker. He talked like one, too, telling the entire staff of **Bild**, the national newspaper, that as both a fan of the movies and the latest costar of Willa Sex (he actually said "Sex" instead of "Sax"), he felt that "Sandra Caspart was the most complimental and sophisticationed of any and all films, for Willa Sex is heroin for our times, and a **woman of the four ages**." Then came the questions.

What is it like working with Willa Sex?
What is it like kissing Willa Sex?
Is that really your butt in the hurricane scene?

"Try not to call her Willa Sex," Irene told him in the car back to the hotel.

"When did I do that?" Rory asked.

"Just now. To Germany's largest daily newspaper."

"Sorry," he said. "I'm no longer sure what the words are that come out of my mouth."

The German screening of the teaser took place later that night, projected onto the Brandenburg Gate to six thousand fans. When she appeared at the balcony of the hotel to wave to them, Willa Sax was disappointed there were no fistfights.

"I guess I'm no Willa **Sex** tonight," she said at the gala dinner afterward, held in the same museum that displays Nefertiti's bust.

By the time Rory and Irene had flown to London (CompuAir into Gatwick), the international press junket had turned Rory into blabbering toast.

DAY 2

7:30—Grooming in room
8:00—Transfer by Car to Gare de l'Est
8:10–9:00—Red Carpet Interviews prior to
  Boarding CASSANDRA EXPRESS

9:05–13:00—Train ride to Aix-en-Provence. En route 15-minute interviews in special Media Car. (Outlet list available on request)

13:00–14:00—Red Carpet interviews upon arrival at Ancient Roman Theater

14:30–16:00—Ancient Roman Theater. Re-creation of Hurricane Scene for Press. (Note: This is broadcast live on RAI-Due TV.)

16:30—Reboard CASSANDRA EXPRESS. Live appearance on "Midi & Madi" TV broadcast from Observation Car.

17:15–21:45—Return to Paris via CASSANDRA EXPRESS. En route 15-minute interviews for non-French media in special Media Car. (Outlet list available on request)

22:00 Transfer by car to Cocktail Reception/ Dinner at Hotel Meurice, hosted by Facebook France.

After dinner you are free to stay or return to hotel.

Irene will be provided the ADVANCE SCHEDULE FOR ASIA before arrival in Singapore/Tokyo.

Getting the job was a fluke, a scratch-off lottery win. Rory had given up on Los Angeles after a six-month stint as a model-actor-bartender with all of two credits on his SAG-AFTRA card. He'd booked a yogurt commercial, playing touch football on a beach. For three cloudy days in San Diego he ran around shirtless—Rory looked damn fine without a shirt—with a group of racially mixed "pals," then they all snacked on yogurt. They were coached on how to dip the spoons into the mini-packs and place the yogurt in their mouths. There was a trick to it.

Nine weeks later he was cast in a one-episode role on the rebranded **Kojak** series for CBS. Rory played a tattooed-shaved-head meth dealer who was **pretending** to be a handicapped Iraq War veteran, so **obviously** he had to die. Rory met his end in high style—shirtless (of course), dragged off the roof of an office building by his fraudulently gained motorized wheelchair, New Kojak jumping to safety just in time.

With little else going on but car payments and gym workouts, Rory grew bored with Southern California, and took his yogurt-**Kojak** money to Utah for the ski season. When New **Kojak** finally aired, one of the several other producers on Cassandra happened to be watching and texted Willa Sax: **Think I saw CR's next bit o' honey.** A few days later, Rory got a call from his agency to get back to town because something **huge** was on deck, in the brew, cooking in the hopper.

The first time Rory met Willa Sax—who was crazy beautiful, beyond-real-life beautiful—was over cups of green tea in her offices in the Capitol Records Building on Vine Street in Hollywood. The home she shared with her venture capitalist husband was somewhere in the hills nearby. She could not have been a nicer person, chatting with Rory about art and raising horses. Rory knew very little about either. Willa changed the subject to Fiji. She had been to the islands to do research for the movie. She told Rory about the beauty of the night sky and the clarity of the water and the happy faces of the locals, especially during the traditional kava ceremonies that were held to welcome visitors. She had learned to surf there. The movie would shoot in Fiji for at least two weeks.

The meeting lasted a little over an hour, but before Rory was in his car and at a standstill in the afternoon traffic of the Hollywood freeway, his phone exploded with texts: **WSaX Loved you!$$$$.** Two weeks later he was officially cast as Caleb with a crazy payday of nearly half a million dollars, to be spread over three films, which could or could not be part of the Cassandra Rampart universe. The next time he saw Willa was at the studio for camera tests. A production assistant took Rory to her trailer. When he climbed up the steps wearing his torso-clinging Caleb Jackson surfing outfit, she sized up her no-name yet gorgeous costar and said, "Well, ain't you hot shit!"

The start date of the movie was delayed for a few months as the script was rewritten, then pushed to after the new year so Willa could enjoy the holidays with her husband; they spent Christmas in a castle in Scotland. Rory's first day playing Caleb Jackson was in late March on a soundstage in Budapest. Willa had been shooting for three weeks and had her own makeup trailer, so the two did not see each other until they were on the set. The scene called for them to make out in a shower, but the water was not hot enough to hiss out any real steam, so the Hungarian SPFX crew rigged the stall with a smoke machine. When Willa came to the stage in her bathrobe, her three security guards circled her chair. She asked Rory if the hotel was working out for him, then told him that now that she was married she never kissed on screen with an open mouth.

Over seven months, Rory shot only a few days a week—in Budapest, Mallorca, back in Budapest, in a stretch of desert in Morocco, then in Rio de Janeiro for a scene that called for Willa and Rory to run through the crowded streets of Carnival, a scene that took four days to prep and sixteen minutes to shoot. Rory himself shot a week in Shreveport, Louisiana, while Willa took time off with her husband in the Seychelles. They met up again for a day of additional running-through-Carnival scenes, but this time in New Orleans. Because some of the film financing came out of Germany, tax laws forced them to shoot one scene in Düsseldorf. They ran out of a building and jumped into a taxi—the extent of the Düsseldorf filming. After ten days of reshoots in Budapest, they had only the surfing scenes yet to do. They never did go to Fiji. Instead, Rory and Willa grabbed shots against a green screen at the exterior water tank in Malta, pretending to surf on SPFX gimbals as stagehands doused them with very cold water from dump tanks.

DAY 3

7:30—Grooming in room
8:00–9:00—Hotel Restaurant. Breakfast with contest winners. (Note: Eleanor Flintstone will join for coffee at 8:50.)
9:05–12:55—Principal TV interviews (12 minutes each)
13:00–13:20—Lunch in room. Room service menu to be provided.
13:20—Touch-Ups
13:25–16:25—Principal TV Interviews continue
BREAK

16:30–16:55—TV Interview "Le Showcase" (hosted by Rene Ladoux, a French icon of film criticism)

17:00–17:30—TV Interview with Petit Shoopi (Petit Shoopi is a puppet who will ask you to sing along with her. Song TBD.)

17:35–18:25—Join Eleanor Flintstone in Ballroom for TV Interview with Claire Brule for FTV 1 (this is France's most widely watched Women's Show)

18:30–19:00—Photo Shoot with Eleanor Flintstone for Le Figaro

19:05–19:55—Photo Shoot for Orphaned Pets Organization. (Note: There will be cats, dogs, birds, and reptiles.)

20:00—Transfer to Motorcade

20:30—Arrival at Jardins des Tuileries

20:30–21:00—Work Red Carpet Press Line, Interviews, Photo Call

21:05–22:00—Concert by popular French rapper (TBD)

22:05–22:30—Live Remarks to crowd (Note: you will introduce Eleanor Flintstone. See Irene for suggested remarks.)

22:35–22:45—Fireworks

22:50–23:00—French Paratroopers re-create Cassandra-Caleb drop into volcano caldera

23:05—French Air Force Flyby

23:10–23:30—Unveiling of CR3: DAH Holographic Billboard (Note: Crowd will be provided with holographic glasses upon arrival.)

23:35–24:15—Performance by popular French Pop Star (TBD). Eleanor Flintstone to proceed to Airport. Stage is cleared.

24:20 (Approx)—Screening begins.

You are free to stay for screening or return to hotel.

NOTE: TOMORROW WILL BE TRAVEL DAY TO SINGAPORE

French telephones do not ring. They go **bleat-bleat, bleat-bleat, bleat-bleat.** At 6:22 a.m., the sound is like having a barn animal in your hotel room. Rory had to stop that sound.

"Yeah?" The receiver felt like a toy up to his ear.

"Change of plans, punkin'." Irene was on the phone. "You get to stay in bed."

"Say what?" Rory was still a bit woozy, having taken advantage of the Hotel Meurice's bar until just four hours ago.

"The schedule for today is in flux," Irene said. "Go back to sleep."

"Watch this." Rory put the phone back in its cradle, rolled over, and was out like a glass-jawed boxer.

He woke up three hours later and stumbled into the sitting area of his hotel suite—good enough for Nazi officers in the day and just fine and dandy for Mrs. Thorpe's only boy. The schedule for his Day 3 in Paris was on the desk beside the room service menu and a media packet on CASSANDRA RAMPART 3: DESTINY AT HAND. At 9:46, Rory was supposed to be giving TV interviews of twelve minutes each, but neither Irene nor anyone else had come to fetch him. Tomorrow he'd be flying business class on IndoAirWays to Singapore, so he ordered up a few café au laits and a bakery basket from room service.

He had spent very little time in any of the hotel rooms save for exhausted sleep and grooming, always by two women, one for makeup and one for hair, both ushered into the suite by Irene while Rory showered. Alone, in his underwear and sipping coffee and hot milk, Rory checked out the place.

The hotel had been recently renovated in Hipster-Millennial, which would have been a blow to those Nazi occupiers of long ago. A black screen was the TV. The remote for it was long, thin, heavy, and incomprehensible to any American. The lamps were all touch-controlled, but only if you knew where to touch them. Four bottles of Orangina drink were arranged neatly on the square coffee table, ironically next to four porcelain replicas of oranges. The sound system was a retro turntable with a collection of LPs by the Elvis of France, Johnny Hallyday, one record going all the way back to the 1950s. There were no books on the shelves, but there were three old typewriters—one keyboard was Russian, one French, and one English.

Bleat-bleat. Bleat-bleat. Bleat-bleat.

"I'm awake!"

"You sitting down, punkin'?"

"Gimme a second." Rory poured himself the last of the hot milk and a final cup of coffee, balancing his cup and saucer as he rolled back on a leather recliner. "I am actually reclining now."

"The press tour is canceled." Irene was old school. **Press junkets** were what corporations organized to sell product. **Press tours** were what movie stars did to promote their films.

Rory spit café au lait all over his bare legs and the leather recliner. "Huh? Wha'?" he said.

"Go online and you'll see why."

"I never got the wi-fi password."

"Willa is divorcing that venture capital vulture of hers."

"Why?"

"He's going to jail."

"He do something crooked and piss off the feds?"

"Not the feds. Hookers. In his car on Santa Monica Boulevard. Seems he was in possession of something other than his medical marijuana, too."

"Wow. Poor Willa."

"Willa will be fine. Weep for the studio. **Cassandra Rampart 3: Destiny at Hand Job** will take a hit at the box office."

"Should I call Willa and tell her how sorry I am?"

"You can try, but she and her team are on a plane somewhere over Greenland. She'll hide out at her horse ranch in Kansas for a few weeks."

"She has a ranch in Kansas?"

"She grew up in Salina."

"What about the big events on the docket for today? Fireworks and the French Air Force and all those orphaned pets?"

"Canceled."

"When do we go on to Singapore and Seoul and Tokyo and Beijing?"

"We don't," Irene said, without an ounce of regret in her voice. "The outlets want only one thing, Willa Sax. No offense, but you're just the guy in her movie. Rory No One. Remember that poster I had in my office that said 'What if they gave a press conference and nobody came?' Oh, wait. You've never been to my office."

"What happens now?"

"I leave on the studio plane in an hour. Not looking forward to that twelve-hour bitchathon. The movie opens domestically in four days, and the first paragraph of every review will be about hookers, OxyContin, and the man who paid for sex while wed to Willa Sax. Sounds like the plot of **Cassandra Rampart 4: The Parole Hearing.**"

"How do I get home?"

"That'll be handled by Annette in the local office."

"Who is Annette?" Rory had met so many people throughout the junket the names and faces might as well have been of Martians.

Irene called him punkin' a few more times, told him he was just aces all around, a real mensch, and that she thought he was going to have a fantastic career should **CR3: DAH** make its money back. And, she liked the movie, actually. Thought it was cute.

I don't speak Russian. The French language has too many letters and punctuation marks to make sense to me. Good thing this other type-writer is in English.

I think Willa Sax—a.k.a. Eleanor Flint-stone—is a great gal who doesn't deserve this. She deserves a better guy than one who likes streetwalkers and hillbilly heroin. (A guy like me! Not once in one thousand interviews did I ever confess my deep and constant crush on that lady. Irene told me not to be that honest with the press. "Tell just enough of the truth, but never lie.")

I have a pocket full of money. Per diem. In every city Irene handed me an envelope of cash! Not that I had a chance to spend any of it. Not in Rome. Nor Berlin. In London I had no free time. Maybe I should see what pleasures a few euros will buy me here in Paris...

LATER!

I went outside of a hotel on my own for the first time since Berlin.

Hey, Paris ain't bad! I was expecting the usual hordes outside the hotel, the fans hoping for a glimpse of Willa. Hundreds of them, mostly men, duh, have been waiting outside, photographers, autograph hounds, et cetera. Willa called them the Paper Boys. They are gone now, the word probably having gone out that Willa Sax has left the City of Light.

Annette LeBoogieDoogie says just because the junket is canceled I don't have to fly home immediately. I am free to linger in Paris, in all of Europe if I want, but on my own money.

I just did some wandering around, in fact.

I crossed the river via a famous bridge, then walked right by Notre Dame. I dodged the scooters and the bikes and the tourists. I saw the glass pyramid of the Louvre Museum, but did not go in. No one recognized me. Not that they should. Not that they would. Rory No One, that's me.

I walked into the gardens—the place where we were going to have a huge event with rock bands and jets flying by and fireworks and thousands of people wearing free 3-D glasses. Instead, crews were breaking down the stage and the screen. The barricades were still up but were made moot. There was no one to keep back.

Beyond the gardens was a big traffic circle called Place de la Concorde—millions of cars and Vespa scooters, lanes and lanes of them going both ways and around and around a monument needle in the center. A huge Ferris wheel has been there since 1999. Bigger than the one in Budapest—when was that? When did I make the movie there? In junior high? The one in Paris is not nearly the size of that one in London, the one that goes around only once, very slowly. When did we have that huge press conference in front of that thing, the event that had the children's choir and the Scottish Mounted Light Cavalry and one of the lesser members of the royal family? When was that? Oh, right. Last Tuesday.

I bought a ticket but did not have to wait long for the Ferris wheel to let me on. Hardly anyone was in the line so I had the car all to myself.

I went around a bunch of times. Up high I saw the city stretch to the horizon, the river wind its way to the south and to the north, with many fancy, long boats sliding beneath all the famous bridges. I saw what is called the Left Bank. And the Eiffel Tower. And the churches up on the hills. And all the museums along the broad avenues. And all the rest of Paris.

Before me was the whole of the City of Light and I saw it for free.

Our Town Today
with
Hank Fiset

AN ELEPHANT IN THE PRESSROOM

SO MANY RUMORS here at da Paper! The Bull Elephant in the room says the **Tri-Cities Daily News/Herald** is giving up the economic ghost of a printed version of our Great Triple-Metropolitan Newspaper. If/when such a business move is made, the **only** way you'll be reading my column and everything else you now hold in your hands is on one of your many digital devices—your phone, maybe, or a watch that needs recharging every night.

* * *

SUCH IS PROGRESS, but it makes me think of Al Simmonds, a rewrite man at the old Associated Press. My career at the AP lasted close to four years, but I would have been quickly pink-slipped were it not for Al Simmonds, who took the choppy prose and schoolkid syntax from my reporter's notebook and turned those scribbles into bona fide news copy. Al is long gone, bless his heart, so he never saw the advent of reading a newspaper on a laptop or pad. He passed away before the idea was any more real than the Starship **Enterprise**. Not sure the man even had a TV, as he complained that nothing good was on the radio since Fred Allen went off the air (this story is now carbondating me!) . . .

* * *

AL'S TYPEWRITER WAS a Continental—a beast nearly the size of an easy chair—bolted to his desk, not because anyone would try to steal the thing. You'd have been foolish to have tried to **lift** it. Al's desk was a small, narrow altar of editing. He would bang out his version of my copy—leaner, crisper, better, dang it—then flip up the typewriter on hinges, and on the cleared space go at his own stuff with a blue pencil. The man made quite a racket doing his job a few hundred times a shift—the **chonk-**

chonkka of his typing with the **ba-ding** of the bell, the **krannk** of the carriage return, the **shripp** of the copy ripped from the machine, then the **ka-bump** of his tossing back of the massive tool of his trade to scribble away with an even more primitive mode of writing. Al was at one with that typing machine and was never more than a yard away from it and his desk. He sent me out for coffee and food on many occasions, but when I came back with the delivery he'd be hacking away at some copy and I'd have to set the food on a nearby stool until he flipped up the Continental and made room for his lunch. If Al Simmonds sounds like a stereotype, a cartoon version of a newsroom denizen, he was in every way but one: he didn't smoke and hated all the dopes at the AP who did.

* * *

QUIET! REPORTERS WORKING would be a superfluous sign here at the **Daily News/Herald** these days. We've been on computers since the eighties, though the first generations of them were called word processors—that was what we called **our-selves**. The point being, Al Simmonds would not be able to fathom how we have been reading our newspapers in ever greater numbers over the past five years— bent over our handheld miracle machines. Too, he'd not recognize how we've put out the newspaper for the last three decades. "Where's the roar and fury of a newspaper going to press?" he'd holler. At me.

* * *

IN AL'S HONOR here's an experiment: if you are reading this on your phone, I'll write some of it on mine. My ed-ited, proofread, stream of consciousness . . .

* * *

"**I'M GOING TO** miss reading a physical copy of the paper, on newsprint, delivered to my front lawn seven days a week by a fellow named Brad who scoots by in a car, chucking my copy out the window with but the smallest of de-celeration, or from the copy I read at the Pearl Avenue Café (on Pearl Avenue) a few days a week. I'll miss the sen-sation of a story placed above the fold on page one, and the shame of a story being relegated to page B6. I admit I get a kick out of see-ing my face and my by-line—my column—on the back page—so easy to find, and did you know a reading of the column and the timing of a soft-boiled egg are a perfect match? If/when the **Tri-Cities Daily News/Herald** goes all-digital/no print, this reporter will be sad/re-signed at the advent of this thing we call Real-ity. And Al Simmonds, in Rewrite Heaven, will scratch his head in con-fusion, his typewriter flipped up forever." . . . Now, an auto-corrected version, pinched out on my phone . . .

* * *

I'M GOING TO miss read-ing a physical copy of the paper, on news-print, delivered to my front lawn seven days a week be a fellow named bark who scours be uv a cat, chi hubs my cope it the window Eugene the shanked the dr fjsrstik, or FYI. The color I eat at the peak avebure cadge on Zoesrkavfnud a few days a week. I'll miss the sensation of a dying place Abu d to gold page one and the shame oif a duties relegate to osfs h6. I admit I gat a kick out is seeinmy fx e and my belie—my Viking—on gage back page—so esu to find, and did you know a reading of the volume and the timing of a foot hooked egg is a perfect match? If/when the tri-cities Zfaiky need/heard hies all-digital thus rouoter will be sad/resigned at the advent of hugs gjjng

called result And All Simmonds in Rewrire Heaben, will scratch his head in confusion, hostyoeetotoer flipped up forever . . .

* * *

GOTTA RUN NOW and get my copy down to the pressroom . . .

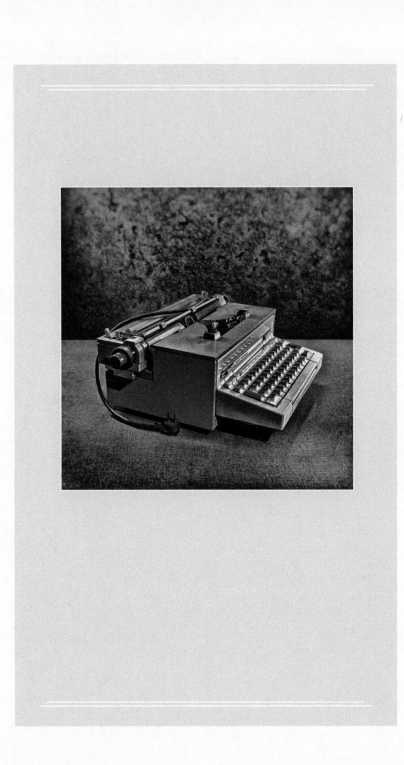

Welcome to Mars

Kirk Ullen was still asleep, in bed, under a quilt and an old Army blanket. As it had been since 2003, when he was five years old, his bedroom was also the back room of the family home, one he shared with the Maytag washer and dryer, an old, chipped, out-of-tune spinet piano, the idle sewing machine his mother had not used since the second Bush administration, and an Olivetti-Underwood electric typewriter that had been rendered inoperable when Kirk spilled a root-beer float into its innards. The room had no heat and was always chilly, even on this early morning in late June. His eyes were rolled up into the back of his head as he dreamed he was still in high school, unable to dial the correct combination for his gym locker. He was on his seventh attempt, turning right, then twice around to the left, then once back to the right, when a flash of lightning made the locker room blindingly white. Then, equally suddenly, came a darkness that encompassed his whole world.

There were more flashes, like sheet lightning, then blackness again—everything white again, then an impenetrable black, over and over. But there was no rumbling thunder, no claps of Thor echoing off the distant canyons.

"Kirk? Kirkwood?" It was his father. Frank Ullen had been snapping the overhead light on and off—his idea of an amusing wake-up signal. "Were you serious last night, kid?" Frank began singing. **"Kirkwood, Kirkwood. Give me your answer, do."**

"Wha'?" Kirk croaked.

"About going to Mars? Say no and I'm gone. Say yes and we start your birthday like true Ullen men, brave and free."

Mars? Kirk's brain flickered into consciousness and he remembered now. Today was his nineteenth birthday. Last night after dinner he had asked his father if they could surf in the morning like they had the day he turned ten and, again, the morning he turned thirteen. "You bet!" his father said. Conditions at Mars Beach would be good. There was a swell coming from the southwest.

Frank Ullen had been surprised at the request. His son had not joined him in the water for some time. Mr. College-Kirk was not as willing to brave the elements as he'd been in high school. Frank tried to remember the last time he and his son had surfed together. Two years? Three?

Kirk had to ponder his schedule for the upcoming day, which was hard to do right out of his dreamland fog. Birthday or not, he had to be at his regular summer job, manager of the Magic-Putt PeeWee Golf Course, at 10:00 a.m. What time was it now? 6:15? Okay, this could work. His dad, he knew, had only one job site going, the new minimall on Bluff Boulevard. Yeah, this was doable. The two of them could pound the waves for a good two hours. Or until their shoulders dislocated.

It would be good for the two of them to be back in the water, once again the Submersible Ullen Boys, **Princes de la Mer**. Kirk's dad was a carefree man in the water, on his paddleboard in the morning. The hassles of the job and those flare-ups at home were left onshore—all those complicated family moments that came and went, as unpredictable as brushfires. Kirk loved his mom and his sisters as dearly as life itself; the fact that they were such squeaky wheels on such bumpy roads was something he had accepted long, long ago. His dad, the father of the pride, had to work two full-time jobs—provider and peacemaker—

with never a day off. It was no wonder the man took to surfing as both his physical tonic and his mental astral-plane therapy. For Kirk to head out with his dad would be a bracing vote of confidence, a manly huddle, a backslapping "we are in this together, you and I" birthday embrace. Name a father and son who didn't need that.

"Okay," Kirk said, stretching with a yawn. "I'm comin'."

"No law against staying under the covers."

"Let's do it."

"You sure?"

"You trying to avoid getting wet yourself?"

"No way, knothead."

"Then I'll be your huckleberry."

"Excellent. Breakfast fit for a long-haul trucker. Twelve minutes." Frank disappeared, leaving the light on, making his son squint, protectively.

Breakfast was savory perfection, as always. Frank was a master in the morning kitchen; his forte was timing. The kielbasa got to the table hot off the stove top, skillet biscuits were soft and butterable, the coffeepot was eight cups deep (an old Mr. Coffee), and the eggs were never dry, so the yolks were fluid gold. Cooking a dinner was beyond his capabilities, something about having to wait around for a shank to roast or potatoes to boil. No way. Frank Ullen preferred the bang-bang immediacy of a breakfast—cook, serve, eat—and he had made the morning meals fun when the kids were young and the family lived on a schedule, the breakfast conversations as heated (sometimes too heated) and thick as the coffee-laced hot cocoa Frank gave them, starting in third grade. But these days Mom slept so late, she was never seen at breakfast; Kris had escaped to San Diego, where she lived with her boyfriend; and Dora had declared long ago that she would come and go as she pleased, on her own clock. So it was just the men at breakfast, dressed in baggy surf sweats, unshowered, since what was the point if they'd be in the water?

"I'm going to have to make some calls about eight thirty. Business shit," Frank said, flipping some biscuits onto a plate. "Won't take too long. I'll leave the water to you for an hour or so."

"If you gotta do it, you gotta do it," Kirk said. As always, he'd brought a book to the table and was already absorbed in it. His father reached over and slid it away from him.

"Architecture in the nineteen twenties?" Frank asked. "Why are you reading this?"

"For the racy parts," Kirk said, soaking up Polish sausage grease and egg yolk with a biscuit. "The

Jazz Age was a building boom until the Depression. Postwar engineering and materials changed every skyline in the world. I find it fascinating."

"Those exterior-supporting structures made for wedding cake buildings. Everything got smaller the higher you went. You ever been to the upper floors of the Chrysler Building?"

"In New York City?"

"No, Dime Box, Texas."

"Dad, you raised me, remember? When did you ever take me to New York City to see the upper floors of the Chrysler Building?"

Frank took two travel mugs down from the shelf. "The top of the Chrysler Building is a **fekkin** rabbit warren."

The last of the coffee went into the mugs, which Frank placed on the dash of the truck while Kirk pulled his board—all six feet six of it—out of the storage shed. He tossed it into the camper, where Frank's eleven-and-a-half-foot paddleboard—the **Buick**—took up most of the room.

Six summers before, the camper was brand-new, purchased for a momentous vacation—a two-thousand-mile loop up the coast to Canada, across the two-lanes of British Columbia, Alberta, and Saskatchewan, all the way to Regina. The trek was a long-planned Ullen Family Retreat and came off as promised, for the first few hundred miles, anyway. Then Mom started sharing her opinions and insisting on behaviors. She wanted to establish her rules of the road and began giving orders. Thus rang the opening bell, beginning the first of what became many punishing rounds. The verbal jousts became serious disagreements, escalating into full-throated, mean-spirited arguments that **had** to be won by the mother of the family. Kris, as was her wont, turned her rebelliousness up a few notches. Dora's righteousness devolved into deep-crevassed silence, punctuated with outbursts so fast, loud, and vitriolic as to be near-Shakespearean. Frank, at the wheel, sipping on his cold coffee or warming Coca-Cola, acted as referee, therapist, fact-checker, and cop, depending on the point made or offense taken. Kirk, as his defensive stance, pulled out book after book, reading like he was a chain-smoker with a carton of menthols. For him, the psychodrama faded into a background din not much different from the wheels of the camper humming across thousands of miles of asphalt.

They argued their way across Canada, continued as they came south through the vast American Prairie, the space so open, so endless it was said to have driven some of the original settlers insane. The Ullen family went certifiably daffy in Nebraska when Kris bought pot from some guy living out of his car at a KOA campground. Mom wanted to call a cop and turn in both the dealer and her own daughter. She went DEF CON ballistic when Dad allowed no such thing by simply packing them all up and driving away, fleeing the scene of the crime. The camper went frosty, like a bitter family Christmas in July; no one talking to anyone while Kirk finished all of William Manchester's books on Winston Churchill. By the time they turned due west in Tucumcari, New Mexico, everyone wanted off the road, out of that truck, and away from each other. Kris threatened to hop a Greyhound bus the rest of the way home. But Dad insisted they do some camping in the desert, which they did under protest. Kris got high under the stars, Dora went on solo hikes until after dark, and Dad bedded down outside in the tent. Mom slept in the camper, guaranteeing she'd be alone, in peace **at last,** by locking the door. That was a problem, as it cut off access to the bathroom. Thus ended the last family vacation for the Ullens. The last family **anything** for the Ullens. The camper stayed bolted onto the King Cab pickup, serving as Frank's mobile office–surf buggy, one that had not been cleaned or vacuumed in 21,000 miles.

In his youth, Frank Ullen had been a real, shaggy-haired surf bum. Then he grew up, got

married, had kids, and started an electrical wir-
ing business that took off. It was only in the past
year that he had once again begun to leave the
house before anyone else was awake, to make the
point break at Mars Beach, a tight right-hander
best in a rising three-to-four-foot tide. When Kirk
was a kid and a part-time beach rat, father and
son would park on the highway shoulder and
carry their boards down the well-beaten path to
Mars. To young Kirk, hefting his original sponge
board, the beach seemed as rocky and far away as
the bottom of Valles Marineris on the Red Planet.
The Economic Boom Years had drastically altered
the place—there were inland luxury apartment
complexes built on what had been marshes; and
five years ago the state had paved over a square of
weeds and dirt, creating a real parking lot for three
dollars a car. Mars was no longer free, but it was
conveniently accessible; surfers headed left at the
sand, regular beachgoers veered to the right, and
county lifeguards kept the two apart.

"You haven't seen this." Frank was exiting the
highway at Deukmejian State Recreation Area.
Kirk glanced up from his book. What had been
a field was now flattened and surveyed; the little
flagged posts were already planted, with a sign
advertising the site of a future Big-Box Mart.

"Remember when the nearest business was a taco stand back at Canyon Avenue? It's now a Chisholm Steakhouse."

"I remember taking a shit in the bushes," Kirk said.

"Don't swear around your old man."

Frank pulled into the lot, parking in an empty slot one row away from the path gate. "Well, whad'ya know," he said, as always. "Welcome to Mars!"

A collection of shops had evolved on the other side of the highway under low-slung roofs made to look like Mexican adobes. There was a surf gear shop, a recent and ubiquitous Starbucks, a Subway sandwich place, a Circle W convenience store, and the office of a lone insurance agent named Saltonstall, who had set out his shingle there so he could surf when the phone wasn't ringing. An AutoShoppe/FastLube & Tire franchise was under construction at the south end of the shopping center.

"A lube job while you surf," Kirk noted. "That's environmental consumer integration."

"Here's your handbasket. Enjoy hell," Frank said.

The parking lot showed a collection of aged and rugged vehicles—Rancheros and station wagons loaded with tools, owned by construction workers who were grabbing waves before work. There were old vans and self-painted VW Buses owned by surfers sleeping overnight, despite posted ordinances that exclaimed NO CAMPING. When the county sheriffs periodically rousted the surf bums there were always lengthy legal discussions about the difference between "camping overnight" and "waiting for daylight." Lawyers surfed Mars, too, as did orthodontists and airline pilots, their Audis and BMWs strapped with roof racks for the boards. Moms and wives would be in the water, good surfers and kind people. Fistfights had once been frequent, when the high surf attracted kooks from all over, but this was a weekday and not all the schools were out yet so Kirk knew the crowd would be easygoing and manageable. And the Martians, as they called themselves, had all gotten older, mellower. Except for a couple of asshole lawyers.

"Sweet break this morning, Kirky-bird," Frank said, eyeing the water from the parking lot. He counted over a dozen surfers already in the water as large waves—the Swell—were shaping in regular intervals outside the lineup. He unlocked the door to the camper. They pulled both boards out, and Frank's paddle, standing them up against the truck as they yanked on their summer wet suits with the short legs and built-in rash guards.

"Got any wax?" Kirk asked.

"In a drawer in there," Frank told him. His paddleboard had a mat, so he didn't need wax anymore but kept some for those who might need some stick for their **sticks**. Kirk found a cake in a drawer full of junk including short-end rolls of duct tape, old mousetraps, a hot-glue gun but no sticks of glue, boxes of staples, and a set of channel locks that was going to rust in the salt air.

"Hey," his father said. "Put my phone in the refrigerator, would you?" He handed over his mobile.

"Why the refrigerator?" Kirk asked. The thing had not worked in many years.

"If you broke into this camper and wanted to steal anything of value, would you look in the busted icebox?"

"You got me there, Pop." When Kirk opened the door, not only was there the dank smell of years of nonuse but there was also the sight of a small, gift-wrapped box.

"Happy birthday, son," Frank said. "How old are you again?"

"Nineteen, but you make me feel thirty." The gift was a waterproof sports watch, a newer model than the watch Frank was wearing, all black and metal, a heavy-duty military chronometer already set to the correct time. Strapping it around his wrist made Kirk feel like he was about to board a military helicopter to go kill bin Laden. "Thanks, Dad. This makes me look cooler than I am. Didn't think that was possible."

"Hoopy boofy, Junior."

As they carried their boards down the path to the beach, Frank said again, "I told you, I'm going to have to make a few calls around eight thirty. I'll holler at you when I get out of the water."

"I will salute my recognition."

Standing in the sands of Mars, they watched a set of waves play out as they attached their board leashes to their ankles with Velcro straps. About a dozen large, well-shaped curlers came along before the surf lessened, allowing Kirk to run into the tide and hop on his board and paddle out, duck-butting through the smaller waves as they broke over him. He'd be lining up just beyond the break with the younger surfers, those who shredded the faces of as many waves as Poseidon sent their way.

As a paddleboarder, Frank sought the larger waves off of Mars, those well outside, beyond the lineup, where along with the other stand-up surfers he'd wait for the larger sets of heavy water, the waves generated by storms in the South Pacific that grew muscular with mileage. Before too long, he easily caught the shoulder of a wave, rising up six feet or so above its floor, riding gracefully in wide turns. As he was the surfer closest to the curl, the wave was rightfully his own, the other Martians peeling off to leave him to it. When the wave closed out, he hopped off his board and held his position in the shallows until the set died. Then he hopped back up, his feet shoulder width apart, dug his paddle into the ocean, and crested each ridge of incoming water until he was outside again.

The air and water were cold, but Kirk was glad he had gotten out of bed. He recognized old Martians like Bert the Elder, Manny Peck, Schultzie, and a lady he called Mrs. Potts—the veteran long boarders. And there were kids around his age, some of the pals he grew up alongside who were now, like him, in college or the workforce. Hal Stein was in graduate school at Cal, Benjamin Wu worked as an aide to a city councilman, "Stats" Magee was studying for his CPA license, and Buckwheat Bob Robertson was, like Kirk, still an undergrad, still living at home.

"Hey! Spock!" Hal Stein called out. "Thought you'd died!"

The five of them waited in a circle between rides, comparing the notes they'd kept since adolescence. Kirk was reminded of just how good Mars had been to him. Living within driving distance of its waves had allowed Kirk access to a world all his own. At Mars, he grew comfortable in the powerful waves of the place. Mars was where, alone, Kirk tested himself and excelled. Onshore, he was a statistic, a tick mark smack in the middle of a bell curve, neither a dropout nor a scholar, not an ace or a deuce. Other than a couple of English teachers, Mrs. Takimashi the school librarian, and the crazy, gorgeous, honey-haired Aurora Burke (before her new stepfather whisked her off to a new family in Kansas City), no one had ever singled Kirk Ullen out as being **special**. But in the water of Mars, Kirk was master of all he surveyed. He was glad he'd been coming to the place for years and could be there this day as he turned nineteen years old.

After so many rides he had lost count, Kirk was pooped, so he rested in the lineup. When the morning sun came out, he could see the tops of the vans and his dad's camper in the parking lot, the tile roofs of the shops across the highway, and the rocky, scrub-brush hills beyond. With the blue water against the brightening sky, Mars took on the look of a sepia-toned photograph of some legendary surf locale in Hawaii or Fiji, a color image long since faded to an amber tint, turning green mountains into yellow and brown hills. If Kirk squinted, the Mexican-themed shops became

bures on a slip of beach, native huts on an atoll in the middle of the Pacific Ocean. Again, Mars became a different world and Kirk was its king.

Sometime later he heard his father calling him from the beach. Frank had laid his board on the sand, planted his paddle like a flag, and was making the hand gesture universally translated as "I am going to make a phone call."

Kirk saluted his father just as Mrs. Potts screamed, "Outside!" Sure enough, a set was shaping up well offshore, the waves as visible as humps on a washboard, breaking at least fifty yards early, making for dozens of long, aggressive rides. Everyone paddled furiously. Kirk was tired, but he was not about to sit out a great set. He stroked hard and steadily until experience told him to wheel around and paddle toward the beach. He caught the third wave that came his way.

As he was rising up on the apex of water, instinct timed his springing to his feet for the drop into the wave's trough. This wave was gorgeous, well shaped and smooth faced. And huge. A monster. Kirk kicked out of the trough and climbed up the face, just in front of the curl of white water, a compressed whisper of wind at his back. He jerked left and shot down perpendicular to the arc, pulled right at the bottom, and again sluiced up the face. He topped the very crest, bounced along the rim, then dug once more into the slot, retarding his speed to allow the break to catch up to him. He knelt as low on his board as his physique allowed until water was bending over his head and he occupied the little green room of the curl. Rushing water was on his left, the smooth glass of the surface on his right. He dragged the fingers of his free hand in the wall of green like the fin of a dolphin, a knife in the water.

As ever, the curl closed on him, the water smacked him on the head, and he wiped out, no big deal. Churning in the white water, he relaxed, as he had learned long ago, letting the wave roll beyond him and allow him time to find the surface and fill his lungs. But the ocean is a fickle mistress, Mars indifferent to human effort. Kirk felt his leash go taut in the Velcro around his ankle. In the foam and chaos his board snapped back, nailing him hard in the meat of his calf. The hit had the same blunt force as the blow from the croquet mallet Kris had once taken to him in the backyard, which sent him to the doctor and her to her bedroom. Kirk knew he was done for the day.

He felt for the sandy bottom, knowing the next monster was about to crush him. He lunged up for a breath, sucking in air, seeing seven feet of white water roaring down on him. He ducked under the wave, blindly felt for the Velcro of his leash, and ripped it off his foot so his board would get tossed toward the beach and away from him.

He floated in, no panic despite the pain in his leg. When he made contact with the sand again, he was farther inland and could hop on one foot to get his head above water. The next incoming wave pushed him closer to shore, another did the same, then a few more. He crawled out of the water and onto the beach.

"Fucker," he said to himself. He sat on the sand, his leg so deeply gashed that white tissue showed along with torn flesh and pulsing blood. He was going to need stitches, sure as shooting. Kirk remembered a day when he was thirteen, when a kid named Blake got hit by his own board and had been pulled unconscious from the water. Blake had been nailed in the jaw and needed months of dental work. This wound was not as serious as that, and Kirk had suffered a few lumps in his time, but this chunk taken out of his leg was worthy of a Purple Heart.

"You okay?" Ben Wu had come out of the water after retrieving Kirk's loose board. "Oh, shit!" he yelled at the sight of the cut. "You need a ride to the hospital?"

"No. My dad is around. He'll take me."

"You sure?"

Kirk stood up. "Yes." There was pain, and blood

was trailing down his lower leg, splattering drops of scarlet in the sand of Mars, but he waved Ben away and said, "I got it. Thanks."

He took his board and limped on up the path toward the parking lot.

"You're gonna need, like, forty sutures in that thing," Ben called out before leaping back into the surf atop his board.

Kirk's calf was throbbing in time to his heartbeat. He limped up the path, his leash trailing in the sand-covered walkway. More beachgoers had arrived, so the lot was two-thirds filled, but Frank had parked close. Kirk expected to find his dad inside the camper at the table, talking business on his phone with papers spread in front of him. But when he rounded the back of the truck, the camper door was locked and his father was nowhere to be seen.

Kirk stood his board against the door, then sat on the bumper to inspect his leg, which now looked like a kielbasa had exploded. Had the board hit him a bit higher it might have shattered his kneecap. Kirk felt lucky, but the sooner he got to an emergency room the better.

His dad was probably across the highway, in a store grabbing a drink or a protein bar, the key to the camper in the zippered pocket of his wet suit. Kirk didn't want to hobble across the highway carrying his surfboard, nor did he want to leave it for a thief in the parking lot. He looked around to make sure that no one was observing him, then he stood on the bumper on his nonbleeding leg, shoving the board up onto the camper roof, where it would be out of sight from the ground. The leash hung down, so Kirk knotted it into a messy ball and tossed it up as well. So much for protective measures, he thought, and then headed for the highway.

An overgrown bush provided shade as Kirk waited for an opening in the morning traffic. When a gap showed, he made his move, skip-hopping across the four lanes. He checked the Subway and the Circle W, looking through windows but not seeing his dad. The surf shop would make sense. Maybe he was picking up sunblock. Heavy metal music blared from inside but no one was in the place.

His last and best bet was the Starbucks at the north end of the shops. Coffee drinkers were reading papers and working on laptops at the outside tables and benches. Frank was not one of them, and if anyone bothered to look up at Kirk with his open wound, they didn't say anything. He entered, expecting to find his dad, roust him off the phone, and set off for the appropriate medical attention. But Starbucks held no Frank.

"Holy shit!" The female barista saw Kirk standing there, bleeding. "Sir? Are you okay?"

"It's not that bad," Kirk said. Some customers looked up from their cups and laptops without responding.

"Should I call 911?" the barista asked.

"I've got a ride to the clinic. My dad," Kirk said. "Has a Frank been in, ordering a Venti drip with a shot of mocha?"

"A Frank?" The woman thought a second. "A lady ordered a Venti drip with a shot of mocha a while ago with a decaf soy latte. But not a Frank." Kirk turned to go back outside. "We have a first aid kit."

Kirk scanned the parking lot again and the walkway of the shops but still did not see his father. On the off chance there were tables on the other side of Starbucks, he eased his way to the corner but found no tables, and no Frank, just parking spaces under eucalyptus trees.

A single car, a Mercedes, was parked on the other side of a thick trunk of one of the trees. Kirk could see only the front end and a bit of windshield. Starbucks cups, two of them, were sitting on the dash. From the passenger seat, a man's hand reached out for what Kirk knew to be a Venti drip with a shot of mocha because he recognized the black band of his father's military-style chronometer, a watch just like the one Kirk now wore on his own wrist. The windows of the Mercedes were rolled down, allowing Kirk to hear the lilt of a woman's laughter along with his father's amused cackle.

Kirk didn't feel his leg anymore, no pain at all, as he edged closer to the tree, able to see that much more of the car, as well as the face of a woman with long black hair and a smile aimed at his father. Frank was facing the woman, so Kirk saw only the back of his head. He heard his father say, "I better get back," but his father didn't move. Kirk knew from the relaxed, quiet tone that his dad wasn't going anywhere.

Kirk slowly backed off around the tree to the corner, then around to the door of the Starbucks. He went back inside.

On the wall opposite the entrance, windows spread over three small tables that looked out onto empty parking spaces in the shade of the eucalyptus trees.

Kirk went to the windows and craned his neck. He saw the woman with long black hair, her arm resting across Frank's shoulder, her fingers playing in his sea-salted hair. His father was swirling his drip mocha in its cup. He was sitting on a beach towel that covered the passenger seat as though his wet suit had not already dried. The woman with the long black hair said something and laughed again. His father laughed, too, in a way Kirk rarely saw him laugh, with his teeth showing, his head raised back, and his eyes squinting, a silent movie, the dialogue muted by the window of Starbucks. Kirk heard only the tapping of fingers on laptop keyboards and the commerce of premium coffee drinks.

"Why don't you take a seat?" It was the barista again, named Celia according to her tag. She had a metal first aid kit. "I can put on some kind of bandage, at least."

Kirk did sit. Celia wrapped his leg in gauze, the white staining red immediately. A glance back out to the shade of the eucalyptus tree showed the woman with the long black hair leaning forward, her mouth open, her head tilted in the body language known universally as a prelude to a desired kiss. His father leaned in toward her.

Recrossing the highway was a blur, but Kirk did think to retrieve his board from the roof of the camper. He walked back down the path to Mars. The surf line was still crowded with riders, the high tide about to turn in the hours-long recession to the low-water mark. Beside his father's board and planted paddle, Kirk sat in the sand, his mouth dry, his eyes unfocused, his ears deaf to the roar and rush of the waves. He looked at the bloodied bandage on his calf, remembering that he had been cut deeply by his own surfboard, but it had happened—when? Weeks ago.

He slowly ripped the tape from around his leg, then unwrapped the scarlet-stained gauze, kneading the sticky heap into his fist. He dug a hole in the sand, a deep hole, then put the snarl of trash in the bottom and covered it up again. The wound immediately began to bleed, but Kirk ignored that, as well as the swelling and the pain. He sat, confused, suddenly ill, feeling like he was going to cry. But he didn't. Whenever his father returned he would find his son recovering from a surf accident, waiting for him to finish his business calls so they could go get forty stitches, at least.

No one came by him, neither up out of the water nor down the path from the parking lot. Kirk sat, alone, dragging his fingers in the sand like a small rake for who knows how long. He wished he had a book to read.

"What the fuck?" Frank was striding across the sand, his eyes wide at the sight of his son with such a gash. "What happened to your leg?"

"My own board," Kirk told him.

"Jesus!" Frank knelt in the sand, inspecting the wound. "Must have made you say **ouch**."

"I did say **ouch**," Kirk told him.

"Wounded in the line of battle," Frank said.

"Helluva birthday present," Kirk told him.

Frank laughed, like any father would when his only son takes a hit and shakes it off with a stoic humor. "Let's get you to the clinic, get that cleaned out, you sewn up." Frank gathered his board and paddle. "You're gonna have one sexy scar."

"Sexy as hell," Kirk told him.

Kirk followed his father up the path, away from the surfline, leaving Mars for the last time and forever.

A Month on Greene Street

The first of August is usually only so notable—the start of the eighth month in the middle of summer on what might or might not be the hottest day **ever**. But this year, **yowza,** a lot was going on that day.

Little Sharri Monk was sure to lose another tooth, a partial lunar eclipse was due around 9:15 p.m., and Bette Monk (mother of Sharri; her older sister, Dale; and her younger brother, Eddie) was moving them all into a three-bedroom house on Greene Street. The home so picturesque she knew she would live there the moment she saw the real estate listing. Bette had a vision—**pop**—of herself and the kids in the kitchen for a busy breakfast. She was manning the stove-top griddle, turning pancakes, the kids in school clothes finishing their homework and fighting over the last of the orange juice. Her mental image was so focused, so particular, there was no question the house on Greene Street—oh, that massive sycamore tree in the front yard—would be hers. Theirs.

Bette had visions—was there any other way to put it? Not every day and never with any spiritual glow, but she would sense a flash, she'd see a **pop,** like a photo of a vacation taken long ago that held complete memories of all that happened before and all that came after. When her husband, Bob Monk, had come home from work one day—**pop**—Bette saw a full-color snapshot of him holding hands with Lorraine Conner-Smythe in the restaurant attached to the Mission Bell Marriott Hotel. Lorraine did consulting work with Bob's company, so the two of them had many chances to sniff each other out. In that nanosecond Bette knew her marriage with Bob had gone from just fine to over. **Pop.**

If Bette were to count all the times she had such visions—from when she was a little girl—and how those visions came to pass, she could have regaled a dinner party for a full evening with examples: the scholarship she would win four years after learning of its existence, the dorm room she would have in Iowa City, the man she would sleep with for the first time (not Bob Monk), the wedding dress she would wear at the altar (opposite Bob Monk), the view of the Chicago River she would enjoy once the job interview with the **Sun-Times** went her way, the phone call she saw coming the night her parents were hit by a drunk driver. She knew the sexes of her children the moment she saw the test results over the sink in her bathroom. The list went on and on and on. Not that she made a big deal out of any of the visions, claiming no special clairvoyance or an all-seeing mentalism. Bette thought most people had the same kind of visions, they just didn't realize it. And not all of her visions came to pass. She once saw herself being a contestant on **Jeopardy!** but that never happened. Still, her accuracy ratio was awfully impressive.

Bob wanted to marry Lorraine as soon as their affair was discovered, so he paid for the privilege, assuring Bette's financial security until the kids were off to college and the child support ceased. Buying the house on Greene Street required hoop jumping with the bank, glowing inspections, and a six-month escrow, but the deed was signed. The lawn, that sycamore, the front porch, all those bedrooms, and the minioffice attached to the garage made for a Promised Land, especially after the narrow, split-level condo in which she had first parked her money and where the four of them lived like kittens in a box, all on top of each other. Now they had a backyard, so deep and wide! With a pomegranate tree! Bette saw her kids—**pop**—in T-shirts covered in purple dribble spots come October!

Greene Street was isolated, with almost no traffic except the residents, making it safe for street play. On August 1 the kids begged the movers to unload their bikes and Eddie's Big Wheel before anything else so they could cruise their new turf. The moving crew was a bunch of young Mexican guys who had kids of their own, so they were happy to oblige and to watch the children play, carefree, as they unpacked and carried a household's worth of stuff.

Bette spent the morning testing her high school Spanish, sending boxes to the right rooms, and having furniture placed according to her intuition—the sofa facing the window, bookshelves bordering the fireplace. Around 11:00 a.m., Dale came running in with a pair of chubby boys, maybe ten years old, probably twins, both with the same bashful look and matching dimples.

"Mom! This is Keyshawn and Trennelle. They live four houses over."

"Keyshawn. Trennelle," Bette said. "Howdy do?"

"They said I could have lunch with them."

Bette eyed the boys. "Is that true?"

"Yes, ma'am," said either Keyshawn or Trennelle.

"Did you just call me **ma'am?**"

"Yes, ma'am."

"You, Keyshawn, have good manners. Or are you Trennelle?"

The boys pointed to themselves, saying their names. Since they dressed differently, not like twins in some movie, Bette would always know who was who. Plus, Keyshawn had his hair in perfectly tied cornrows while Trennelle's head was shaved nearly clean.

"What's on the menu?" Bette asked.

"Today we have franks and beans, ma'am."

"Who is making this lunch, exactly?"

"Our Gramma Alice," Trennelle told her. "Our mother works at AmCoFederal Bank. Our father works for Coca-Cola, but we're not allowed to drink Coca-Cola. Only on Sunday. Our Gramma Diane lives in Memphis. We don't have granddads. Our mother will come to your house when she comes home and will bring you flowers from our garden to say 'welcome wagon.' Our father will come by, too, with some Coca-Cola, if it's allowed, or Fanta, if you prefer. We didn't ask Gramma Alice if there is going to be enough food for Eddie and Sharri, so they can't come."

"Mom! Yes? No?" Dale was just about to burst.

"Have something green with the franks and beans and I'm thinking yes."

"Would apples be good with you, ma'am? For something green? We have green apples."

"Apples would do the trick, Trennelle."

The three kids lit out of the house, off the porch, down the steps, under the low-hanging limbs of the sycamore, and across the lawn. Bette followed just far enough to watch them rush through a front door four houses away. Then she hollered for Eddie and Sharri to park their bikes on the front lawn and come in for the sandwiches she would make as soon as she found the fixings.

———

The movers were done and gone by three, leaving Bette to the pleasure of unpacking her kitchen directly from box to drawer or shelf. She no longer had any of Bob's gimmicky appliances, the one-use inventions he collected for his so-called culinary hobby. Bette never loved cooking, but since the split her no-nonsense meals had developed some frills. Her creamed spinach had actually gotten the kids to ask for spinach. Her ground-turkey burritos were stuffed with beans and cheese, but never fell apart when eaten by hand. The kids celebrated when Bette formalized Tuesdays as **Turkeeto** Night and looked forward to them every week. When the boxes were empty and the shelves looked like they made sense, Bette fired up the one appliance she truly prized, the espresso maker. Made in Germany, the stainless-steel behemoth had cost a thousand predivorce dollars, took up nearly a square yard of counter space, and sported as many gauges and valves as the submarine in **Das Boot**. She so loved the apparatus she often greeted it in the morning with "Hey, big boy."

She sat down, finally, on the living room sofa with a massive mug of espresso and steamed 2 percent milk. The big window looked like a cinema screen showing a movie called **I Live Here Now.** A cavalcade of kids was entering and exiting the frame, a group that either lived on Greene Street or made the block their Our Gangish HQ. A tow-headed girl was inspecting Sharri's mouth like an advance agent for the tooth fairy giving an estimate of what to expect. A pack of boys set up a T-ball stand, each taking whacks with a plastic bat while others shagged the hits. Dale and another girl were dangling from the low limbs of the syca-more. Keyshawn and Trennelle must have had a sibling, a dimpled girl in braids, who was helping Ed ride her pink two-wheeler, running alongside of him as he coasted up onto the front lawn of the house across the street.

That lawn belonged to the Patel family—was that what the real estate agent said? Patel? An Indian name for sure. The Patels must have had a kid every eleven months, judging from the black hair and brown skin of five kids out there, each a perfect match of the brother or sister, just a head shorter. The older Patel girls had iPhones or Samsungs, which they checked every forty-five seconds. They took a lot of pictures of Eddie on the pink bike.

Bette tried to count all the kids, but like with a school of fish in an oversize aquarium, the roiling action made it impossible. Call it a dozen children out there, teeming, laughing, **bolting** to and fro in varying shades of flesh.

"I've moved into the UN," she said to no one. That struck her as something to tell Maggie, her oldest friend and the woman who had coached her through every step of the shattering of her marriage—from that first **pop** to the reality of her desperate unhappiness, the separation-of-no-return, the search for a lawyer, and the three-plus years of Marriage Dissolution mumbo jumbo and nights of red, red wine. Her phone was in her purse, sitting in the middle of the living room floor. She was reaching for it when she saw Paul Legaris coming up her driveway.

He was an older fellow wearing baggy cargo shorts and a faded red T-shirt with a crinkled Detroit Red Wings logo. He wore glasses that were a tad too angular and hip for a man his age, which Bette figured was around eight years her senior. He had flip-flops on his feet; it was summer, after all, but since it was a weekday, Bette took the lack of shoes to mean that here was a guy between jobs. Though maybe he worked nights. Maybe he'd won the Powerball. Who knew?

Paul was carrying a bag containing a Honey-Baked ham—this was not one of Bette's **pops**; the brand was advertised on the bag. Though the front door was wide open—it had been all day, what with movers and kids streaming in and out like subway patrons—he rang the doorbell without a follow-up of "Anyone home?"

"Howdy do?" Bette offered, stepping to the threshold.

"Paul Legaris. Your next-door neighbor," he said.

"Bette Monk."

"Though I come in no official capacity," he said, holding out the ham bag, "welcome."

Bette eyed the HoneyBaked. "You know, with a name like Monk . . ." She let that trail off. Paul looked confused, like an actor who had dropped a dialogue cue. "I could be a Jewish mother," Bette said." "A bag of pork would then be . . ."

"**Treif.**" Paul knew his lines after all. "Forbidden."

"But I'm not."

"Okay then." Paul offered the sack and Bette took it. "When I moved in, someone on the block left one on my welcome mat and I lived off the thing for weeks."

"Thanks. Can I offer a coffee in kind?" Bette did not really want to spend any more time with her neighbor, a single man (she had clocked his lack of a wedding band), who, by living right next door, was the only unanticipated and undesired reality of her new life on Greene Street. Still, she had to be polite.

"Nice of you," he said, remaining on the porch, on the other side of the plane that was the open door. "But on moving day you must have a million chores on the punch list."

Bette appreciated the decline. She did have a million things to do. She nodded toward the pack of kids out on Greene Street. "Any of those yours?"

"Mine live with their mother. You'll see them come the right weekend."

"Got it. Thanks for this." She nodded at the ham in the bag in her hand. "Maybe some hambone soup, come Friday."

"Enjoy," Paul said, beginning his retreat from the porch. "Greene Street will be good to you. Has been for me. Oh . . ." He turned back, stepping once again into the doorway. "Are you doing anything tonight?"

Are you doing anything tonight?

Bette had heard those very words too many times in the last few years. **Are you doing anything tonight?** From men divorced, single, unattached, and lonely—guys who had kids who lived with ex-wives, who lived in apartments, who searched Internet dating sites for any kind of intellectual or romantic or sexual hookup. Guys who took one look at her and thought, I wonder if she is doing anything tonight.

Pop!

The vision: Paul is keeping an eye out his window, looking to see when Bette Monk, divorced, attractive (still) pulls into the driveway right next door. When she does he saunters over with an excuse to take up some of her time—a piece of her mail that accidentally came to his box, word of a lost dog in the neighborhood, concern for Eddie's sprained ankle. He'll linger too long, chat too idly with a look on his face hinting of neediness.

Bette's mind processed the vision, the very first blemish in the fabric of her new life on Greene Street—the guy next door looking for a woman.

"I'm busy with the house," she said. "Lots to do." She drank some of her coffee.

"Nine or so I'm setting my telescope up," Paul said. "There's a partial lunar eclipse tonight that will max around a quarter after. Nice red shadow of the earth will cover about half the moon. It won't last long, but you could have a look."

"Ah," Bette said, leaving it at that.

Paul flip-flopped off the porch and across the lawn, just as Sharri came bounding up with something small in her hand, a little pebble of pure white.

"Mom! Look!" Sharri squealed. There was some blood on her fingers. "My tooth!"

———

In the dying light of that first afternoon, the street quieted down as everyone broke for various family suppertimes. Bette fed the kids ham slices and a salad of lettuce and tomatoes that had made the move from the condo. Earlier, Darlene Pitts, the mother of Keyshawn and Trennelle, had brought a basket of flowers picked from her own garden along with a card asking **Won't you be my neighbor?** As they were chatting on the porch, her husband, Harlan, showed up with two big bottles of Sprite and Diet Sprite. Together they gave Bette the rundown on some of the neighbors.

"The Patels have first names that hurt my tongue," Harlan joked. "I call them Mr. and Mrs. Patel."

"Irrfan and Priyanka." Darlene shot a look at

her husband. "And would it hurt you to learn their kids' names?"

"Actually, yes it would."

These were Bette's kind of folks.

Darlene rattled off the names. "Ananya, Pranav, Prisha, Anushka, and the youngest boy is Om."

"Om, I got," Harlan said.

The Smiths **over there** gave away apricots from their tree by the bushel. The Ornonas **over there** had the ski boat that never left their driveway. The Bakas family in the big blue and white house had huge parties every Greek Easter and if you didn't show up the family would bring up your absence for the rest of the year. Vincent Crowell operated a ham radio at all hours. His was the house with a huge antenna on the roof.

"And Paul Legaris teaches science at Burham. The college. Has two older kids." Harlan reported. "Heard his son is joining the Navy."

"A teacher," said Bette. "Thus the footware."

"Come again?" Darlene asked.

"He gave us a ham in flip-flops. On his feet, not on the ham. I thought a man wearing flip-flops in the middle of a weekday was, you know . . ."

"Comfortable?" said Harlan.

"Unemployed."

"No classes in session in August." Harlan sighed. "I envy a man in flip-flops on a day like today."

Pop! Bette saw Paul on campus, between classes, sitting on a bench on the quad, surrounded by coeds, pretty girls who had Legaris for Introduction to Biology, and he was always so free with his time. One of those coeds was sure to have a thing for older men in positions of authority, or so Paul Legaris hoped.

The warm summer evening beckoned the kids back out onto Greene Street as Bette cleaned the dishes, then headed upstairs to find linens and make the beds. From the window of the bedroom shared by Dale and Sharri, Bette saw Paul wheeling a large tube out of his garage—his aforementioned telescope—on a hand-made dolly, aided by some kids. By the time darkness fell completely, Bette had plugged in her Bluetooth speaker and paired it with her phone so Adele could provide a mournful score for the evening's chore of lining closet shelves and untangling hangers. Bette was still organizing dresser drawers when she heard one of the kids slam the front door and stomp up the stairs.

"Mom?" Eddie yelled, coming into what was going to be his room. "Can I make a telescope?"

"I admire your spunk."

"Professor Legaris made his own telescope and it's **amazing** to look through."

"**Professor** Legaris, huh?"

"Yeah. The man who lives right next door. His garage is full of **amazing** stuff. He keeps a bunch of wires and tools in a big wooden thing called a chifforobe. He has three old TVs with knobs on the side of them and a sewing machine you have to pedal." Eddie jumped onto his bed. "He let me look into the Cosmos, whatever that is, through his telescope. I saw the moon and, like, a shadow of the sun was covering part of it."

"I'm no professor, but I think it's the shadow of the Earth."

"It was funny. With just my eye, the moon looked like it was being sliced out of the sky, but through the telescope, you could still see the cut-up part, but it was red. Craters and everything. He made the telescope himself by hand."

"How do you make a telescope?"

"You get a round piece of glass and grind on it for a long time, then make that part shiny, then put it on one end of a tube, like for carpets. Then you buy eyehole things."

"Lenses?"

"Opticons, I think he called them. He teaches a class on how to make your own telescope. Can I?"

"If we can find a tube, like for carpets."

The kids went to bed late that first night on Greene Street, but having spent so much energy running around they all conked out, pronto. Before she could forget, Bette put three dollars under Shar-ri's pillow in exchange for that tooth, the fairy being rather flush with cash.

The day finally over, Bette opened a bottle of red, red wine and called Maggie, telling her about all the neighborhood kids, the Pittses and the Coke connection, and yes, her vision of Paul Legaris.

"What is with your luck with men?" Maggie asked.

"It's not my luck," Bette said. "It's the men. They are all so sad. So obvious. So desperate for a woman to define them."

"Desperate to fuck you," Maggie deemed. "And there you are, right next door. If he comes over next time smelling of some Rat Packesque cologne? Bolt the door. He's after you."

"I hope he's aiming for his students. Teaching assistants. Sorority girls."

"Those could get him fired. The hot divorcée who moved in next door is legal game. He may have binoculars trained on your windows right now."

"If he does he'll see Eddie's Star Wars curtains. My room is on the other side of the house."

———

As August yawned deeply into its dog days, Bette avoided contact with her next-door neighbor, not wanting to hear **Are you doing anything tonight?** again. She drove home, scanning Greene Street for signs of Paul Legaris. Once he was on his front lawn and he waved as she pulled into the driveway, calling out, "How you doing?"

"Just super, thanks!" she said. She hustled inside like she was very busy with something when, in fact, she had nothing going on. Another time, there he was watching the neighbor kids kicking footballs in a game called Pig on the Fly, so she grabbed her idle phone and pretended to be on a call as she went into the house. Paul waved at her, but she just nodded back. During the evenings she feared the doorbell would ring and there he would be, freshly showered and smelling of Creed, asking if she wasn't doing anything, would she be interested in dinner at the Old Spaghetti Factory? She had once taken her dentist up on that very offer. He turned out to be such a narcissistic bore she changed her dental care provider. Around then she declared an Armistice in the Dating War, and now she was hell-bent on keeping her new life on Greene Street void of attachments and thus disaster free.

As it turned out, the kids saw more of Paul Legaris than she did. He was washing his car on a Friday evening (who washes a car on Friday evening?) when Bob picked them up for his weekend of custody. Bette showed her ex-husband around the lower floor of her new house as the kids packed their weekend bags, then she watched as they all piled into Bob's car. Paul came over when Eddie wanted to introduce his dad to the guy who taught Cosmos at the college. The two men chatted longer than necessary, Bette decided. When Bob and the kids drove off, Paul went back to washing his car. Though she did not have a vision about the exchange, she wondered if the two men had compared notes on, well, **her**.

The next morning Bette slept in, wonderfully late on a Saturday morning without the kids. She came down the stairs of the quiet house barefoot, in a pair of yoga pants and a light cotton hoodie, carrying her iPad.

"Hey, big boy." In bare feet she steamed up her morning elixir, taking it out to the backyard before the sun broke over the roof and the heat became too much. She took her iPad with her; it seemed like years since she had used the thing anyplace other than in bed. She sat in a plastic Adirondack chair under the backyard tree, scrolling through back issues of the Chicago **Sun-Times** Sunday magazine, then lingering too long on the **Daily Mail** website, when she heard **klock klock klock klock klock**.

A woodpecker was doing the woodpecker thing somewhere.

Klock klock klock klock klock.

She scanned the branches of the trees for a sign of the bird but found none. **Klock klock klock klock klock.**

"Persistent fives," Bette said, counting the **klocks**.

She looked at the exterior of the house, happy she didn't see the bird damaging the siding by digging for insects, then came again **klock klock klock klock klock.**

The sound was coming from over the fence, from Paul Legaris's backyard. The tall fence—which even on Greene Street made for good neighbors—blocked any view of next door, save the higher tree branches. There were no signs of Mr. Peckerhead up in them, but the **klock klock klock klock klock** sounds kept coming, which made Bette curious. She wanted to see how big this woody-bird was, so she moved her chair to the fence and stood on it, hoping to see the bird in action.

Klock klock klock klock klock.

Paul Legaris kept his backyard neat and organized, with a vegetable garden with drip irrigation and beanpoles. An antique plow, rusted and in need of a horse, sat in the center of a patch of grass beside, incongruously, an array of solar panels. Toward the back of the yard, distant from the patio, was a massive brick BBQ and one of those freestanding, mail-order-catalog hammocks.

Klock klock klock klock klock.

Paul himself was sitting at a picnic table on a redwood deck under a sloping canopy, already dressed in his uniform of baggy shorts, polo shirt, and those flip-flops. His too-cool eyeglasses were set on the top of his head, and he was bent in concentration over a hunk of machinery that looked like it had been made in the 1800s.

Klock klock klock klock klock.

The machine was a typewriter, though it looked like no typewriter Bette had ever seen. The thing was ancient, something out of the Victorian era, a mechanical printing apparatus with hammers arcing onto paper rolled into the carriage. Paul hit a key five times—**klock klock klock klock klock**—added a touch of oil to the inner levers of the typewriter, and repeated.

Klock klock klock klock klock.

This was how Paul Legaris could ruin a peaceful morning on Greene Street, servicing a writing gimcrack straight out of Jules Verne.

Klock klock klock klock klock.

"Yowza," Bette mumbled. She went back inside

for another jolt of caffeine and stayed there, reading her iPad in the relative quiet at her kitchen table, still hearing the muffled **klock**ing of her neighbor's ironclad word processor.

That afternoon, when the sun was turning Greene Street into both the frying pan and the fire, Bette was on the phone with Maggie.

"So he's got telescopes and typewriters laying around his house. I wonder what else," Maggie wondered.

"Old toasters. Dial telephones. Washtubs with wringers. Who knows?"

"I checked some of the dating sites on the Web. Couldn't find him."

"CreepyNeighbor.com? SadSacks4U?" Bette was looking out the front window when an unfamiliar car pulled up across the street—one made in Korea the color of red nail polish. A young man, the driver, got out along with a girl a few years younger, no doubt his sister. As they walked across the street, angling toward Paul Legaris's front door, Bette recognized the Legaris gait in the boy.

"Kid alert," Bette told Maggie. "Guess who just showed up."

"Who?" Maggie asked.

"Pretty sure it's the offspring of Professor Lonesome next door. Son and daughter."

"They showing tattoos or Birkenstocks?"

"Nah." Bette eyed the kids for signs of youthful rebellion or oddity. "They look normal."

"Normal is a setting on a washing machine."

The girl let out a squeal and ran toward the front door of the house. Paul Legaris was heading for her when they intersected on the lawn. She took him in a headlock and bulldogged him into the turf, laughing. The son joined the fracas, two kids dog-piling on the father they had clearly not seen in a while.

"I may have to call 911 soon. I think a separated shoulder is due," Bette opined.

That night Bette, Maggie, and the Ordinand sisters met for dinner at a Mexican cafe made of cinder block and with paper shades over the lights, a place so authentic they were afraid to drink the water, but not the margaritas. The night filled with laughter and stories about former husbands, lousy ex-boyfriends, and men who lacked both common sense and sanity. The talk was fun and saucy, much of it about Paul Legaris, none of it flattering.

When her Lyft driver dropped her off at Greene Street, the sky had been dark for two hours and once again the telescope had been wheeled out onto Paul's front yard. His car was not in the driveway; his kids were manning the search of the heavens. Bette was making straight for her door when the son's voice reached across the driveway.

"Good evening" was all he said.

Bette gave a nod and made a sound like **g'deve** but didn't slow.

"Wanna see the moons of Jupiter?" This was the girl asking. "Smack in the middle of the sky and cool as hell?"

"No, thank you," Bette said.

"You're missing one gorgeous show!" The girl had a voice like Dale's, open and friendly, prone to enthusiasm over the smallest things.

"No eclipse tonight?" Bette was getting her front door keys from her purse.

"Those are infrequent. Jupiter is out all summer long," the girl said. "I'm Nora Legaris."

"Hi. Bette Monk."

"Mother of Dale and Sharri and Eddie? Dad said your kids are a hoot." The girl headed Bette's way, stepping onto the driveway. "You bought the Schneiders' house. They moved to Austin, the lucky punks. That's my brother." Nora pointed to the telescope. "Tell Ms. Monk your name!"

"Lawrence Altwell-Chance Delagordo Legaris the Seventh," he said. "You can call me Chick."

Bette looked confused, like a woman with three margaritas in her, which she was. **"Chick?"**

"Or Larry. Long story. You want to see what Galileo saw centuries ago? Changed the course of human history."

To wave off such an invitation, to flee into her house, would have been rude, very un–Greene Street. Nora and Chick were charming kids. So Bette said, "Put that way, guess I better."

Bette crossed the boundary of her house into Legaris territory, her first ever visit. Chick stepped back from the telescope, offering Bette access. "Behold Jupiter," he said.

Bette put her eye up to the lens at the open end of the carpet tube.

"Try not to bump the telescope. It should be lined up right."

Bette blinked. The glass of the lens brushed her eyelash. She couldn't make any sense of what she was looking at. "I don't see a thing."

"Chick," Nora sighed. "You can't say 'behold Jupiter' and fail to have Jupiter beholdable."

"Sorry, Ms. Monk. Let me see." Chick looked through a much smaller telescope mounted on the huge carpet tube and made adjustments up and down and left and right. "Bang solid fat as a goose!"

"I sure hope you behold Jupiter now," said Nora.

With her eye again so close to the lens her mascara could have marred it, Bette saw, at first, nothing, and then a brilliant pinhole of light. Jupiter. Not only Jupiter but four of its moons in a straight line, a single moon to its left, and three to its right, as clear as could be.

"Yowza!" Bette cried. "It's as clear as can be! That's **Jupiter**?"

"King of the planets and the Jovian moons," Chick said. "How many can you see?"

"Four."

"Just like Galileo," Nora said. "He put two bits of glass in a brass pipe, pointed it at the brightest object in the Italian sky, and saw just what you are looking at. Slammed the door on the Ptolemaic theory of the universe. Got him in some hot water."

Bette could not take her eye away. She had never looked deep into the Cosmos and seen another planet with her own eyes. Jupiter was gorgeous.

"Wait till you see Saturn," Chick said. "Rings and moons and the whole shebang."

"Show me!" Bette was suddenly hooked on celestial views.

"Can't," Chick explained. "Saturn doesn't rise until very early morning. If you want to set your alarm for quarter to five, I'll meet you here and line it up for you."

"Four forty-five a.m.? That will not happen."

Bette stepped away from the telescope and those Jovian moons. "Now, explain Chick to me."

Nora laughed. "Abbott and Costello. The skinny one was Chick in one of their movies. We watched it about a thousand times and I started calling my brother by it. Chick stuck."

"Better than La-La-La-Larry Le-Le-Legaris."

"I get that," Bette said. "I was Elizabeth, along with seven other girls in fourth grade." She looked at Jupiter again through the telescope and once more marveled at the sight.

"Here comes the old man." Nora saw the headlights of her father's car coming down Greene Street. Bette thought to bolt for her front door, but to do so now would be such an obvious dis that she waved off her flight instinct.

"What are you punks doing on my lawn?" Paul said, getting out of his car. Another fellow, a redhead not much older than Chick, climbed out of the passenger seat. "Not you, Bette. These two scalawags."

Nora turned to Bette. "Dad uses words like **scalawags**. Sorry you witnessed it."

"This is Daniel," Paul said, pointing to the redheaded fellow, who, Bette could not help but notice, was very, very thin, possibly malnourished. He was wearing clothes that were brand new and surely not of his own taste, he wore them so uncomfortably. The kids exchanged greetings and Bette said hello.

"You have the Big Guy in sight?" Paul looked at the gas giant in the sky. "Daniel, you ever see Jupiter before?"

"I have not." With no other comment, Daniel stepped to the big tube and looked into its eyepiece. "Wow," he said with no expression.

"Bette? You have a gander?" Paul asked.

"I did. Made me say **yowza**." Bette looked at Nora. "Sorry you witnessed me saying **yowza**."

"**Yowza** is good," said Nora. "A catchall superlative. Like **big-time** or **super-duper**."

"Like **swingin'**," said Chick.

"Or **bodacious**," said Paul.

"Or **tits**," said Daniel. Again, no expression.

No one knew what to say to that.

———

The Daniel fellow spent a few days at the Legaris place. Bette heard the two men talking in the mornings, their distant voices coming over the fence in the backyard. She saw them leaving together in the evenings around 7:00 p.m., and then one night the skinny redhead was gone. Greene Street became, once again, a place of bikes, balls, and kids playing with a decided headiness since the beginning of school was bearing down. The end of summer was suddenly in the air, palpable.

On the final evening of August, Bette took the kids for pizza at a place that was wall-to-wall arcade games. When they returned home, the block was a quiet heaven after all that noise. The Patel kids were playing with a garden hose on their lawn, so Eddie and Sharri joined them. Dale went into the house. Bette lingered out front in a cooling, lovely breeze that stirred the leaves of her sycamore. Some of the spare pizza made it from the take-home box and into her hand as she leaned against one of the lower limbs, nibbling away.

There was no sign of Paul Legaris. His car was not in his driveway, so she felt relaxed in the calm of Greene Street, though guilty over what was her fourth slice of pepperoni, olive, and onion. As she tossed the thin crescent of uneaten crust into the grass—some bird would soon find it—she thought she saw a very large insect crawling across Paul Legaris's driveway.

She nearly let out an **eek** of terror—that could have been a huge spider—but then realized it was only a set of keys lying on the ground, right where Paul's car would have been parked.

Bette, then, found herself in something of a dilemma—what was a neighbor to do? She **should** pick up the keys, hold on to them until Paul came home, then knock on his front door and return them. If indeed they were his keys, as was most probable, she would save him the angst of a fruit-less search. Anyone **would** do that, but—**pop**—Paul would be so happy at getting his keys back he would insist on repaying Bette with a dinner he would cook himself. Say! How's about I BBQ some ribs in the backyard with my own sauce recipe!

Bette did not want to go there. The simple solution would be for her to have Eddie return the keys. When Paul came home her son would scamper over and do the good deed and Bette would be inside her own house and that would be that.

She reached down and picked up the keys. There was a fob with the seal of Burham Community College, a couple of house keys and two industrial types with serial numbers stamped into them, a bike-lock key, and, the largest item on the ring, a plastic poker chip held in place by a hole drilled through its rim.

The chip was worn down, its serrated edges smoothed over. It had once been red but now was only flecked with faded spots. Still visible in the center was a big number 20. Paul must have won twenty bucks at one of the fake riverboat casinos at the state line. Or maybe the chip was all that remained of a two-thousand-dollar stake. She turned the chip over and saw **NA** on the other side. The letters were exotic and stylized, like a tattoo, sitting inside a square set on its corner like a baseball diamond. In the fading evening light, she saw some writing in the open areas of the chip, but it, too, was worn down and illegible save for a few letters—a **g** here, an **oc,** and what looked like **vice** but could have been **riot** or **ribs** or any four-letter word.

Across the street, the kids were playing Punch Ball against the Patel garage door. Bette took the keys inside to hold on to until she could assign Eddie the mission to return them.

Dale was on her laptop in the living room, watching YouTube videos of horse jumping.

"You busy?" Bette asked her. Dale did not answer. "Hey, kid-o-mine," she said, snapping her fingers.

"What?" Dale did not look up from her computer.

"Can you google something for me?"

"Google what?"

"This poker chip." Bette held up the key chain.

"You want me to google 'poker chips'?"

"This poker chip."

"I don't need Google to tell you. That is a poker chip."

"Where is it from?"

"A poker chip factory."

"I am going to bounce this off your head if you don't google this."

Dale sighed and looked at her mother and the key ring and the poker chip and rolled her eyes. "Okay! But can I just finish this?"

Bette showed Dale the detail of the chip—the faded red, the 20, the **NA** on the other side with the rubbed-out letters—leaving the key chain behind to go wash her hands of pizza crumbs. She was loading the dishwasher when Dale hollered something from the living room.

"What?" Bette called back.

Dale came into the kitchen carrying her laptop. "It's a thing for narcotics."

"What is?" Bette was putting silverware into the top rack of the dishwasher.

"The poker chip," Dale said, showing her mother a collection of images on her computer. "**NA** is for Narcotics Anonymous. Like AA, but for narcotics. I entered **poker chips with NA** and a site came up, then I searched for images and there you go."

Bette was looking at the same design as was on the key ring. **NA** was in a baseball diamond, with the words **Self, God, Society, Service** in the open spaces.

"They give them out to celebrate 'sobriety,'" Dale said. "That means for not doing drugs. For thirty days on up."

"But this one says twenty." What was Paul Legaris doing with a poker chip from Narcotics Anonymous?

"I think that means twenty years," Dale said. "Where did you find these keys?"

Bette hesitated. If Paul Legaris had anything to do with drugs or Narcotics Anonymous, she didn't want Dale to know until she knew more herself.

"Found it someplace," Bette said.

"I need to google anything else? Potato chips or the rules for poker?"

"No." Bette went back to loading the dishwasher. When she was finished she called Maggie.

"Sure, Narcotics Anonymous," Maggie told her. "AA for drunks. CA for cokeheads. They have an Anonymous for everything."

"NA is for junkies?"

"Not narcoleptics." Maggie was curious. "You sure they are **his** keys?"

"No. But they were in his driveway, so let's assume—which will make an ass out of you and me . . ."

"Guys in twelve-step programs always sleep with someone else in the twelve-step program.

Sarah Jallis had a niece who married a guy from her AA group, but I think they divorced later."

"If Paul Legaris is in NA, has **been** in NA for twenty years, I wonder what for."

"Well." Maggie paused. "I'd guess narcotics had something to do with it."

Eddie and Sharri came in an hour later, wet from the Patels' garden hose. An hour after that, all three kids were bathed and in front of the PlayStation watching a movie in HD. Bette was in the kitchen on her iPad, looking up Narcotics Anonymous on website after website. She did not hear the knock on the front door.

"Professor Legaris is here." Eddie had come into the kitchen. Bette looked at her son with no reaction. "He's at the front door."

And there he was, on the porch, just on the other side of the doorway, dressed in jeans and a white shirt with leather deck shoes on his feet. Bette closed the door slightly behind her to block the sound from the movie.

"Hi," she said.

"Sorry to bother you. I wonder if I can use your backyard to access my backyard."

"Why?"

"Because I am a knucklehead. Locked myself out of my house. I think my sliding door is unlocked.

I'd go over my own fence but I'd land in my garbage cans."

Bette looked at Paul, at the same face that had brought her a HoneyBaked ham a month before, at the same guy who washed his car on Friday and thought her kids were a hoot, the neighbor who made his own telescopes and fixed old typewriters. **Pop!** Paul Legaris is sitting in a circle of men and women, all on folding chairs. He is listening to Daniel, the skinny redhead, talking about his days scoring heroin. Paul nods his head, recognizing his own behavior of twenty years prior.

"Wait right here," Bette says.

She returned seconds later with the key chain in her hand.

"My keys," Paul murmured. "You swiped my keys? That's a joke."

"They were in your driveway. I thought it was a big bug, but nope."

"My car remote must have fallen off without me noticing, one more event to which I am oblivious. I had no clue where I'd lost them, so thanks."

"Credit Greene Street and its good neighbor policy," Bette said. Now would have been the time for her to close the door on any more interaction with the guy who lived next door, the guy who wore flip-flops, the guy whom she had been avoiding since she had moved in. But she surprised herself with a question. "What happened to that Daniel fellow with the red hair and the lofty vocabulary?" she asked.

Paul had turned to go but stopped, facing Bette in the doorway. "Ah, Danny." Paul paused. "He's in Kentucky."

"Kentucky? He from there?" Bette was now leaning in the doorway, casually, comfortably. She found herself relaxed with Paul in her doorway, something she had never felt, not since that first **Are you doing anything tonight?**

"He's from Detroit. A spot opened up at a place in Kentucky, so he took it for ninety days, if all goes well. I hope there was no problem during his stay with me."

"No. I did want to give the guy a sandwich to fatten him up."

"Yeah. Danny needs to eat better." Paul stepped away again, leaving.

"You know," Bette said, "in olden times red-heads like him were considered demons. Because of the devil-colored hair."

Paul laughed. "He's got his demons, but no more than any of us."

Bette looked down at the keys in Paul's hand, at the poker chip that celebrated twenty years of sobriety, two decades narcotics-free. She did some math in her head. Chick Legaris was at least twenty-one years old, which would have made him a baby when his father hit his own rock bottom, when Paul began his journey from wherever that was to this night in August.

In that wink of an eye, Bette was even more assured she and the kids belonged here, on Greene Street.

"Thanks for saving me a ton of hassle," Paul said, waving his keys.

"**De nada,**" Bette said, watching him step away toward his house next door.

She was just turning back into her house when—**pop**—she saw herself in her kitchen, early in the morning, with dawn still hours away and kids all still asleep in their beds.

"Hello, big boy," she is saying to her espresso machine, steaming her morning latte and, in another mug, a double cappuccino with just a frothing of foam.

Then she is carrying both wake 'em ups out her front door, down her porch steps, across her lawn, and under the low hanging limbs of her sycamore.

Paul Legaris has set up his telescope on his driveway. The instrument is pointing at the deep, dark blue of the eastern sky over Greene Street.

Saturn is just rising. Through the eyepiece, the ringed planet is a glory, bang solid fat as a goose and cool as hell.

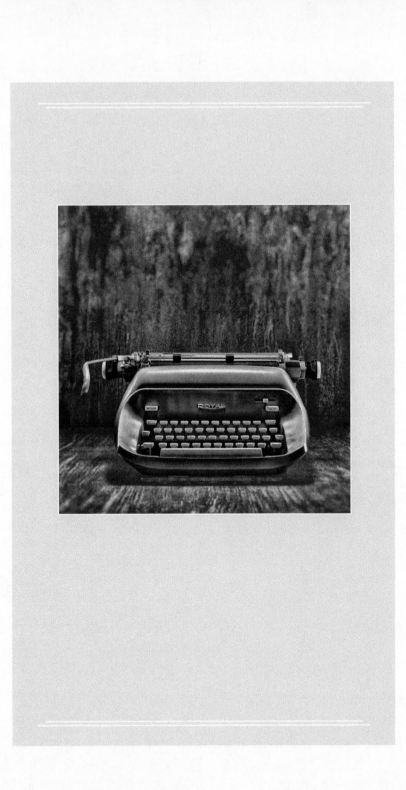

Alan Bean Plus Four

———————◆———————

Traveling to the moon was way less complicated this year than it was back in 1969,
as the four of us proved, not that anyone gives a
whoop. You see, over cold beers in my backyard,
with the crescent moon a delicate princess finger-
nail low in the west, I told Steve Wong that if he
threw, say, a hammer with enough muscle, said
tool would make a 500,000-mile figure eight, sail
around that very moon, and return to Earth like a
boomerang, and wasn't that fascinating?

Steve Wong works at Home Depot, so has
access to many hammers. He offered to chuck a
few. His co-worker MDash, who'd shortened his
given name to rap-star length, wondered how one
would catch a red-hot hammer falling at a thousand miles an hour. Anna, who runs her own
graphic design biz, said that there'd be nothing to
catch, as the hammer would burn up like a meteor,

and she was right. Plus, she didn't buy the simplicity of my cosmic throw-wait-return. She is ever doubtful of my space program bona fides. She says I'm always "Apollo missions this" and "Lunokhod moon landing that," and have begun to falsify details in order to sound like an expert, and she is right about that, too.

I keep all my nonfiction on a pocket-size Kobo digital reader, so I whipped out a chapter from **No Way, Ivan: Why the CCCP Lost the Race to the Moon,** written by an émigré professor with an ax to grind. According to him, in the mid-sixties the Soviets hoped to trump the Apollo program with just such a figure-eight mission: no orbit, no landing, just photos and crowing rights. The Reds sent off an unmanned Soyuz with, supposedly, a mannequin in a spacesuit, but so many things went south that they didn't dare try again, not even with a dog. **Kaputnik.**

Anna is as thin and smart as a whip, and driven like no one else I have ever dated (for three exhausting weeks). She saw a challenge here. She wanted to succeed where the Russians had failed. It would be fun. We'd all go, she said, and that was that, but when? I suggested that we schedule liftoff in conjunction with the anniversary of **Apollo 11,** the most famous space flight in history, but that was a no-go, as Steve Wong had dental work scheduled for the third week of July. How about November, when **Apollo 12** landed in the Ocean of Storms, an event now forgotten by 99.999 percent of the people on Earth? Anna had to be a bridesmaid at her sister's wedding the week after Halloween, so the best date for the mission turned out to be the last Saturday in September.

Astronauts in the Apollo era had spent thousands of hours piloting jet planes and earning engineering degrees. They had to practice escaping from launchpad disasters by sliding down long cables to the safety of thickly padded bunkers. They had to know how slide rules worked. We did none of that, though we did test-fly our booster on the Fourth of July, out of Steve Wong's huge driveway in Oxnard, hoping that, with all the fireworks, our unmanned first stage would blow through the night sky unnoticed. Mission accomplished. That rocket cleared Baja and is **right now** zipping around the Earth every ninety minutes and, let me state clearly, for the sake of multiple government agencies, will probably burn up harmlessly on reentry in twelve to fourteen months.

MDash, who was born in a sub-Saharan village, has a super brain. As a transfer student at St. Anthony Country Day High School with minimal English skills, he won a science-fair Award of Merit with an experiment on ablative materials, which caught fire, to the delight of everyone. Since having a working heat shield is implied in the phrase "returning safely to Earth," MDash was in charge of that and all things pyrotechnic, including the explosive bolts for stage separation. Anna did the math, all the load-lift ratios, orbital mechanics, fuel mixtures, and formulas—the stuff I pretend to know, but which actually leaves me in a fog.

My contribution was the Command Module—a cramped, headlight-shaped spheroid that was cobbled together by a very rich pool-supply magnate, who was hell-bent on getting into the private aerospace business to make him some big-time NASA cash. He died in his sleep just before his ninety-fourth birthday, and his (fourth) wife-widow agreed to sell me the capsule for a hundred bucks, though I would have paid twice that. She insisted on typing a receipt on one of her husband's old typewriters, a green Royal Desktop, a behemoth, just one of many that he collected but failed to maintain, as there was a stack of them growing rust in a corner of the garage. MUST TAKE DELIVERY IN 48 HOURS she typed, as well as NO RETURNS/CASH ONLY. I named the capsule the **Alan Bean**, in honor of the lunar-module pilot of **Apollo 12**, the fourth man to walk on the moon and the only one I ever met, in a Houston-area Mexican restaurant in 1986. He was paying the cashier, as anonymous as a balding orthopedist, when I yelled out, "Holy cow! You're Al Bean!" He gave me his autograph and drew a tiny astronaut above his name.

Since four of us would be a-comin' round the moon, I needed to make room inside the **Alan Bean** and eliminate pounds. We'd have no Mission Control to boss us around, so I ripped out all the Comm. I replaced every bolt, screw, hinge, clip, and connector with duct tape (three bucks a roll at Home Depot). Our privy had a shower curtain for privacy. I've heard from an experienced source that a trip to the john in zero gravity requires that you strip naked and give yourself half an hour, so, yeah, privacy was key. I replaced the outer-opening hatch and its bulky lock-EVAC apparatus with a steel-alloy plug that had a big window and self-sealing bib. In the vacuum of space, the air pressure inside the **Alan Bean** would force the hatch closed and airtight. Simple physics.

Announce that you are flying to the moon and everyone assumes you mean to land on it—to plant the flag, kangaroo-hop in one-sixth gravity, and collect rocks to bring home, none of which we were going to do. We were flying **around** the moon. **Landing** is a whole different ball game, and as for stepping out onto the surface? Hell, choosing which of the four of us would get out first and become the thirteenth person to leave bootprints up there would have led to so much bad blood that our crew would have broken up long before T minus ten seconds and counting. And let's face it, that crewman would have been Anna anyway.

Assembling the three stages of the good ship **Alan Bean** took two days. We packed granola bars and water in squeeze-top bottles, then pumped in the liquid oxygen for the two booster stages and the hypergolic chemicals for the one-shot firing of the translunar motor, the minirocket that would fling us to our lunar rendezvous. Most of Oxnard came around to Steve Wong's driveway to ogle the **Alan Bean,** not a one of them knowing who Alan Bean was or why we'd named the rocket ship after him. The kids begged for peeks inside the spacecraft, but we didn't have the insurance. What are you waiting for? You gonna blast off soon? To every knothead who would listen, I explained launch windows and trajectories, showing them on my MoonFaze app (free) how we had to inter-sect the moon's orbit at exactly the right moment or lunar gravity would . . . Ah, hell! There's the moon! Point your rocket at it and put on a show!

———

Twenty-four seconds after clearing the tower, our first stage was burning all stops, and the Max-Q app ($0.99) showed us pulling 11.8 times our weight at sea level, not that we needed iPhones to tell us this. We . . . were . . . fighting . . . for breath . . . with Anna . . . screaming . . . "Get off . . . my chest!" But no one was on her chest. She was, in fact, sitting on me, crushing me like a lap dance from an offensive lineman. **Kaboom** went MDash's dynamite bolts, and the second stage fired, as programmed. A minute later, dust, loose change, and a couple of ballpoint pens floated up from behind our seats, signaling, Hey! We'd achieved orbit!

Weightlessness is as much fun as you can imagine, but troublesome for some spacegoers, who for no apparent reason spend their first hours up there upchucking, as if they'd overdone it at the prelaunch reception. It's one of those facts never made public by NASA PR or in astronaut memoirs. After three revolutions of the Earth, as we finished running the checklist for our translunar injection, Steve Wong's tummy finally settled down. Somewhere over Africa, we opened the valves in the translunar motor, the hypergolics worked their chemical magic, and—**voosh**—we were hauling the mail to Moonberry RFD, our escape velocity a crisp seven miles per second, Earth getting smaller and smaller in the window.

The Americans who went to the moon before us had computers so primitive that they couldn't get email or use Google to settle arguments. The iPads we took had something like 70 billion times the capacity of those Apollo-era dial-ups and were mucho handy, especially during all the downtime on our long haul. MDash used his to watch the final season of **Girls.** We took hundreds of self-ies with the Earth in the window and, plinking a Ping-Pong ball off the center seat, played a table-less table-tennis tournament, which was won by Anna. I worked the attitude jets in pulse mode, yawing and pitching the **Alan Bean** for views of some of the few stars that were visible in the naked sunlight: Antares, Nunki, the globular cluster NGC 6333—none of which twinkle when you're up there among 'em.

The big event of translunar space is crossing the equigravisphere, a boundary as invisible as the International Date Line but, for the **Alan Bean,** the Rubicon. On this side of the EQS, Earth's gravity was tugging us back, slowing our progress, bid-ding us to return home to the life-affirming ben-efits of water, atmosphere, and a magnetic field. Once we crossed, the moon grabbed hold, wrap-ping us in her ancient silvery embrace, whispering to us to **hurry hurry hurry** to wink in wonder at her magnificent desolation.

At the exact moment that we reached the threshold, Anna awarded us origami cranes, made out of aluminum foil, which we taped onto our shirts like pilots' wings. I put the **Alan Bean** into a Passive Thermal Control BBQ roll, our moon-bound ship rotating on an invisible spit so as to distribute the solar heat. Then we dimmed the lights, taped a sweatshirt over the window to keep the sunlight from sweeping across the cabin, and slept, each of us curled up in a comfortable nook of our little rocket ship.

When I tell people that I've seen the far side of the moon, they often say, "You mean the dark side," as though I'd fallen under the spell of Darth Vader or Pink Floyd. In fact, both sides of the moon get the same amount of sunshine, just on different shifts.

Because the moon was waxing gibbous to the folks back home, we had to wait out the shadowed portion on the other side. In that darkness, with no sunlight and the moon blocking the Earth's reflection, I pulsed the **Alan Bean** around so that our window faced outbound for a view of the Infinite Time-Space Continuum that was worthy of IMAX: unblinking stars in subtle hues of red-orange-yellow-green-blue-indigo-violet, our galaxy stretching as far as our eyes were wide, a diamond-blue carpet against a black that would have been terrifying had it not been so mesmerizing.

Then there was light, snapping on as if MDash had flipped a switch. I tweaked the controls, and there below us was the surface of the moon. Wow. Gorgeous in a way that strained any use of the word, a rugged place that produced oohs and awe. The LunaTicket app ($0.99) showed us traversing south to north, but we were mentally lost in space, the surface as chaotic as a windblown, gray-capped bay, until I matched the Poincaré impact basin with the "This Is Our Moon" guide on my Kobo. The **Alan Bean** was soaring 153 kilometers high (95.06 miles **Americanus**), at a speed faster than that of a bullet from a gun, and the moon was slipping by so fast that we were running out of far side. Oresme Crater had white, finger-painted streaks. Heaviside showed rills and depressions, like river washouts. We split Dufay right in half, a flyover from its six to its twelve, the rim a steep, sharp razor. Mare Moscoviense was far to port, a miniversion of the Ocean of Storms, where four and a half decades ago the real Alan Bean spent two days, hiking, collecting rocks, snapping photos. Lucky man.

Our brains could take in only so much, so our iPhones did the recording, and I stopped calling out the sights, though I did recognize Campbell and D'Alembert, large craters linked by the smaller Slipher, just as we were about to head home over the moon's north pole. Steve Wong had cued up a certain musical track for what would be Earthrise but had to reboot the Bluetooth on Anna's Jambox and was nearly late for his cue. MDash yelled, "Hit PLAY, hit PLAY!" just as a blue-and-white patch of life—a slice of all that we have made of ourselves, all that we have ever been—pierced the black cosmos above the sawtooth horizon. I was expecting something classical, Franz Joseph Haydn or George Harrison, but "The Circle of Life," from **The Lion King,** scored our home planet's rise over the plaster-of-Paris moon. Really? A Disney show tune? But, you know, that rhythm and that chorus and the double meaning of the lyrics caught me right in the throat, and I choked up. Tears popped off my face and joined the others' tears, which were floating around the **Alan Bean.** Anna gave me a hug like I was still her boyfriend. We cried. We all cried. You'd have done the same.

Coasting home was one fat anticlimax, despite the (never spoken) possibility of our burning up on reentry like an obsolete spy satellite circa 1962. Of course, we were all chuffed, as the English say, that we'd made the trek and maxed out the memory on our iPhones with iPhotos. But questions arose about what we were going to do upon our return, apart from making some bitchin' posts on Instagram. If I ever run into Al Bean again, I'll ask him what life has been like for him since he twice crossed the equigravisphere. Does he suffer melancholia on a quiet afternoon, as the world spins on automatic? Will I occasionally get the blues, because nothing holds a wonder equal to splitting Dufay down the middle? TBD, I suppose.

"Whoa! Kamchatka!" Anna called out as our heat shield expired into millions of grain-size comets. We were arcing down over the Arctic Circle, gravity once again commanding that we who went up must come down. When the chute pyros shot off, the **Alan Bean** jolted our bones, causing the Jambox to lose its duct-tape purchase and conk MDash in the forehead. By the time we splashed down off Oahu, a trail of blood was running from the ugly gash between his eyebrows. Anna tossed him her bandanna, because guess what no one had thought to take around the moon? To anyone reading this with plans to imitate us: Band-Aids.

At Stable One—that is, bobbing in the ocean, rather than having disintegrated into plasma—MDash tripped the "Rescue us!" flares that he'd rigged under the Parachute Jettison System. I opened the pressure-equalizing valve a tad early, and—oops—noxious fumes from the excess-fuel burnoff were sucked into the capsule, making us even queasier, what with the mal de mer.

Once the cabin pressure was at the same psi as

outside, Steve Wong was able to uncork the main hatch, and the Pacific Ocean breeze whooshed in, as soft as a kiss from Mother Earth, but owing to what turned out to be a huge design flaw, that same Pacific Ocean began to join us in our spent little craft. The **Alan Bean**'s second historic voyage was going to be to Davy Jones's locker. Anna, thinking fast, held aloft our Apple products, but Steve Wong lost his Samsung (the Galaxy! Ha!), which disappeared into the lower equipment bay as the rising seawater bade us exit.

The day boat from the Kahala Hilton, filled with curious snorkelers, pulled us out of the water, the English speakers on board telling us that we smelled horrid, the foreigners giving us a wide berth.

After a shower and a change of clothes, I was ladling fruit salad from a decorative dugout canoe at the hotel buffet table when a lady asked me if I had been in that thing that came down out of the sky. Yes, I told her, I had gone all the way to the moon and returned safely to the surly bonds of Earth. Just like Alan Bean.

"Who's Alan Bean?" she said.

Our Town Today with Hank Fiset

AT LOOSE IN THE BIG APPLE

NEW YORK CITY! On my own for three days as my wife let me tag along as she celebrated her Twenty-fifth College Reunion with her Sorority Sisters of Gotta Getta Guy. I had not been to the isle of Manhattan since **Cats** was on B'way and hotel TVs were not high-def.

* * *

SO, WHAT'S NOO in Noo Yawk? Too much, if you have fond memories of the place, but little if the Naked City leaves you feeling, well, **naked.** I think NYC comes off way better on TV and in the movies, when a taxi is just a whistle away and superheroes save the day. In the real world (ours) every day in Gotham is a little like the Macy's Thanksgiving Day Parade and a lot like Baggage Claim after a long, crowded flight.

* * *

HITTING THE STREETS of the Big Town ASAP is a requirement, especially when the Mrs. takes the family credit history off to all those big stores with one name: Bergdorf's, Goodman's, Saks, Bloomie's, not a one of which is any better than our own Henworthy's, which has been open at Seventh and Sycamore since 1952. For my money (a dwindling supply) those fancy places charge too much for just shopping bags. But give NY, NY, this—walking those streets is a show unto its own. I mean, where is everyone **going**?

* * *

CENTRAL PARK, MAYBE? That big rectangle of greenery has more musicians than the East Valley High School Marching Band, but they're all solo acts. Those sax blowers, horn players, violinists, accordion squeezers, and at least one Japanese samisen musician are all in competition with the fellow starving musical artist who performs a few yards away, making for a funky fugue that mars the relative peace of the park. Add in hundreds of serious joggers, power walkers, cyclists, an equal number of lollygaggers, tourists on rental bikes, tricycles towing passengers, and the horses and buggies that make the park smell of a petting zoo, and you'll yearn for our own Spitz Riverside Park, with less postcard views, true, but at least our Tri-Cities squirrels look a lot happier. On foot, you cross the park from the East Side streets tall with former tycoon mansions to the West Side avenues jammed with Starbucks, the Gap, and Bed Bath & Beyond. Had I just stumbled into our own Hillcrest Mall in Pearman? Looked like it, but where was the convenient parking?

* * *

NOT WITHOUT MAGIC is Metropolis, a.k.a. New York City, I admit. When the sun drops behind the towers and stops baking the pavement, it's nice to cool one's heels at a curbside table with a cocktail in your fist. That's when Yankee-Town has the charm of our own Country Market Patio Bar and Grill. I sat and sipped and watched as a world of Knickerbocker oddballs strolled by. I saw a man with a cat on his shoulders, European tourists in the tightest pants imaginable, a team of firemen pull up in an engine, go into a high-rise apartment, only to come out later talking about a bad smoke detector, a man rolling a homemade telescope up the street, the actor Kiefer Sutherland walk by, and a woman with a big white bird on her shoulder. Hope she avoided the guy with the cat.

* * *

A CAESAR SALAD is the true test of any hotel restaurant—write that down! Our own Sun Garden/Red Lion Inn at the airport serves a beauty, but at a Times Square eatery—pretheater dinner with the Wife and still-foxy coeds—my salad was limp and the dressing too tart. **Hell, Caesar!** After I picked up the check, the girls headed off to see the B'way production of **Chicago**—like the movie, but without the close-ups. I don't know much about musical theater, but I bet cash money what the girls saw that night was not any better than the Meadow Hills Community College

Drama Department's production of **Roaring-Twenty-Somethings**, which went to the American College Theater Festival last year. Does the Great White Way beat out the best of the Tri-Cities? Not according to this reporter.

* * *

IF YOU'RE HUNGRY and crave a frankfurter, they're for sale all over Manhattan—on street corners, every few yards in the park, in subway stations, with papaya juice. None of them beat a tube steak from Butterworth's Hot Dog Emporium on Grand Lake Drive. A bagel in Manhattan is the stuff of theologians, but Crane's West Side Cafeteria serves up a heavenly leavened bun to all in the Tri-Cities. Much is made of N'york, N'york–style pizza, but I fork my money over for a slice of Lamonica's Neopolitan, and, yes, they deliver within a ten-mile circle of each of their fourteen locations. And speaking of Italian food, Anthony's Italian Cellar in Harbor View has all the authenticity of any joint in Little Italy without the mobster rubouts.

* * *

ANYTHING NEW YORK has that we lack in our own Tri-Cities? Not so much, since TV gives us all the sports and media in the world and the Internet provides all else. I admit the multitude of museums on Manhattan is fine, dandy, impressive, et cetera. Being able to walk into, say, an ancient temple from Dendur or a hall full of assembled dinosaur bones makes for a great excursion, even when you have to share it with schoolkids from all over the state and tourists from all over the world. I had a whole day of museums when the women booked facials, massages, and pedicures—a.k.a. hangover cures. I saw paintings I will never understand, an "Installation" that was nothing more than a room filled with torn-up carpet samples, and a sculpture that looked like a huge, rusted, dented refrigerator. **Ars Gratia Artis** (Art for Art's Sake), moaned the MGM lion.

* * *

MY FINAL MUSEUM was the place for Modern art, where I saw a movie that was nothing more than time passing—really, a lot of clocks ticking and people looking at their watches. I gave it ten minutes. Upstairs, there was a blank canvas with a knife slice down its middle. Another canvas was colored a light blue at the bottom that became a dark blue at the top. In the stairwell, an actual helicopter was hanging from the ceiling, a whirlybird frozen in flight. Up the steps a pair of Italian typewriters, large and small versions of the same model, were kept behind glass as if they were studded with valuable gems but they weren't! Nor were the machines more than fifty years old. I couldn't help but think the Tri-Cities could put together a collection of used typewriters and charge admission. The now vacant Baxter's Ham Factory on Wyatt Boulevard is available. Anyone civic-minded enough to get cracking on that?

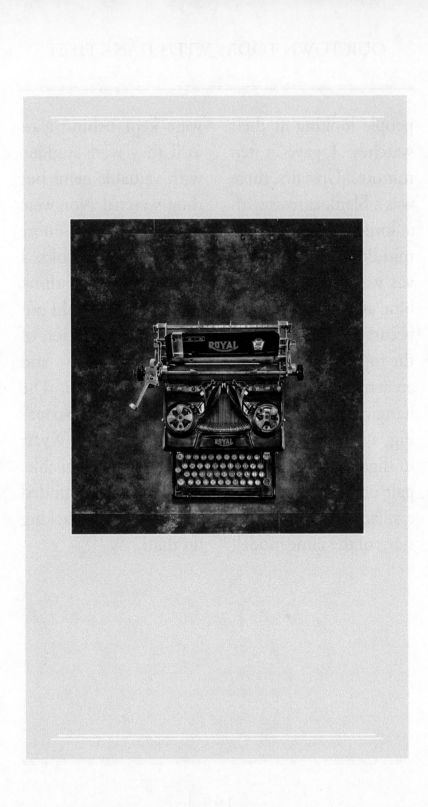

Who's Who?

On a Monday morning in early November of 1978, as she had been every day for the past six weeks, Sue Gliebe was up and out of the apartment before her roommates were awake. Rebecca was asleep, eight feet off the floor in the loft bed in the living room, and Shelley, probably, was still conked out behind the locked door of the apartment's single bedroom.

Sue had showered quickly and quietly in the half tub with the rubber hose running up from the faucet, the dribbling water a weak stream that was alternately tepid and then as hot as the surface of the planet Mercury. Since she had come to New York, she had yet to feel truly clean and her scalp had begun to itch. She dressed in the fog of the tiny bathroom, slipped on her shoes from under the living room sofa, where she slept, strapped her big leather purse crossways from shoulder to opposite hip, then grabbed the umbrella she had bought on Friday. Another storm was due, the news said, and Sue was prepared; she had already paid five of her dollars to one of the many men who appeared with boxes of umbrellas the moment the clouds grew thick with rain. As quietly as possible, Sue exited through the front door, making sure the lock clicked behind her. She had once failed to confirm that click and Shelley had angrily lectured her on the dangers of an unlocked apartment door in New York City in 1978. No click was a major no-no.

Her roommates had come to view her as an unexorcised poltergeist, one that had to be negotiated around. Then again, they were not really her roommates but her hosts, making Sue feel as welcome as an abdominal parasite. Rebecca had been so friendly the last summer when she was working costumes for the Arizona Civic Light Opera, and Sue, a local hire, was playing three featured roles. They were gal pals, then. On days when her duties were slack, Rebecca swam in the pool at the Gliebe family home and partied with the company on the Gliebe patio. She had offered Sue her couch for "a while" whenever—if ever—she came to New York City. When Sue showed up with three suitcases, eight hundred dollars in savings, and a dream, Rebecca's **actual** roommate, Shelley, nodded her assent to the deal with a "yeah, okay." But that was seven weeks ago and Sue was still spending every night on the couch in the small living room. The vibes in the one-bedroom apartment just off Upper Broadway had gone from benign acceptance to Arctic-level iciness. Rebecca wanted Sue out; Shelley wanted her dead. Sue hoped to purchase extra sofa time and goodwill with contributions of fifty dollars to the rent as well as providing milk, Tropicana orange juice, and, once, a thing called blackout cake that Shelley ate for breakfast. Such gestures were not so much appreciated as expected.

What could Sue do? Where could Sue go? She was hunting for her own New York City apartment every single day, but the agencies named Apartment Finders and Westside Spaces had "listings" that were in dark, urine-stained tenements where no one answered the buzzer, or were no longer available, or never existed in the first place. Shelley told her to post a Need a Roommate notice on the board at Actors' Equity, but Sue confessed that she had yet to join the union—she couldn't until she had an acting job. Shelley gave her a half-lidded look of supreme disappointment and another "yeah, okay," then added, "Next time you go to ShopRite, get a big can of Chock Full O'Nuts, please." In this eighth week—the start of her third month on the isle of Manhattan—the bundle of Arizona talent who had played Maria in **West Side Story** (just last season at the ACLO) was prone to weeping at night, silently, in her bedroll on the couch, in the diamond-shaped silhouettes made by the window's security gates (were such things actually burglarproof?). On the subway, which cost her fifty cents a ride, she often fought back tears, worried that someone would see a pretty young girl undone by her struggles and, well, rob her or worse. For Sue, moving to New York was an act of faith, faith in herself, in her talent, and in the promise of the city that never slept. It was supposed to be an adventure, like something out of the movies, where she would come out of a stage door after a performance and kiss a handsome sailor on shore leave, or a TV show like **That Girl,** where she'd have an apartment with a big kitchen and louvered shutters and a boyfriend who worked for **Newsview** magazine. But New York was not cooperating. How could things be going so sadly for Sue Gliebe, who was the very definition of a triple threat; she could sing, dance, and act! Her parents had recognized her raw talent when she was a little girl! She had starred in all the high school plays! She had been selected from the chorus at the Civic Light Opera to become their lead actress for three seasons running! She had done **High Button Shoes** with Monty Hall, the host of TV's **Let's Make a Deal**! She had had a going away party with a big banner reading ON TO BROADWAY!

So why was New York, New York, making her cry? Her first night in the city, when Rebecca took her via the bus to see Lincoln Center, Sue had looked at all the locals along upper Broadway and actually asked, "Where is everyone going?" She now knew that everyone was going everywhere. This morning, she was going to the bank, the Manufacturers Hanover branch where she had opened an account five weeks before. From behind a Plexiglas (bulletproof) wall, a disinterested female teller slid a ten-dollar bill, a fiver, and five ones through a slot, leaving it to Sue to note that her savings were now down to exactly $564. She had spent more than $200 in New York City and had nothing to show for it but a five-buck umbrella, a blue one with a telescoping handle.

From the bank, Sue went to a donut shop for one plain cake—which was the least expensive—and a coffee with sugar and half-and-half. That was breakfast. She ate standing at a counter sticky from bits of sugar glaze and spilled java. Barely fortified, she walked to the office of Apartment Finders on Columbus Avenue, which was up a wide flight of stairs and above a Hunan Chinese restaurant. The posted listings on the wall had not changed since Saturday, but Sue searched the bulletin board anyway, for a diamond chipped off a ring, for an overlooked gem, for a place with her name on it. Apartment Finders had cost her fifty dollars a month, money she might as well have used to light candles. She would come back later in the day, when, supposedly, new listings were posted, but she already knew her hopes were sure to be dashed again.

Sue decided she was adapting to Gotham, because she turned on her heel and headed back over to Broadway with an agenda for the day. She would not blow time by idly walking in Central Park, with its weedy lawns and cracked benches, dirty sandlots and pathways littered with discarded coffee cups, spent condoms, and other trash. She would not filter through the record stores and bookstores without buying any of the titles. She would not spend money on the trade papers—**Show Biz, Back Stage,** or **Daily Variety**—looking for notices of Equity Principal Interviews or auditions for Non-Equity Showcases. Not today. Today, she was going to the Public Library, the famous building at Forty-Second and Fifth, the landmark building with the stone lions in front.

Two blocks from the Eighty-Sixth Street subway station, the rain started. Sue halted, reached for her umbrella, pushed the button on the telescoping handle, but the handle did not telescope. She pulled on the fabric of the thing, forcing it open, but in doing so bent some of the spokes. When she tried to slide the plastic knob up the shaft, the umbrella bent like the leg of a card table. She shook the umbrella and tried forcing the knob, but only half of the cover deployed. With the rain getting heavy, she recocked and again tried to get the umbrella open, but it inverted into a scoop and more of the spokes disconnected like severed ribs.

Giving up, she tried to jam the worthless skeleton into an overflowing trash bin at Broadway and Eighty-Eighth, but the umbrella seemed to fight back, refusing to go in with the other garbage. It took her four tries before it stayed put.

Sue hurried to the subway station. Her hair was dripping from the rain as she stood in line at the kiosk to purchase the two tokens she would need for the day's travels.

The local trains were delayed. A flood on the uptown tracks. The crowd grew on the platform, large enough that Sue was edged ever closer to the yellow safety line. One bump and she could have fallen onto the tracks. Forty minutes later, she was standing in a subway car so crowded the riders were crammed against each other, their body heat making steam rise from their heavy, rain-soaked coats. The car was so stuffy and hot Sue began sweating. At Columbus Circle the car stopped and did not move for ten minutes, the doors jammed shut, preventing escape. Finally, at Times Square, Sue pushed herself out of the car and into the stream of people who had managed to find the stairs. She tramped up and up and through the turnstiles, then up more stairs and out into the chaos of the Crossroads of the World, where everybody was going everywhere.

Times Square was an exterior version of the station below—filthy, flooded, and overcharged with people. Sue had learned a primary lesson since her arrival in the city, to **keep moving,** to walk with purpose even when she had none, especially along Forty-Second Street, dodging the human debris that collected there for the drugs, the porn, and, in the rain, to peddle five-dollar umbrellas.

She'd navigated the area before, seeking appointments at the lesser talent agencies, those with offices close by the big X where Broadway crossed Seventh Avenue. She had been surprised to find normal people at normal desks doing normal business just floors above the hissing concrete of Times Square. She had no luck with any of the agents—she never made it past the outer offices—so was reduced to leaving her résumé with secretaries who would say, "Yeah, okay," in a tone remarkably similar to her temporary cohost Shelley's.

On this Monday, her agenda **was** her résumé.

During her last month in Scottsdale, Sue had done two TV commercials for Valley Home Furniture, sweeping her arms wide, exclaiming, "Every room, every style, every budget!" Then, for four weekends, she had acted at the Autumnal Renaissance Faire, quoting Shakespeare as a Lusty Wench for thirty dollars a day. She had added those credits to her résumé with a ballpoint pen, but she knew it looked, well, **amateurish**. So she was going to retype the whole thing, get an offset printer to make a hundred copies, then staple one each to the backs of her head shots, the photo that made her look like Cheryl Ladd from **Charlie's Angels** but with real cleavage.

The problem was that she had no typewriter, nor did Rebecca. When Sue asked Shelley if she had a machine she could use, she didn't say no but did tell her, "They rent them at the library." That's why Sue Gliebe was umbrellaless, navigating eastward on Forty-Second Street, passing a stoned-looking teenager who had pulled his penis out of his pants and was pissing as he stumbled along. Not a single person made note of the sight.

The exact moment Sue discovered that the

Main Library was closed on Mondays, a flash of lightning bleached the scraped sky of Mid-Manhattan. She stood at the side entrance to the landmark building, its door locked, unable to comprehend the meaning of those three simple words: **Closed on Mondays**. Just as a roll of thunder outblared the honking horns of traffic, she lost the battle against tears, the collective disappointments simply too much: New York City roommates were not friendly soul sisters; Central Park was a place of naked trees, unusable benches, and spent rubbers; windows had security gates that locked rapists out and victims in; no cute sailors were waiting to meet a girl and get a kiss. No. In New York City real estate parlors took your money and lied to you, drug addicts relieved themselves in plain sight, and the Public Library was closed on Mondays.

Sue was crying, right there on Forty-Second Street between Fifth Avenue and Sixth or, according to the map, the Avenue of the Americas. Sobbing, gasping, tears, the big show. As many people as had made note of the stoned guy's penis stopped to help or even look at the girl who was having so terrible a day that she was weeping aloud in public. Until . . .

"Sue Gliebe!" a man's voice called out. "You little titmouse!"

Bob Roy was the only man in the world who called her a titmouse. Bob Roy had been the general business manager of the ACLO but lived in New York City. He was a Theater Professional contracted for the season and a homosexual. He had once been an actor on Broadway and he'd done commercials in the 1960s but went into theater management for steady work. Running the Civic Light Opera out west was a summer camp for him—he did it every year—and took his duties a little less seriously than he did laughing and gossiping. Bob Roy seemed to know everything about the Theater, and if you worked in his company, if he signed your paychecks, he either loved you or loathed you. Your treatment completely depended on which way his judgmental wind blew.

He loved Sue Gliebe from the moment he saw her at a dress rehearsal for **Brigadoon** in the summer of '76. He delighted in her youth, her halo of honey-blond hair, her clear eyes full of good nature, and her conscientious work ethic. He adored her for showing up on time, knowing her lines, and having ideas for her onstage business. He was fascinated by her tanned body and firm boobs and her lack of self-consciousness, ego, and spite. Every straight man—all seven of them—at the ACLO wanted to fuck her, but she wasn't that way. Most actresses craved such adoration and demanded the largest dressing room, but Sue Gliebe wanted nothing more than to be onstage. After three seasons, she had not changed a whit and Bob Roy loved her all the more.

He was in a taxi at the curb, the window rolled down with the rain falling between them. "Get in this cab right now!" he ordered.

He slid over to make room for her and the cab moved along. "I'd have bet on seeing Eva Gabor on Forty-Second Street before you. Are you **crying?**"

"No. Yes. Oh, **Bobby!**"

Sue explained: She had been in the city for two months, sleeping on Rebecca's couch. Her savings were running out. No agents would give her the time of day. She saw a man pissing in the street. She was crying now, in particular, because the only movies that told the truth about New York City were about needle parks and taxi drivers on killing sprees. Bob Roy laughed out loud! "You've been in **Noo Yawk** for two months and haven't called me? Naughty, Sue. Naughty, naughty."

"I didn't have your number."

"What were you doing in Slime Square?"

"Going to the library."

"To check out the latest Nancy Drew mystery? I'd have guessed you'd read them all by now."

"They have typewriters. I need to create a new résumé."

"Titmouse," Bob said. "Start with a new **you** first. How about a cup of tea or hot Postum? Whatever soothed Baby Sue growing up in Indian Country."

The taxi took them to Bob's apartment downtown—to a terrible neighborhood where all the buildings were six-story tenements and the sidewalks were lined with beaten-up trash cans. He gave the driver six dollars and asked for no change. She followed him out into the rain, up the stoop, through the heavy main door, then four flights up a narrow, zigzagging stairway to apartment 4D. He needed keys for three different locks on the door.

From the dingy, dimly lit hallway, the walls more dirty gray than the original green, the floor a maze of broken and mismatched tiles, Sue stepped into a haven that smelled of candles and lemon-scented dish soap, a cabinet of curiosities, one of which was the bathtub smack dab in the middle of the small kitchen. Bob Roy's railroad flat was four tight, connected rooms, each stuffed with koombies, knickknacks, doodads, furniture pieces of any style, shelves, books, photos in frames, trophies bought from flea markets, old records, small lamps, and calendars from decades before. "I know," he said. "It looks like I sell magic potions in here, like I'm an animated badger from a Disney cartoon." He lit a burner on the stove with a huge kitchen match, then filled a shiny, Olde English–style kettle with water from the tap. As he prepared cups on a tray he said, "Tea in minutes, titmouse. Make a home for yourself."

The room off the kitchen was really a hallway, a narrow passage through treasures and castoffs. The sitting room featured three large chairs of different eras, one a La-Z-Boy, each covered with a colorful throw of some kind. A circular coffee table, nearly too large for the square space, was covered with stacks of books, a cigar box full of sharpened pencils, a vase with an artificial orchid, and two assembled toy bugs from the Cootie game, posed like they were either fighting or mating. The rain was still coming down hard outside, but window curtains that could have come from an antebellum mansion muffled the roar of the storm. The last room in the railroad flat was Bob's bedroom, most of it taken up by a four-poster bed.

"I can never move out of this place, it would take me years to pack," Bob called from the kitchen, only eight feet away. "Turn on the radio, would you?"

"If I can find it," Sue said and heard his laugh in response. She had to focus out so much clutter, like she was in a Lost and Found Forgotten by Time, until she saw it. The radio was a blond-wood-paneled box as big as an ice chest, with circular knobs like thick poker chips and four lines of numbers for different frequencies. She turned the ON/OFF VOLUME until its satisfying **kock** was so loud Bob heard it from the kitchen.

"The tubes have to warm up," he said.

"Does this get shortwave from the Soviet Union?"

"How'd you know?"

"My grandma had a radio like this."

"So did mine! In fact, that's it."

Bob came in with a tray on which were two cups, a pitcher of milk, a sugar bowl with a painted honeybee on the lid, and a plate stacked with Oreo cookies. "Feel free to take off your coat, unless you like being damp." Orchestral music came from the radio just as the teakettle sounded its harmonic **toot**.

Sweet tea with milk, three Oreos, and Bob Roy's snug and cozy flat helped Sue breathe deeply for the first time in months. She let out a sigh as big as a cresting wave and leaned back into a chair so soft it put the **z** in **cozy**.

"Okay," Bob said. "Tell me everything."

She opened up about, well, **everything,** cued by Bob's sympathy. He uttered his support at every story, every anecdote: New York was the only place for Sue to be! Shelley and her "yeah, okay" attitude were to be expected from such a **see-you-next-Tuesday!** The subway was survivable as long as you never made eye contact with anyone. You found an apartment by reading the Rental classifieds in the **Times** and **The Village Voice,** but you had to get them early, at seven in the morning, and then you had to hightail it to the apartments with a bag of donuts because the super would always open up for a pretty girl who shared her donuts. From there, they moved back in time, reminiscing about the summer seasons in Arizona, comparing the backstage gossip to that from the front office, the love affairs gone horrible, and how Sue thought Monty Hall was a solid professional. Bob spilled his tea, laughing.

"Have you had any lunch?"

"No. I was going to treat myself to a slice of pizza pie." At half a dollar per wedge, pizza had become Sue's standby meal at midday.

"Let me go out for deli. You strip out of that uniform of yours and take a hot bath. I'll leave you a robe I stole from a spa in the desert, then we'll eat like middle class Jews."

In the kitchen, he removed a large butcher board that covered the bathtub. Why a tub was in the kitchen had something to do with the original plumbing of the old building. He turned on the water, so hot plumes of steam hazed the security-gated window, and laid the robe across a chair. A delicate wicker basket held scented soap, shampoo, conditioner, an organic sponge, and a pitcher to fill with water and rinse with.

"I'll take my time. You soak." Bob locked two of the front door locks behind him.

After the weak, abbreviated showers uptown, Sue relished the feel of hot water on her skin and the pouring of water over her head. It was funny, taking a bath in a kitchen like this, but she was alone, the bath was like the hot tub on the Gliebe family patio, and Sue scrubbed, rinsed, and soaked her way to being truly, wonderfully **clean**. She was still soaking when the front door locks were opened and Bob returned carrying a large bag of deli.

"Still naked, I see." Bob didn't bother averting his eyes, and Sue didn't mind. If "backstage was no place for modesty," as they said in the Theater, Bob Roy's kitchen was no place for blushing.

Sue's now pale limbs were swimming in the man-size terry-cloth robe as she sat at the coffee table, running a comb through her damp hair.

Bob set down some half sandwiches, small cartons of soup, coleslaw, pickle wedges, and cans of what was called seltzer and, over lunch, they talked about movies and plays. Bob said he could get her free tickets to the lousy shows on Broadway and cheap seats for the hits, so there would be no more evenings in New York with nothing to do but be unpopular on Rebecca's couch. He'd call around to his friends for tips on agents who could arrange a meeting or two, no promises beyond that. He knew a few rehearsal pianists who would help with her audition numbers, with sheet music, transposed for her key. "Okay, titmouse," Bob said, clapping rye crumbs from his fingers. "Let me see this résumé of yours."

Sue pulled the old version out of her purse as Bob grabbed a pencil. After a quick once-over, he drew a big X on the paper with a sigh. "Standard. So standard."

"What's wrong with it?" Sue was hurt. She had worked hard on the thing. Her stage career was on that piece of paper. All the plays she had done in high school, including the one-acts, asterisked with *Thespian Society Award*. Every performance she had ever given at the ACLO, from member of the chorus right up to last year's turn as Nellie Forbush in **South Pacific**. Five seasons and eighteen musicals! The productions at the Gaslamp Play-house Dinner Theater—Emily in **Our Town** and the Ensemble in **Zoo Story**. The Narration she did for the Diabetes Walk-a-thon public service message. Every performance Sue Gliebe had ever given was listed on that résumé.

"As we jaded queens say, 'Nobody gives a shit, honey.'" Bob stood up and went into his bed-room. From under his bed he pulled out an old typewriter protected by a clear plastic dustcover. "This beast is so heavy. I really should keep it out. Make space on the table, would you?" Sue moved away the deli leftovers and a stack of books.

Bob's typewriter was nearly as big as his grand-mother's radio, a black metal antique, fitting for an apartment crammed with old, peculiar things. The typewriter was a Royal, with glass sections on the sides, like opera windows for any titmouse that might take up residence among the keys.

"Does that still work?" Sue asked.

"It's a typewriter, child. Ribbon. Oil. Paper. Happy fingers. That's all it needs. **This**, how-ever . . ." He disdainfully picked up the record of Sue's life's work, holding it with two fingers like it was rancid melon rind. Then he grabbed a pencil and used it as a pointer. "You list only the roles you've played, not the high school you went to or the Gasbag Amateur Play School Diner. The only pro credit you have is the Arizona CLO, so you can't lie about those credits. You put it at the top in big capital letters, then list the best plays and the best roles first, not in the order you performed them. If you were in the chorus, name your part like 'Ellen Craymore' or 'Candy Beaver' toward the bottom. If anyone questions you, then say you were in the chorus. These other roles? In high school and all that?"

"Yes?"

"They go under the heading 'Regional Theater.' Embellish. Don't tell them the plays were one-acts. Don't tell them you won any trophies. Don't tell them they only ran two weekends. The play. The role. You were a working actress in the Region of Pile-of-Rocks, Arizona, and you have the credits to prove it."

"Isn't that lying?"

"They don't care." Bob took his pencil to the résumé again. "Oh, look! You've done commercials! Valley Furniture! The disease of the month! No, no, no. You put right here, 'Commercials on Request.' They will see that you have done commercials but will request not a single one."

"Really?"

"Trust Bobby Roy, Sue. The great ones all do.

Now, this last bit, this sad paragraph listing your **Special Skills**. This is bullshit to anyone on the other side of the casting desk. Notice I did not say 'couch.'"

"What if they're looking for special skills?"

"They ask you. But this list? Guitar. You know three chords, right? You can juggle. Three oranges for a few seconds, right? You roller-skate. What kid doesn't? You can ski and ride a bike and skateboard. BFD! Did you actually put **Sign Language** here?"

"I learned some for Tribal Heritage Day. This means 'awkward.'"

Bob gave the one bit of sign language he knew. "This means 'bullshit.' Understand that your résumé will receive all of five nanoseconds of attention. Casting people look at your picture, then at you to see if it matches. Are you actually a girl? Do you have blond hair? You sporting a rack of any significance? If you're what they are looking for, they turn over to your résumé, scan your credits and your lies, then scribble down this magic word: **callback**."

Bob rolled paper into the old Royal, adjusted the margins and tabs, and within minutes had typed out a crisp, clear, and clean résumé that made Sue look like she was as experienced a dreamer as ever hopped a bus to the big city. She could boast of thirty roles. The one thing missing from the paper was her name at the top.

"Let's think about this for a moment," Bob said. "Over more tea." He removed the deli tray to the kitchen and lit another big match for the burner. "I'd get out more Oreos but then we'd just eat them."

"Think about what?" Sue studied her new professional call sheet. She liked herself more because of what Bobby had typed.

"Have you ever thought of changing your name?"

"My real name is Susan Noreen Gliebe. I've always been just Sue."

"Joan Crawford had always been Lucy LeSueur. Leroy Scherer was called Junior till he became Rock Hudson. You ever hear of Frannie Gumm?"

"Who?"

Bob sang the opening lines of "Over the Rainbow."

"Judy Garland?"

"**Pal of Frances** lacks the **panache** of **friend of Dorothy**, doesn't it?"

"My parents will be disappointed if I don't use my real name."

"Disappointing your parents is the first thing to do when you come to New York." When the kettle sounded off, Bob refilled the teapot sitting beside the Royal. "And say you make it big on the Great White Way—which you will. Do you really want to see **that** name in lights: Sue Gliebe?"

Sue blushed, not out of embarrassment at such praise, but because, deep inside her, she knew she had a future as an actress. She **wanted** to be big. Yes, as big as Frances Gumm.

Bobby poured more tea in both cups. "And how do you pronounce that? 'Gleeb'? 'Glee-bee'? 'Glibe'?" He pantomimed a big, fake yawn. You know what Tammy Grimes's stage name was? Tammy Grimes." He fake-yawned even wider.

"How about . . . Susan Noreen?" Sue could imagine that name up in lights, no problem.

Bob flicked the paper in the Royal typewriter, snapping the new résumé with his finger. "This is a birth certificate for the new Sue. If you could go back in time and pick a brand-new name for yourself and your ma and pa, what would that name be? Elizabeth St. John? Marilyn Conner-Bradley? Holly Woodandvine?"

"I can call myself something like **that**?"

"We'll check with the union, but yes. Who do you want to be, titmouse?"

Sue held her tea. There was a name she'd once dreamed of having, in junior high school, when she sang in a folk group for her chapter of Young

Life. Everyone was making up groovy names like Rainbow Spiritchaser. She came up with hers, imagining the name on the cover of her first LP.

"Joy Makepeace." She said it out loud. Bobby's face showed no reaction.

"Heap big trouble with that'um smoke signal," he said, "unless you have some Native American DNA in the Gliebe bloodline."

So it went as the afternoon wore on. Bobby came up with a constant stream of stage names, the best of which was Suzannah Woods, the worst being Cassandra O'Day. The Oreos had come back out and were now all eaten. Sue kept working the Joy angle. Joy Friendly. Joy Roarke. Joy Lovecraft.

"Joy Spilledmilk," Bobby said.

Sue used the bathroom. Even Bob's water closet was replete with estate-sale booty. She could not imagine why anyone would want a toy bowling set with Fred Flintstone tenpins, yet there they were.

When she came out, Bobby was holding a stack of vintage picture postcards from Paris. They had considered French names like Joan (of Arc), Yvette, Babette, and Bernadette, but none of those sang out.

"Hmm." Bobby held one of the cards. He

showed it to Sue. "The Rue Saint-Honoré. Pronounced 'Honor-ray.' That's the masculine. The feminine has an extra **e** on the end and is pronounced the same. **Honorée.** Isn't that lovely?"

"I'm not French."

"We could try an Anglo-Saxon surname. Something simple, one syllable. Bates. Church. Smythe. Cooke."

"None of those are good." Sue flipped through the stack of old postcards—the Eiffel Tower. Notre Dame. Charles de Gaulle.

"Honorée Goode?" Bob repeated the name and liked the sound of it. "**E**'s on the ends of both."

"They'd call me Honorée Goody Two-shoes."

"No, they wouldn't. Everyone pretends they speak French, **mon petite teet-mouse.** Honorée Goode is honestly good." He reached over and pulled a black Princess-model phone off a bookshelf and dialed a number.

"I have a friend at Equity. They have a computer so no names get duplicated. Jane Fonda. Faye Dunaway. Raquel Welch. Taken!"

"Raquel Gliebe? My parents would have no problem with that."

Bob was connected to his friend Mark. "Mark-y Mark-a-lot, Bob Roy. I know! It has? Not since she went out of town, on that cruise liner. It's good money! Can you do me a little service? Check the database for a stage name. No, for one **not** taken. Last name Goode with an **e** on the end. First name Honorée." He spelled it out. "With an accent or **schwa** or whatever on the first **e**. Sure, I'll hold."

"I don't know, Bobby." Sue was running the new name over and over again in her head.

"You can decide when you march into Equity with your first contract and a check for the dues. Then, you can be Sue Gliebe or Catwoman Zelkowitz. But I have to tell you . . ." Someone came on the phone, but it wasn't Bob's friend. "Yes, I am holding for Mark. Thank you." He turned back to Sue. "I walked into that run-through of **Brigadoon**. Up there onstage was a girl playing Fiona who was going to have a **career**."

Sue smiled and blushed. She was that Fiona. She had crushed that role, her first out of the chorus. Her Fiona had led to all the roles the ACLO had given her, had pushed her off to NYC, and had made her clean in Bob Roy's kitchen tub.

"I loved that girl," Bob said. "I loved that actress. She wasn't some bitter leading lady pissed off that New York had had enough of her. Or a painted starlet doing Civic Light Opera because the distance and makeup hid the fact she was forty-three years old. That Fiona was no mutton. No, she was a local lamb, an Arizona gal who could hold the stage like a Barrymore, sing like Julie Andrews, with a set of boobs that set the boys a-flutter. If you had introduced yourself to me as Honorée Goode, I would have said, 'Well, you certainly are!' But no, you were Sue Gliebe. I thought, Sue Gliebe? That's just not going to fly."

Sue Gliebe felt warm inside. Bobby Roy was her biggest fan and she loved him. If he had been fifteen years younger, forty pounds lighter, and not a homosexual she would have spent the night in his bed. Maybe she would, regardless.

Mark came back on the phone. "Are you sure?" Bob asked. "That spelling, with the e? Okay. Thanks, Marco. I will. Thursday? Why not! Bye!" He hung up the phone, tapping it with his running fingers, and said, "Big decision time, titmouse."

Sue leaned back in her overstuffed chair. The rain had stopped outside. Her skin had been dried by the terry cloth of the robe and she smelled of delicate rosewater from the bath soap. The big radio was softly playing an orchestration of a nightclub standard, and, for the first time ever, New York City seemed like the place Sue Gliebe belonged . . .

EXACTLY ONE YEAR LATER:

WHO'S WHO IN THE CAST

HONORÉE GOODE (Miss Wentworth)—Ms. Goode trained at the Arizona Civic Light Opera. She was nominated for an Obie last year for her role as Kate Brunswick in Joe Runyan's Backwater Blues. This marks her Broadway debut. She thanks her supportive parents and Robert Roy, Jr., for making it all possible.

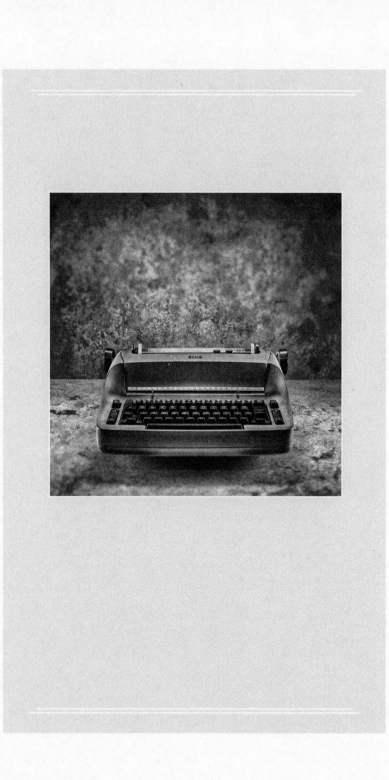

A Special Weekend

It was the early spring of 1970 and because his tenth birthday was in a week and a half, Kenny Stahl, still thought of as the baby of the family, did not have to go to school. He was going to be picked up by his mother around noon to spend a special weekend with her, so he came to the breakfast table in his ordinary, nonschool clothes. His older brother, Kirk, and older sister, Karen, both in their uniforms for St. Philip Neri School, thought the deal was unfair. They wanted their mom to come and pick them up, too—to take them away, out of the house they had been moved into, to live again in Sacramento or anyplace else as long as they were the only kids and the dark moodiness of their father and the constant, sunny practicality of his second wife would not make their lives an emotional teeter-totter.

Kenny's three stepsisters were seventeen, fifteen,

and fourteen years old. His stepbrother had two years on him. None of them had opinions as to the fairness of the birthday plan. They had always lived together in Iron Bend, attended the unified public schools, and never had to wear uniforms. This weekend didn't strike them as interesting, notable, or in any way special.

The small house they all lived in was far out of town on Webster Road, closer to Molinas than to Iron Bend, which was the county seat and where Kenny's father was head cook at the Blue Gum Restaurant. Eucalyptus trees—blue gums—lined both sides of Webster Road for most of the miles between the two towns, scattering their leaves and nuts all over the two lanes and both shoulders. Decades ago the messy imports from Australia were planted as windbreaks for the almond groves as well as in a misinformed attempt to farm the trees for railroad ties. This was back when big money could be made in railroad ties, as long as they were not made of eucalyptus. Fortunes were lost on the twisting, peeling, gnarly-growing trees, three of which were spaced across the front yard of Kenny's house; the constant rain of debris laid waste to every attempt to plant decent grass there. The backyard had sort of a lawn, a patch of weed-studded green, which the kids took turns mowing on occasion. Across the road were almond orchards. Almonds were a big industry then and still are now.

Kenny's father had found a new job in Iron Bend, a new home, a new school, and, it turned out, a new family. He'd moved his three kids into the small house the very same night they had left Sacramento. All the boys slept in what had been a screened-in porch. All the girls were in one bedroom with twin bunk beds.

After two school buses had come and gone, Kenny spent the morning shuffling around the house as his father slept and his stepmother quietly cleaned up the breakfast dishes. He had never been at home without the other kids and was thrilled to have the run of the place. His only instruction was that he was to keep quiet. For a while, he watched TV with the volume nearly mute, but there was just one channel, Channel 12 from Chico, and during school hours there was nothing on that interested him. He played with the model ships and planes he had made from kits, using the top of the living room coffee table as the vast sea. He went through the dresser drawers of his brother and stepbrother looking for secrets, but their treasures were hidden elsewhere. In the backyard, he punted a football, trying to clear the nearest almond trees, gambling that in failure the ball wouldn't get stuck in their branches. He tied a cut of an old bedsheet to a discarded beanpole, making a flag that he ran around with like he was leading a charge in the Civil War. He was trying to plant the flag into a hole when his stepmom called to him from the kitchen window she had cranked open.

"Kenny! Your mother is here!"

He hadn't heard the car.

In the kitchen, he was caught short by a sight he had never seen in the near decade of his life; his dad was awake and sitting at the table with his morning coffee. His mother, his real mom, was sitting at the table as well, a cup of coffee of her own. His stepmother was on her feet, leaning against the counter, sipping coffee, too. The three caretakers of his world had never been in the same room at the same time.

"There's the Kenny Bear!" Kenny's mom was beaming. She looked like a secretary in a TV show—professionally dressed, wearing heels, her trim black hair neat, her makeup showing red lips that left marks on her coffee cup. She stood and hugged him with perfumed arms, kissing the top of his head. "Go get your bag and we'll hit the road."

Kenny had no idea about any bag, but his stepmother had put some clothes into one of her daughter's small pink suitcases. He was packed. His father stood up and frazzled Kenny's hair. "I gotta shower," he said. "Go check out your mother's hot wheels."

"You got me Hot Wheels?" Kenny asked, thinking that his birthday present was going to be some miniature cars made of die-cast metal.

But no. In the driveway was an actual sports car, red, a two-seater, with wire wheels. The top was up and already littered with eucalyptus fallings. The only sports cars he'd ever seen were on television, driven by detectives and young doctors.

"Is this yours, Mom?"

"A friend let me borrow it."

Kenny was looking through the driver's side window. "Can I sit in it?"

"Go ahead."

Kenny figured out how to open the door and sat behind the wheel. The dials and switches of the car looked like they came from a jet plane. The wood paneling was like furniture. The seats smelled like leather baseball mitts. The red circle in the middle of the steering wheel said FIAT. After his mother put the pink suitcase in the car's trunk, she asked for Kenny's help putting the top down.

"We'll let the wind blow through our hair until we get to the highway, okay?" She undid the latches of the top and Kenny helped fold it back, bending the clear plastic window in on itself. His mother fired up the engine, which sounded like a dragon clearing its throat, then she backed out of the driveway—she had taken off her heels to work the pedals and put on a pair of sunglasses, the kind worn by snow skiers. Mother, son, and Fiat roared away from the house, down Webster Road, the gum tree shadows making the sunlight strobe in Kenny's eyes, the wind sounding in his ears and whipping his hair from back to front. The car was the coolest, most **boss** ride Kenny had ever seen. He was the happiest he had been since he was a little kid.

———

The attendant at the Shell station in Iron Bend was all over the car, giving it and the woman driving it his keen attention. He filled the tank, wiped the windshield, checked the oil, and marveled at the "dago motor." Kenny was offered a free soda pop from the vending machine. While he was pulling a bottle of root beer (always his choice) from the cold box, the man was helping his mother put the top back up and close the latches. The man was smiling and chatting, asking questions about if his mother was headed north or south and if she planned on coming back to Iron Bend soon. When they were back in the car and on the highway (heading south), she told her son the Shell man had "cow-eyes" and she laughed.

"Find us some music, honey," she said, pointing to the tiny radio in the wooden dashboard. "Turn that knob, then that one for a station."

Like a radio operator on a bomber, Kenny moved the red line of the dial along the numbers. The local radio station had a commercial for Stan Nathan's Shoes for the Family, a store in town. Static and voices came and went until Kenny located the beam from a station that came in loud and clear. A man was singing about raindrops on his head. Kenny's mom knew the words and sang along as she dug around in her purse at the same time she steered. She found a little leather case with a clasp on it, which she unsnapped to reveal the tips of cigarettes. They were long cigarettes, longer than those his father smoked. She had one in her lips, the red lipstick already staining the white filter, when she pushed a button on the dash. In a few seconds the button popped and she pulled the whole thing out. There was a glowing red coil on the end of the button, so hot she used it to light her long cigarette. She put the hot button back in its hole, then switched hands on the wheel to open a small, triangular window. As soon as there was a whistling crack, the smoke from her long cigarette was sucked out the window like a magic trick.

"Tell me about school, sweetie," she said. "You like school?"

Kenny told her that St. Philip Neri wasn't like St. Joseph, the only other school he had gone to, back in Sacramento. St. Philip Neri was small, not many kids went there, and some of the nuns didn't dress like nuns. As he savored his bottle of root beer with short, airy sips, he told his mom about the bus rides to school, how the uniforms were red plaid instead of blue plaid and they had some days when they didn't have to wear them, and that a kid in his class named Munson made models like he did and lived in a house with a pool, but not an inground pool like at the city park, but a circular aboveground pool. From just the one question, Kenny talked all the way from Iron Bend to the Butte City cutoff as his mother smoked. When the one radio station faded, Kenny found another, then another. His mom let him signal to the truck drivers they passed to blow their air horns. He would pump his fist up and down, and, if the drivers saw him, more often than not they would send out a toot. Once, Kenny saw a truck driver looking at them in his sideview mirror and got a blast on the horn without having to pump for it. The driver blew a kiss that was probably meant for his mom, not for Kenny.

They stopped for lunch in Maxwell at a diner called Kathy's Kountry Kafe, a place for travelers and, in season, duck hunters. The Fiat was the only sports car in the parking lot. The waitress seemed to love chatting with Kenny's mom—they talked like old friends or sisters. Kenny noticed that the waitress had very red lips, too. When she asked what to bring for the young man, he asked for a hamburger.

"Oh no, honey," his mother said. "Hamburgers are for anytime. At a restaurant we should order from the menu."

"Why not, Mom? Dad doesn't care. And Nancy lets us." Nancy was Kenny's stepmother.

"What say we make this a special rule," his mother said. "Just for you and me." This seemed like an odd rule to suddenly impose. Kenny had never been told what to order or what he could not have. "I think you'll like the hot turkey sandwich," his mother said. "We'll split it."

Kenny thought she meant a sandwich that was going to be steaming hot and was not sure he was going to like it. "Can I have a milkshake?"

"Yep." She smiled. "I'm flexible!"

Truth be told, Kenny liked the open-faced sandwich that was swimming in brown gravy and was not too hot at all. The white bread that sucked up all the gravy was just as good as the turkey meat, and mashed potatoes were his favorite food of all time. His mom had an igloo-shaped scoop of cottage cheese on tomato slices but cut up a few bites of the hot turkey for herself. His vanilla milkshake came in the freezing steel cup it was made in and twice filled up a fancy glass. He poured it himself, tapping the steel against the glass to help it along. This was so much milkshake, Kenny couldn't finish it.

When his mother went to the restroom, Kenny noticed all the men travelers following her with their eyes, turning their heads to watch her go. One of them got up to pay his check, stopping by the booth where Kenny sat alone.

"Is that your mommy, slugger?" the man asked. He wore a brown suit with a tie partly undone. His eyeglasses had flip-up sunshades that stuck out like small visors.

"Um-hmmm," Kenny said.

The man smiled. "You know, I got a boy at home just like you. But not a mommy like you got." The man laughed out loud, then paid at the register.

When his mom came back from the restroom, her lips were freshly painted. She took a sip from what was left of Kenny's milkshake, leaving red marks on the paper straw.

———

Sacramento was more than an hour down the highway. Kenny had not been to his hometown since his father packed their stuff into the station wagon, the day they moved to Iron Bend. The buildings had a look of comforting familiarity, but when his mom turned the Fiat off the highway it was at a street he had never traveled. When he saw the sign for the Leamington Hotel he felt a smile on his face—his parents had both worked at the Leamington, but now only his mom did. He and his brother and sister had spent time there, tagging along on some weekends when their folks were still married. They played in the big conference room when it was empty and would eat at the counter of the coffee shop when the place was not busy. Dad would pay them a nickel for every tray of potatoes they would wrap in tinfoil for baking en masse. If they asked permission, they could get their own chocolate milk from the dispenser, as long as they used the small glasses. This was long ago; a big chunk of Kenny's life had passed since then.

His mother parked the Fiat in the back of the hotel and they entered through the kitchen—just as Kenny remembered doing in his dad's station wagon and his mom's Corolla. The staff all welcomed his mother and she greeted each person by name in response. A lady and one of the cooks could not believe that Kenny had grown up so much since they had last seen him, but Kenny could not remember who those people were, though he thought he recognized the lady's cat's-eye glasses with the thick lenses. The kitchen looked smaller than Kenny remembered it.

When he was little, Kenny's mother was a waitress in the Leamington Hotel coffee shop and his father one of the cooks. She wore a uniform then, but now dressed in business clothes and had an office off the hotel lobby. Her office had a desk stacked with papers and a wall covered by a bulletin board that had many index cards, all written upon in different colored inks and arranged in neat columns.

"Kenny Bear, I have a few things to do, then I'll tell you about your birthday surprise, okay?" She was sliding some papers into a leather folder. "Can you sit here for a bit?"

"Can I pretend this is my office and I work here?"

"Sure," she said, smiling. "Here're some notebooks, and look, this is an electric pencil sharpener." She showed him how to push a pencil into the opening of the machine and make the grinding noise that produced a pencil point as sharp as a sewing pin. "Don't answer the phone if it rings."

A lady named Miss Abbott came into the office and asked, "So this is your little man?" She was older than his mom and wore glasses on a chain around her neck. Miss Abbott would keep an eye on Kenny and would know where his mother was if he needed her.

"Kenny is going to do some work for us today."

"Wonderful," Miss Abbott said. "I'll give you some stamps and an ink pad to make everything official. Would you like that?"

His mother left, carrying her leather folder. Kenny sat in her chair behind her desk. Miss Abbott brought him some stamps that said the date on them and INVOICE and RECEIVED as well as a metal rectangular box with blue ink on a pad.

"You know," Miss Abbott said, "I have a nephew just your age."

———

Kenny used the stamps and ink on a few pages of a notebook, then, bored, looked through the top drawers of the desk. One drawer had dividers that separated paper clips, boxes of staples, rubber bands, pencils, and some pens that said LEAMINGTON HOTEL on the sides. Another drawer had envelopes and letter paper that said LEAMINGTON HOTEL with a little drawing of the building at the top of each sheet.

He got up from the desk, went to the door, and saw Miss Abbott at a desk of her own, typing some kind of letter.

"Miss Abbott," Kenny said. "May I use some paper that says 'Leamington Hotel' on it?"

Miss Abbott kept typing. "What's that?" she asked without looking up.

"May I use some paper that says 'Leamington Hotel' on it?"

"Go ahead," she said as she kept on typing.

Kenny used the stamps and hotel pens on the paper, drawing lines and signing his name next to the stamps. Then he had an idea.

He took the cover off the typewriter that was on its own little desk beside his mother's. The machine was light blue, had the letters **IBM** on the front, and was really big, taking up most of its special table. He rolled a sheet of paper into the workings of the typewriter and pressed on the keys, but they were dead. Nothing happened. Kenny was about to ask Miss Abbott why the typewriter didn't work but then he saw the rocker switch that said ON/OFF and that the OFF part was depressed. He rocked it to ON and the machine hummed and vibrated. The mechanical ball with the letters on it swept back and forth once, then stopped on the left side. The carriage with the paper in it did not move, which made Kenny think the typewriter must be part computer or one of those Teletype machines.

He tried to type his name, but it came out **kkkkkkkkkkkkk**. That's when he discovered that if he kept the key pressed down, the letter repeated, sounding like a machine gun—**kkkk kkkkkk kkkk keeee eeeenn nnnnnnnn n n n yyyy yyy**. What confused him the most was the lack of a handle he was supposed to slap to make the page go back. There was none. There was a very big button that said RETURN on it. When he pressed that the ball moved back with a **chunk** and he could type a new line. This was now, officially, the most amazing typewriter Kenny had ever seen or heard of.

Kenny did not know how to type like a grown-up—like Miss Abbott or his mom—so he used just one finger, finding the letters he wanted but sometimes hitting ones he didn't—**kennnystdahlkl kjenny stanhl kenn sath**. By going very slowly and being very careful he finally typed his name correctly—**kenny stahl**—and rolled that page out of the IBM. He put the date stamp next to his name along with **INVOICE**.

"How about a coffee break?" Miss Abbott was standing in the door.

"I don't drink coffee," Kenny said.

Miss Abbott nodded. "Well, let's see what else we can find, shall we?"

He followed her into the lobby, where Kenny saw his mother standing with a group of men. They were all talking business, but Kenny still called out to her.

"Mom!" he hollered, pointing toward the hotel kitchen. "I'm taking a coffee break!"

She turned to him and smiled and gave a little wave, then turned back to the businessmen.

In the kitchen, he asked Miss Abbott if he could get his own chocolate milk like he used to, but the dispenser no longer held chocolate milk. Just regular milk and something called Skim. Instead, Miss Abbott went to a silver refrigerator and pulled out a carton of chocolate milk, grabbed one of the big drinking glasses, and filled it to the top. This was more chocolate milk than Kenny had ever been allowed, which he thought was great. Miss Abbott got herself some coffee out of a round, glass pitcher that sat on a Bunn Coffee Service maker. They could not take their drinks back through the lobby, so they went into the coffee shop, which looked and smelled exactly the same as when Kenny was little. They sat in an empty booth, not at the counter.

"Do you remember me?" she asked him. "I worked here with your daddy. Before your mommy started." Miss Abbott asked Kenny more questions, mostly if he liked the same things her nephew liked—baseball, karate class, and TV shows. Kenny told her they only got Channel 12 from Chico.

———

Back in his mother's office he decided to write her a letter on the IBM typewriter. He started with a new sheet of Leamington Hotel paper and went very slowly.

Deear Mom,

How are you I am fine
   Your friends sport car is like a racecar. I like how loud the motor goes and working the radio.
   I saw you in the hotel just now and wonder what is my big sur-prise?????? ?
   I am going to leave this let-ter in a place where it will be a SURPEIZE for you. After you find it right me back on this tiperighter that is so cooooool and esy to do.

Love
Kenny Stahl RECEIVED RECEIVED INVOICE

Kenny folded the letter as best he could and put it into a hotel envelope and licked the seal, careful not to cut his tongue on the sharp edge. He wrote **TO MOM** on the front with a Leamington Hotel pen, then looked for a place to hide the letter, deciding the best place would be in a desk drawer under a few pages of Leamington Hotel stationery.

Kenny was playing with some rubber bands when his mom came back into her office. She was with a man who had dark brown skin and the straightest, blackest hair. "Kenny, this is Mr. Garcia. He let us borrow his car for the ride down today."

"Hello," Kenny said. "That's your car? The sports car?"

"It is," Mr. Garcia said. "I'm glad to meet you. But let's do it proper, shall we? Stand up."

Kenny did as he was told.

"Now," Mr. Garcia continued, "we shake hands. Grab firm now."

Kenny squeezed Mr. Garcia's hand as hard as he could.

"Don't hurt me." Mr. Garcia chuckled. Kenny's mom beamed at the two men. "Now, look me in the eye, just like I look at you. Good. Now you say, 'It's a pleasure to meet you.'"

"It's a pleasure to meet you," Kenny repeated.

"Now comes the most important part. We ask each other a question, engage each other, man to man, see? I'm going to ask you this—do you know what 'Fiat' stands for?"

Kenny shook his head, because he was confused by the question and because he had no idea what was going on. No one had ever explained to him how to shake hands.

"'Fix it again, Tony.'" Mr. Garcia laughed. "Now you ask me a question. Go ahead."

"Um." Kenny had to think of something to say. He was looking at Mr. Garcia's head of thick, jet-black hair, held stiffly in place and so shiny. That was when he remembered seeing Mr. Garcia before, when he was little, when he was playing in the hotel with his brother and sister. He remembered that Mr. Garcia did not work in the kitchen with his dad, but would come in from the lobby wearing a suit. "You work here, too, like my mom, don't you?"

Mr. Garcia and his mom shared a glance and a smile. "I used to, Kenny, but not anymore. Now I'm at the Senator."

"You're a senator?" Kenny knew what a senator was from the news on Channel 12.

"Mr. Garcia works at the Senator Hotel, Kenny," his mother said. "And he has a big surprise for you."

"You haven't told him?" Mr. Garcia asked.

"I thought it should be your treat," she said.

"Okay." Mr. Garcia looked at Kenny. "I hear you have a birthday coming up, is that right?"

Kenny nodded. "I'm going to be ten."

"Have you ever flown?"

"You mean, in an airplane?"

"Have you?"

Kenny looked at his mother. Maybe, when he was a baby, she had taken him on an airliner but he had been too little to remember. "Have I, Mom?"

"Jose is a pilot. He has a plane and wants to take you up for a ride. Won't that be fun?"

Kenny had never met a pilot before who owned his own airplane. Where was Mr. Garcia's uniform? Was he in the Air Force?

"What are you doing tomorrow?" Mr. Garcia asked. "Want to go up?"

Kenny looked at his mother. "Can I, Mom?"

"Yep," she said. "I'm flexible."

Kenny and his mother had their dinner at a restaurant called the Rosemount. She knew everybody who worked there. The waiter took away two place settings because his mom said that she was on "a special date with this young man," meaning Kenny. The menus were as big as newspapers. He had spaghetti and, for dessert, the waiter brought him a piece of chocolate cake as big as his shoe. He couldn't finish it all. His mother smoked her long cigarettes and drank an after-dinner coffee. One of the cooks came out, a fellow Kenny remembered from his days at the Leamington. The cook's name was Bruce. He sat at the table with the two of them and talked with his mom for a while, mostly laughing.

"Good God, Kenny," Bruce said to him. "You are growing up as fast as alfalfa." Bruce could do an amazing trick—he could throw a drinking straw into a raw potato and make it stick like an arrow. On the way out through the kitchen—Mom had parked the Fiat in the back—Bruce did the trick for Kenny. **Whap!** And the straw almost went all the way through the potato. It was amazing!

His mom lived in a two-story building with a stairway in the middle that separated the two apartments on each floor. The living room of her place had something called a Murphy bed that folded up and disappeared into the wall. When his mom pulled the bed down, it was already made. She had a small color TV on a rolling stand that she turned to face the bed, but before he could watch it she made Kenny take a bath.

The bathroom was small and the tub was tiny, so it quickly filled up with water. On one shelf there were bath soaps and other girlie things, all in colorful bottles and tubes with flowers on the labels. On another shelf was a can of Gillette shaving cream and a man's razor made by Wilkinson Sword. Kenny played in the tub until his fingers wrinkled and the water got cold. Pajamas had been packed in the pink suitcase from home, and, as he put them on, he smelled popcorn. His mom had made some, shaking it to life in a pot on her little kitchen stove.

"Find something to watch on TV, honey," she called out as she melted butter in a saucepan to pour over the popcorn.

Kenny turned on the TV and it came to life immediately, without having to warm up like the one at home. He was delighted to see all the old channels, the ones he had watched before his mom moved out of the house and his dad got married again. There were shows on Channels 3, 6, 10, and 13. And, on the other channel knob, the one that turned rather than **clicked,** there was a Channel 40. Every channel was in color, too, except the old movie on Channel 40. He settled on a show called **The Name of the Game,** which was fine with his mom.

They lay on the Murphy bed together, eating popcorn. His mom kicked off her shoes and put her arm around her son's shoulders, her fingers playing in his hair. At one point she sat up and said, "Rub Momma's neck some." Kenny rose onto his knees and tried to give her neck a massage, moving her hair out of the way and avoiding the little chain around her neck. After a few minutes she thanked him and said that she loved her little Kenny. They both lay back down. The next TV show came on—**Bracken's World**, in which grown-ups went on and on about things Kenny could not understand. He was asleep before the first commercial.

———

Music was playing on a radio when Kenny woke up in the morning. His mother was in the kitchen, having already made coffee in a glass percolator on the stove. Kenny had to hop down from the Murphy bed because it was a bit high.

"Well, hello, sleepy-bear." His mother kissed his head. "We have a big problem."

"What?" Kenny rubbed his eyes as he sat at the two-seat kitchen table.

"I didn't get milk yesterday." She did have a can of something called Evaporated Milk—there was a cartoon cow on the label—that she was using for her morning coffee. "Can you go around to Louie's Market and get a half gallon of milk? You'll need some for your cereal."

"I can."

Kenny had no idea where Louie's Market was. His mom explained that it was out the front door, one right turn, then one left turn. A three-minute walk. There were some dollar bills on her dresser in the bedroom, he could take two and buy himself a treat for later.

Kenny dressed in the same clothes he wore the day before and went into his mom's tiny bedroom. There was money on her dresser, so he took two one-dollar bills. Her closet door was open with the light on inside; Kenny could see all her shoes on the floor and her dresses and skirts on hangers. There was also a man's suit jacket and pants hanging in the closet and some ties on little hooks. A pair of man's shoes were in there with her high heels.

The streets around the apartment were lined with big trees, but not the blue gums of Webster Road. These trees had wide green leaves and branches that were thick and high. The roots of the tall, old trees had grown so large they buckled the sidewalks and made them uneven. Kenny carried the two one-dollar bills in his hand as he turned right, then left, finding Louie's Market in less than three minutes.

A Japanese man was behind the cash register, surrounded by candies and sweets on display.

Kenny found the dairy case and carried a half gallon of milk over to pay for it. As the Japanese man rang up the sale he asked, "Who are you? I've never seen you before."

Kenny told him his mother lived nearby and had forgotten to buy milk.

"Who is your mother?" the man asked. When Kenny told him, he said "Oh! Your mother is a nice lady. A very pretty lady. And you are her boy? How old are you?"

"In nine days ten," Kenny said.

"I have a girl just like you," the grocer said.

For the treat he would have later, Kenny picked out a twin pack of Hostess CupCakes, chocolate with the swirl of white icing down the middle. They cost twenty-five cents, which Kenny hoped was not too much. His mother said nothing when he got back with the milk. She made him toast to eat along with his bowl of Rice Krispies and cut up sections of a seedless orange.

Kenny was watching Channel 40—a whole morning of cartoons and commercials for toys—when the phone on the wall of the kitchen rang. After saying hello, his mother said something he did not understand.

"**Que paso, mi amor?** What? Oh, no! He was looking forward to it. Are you sure?" Kenny looked at his mom, she at him as she listened. "Oh! Yes, that could work. Yes, two birds with one stone. Love it. Okay." She listened on the phone for a moment more, then giggled as she hung up.

"Kenny Bear," she sang, coming into the room. "Change of plans. Jose, Mr. Garcia, had business come up and he can't fly you in his plane today. But . . ." She cocked her head, as though a more exciting possibility was about to be floated, like there was a trip on a rocket ship available instead. "He can fly you all the way home tomorrow! We won't have to drive."

Kenny did not quite understand how a flight home on an airplane was possible. Would the plane land on Webster Road right at his house? Wouldn't they crash into the blue gum trees?

With the whole day now to fill, Kenny and his mom spent the late morning at Fairytale Town, a place for kids run by the Parks Department. There were little houses painted to look like they were made of straw, sticks, and stones; a long and curling version of a yellow brick road; and puppet shows every hour until 3:00 p.m. The whole family used to visit the storybook village when Kenny was little, although never with Dad, who was always sleeping at home. Since Kenny was now nearly ten years old, the fairy-tale sets were too young for him. Even the swings were for kids littler than Kenny.

The zoo was nearby. That, too, had been a favorite destination when Kenny was smaller. The monkeys still aired out their limbs by swinging on the rings in their cage, the elephants were still in a pen on the other side of the fence that was no longer as tall as it had been, and the giraffes could still be fed carrots from pails full of them, kept on hand by the zookeepers. He and his mom stayed at the zoo longer than they did Fairytale Town, lingering in the Reptile House. There was a huge python in there, wrapped around part of a tree with his head, as big as a football, right next to the window glass.

For lunch they ate at a little market that also had sidewalk tables with checkerboard cloths. Kenny had a tuna sandwich with no lettuce or tomato, just the tuna, and his mother had a small tub of pasta salad. To drink, there was golden juice that came in bottles shaped like apples—this was instead of a Coke. Kenny was disappointed at first, but the apple juice was so sweet, so thick that his whole body felt good when the drink slid down his throat and into his tummy. He imagined that must be what drinking wine was like, since grown-ups were always making such a big deal about "fine wines." He had his Hostess cupcakes for dessert.

"What shall we do now, Kenny Bear?" his mom asked. "What if we tried our hands at peewee golf?"

She drove the red Fiat onto the freeway, heading west toward the foothills. When they crossed the river, Kenny realized they were near the exit for Sunset Avenue, which was the off-ramp they used to take to get home, to his old house. He recognized the big green sign with the white arrow and SUNSET AVE, and he saw the Chevron station on one side and the Phillips 66 station on the other. But his mom didn't merge into the exit lane. She kept going. Farther down the highway a colorful little town of tiny windmills and castles appeared, the Miniature Golf & Family Fun Center. The place looked brand-new and magical.

Because it was a Saturday, there was a pretty good crowd made up of carloads of families and idle kids who had ridden their bikes or been dropped off, kids who were supplied with enough money for a day of Fun-with-a-capital-F. There was a circle of baseball batting cages with automatic pitching machines, an arcade filled with pinball and shooting games. A snack bar served corn dogs and giant pretzels and Pepsi-Cola. Kenny and his mom had to wait in line to get the balls and the right-size putters from a teenage boy who smiled at his mom with the same cow eyes as the man at the Shell station in Iron Bend. There was a choice of two courses to play and the young man behind the counter not only suggested the Magic-Land course, with the castle, but also walked them to the first hole and took pains to explain how to use the little pencil to keep score on the card. He also explained that if they got a hole in one on the eighteenth, they'd win a free game.

"I think we have the gist of it," his mom said to the kid, hoping to get rid of him. Still, he lingered until they both putted. He wished them a good round and went back to the counter to hand out more putters and colored golf balls.

They never bothered to keep score. Kenny hacked at his ball, the purple one, caring more about distance than accuracy, taking as many strokes as necessary to make the hole. His mom was a bit more careful. The most fun hole was the one where Kenny hit his ball into a polka-dotted toadstool and it disappeared for a few seconds before coming out of one of three tubes onto a lower circular green. From there, he had to hit the ball into a giant frog's mouth that moved up and down like the drawbridge on a castle. Again, the ball disappeared, coming out at an even lower green and nearly rolling right into the cup. He only had to tap the purple ball with his short putter. His mom took forever to make it through the frog's mouth.

"Peewee golf is pretty fun," he said to his mom when they were back in the Fiat. She had gotten him a corn dog, which he ate before getting into the sports car.

"You're awfully good at it," she said, shifting gears as they pulled out of the Family Fun Center parking lot and headed back into the city, back toward the Sunset Avenue off-ramp.

"Mom?" he asked. She was lighting another of her long cigarettes with the Fiat's lighter. "Can we go see the old house?"

His mother blew smoke out of her mouth, and she watched it disappear into the wind. She did not want to see the old house. She had brought Kenny home from the hospital to that house two days after he was born. His brother and sister had been born in Berkeley, but they had few memories of the apartment there. She had watched her older kids play in the backyard of that house as she carried little Kenny around in the crook of her hip. Kenny had crawled on the hooked rug—her mother's old hooked rug—in the living room until he learned to walk on it. That house carried memories of Christmases and Halloweens, of birthday parties for the kids in the neighborhood, the sweeter memories of her marriage and her life as a mother.

But unhappiness also lingered in the corners of the place, arguments sure to be echoing still, a loneliness that haunted the nights after the kids were asleep as well as the days when they were a maddening handful. To escape—the house, the kids, the boredom found in the shadows of discontent—she took a job at the Leamington Hotel. There was an opening for a waitress. She'd drive in early, before her husband came in for the lunch and dinner shift, leaving the kids with one of the Mormon teenage girls who lived down the block. The money was nice, of course, but the activity was what she looked forward to every day—having a place to go, work to do, and people to talk with. She was still Mrs. Karl Stahl, and her husband was the head of the kitchen, but everyone, including Jose Garcia, called her by her first name. She proved to be so very good with numbers that the hotel's general manager moved her from the coffee shop to a bookkeeper's desk. She had risen to the sales office after she divorced Kenny's father and was no longer Mrs. Karl Stahl.

She had walked away from that old house a lifetime ago. She did not want to see the place again.

"Sure," she said to her son. "I'm flexible."

She turned off the freeway, made a right at the Phillips 66 station, and continued down Sunset Avenue to Palmetto Street. She turned left on Palmetto to Derby Street, downshifted as she made the right turn, crossed Vista and Bush Streets, then pulled over and stopped in front of 4114.

Kenny had just two homes, and this was his first. He stared at it. The mailbox by the driveway was the same, the X-frame railing on the porch was as he remembered, but the tree in the front yard looked weirdly small. The lawn was mowed, he'd never seen the grass so neat, and flowers were planted in arrangements along the front of the house. They had never had flowers along the front of the house. The big window had blue curtains in it, not the white ones from when he was a kid. The garage door was closed, unlike when he lived there and it stayed open for easy access to all the bikes and toys and the back rooms of the house. Rather than his father's old station wagon or his mother's Corolla, a new Dodge Dart was parked in the driveway.

The Anhalters had lived next door. Kenny expected to see their white pickup truck, but it was not around. The house across the street had a For Sale sign in the front yard. "The Callendars are selling their house," Kenny said.

"Looks like they've already moved," his mother told him. Yes, the house looked empty. The Callendar kids, Brenda and Steve, were not twins but looked like they'd been born on the same day. They rode Schwinn bikes, had a dog named Biscuit, had been on a swimming team, and now lived somewhere else.

Kenny and his mom sat in the Fiat for a few minutes. Kenny looked at the window of what had once been his bedroom. The shutters with the moving slats were still there, but had been painted blue, like the living room curtains. The shutters had been a natural wood when he and Kirk slept in their twin beds in that bedroom. It didn't seem right that they were now blue.

"I was born here, right, Mom?"

She was looking down the street, not at the house with the blue window shades. "You were born in the hospital."

"Oh, I know that," he said. "But I was a little baby here, right?"

His mother started the Fiat and put it into gear. "Yep," she said over the growl of the motor. On the night she left the house at 4114 Derby, her children were asleep in their beds and their father was standing in the kitchen, silent. She did not see any of them again for seven weeks. Kenny was five years old.

By the time they had driven back to the apartment, she had smoked three of her long cigarettes, the smoke sailing away in the wind of the open-top sports car.

———

She took him to dinner at the Senator Hotel, which was downtown like the Leamington, but much fancier and crowded with men in suits who all wore name tags. They ate in the coffee shop. Jose Garcia stopped by to see them as Kenny was eating his dessert, a huge slice of cherry pie with ice cream on top of it—à la mode, the waitress called it. Kenny didn't care too much for the cherries, but he finished every bite of the ice cream.

"What say we wheels up at noon?" Mr. Garcia said. "We'll see the delta for a while then head up north. Have you ever been in a plane before, Kenny?"

He had already been asked that question but politely answered again. "Never."

"You may just fall in love with the sky," Mr. Garcia said. As he left, he kissed Kenny's mom on the cheek. Kenny had never seen that happen in real life before, a man kissing a woman on the cheek. His dad never kissed Kenny's stepmom like that, just because he was leaving the room. Kissing on the cheek was something men and women did on TV.

———

Jose Garcia took them to breakfast the next morning, to a coffee shop called Pancake Parade with a décor that made the place look like a circus. The two men ordered waffles and, for Kenny's mom, another igloo of cottage cheese. As they were eating, car after car of well-dressed families came in, filling up the place. They were all in Sunday church clothes—the dads wore suits, the moms and girls were in nice dresses. Some of the boys wore neckties and were the same age as Kenny. With all those people talking and ordering breakfast the place **sounded** as loud as a circus.

When Jose and his mom finally finished their coffee—the waitress kept coming over and offering refills—Mom re-redded her lips and they went back out to the Fiat. Mr. Garcia drove, wearing a pair of gold metal-frame glasses with mirror lenses and hooks to go around his ears. His mom had on her skier's shades. Kenny sat in the little area behind the seats, where the wind was the wildest and made it difficult to hear. For the whole ride, he never knew what the grown-ups were saying.

He had fun back there, though, sitting sideways and waving his hands up in the slipstream of the open top. They drove past solid brick houses with wide lawns and a huge green park with a golf course. They came to a place called Executive Field, which turned out to be an airport, but Jose did not use the parking lot. He drove around to a gate that opened and stopped by some small airplanes that were parked side by side.

"Ready to cheat fate, Ken?" Mr. Garcia said.

"Are we flying in one of those?" Kenny pointed to the planes. They were not like the model airplanes he had at home, which were from the war—fighters and a B-17 bomber. These planes were small and had no machine guns, and they did not look like they could go very fast, even though some had two motors.

"The Comanche," Mr. Garcia said. He was walking toward a white plane with a red stripe, one of the single-engine aircraft.

The doors opened on the plane just like a car, and Mr. Garcia left them ajar to cool off the inside. Kenny got to stand on the wing and look inside, at the gauges and the dials and the steering wheel and the foot pedals. There were two of everything—plus some odd switches and controls that all looked very scientific. Mr. Garcia walked around the plane a few times, then looked at some papers he had folded into sleeves on one of the doors.

Kenny's mom came from the car with the pink suitcase. "I think you want to ride up front, don't you?" she said to him. She folded down one of the seats and climbed into the back, setting the pink case beside her.

"I get to sit **here**?" Kenny meant behind the wheel, like the copilot.

"I need a copilot," Mr. Garcia said. "Your mom's shaky on the stick." He laughed, then showed Kenny how to buckle his harness. Mr. Garcia had to pull the straps tight for him, though. Then he pulled a small pair of dark sunglasses out of his pocket and handed them to Kenny. "The sun is bright up there."

The glasses were gold metal–framed like Mr. Garcia's, but not nearly as expensive. They, too, had hooks that went around the ears. The sunglasses were oversize for Kenny's almost-ten-year-old head, but he didn't know that. He turned to show his mom how he looked. He gave her the thumbs-up and all of them laughed.

The starting of the engine was very loud, and not just because the Comanche's doors were still open. The body of the plane shook and the propeller seemed to **snap** with each turn. Mr. Garcia worked switches and knobs and made the engine roar a few times. He put on a set of earphones and did something that got the plane moving even though the doors were still open. They passed other parked planes, then wide strips of grass where little signs with letters and numbers were planted. At one end of the long runway, the plane came to a stop. Mr. Garcia reached across Kenny and latched his door closed, then did the same to the door on his own side. The motor was still very loud, but the plane was not as wobbly.

"Ready?" Mr. Garcia shouted. Kenny nodded. His mother flashed another thumbs-up. She reached forward and rubbed her son's head. If she said something, Kenny did not hear her, but he could see her large grin.

As the plane sped up and the noise got louder, a feeling came over Kenny that he had never, ever had before. They were moving faster and faster and then lifting up, making his stomach go down but the top of his head feel like it was rising. The ground quickly got smaller; soon the streets and houses and cars no longer looked real. Kenny turned to look out the side window. The wing of the plane blocked his view, so he leaned forward to see the earth and sky in front of the plane.

He saw the buildings downtown and recognized what had once been his world: the Tower Theatre and the grid of the streets, the Old Fort—Sutter's Mill, it was called, where gold was discovered in pioneer days—and there was the Leamington Hotel. He could read the sign.

Kenny's first flight in an airplane was the most amazing event of his life. His head seemed to fill up with air and his breath went short. The sun was brighter than it had ever been before, and Kenny was glad he had dark glasses. When Mr. Garcia turned the plane by dipping the wings to the left, the vast delta area of the river took up the view. There were islands down there, separated by twisted waterways and dikes. Right next to the town where Kenny was born lived farmers who needed a boat to get to town. Kenny had no idea!

"That's what the Mekong looks like!" Mr. Garcia shouted. He was pointing out the window. Kenny nodded out of habit, not sure if he was expected to say something. "That's the bargain you make with Uncle Sam! He teaches you to fly then sends you bird-dogging in Vietnam!"

Kenny knew about Vietnam because the war was on Channel 12 from Chico. What a Mekong was, he had no idea.

They flew southwest, ascending so high in the sky the cars and trucks on the highways looked like they were barely moving. The waters of the river grew wide and changed hue when they met the salt water of San Francisco Bay. Ships were down in the wide river, big ships that now looked like the toy models Kenny played with on the coffee table. When Mr. Garcia dipped the wings again, Kenny's tummy went floppy, but just for a moment.

Now they were flying north. Mr. Garcia slid half of his headset off one of his ears. "I need you to fly for a few minutes, Kenny," he said loudly.

"I don't know how to fly a plane!" Kenny looked at Mr. Garcia as if he were a crazy person.

"Can you imagine driving a car?"

"Yes."

"Take hold of the yoke," Mr. Garcia said. The yoke was half steering wheel, half handlebars. Kenny had to sit up straight to reach the handles. "The plane will go where you point it. Pull back some and get the feel of the stick."

Kenny used more muscle than he thought he had and, sure enough, the yoke came back toward him. As it did, the sky filled the front window and the engine slowed.

"See?" Mr. Garcia said. "Now level off just as easy."

The grown man had his hand on his flight controls, but let Kenny do the work of pushing the nose of the plane back down. The earth below took up some of the window again.

"Can I turn?" Kenny yelled.

"You're the pilot," Mr. Garcia said.

Very, very carefully, Kenny turned the handlebar-yoke to the right, and the plane tipped ever so slightly. Kenny could feel the change in direction. He reversed his piloting motion and felt the plane ease back.

"If you were a little taller," Mr. Garcia said, "I'd let you work the rudder, but you can't reach the pedals. Maybe in a year. Next year."

Kenny imagined himself, at age eleven, flying the Comanche all by himself with his mom in the backseat.

"What I need you to do now is, see Mount Shasta up ahead?" Shasta, the massive volcano that loomed over the valley up north, was forever covered with snow. On clear days in Iron Bend the mountain looked like an enormous painting off in the distance. From Kenny's seat in the front of the airplane, Shasta was a triangle of white, poking up over the horizon. "Fly directly at it, okay?"

"Okay!" Kenny set his eyes on the mountain and tried to keep the nose of the plane smack on target while Mr. Garcia pulled some papers out of the side of his seat and a ballpoint pen from his pocket. He wrote some things down, then studied a map. Kenny wasn't sure how much time went by as he flew the plane straight and true, it could have been a few minutes or most of the flight home, but he never let the plane stray. More of Mount Shasta was visible by the time Mr. Garcia folded up the map and clicked his pen closed.

"Atta boy, Kenny," he said as he took over the yoke. "You have the makings of a pilot."

"Good job, honey!" his mom called from the back of the plane. When Kenny looked over his shoulder, her smile was nearly as big as the one on his face.

Looking out the window, Kenny saw the lanes of the highway that led straight up the valley through towns like Willows and Orland leading to Iron Bend and beyond. Just two days ago he and his mom had been down below on that highway. Now, he was miles above it.

After Kenny had flown the plane he had to pop his ears, yawning widely and blowing his nose with his mouth closed. It didn't hurt. The plane was descending, the engine sounding louder as the ground grew closer and the landmarks of Iron Bend showed themselves. There was the logging yard south of town, then the two motels off the highway, the old grain silos that held no grain, and the parking lot of the Shopping Plaza with the Montgomery Ward. Kenny had never been told there was an airport in Iron Bend, but there it was, beyond the Union High football field.

The plane jiggled and shook as Mr. Garcia came in for the landing. He did something to the engine that made it go soft and nearly silent just before the wheels **squeech**ed on the concrete runway. He drove the airplane like a car and came to a stop a few feet from where other planes were parked. When he shut the engine off, the propeller kept going around a few times until seizing up with a jerk. Without the engine, the quiet was odd, making the unclicking of the seat belts sound crisply clear, like something from a movie at the State Theater.

"Cheated death again," Mr. Garcia said without having to shout.

"Honestly," said Kenny's mom. "Do you **have** to put it that way?"

Mr. Garcia laughed, leaned back, and kissed her on the cheek.

———

The airport had a very small coffee shop. There were no customers and, it appeared, no staff. Kenny, still wearing his dark pilot glasses, sat at a table, the pink suitcase on the floor at his feet while his mom put coins into a pay phone on the wall. She dialed, waited, then hung up and put the same coins back into the phone. She dialed another number before she was able to talk to anyone.

"Well, the line was busy," she said into the phone. "Can you come get him? Because we have to get back. How long? All right." She hung up and came over to the bench. "Your dad is coming from work to pick you up. Let's see if there's some hot cocoa for you and coffee for me."

Kenny could see through the glass coffee shop door into the office of the airport. Mr. Garcia—still wearing his dark glasses, too—was talking to a man who was sitting at a desk. Kenny heard a loud **whirring** noise that turned out to be a machine that made hot chocolate. When his mom brought it to him in a Styrofoam cup, one sip told Kenny the cocoa was too watery. He didn't finish it.

His dad came, driving the station wagon. He left the motor running as he got out of the car, wearing his cook's pants and heavy shoes. He shook hands with Mr. Garcia, said a few words to Kenny's mom, then picked up the small pink suitcase and carried it out to the car.

Kenny sat in the front seat, just like he did in the airplane. As they drove out of the parking lot, his father asked him about his dark glasses.

"Mr. Garcia gave them to me," Kenny said.

Kenny told his father about aiming for Mount Shasta, then about going to the zoo and the pee-wee golf and seeing the old house.

"Ah," his father said. He said it again when Kenny told him the Callendars had moved away.

As they rode into town and back to the Blue Gum Restaurant, Kenny looked out the window, his eyes tinted a deep blue by his metal-framed sunglasses, scanning the sky. Mr. Garcia had probably taken off by now, and Kenny hoped to see the plane up there. His mom would be sitting in the copilot's seat.

But there was no sign of them. None at all.

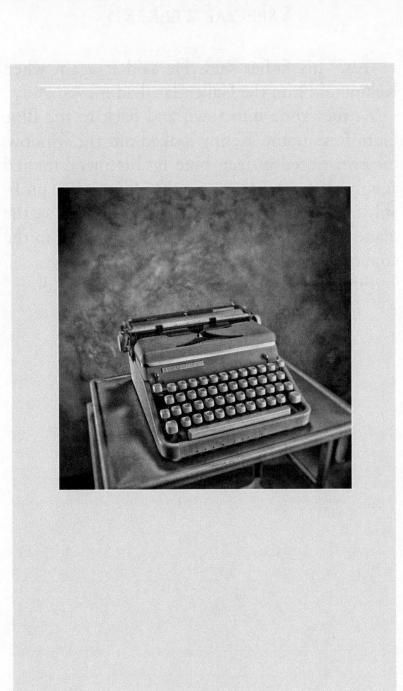

These Are the
Meditations of My Heart

———

S he was not looking to buy an old typewriter. She needed nothing and wanted no more possessions—new, used, antique—not a thing. She had vowed to weather her recent personal set-backs with an era of Spartan living; a new mini-malism, a life she could fit in her car.

She liked her small apartment west of the Cuyahoga River. She'd tossed away all the clothes she'd worn with him, the Knothead; she cooked for herself almost every night and listened to a lot of podcasts. She had enough money saved to see her to the New Year, allowing a lazy, agenda-free summer. January would freeze the lake and prob-ably burst the pipes of her building, but by then she would be gone. New York or Atlanta or Austin or New Orleans. She had options galore as long as she traveled light. But the Lakewood Methodist

Church on the corner of Michigan and Sycamore was having a Saturday Parking Lot Sale, raising money for community service programs like Free Day Care, twelve-step program meetings, and, she didn't know, maybe Meals on Wheels. She was neither a churchgoer nor a baptized Methodist, but she was fairly certain that sauntering through a parking lot full of card tables brimming with yard sale debris was not an act of worship.

As a hoot she almost bought a set of aluminum TV dinner trays, but three of them showed signs of rust. Boxes of costume jewelry revealed no treasures. But then she saw a set of Tupperware ice pop makers. As a kid, she had been in charge of pouring Kool-Aid or orange juice into the molds and inserting the patented plastic handles, which, when the freezer had done the physics, made for inexpensive icy treats. She could almost feel the hot wind of summer in the foothills, her hands sticky from melting, fruity ice. With no haggling, she got the set for a dollar.

On the same table was the typewriter, the color of faded Pop Art red—not an attraction. What got her eye was the adhesive label glued to the top left corner of its housing. In lowercase letters and underlined (by using the Shift and 6 key) the original owner had typed

<u>these are the meditations of my
heart</u>

The words had been typed as many as thirty years ago, when the machine was brand new, just out of the box, perhaps a gift on a girl's thirteenth birthday. A more recent owner had typed BUY ME FOR $5 on a piece of paper and rolled it into the carriage.

The machine was a portable; the body was plastic. The ribbon was two-tone, black over red, and there was a hole in the lid where the name Smith Corona or Brother or Olivetti had once been plugged. There was also a reddish leatherette carrying case with a half-sleeve opening and push-button latch. She punched three of the keys—A, F, P—and they all **clacked** onto the paper and settled back again. So, the thing worked, sort of.

"Is this typewriter really only five dollars?" she asked of a Lady Methodist at a nearby card table.

"That?" the woman said. "I think it works but nobody uses typewriters anymore."

That was not the question she had asked, but she didn't care. "I'll take it."

"Show me the money."

And just like that the Methodists were five bucks richer.

At her apartment, she prepped a supply of pine-apple juice ice pops for later that night. She'd have a couple when the day cooled, when she could have her windows open and watch for the first fireflies of the evening. She pulled the typewriter from its cheap case, set it out on her tiny kitchen table, and rolled in a piece of printer paper from the feed of her LaserWriter. She tried each of the keys—many stuck. One of the four rubber feet on the bottom of the body was missing, so the machine rocked a bit. She pounded each of the keys from the top row straight across, shifting to caps as well, trying, with some degree of success, to shake loose the stickiness. Though the ribbon was old, the letters were legible. She tried the spacing of the carriage return—single and double—which worked, although the bell did not. The margin sliders scraped and then jammed in place.

The typewriter needed a firm scrubbing and a lube job, which she expected to run, say, twenty-five dollars. But she pondered the greater conundrum, one that faces all who buy a typewriter in the third millennium: what is its purpose? Addressing envelopes. Her mom would enjoy typewritten letters from her wandering daughter. She could send poison-pen messages to her ex, like, "Hey, Knothead, you made a big fucking mistake!" with no fear of an email record. She could type out some remark, take a digital photo of it with her phone, then post that onto her blog and Facebook page. She could make to-do lists for the refrigerator door. That made for five Hipster-Retro reasons for her to own a new-old typewriter. Chuck in a few heartfelt meditations and she had six valid uses.

She typed the original owner's intent for the machine.

```
T hes ea re t he med it a tio n s o f
m yh ea r t.
```

The space bar skipped, which would not do. She grabbed her phone and googled **old type-writer repair**.

Three listings gave her the choices of a shop two hours away near Ashtabula, a place downtown that did not answer its phone, or, crazily enough, Detroit Avenue Business Machines, which was just a few minutes' walk away. She knew the shop—it was next to a tire store. She had strolled past it many times on her way to a great pizzeria and, a few doors down, to the art supply store that was soon to go out of business. She thought the small shop was for computers and printer repair so, after taking the few-minutes' walk, was amused to see, upon closer inspection of its front window, an old adding machine, a thirty-year-old telephone answering machine, something called a Dicta-phone, and an ancient typewriter. The bell over the door tinkled when she entered.

One side of the shop was nothing but printers—boxes of them along with toner cartridges for any model. The other side of the shop was like a Museum for Yesteryear's Tools of Commerce. There were adding machines with eighty-one keys and pull handles, single-use ten-key calcu-lators, a stenographer's machine, IBM Selectric typewriters, most in beige housings, and, on wall-mounted shelves, dozens of assorted typewriters gleaming black, red, green, even baby blue. They all appeared to be in perfect working order.

The service counter was in the rear of the shop. Behind it were desks and a workbench, where an old fellow was going over papers.

"How can I help the young lady?" he asked with a slight accent, most likely Polish.

"I'm hoping you can save my investment," she said. She laid the leatherette case on the counter. She unclasped the case and produced the type-writer. The old man let out a sigh at the sight of it.

"I know," she said. "This gem needs work. Half the keys are gummed up. It rocks when I type, and the space bar is kablooey. And no bell."

"No bell," he said. "Ah."

"Can you help a girl out? I have five bucks sunk into this thing."

The old man looked at her, then back at the machine. He let out another sigh. "Young lady, there is nothing I can do for you."

She was confused. From what her eyes took in, this was **the** place to get a typewriter back into working order. On the workbench behind the old man she could see disassembled machines and parts of typewriters, for crying out loud. "Because none of those parts back there match my typewriter?"

"There are no parts for this," he said, waving his hand over the dull red typewriter and leatherette case.

"You'd have to order some? I can wait."

"You don't understand." On the edge of the counter was a little case for his official business cards. He took one and handed it to her. "What do you read on this, young lady?"

She read the card. "DETROIT AVENUE BUSINESS MACHINES. **Printers. Sales. Service. Repair.** Closed Sunday, which is tomorrow," she said. "Office Hours nine a.m. to four p.m. Saturdays, ten a.m. to three p.m. My watch and your clock both show twelve nineteen." She turned the card over. Nothing on the back. "What am I getting wrong?"

"The name of this shop," the old man said. "Read the name of my shop."

"Detroit Avenue Business Machines."

"Yes," he said. "Business **Machines**."

"Okay," she said. "Yeah."

"Young lady, I work on machines. But **this**?" Again, a wave of his hand over her five-dollar typewriter. "This is **toy**." He said the word like he was cussing: **turd**.

"Manufactured of plastic to look like a typewriter. But this is not a typewriter."

He detached the lid on the top of what he called a toy, the plastic bending until it came off with a snap to reveal the workings inside. "The typebars, the levers, the ribbon spools—plastic. The ribbon reverse. The vibrator."

She had no idea there was a vibrator in a manual typewriter.

He banged on some of the keys, flipped levers, slid the carriage back and forth, spun the platen, hit the backspace key, all in disgust. "A typewriter is a tool. In the right hands, one that can change the world. This? This is meant to take up space and make noise."

"Can you at least give it a little oil so I can take a whack at changing the world?" she asked.

"I could clean it, oil it, tighten every screw. Make the bell ring. Charge you sixty dollars and sprinkle fairy dust upon this typewriter. But I would be taking advantage of you. In a year, the space bar would still be . . ."

"Kablooey?"

"Better you take it home and put a flower in it." He slid the typewriter back into its carrying case, like he was wrapping a dead fish in newspaper.

She felt bad, as though she had disappointed one of her teachers with a lazy effort, handing in a poorly structured essay. If she had still been with the Knothead, he'd be standing next to her agreeing with the old man, saying, "I told you the thing was a hunk of junk. Five dollars? Gone!"

"Look here." The old man waved his arm at the typewriters that lined the wall-mounted shelves. "These are machines. They are made of steel. They are works of engineers. They were built in factories in America, Germany, Switzerland. Do you know why they are up on that shelf right now?"

"Because they are for sale?"

"Because they were built to last forever!" The old man actually shouted. In him, she heard her father hollering, "Who left those bikes on the front lawn? . . . Why am I the only one dressed for church? . . . The father of this house is home and needs a hug!" She realized she was smiling at the old man.

"This one," he said, moving to the shelves.

He took down a black Remington 7 typewriter, a model called Noiseless. "Hand me that tablet, there." She found a pad of blank paper on the counter and gave it to him. He ripped off two pages and rolled them into the gleaming, shining machine. "Listen." He typed the words

Detroit Avenue Business Machines.

The letters whispered onto the page one by one. "America was on the move," he said. "Work was being done in crowded offices, small apartments, on trains. Remington had sold typewriters for years and years. Someone said, 'Let's make a smaller, quieter machine. Bring down the racket.' And they did! Did they use plastic parts? No! They reengineered the tension, the force of the keystroke. They made a typewriter so quiet it could be sold as **noiseless**. Here. Type."

He spun the machine to face her. She pecked out

Quiet down. I am typing here.

"I could hardly hear a thing," she said. "I'm impressed." She pointed to a two-tone machine, bone white and blue with a rounded body. "How quiet is that one?"

"Ah. A Royal." He replaced the black Remington 7 and pulled down a gorgeous little writing machine. "A Safari portable. A decent piece of work." He rolled in two more sheets of paper and let her go at the keys. She thought of safari-themed words to type.

```
Mogambo.
Bwana Devil.
"I had a farm in Africa . . ."
```

The machine was louder than the Noiseless and the keys did not fly as effortlessly. But there were features on the Royal that postdated the engineering of the Remington. The number 1 with an ! A button that said MAGIC COLUMN SET. And, it was two-tone!

"Is this bit of Royalty for sale?" she asked.

The old man looked at her with a smile and a nod. "Yes. But tell me. Why?"

"Why do I want a typewriter?"

"Why do you want **this** typewriter?"

"You trying to talk me out of it?"

"Young lady, I will sell you any typewriter you want. I will take your money and wave you goodbye. But tell me, why this Royal Safari? Because of the color? The typeface? The white keys?"

She had to think about it. Again, she felt like she was in school, about to take a test she could fail, a pop quiz when she hadn't done the reading.

"Because of my fickle taste," she said. "Because I brought that toy typewriter home and got to thinking I would like to write on a typewriter rather than in pen and pencil but the dang thing is gummed up and guess what? My local typewriter shop refuses to touch it. In my mind, I see myself at my little table in my little apartment, pecking out notes and letters. I own a laptop, a printer, an iPad, and this, too." She held up her iPhone. "I use them as much as any modern woman does, but . . ."

She stopped. She was thinking now, about what it was that had moved her to buy a five-dollar typewriter—one with an unreliable space bar and no bell—and why she was now in this shop more or less arguing with an old man, when just the day before she'd had no opinion whatsoever about old manual typewriters.

She continued. "I have loopy penmanship, like a little girl, so anything I write looks like a motivational poster in a health clinic. I'm not one who types between sips from a tumbler of booze and drags from a pack of smokes. I just want to set down what few truths I've come to know."

She went back to the service counter and

grabbed the leatherette carrying case. She yanked the plastic typewriter from inside, carried it over to the shelves, and nearly threw it beside the Royal Safari. She pointed to the sticker on the top.

"I want my yet-to-be-conceived children to someday read **the meditations of my heart.** I will have personally stamped them into the fibers of page upon page, real stream-of-consciousness stuff that I will keep in a shoe box until my kids are old enough to both read **and** ponder the human condition!" She heard herself shouting. "They will pass the pages back and forth between them and say, 'So that's what Mom was doing making all that noise with all that typing,' and I am sorry! I'm yelling!"

"Ah," he said.

"Why am I yelling?"

The old man blinked at the young lady. "You are seeking permanence."

"I guess I am!" She paused long enough to take a deep breath, letting her lungs empty in a cheek-puffing sigh. "So, how much for this Jungleland typewriter?"

The shop was quiet for a moment. The old man held a finger to his lips, thinking, wondering what to say.

"This is not the typewriter for you." He picked up the two-tone Royal and placed it back on the wall-mounted shelf. "This was made for a young girl going off to her first year of university, her head filled with nonsense, thinking she would soon find the man of her dreams. It was meant for book reports."

He pulled down a compact typewriter with a body the color of green seafoam. Its keys were just a shade lighter.

"This," he said, again rolling two sheets of paper into the carriage, "was made in Switzerland. Along with cuckoo clocks, chocolate, and fine watches, the Swiss once produced the finest typewriters in all the world. In 1959, they made this one. The Hermes 2000. The apex, the state of the art in manual typewriters, never to be bested. To call it the Mercedes-Benz of typewriters is to inflate the quality of Mercedes-Benz. Please. Type."

She felt intimidated by the green mechanical box in front of her. What in the world could she possibly say on a sixty-year-old marvel of Swiss craftsmanship? Where would she drive a vintage Benz?

**In the mountains above Geneva
The snow falls white and pure
And children eat cocoa krispies
From bowls with no milk.**

"The typeface is Epoca," he said. "Look how straight and even it is. Like a ruled line. That's the Swiss. See these holes in the paper guide, on either side of the vibrator?"

So, **that's** the vibrator.

"Watch." The old man took a pen from his shirt pocket and put the point into one of the holes. He released the carriage, sliding it back and forth, underlining what she had written.

In the mountains above Geneva
The snow falls white and pure

"You can use different-colored inks for different emphasis. And see this knob here on the back?" There was a thimble-size knob with a softly serrated edge. "Tighten it or loosen it to adjust the action for the keys."

She did. The keys stiffened considerably under her fingertips and she had to muscle through.

Cuckoo clocks.

"When carbon paper was needed to make three or four copies of a letter, the firm setting would strike all the way to the last page." He chuckled. "The Swiss kept a lot of records."

Turning the knob the opposite way made the keys feather light.

Clocks. Mercedes Hermes 2000000

"Nearly noiseless, as well," she said.

"Indeed, yes," he said. He showed her how easy it was to set the margins by pressing the levers on each side of the carriage. As for tabs, they were set by pressing TAB SET. "This Hermes was made the year I turned ten years old. It is indestructible."

"Like you," she said.

The old man smiled at the young lady. "Your children will learn to type on it."

She liked the idea of that. "How much is it?"

"Never mind," the old man said. "I will sell it to you with one condition. That you use it."

"Well, not to be impolite," she said, "but **duh**!"

"Make the machine a part of your life. A part of your day. Do not use it a few times, then need room on the table and close it back into its case to sit on a shelf in the back of a closet. Do that and you may never write with it again." He had opened a cupboard under the displays of old adding machines, searching through spare carrying cases. He pulled out what looked like a square green suitcase with a flap clasp. "Would you own a stereo and never listen to records? Typewriters must be used. Like a boat must sail. An airplane has to fly. What good is a piano you never play? It gathers dust and there is no music in your life."

He placed the Hermes 2000 into the green case. "Leave the typewriter out on a table where you see it. Keep a stack of paper at the ready. Use two sheets to preserve the platen. Order envelopes and your own stationery. I will give you a dustcover—free of charge—but take it off when you are at home so the machine is ready to use."

"Does that mean we are now discussing the price?"

"I suppose so."

"How much?"

"Ah," the old man said. "These typewriters are priceless. The last one I sold for three hundred dollars. But for young ladies? Fifty."

"How about something for my trade-in?" She pointed to the toy typewriter she had brought in. She was haggling.

The old man looked at her with something akin to the Evil Eye. "What did you pay for that again?"

"Five dollars."

"You were taken." He pursed his lips. "Forty-five. If my wife ever finds out I made such a deal she will divorce me."

"Let's keep it between us, then."

One thing about the Hermes 2000, it was a lot heavier than the toy. The green carrying case banged against her legs as she carried it home. She stopped twice, putting the machine down not because she needed to rest but because her palm had gotten sweaty.

In her apartment, she did as she had been instructed, as she had promised. The seafoam green typewriter went on her little kitchen table, a stack of printer paper next to it. She made herself two pieces of toast with avocado and sliced a pear into sections, her dinner. She pulled up her iTunes on her phone and hit PLAY, putting the phone into an empty coffee mug for amplification, letting Joni sing her old songs and Adele her new stuff as she nibbled at her meal.

She wiped her hands of crumbs and, finally, in the blush of ownership of one of the finest typewriters ever to come down from the Alps, she rolled two sheets into the carriage and began to type.

TO DO:

STATIONERY—ENVELOPES & LETTER PAPER.
WRITE MOM ONCE A WEEK?
Groceries: yogurt / honey/ 1/2 & 1/2 .

Our Town Today with Hank Fiset

BACK FROM BACK IN TIME

OCCASIONALLY THE TY-RANTS (did I say "tyrants"? I mean "Titans") who publish the **Tri-Cities Daily News/ Herald** pay me for taking my wife on trips that mix business with pleasure—paid vacations to the likes of Rome (Ohio), Paris (Illinois), and the Family Compound (hers) on the shores of Lake Nixon, short trips that I then turn into a thousand words or so of A-One quality journalism, or so my staff tells me. This past week I went off on a **doozy** of a salaried adventure. I went back in time, you see! Not to the age of the dinosaurs, nor to witness the fall of the czars or to talk some sense into the captain of the **Titanic**. Rather, I time-slipped back into my own past, my hazy self-conscious, transported by a certain simple, yet magical machine . . .

* * *

INNOCENCE BREEDS ADVENTURE: I had set out to provide you readers with a column on the workings of the weekly swap meet at the old Empire Auto Movie Drive-In in Santa Alameda, a monster of a flea market, now in its thirty-ninth year and chockablock with sentimental debris and used hard goods. Old kitchen utensils, old clothes, old books, millions of objets d'art, both nice and rather crummy, piles of used tools and racks and racks of new ones, toys, lamps, odd chairs, and a display of hundreds of brand-new sunglasses now bring in cash where carloads of moviegoers once parked to see, say, **Krakatoa, East of Java** on a distant billboard of a screen. They heard the movie from toaster-size speakers that hooked onto the car's window. Movies in mono . . .

* * *

IMAGINE THE LARGEST yard-attic-estate sale in the Western World combined with the **Going out of Business Blowout** of every Sears store in the country and you'll have an idea of the scope of the Swap, as the regulars call it. All day, you can wander the rows of stalls, set on the hillocks between speaker posts, nibbling on chili dogs and kettle corn, wanting to buy everything the eye fancies, limited only by the cash in your pocket and the cargo space of your car. Had I wanted to, I could have paid less than two hundred dollars for a redwood burl table, a 1960s Amana refrigerator-freezer, or the front and back seats yanked out of a Mercury Montego. Luckily, I already have those things at home!

* * *

I WAS ABOUT to retire to the snack bar for a lime shave ice when I set my eyes on an old typewriter, an Underwood portable of ebony that, I kid you not, gleamed in the sun like a Springsteen hot rod. A quick inspection showed the ribbon was good once you advanced the spool a few inches, and the broken-handled case held a small supply of erasable onionskin paper. Even though a man needs a typewriter these days like he needs a timber ax, I offered the kid running the stall all of "forty dollars for this old typewriter with the broken case," and he said, "Sounds good." Should have offered a twenty. Or a fiver.

* * *

ONCE HOME, I set the machine out on the kitchen table and gave it the quickbrownfox- jumpedoverthelazydogs test. The **D** key stuck some, and the **A** key had a slight drop in it. The numbers all worked, and with some repeti- tive strikes the punctu- ation keys loosened up. I typed, I bought this typewriter today, and what do you know, the thing works . . . when the bell at the end of the line sounded

out clear and clean— and just like that, I was **whooshed** into the space-time continuum for a voyage back in time which lasted ei- ther a wink of an eye or for each moment of the last forty-nine years . . .

* * *

DING! First stop was the back room of my dad's old auto parts store, which is now the site of Public Park- ing Lot Number 9 at Webster and Alcorn. He had a big old type- writer in there though I never saw him use it. On weekends as a kid I'd poke out my name on it with my little fingers. When I grew into a teenager I avoided the store as much as I could because if I showed my face at the shop, Dad would put me to work doing inventory for the rest of the day . . .

* * *

DING! I'M IN the eighth grade, the editor of the **Frick Junior High School Banner** (Go, Bobcats!), watching Mrs. Kaye, the journalism teacher, type out my "Welcome, Scrubs!" column on the ditto master that would become 350 copies of the school paper, a volume read by at least forty students. I was busting with pride at seeing my first ever byline in a published newspaper . . .

* * *

DING! I'M IN high school now, the old campus of Logan High, on the upper floor of a building that was not earthquake safe (never felt a shudder) in a room that was meant for one subject only—Typing, levels 1, 2, and 3, for kids wanting to be professional office secretaries. Nothing but desks and indestructible typewriters overseen by a teacher so disinterested in his/her charges that I don't recall seeing our instructor. Someone put a record on a phonograph and we pecked at whatever letter was called out. One semester of Typing 1 was all I needed before volunteering for the audio-visual crew. Instead of being in a classroom, I roamed the halls of Logan, delivering movie projectors and threading up the films for teachers who didn't know how. So I never learned the many formats of business letters or what the heck a "salutation" is. I would have made a lousy secretary. Anyhow, I've been typing ever since . . .

* * *

DING! IT IS 2:00 a.m. in my dorm room at Wardell-Pierce College, and I'm pounding out a paper (due in eight hours) for a rhetoric class—and yes, there was such a subject. My title was "Comparative Criticism in Sports Reporting: Baseball/Track," chosen because I was a sports reporter for the **Wardell-Pierce Pioneer** and that week I had covered both a ball game and a track meet. My roommate, Don Gammelgaard, was trying to sleep, but I was on a deadline. And because it was raining there was no way I was going to tramp all the way across the quad to the Student Service Building. As I recall, I aced Rhetoric.*

* * *

DING! I'M AT a so-called desk in the so-called office of the **Green-sheet Give-Away,** the free shoppers' guide that once provided the Tri-Cities with oodles of coupons, advertisements, and, in the back pages, local-interest stories where regular folks could see their names in print. I was crafting a piece on a dog show just held at the old Civic Auditorium—my pay was fifteen bucks!— when the most beauti-

ful woman who ever started a conversation with me walked by and said, "You type fast." She was right, and since I was the fast type, I wooed her, wed her, and have been her main squeeze for over forty years.

* * *

THAT SAME DISH of American Womanhood brought me back from back in time when she came into the kitchen, telling me to move that typewriter and set the table for dinner. The grandchildren were coming over and it was going to be Make Your Own Taco Night, so a mess was due. The Underwood has powers unexplained, a vehicle for my dreams, so I locked it back into its case and carried it to a shelf in my home office, pronto. At night I think it glows in the dark . . .

* Note: A check of transcripts shows I got a B minus in Rhetoric at W-P. My mistake . . .

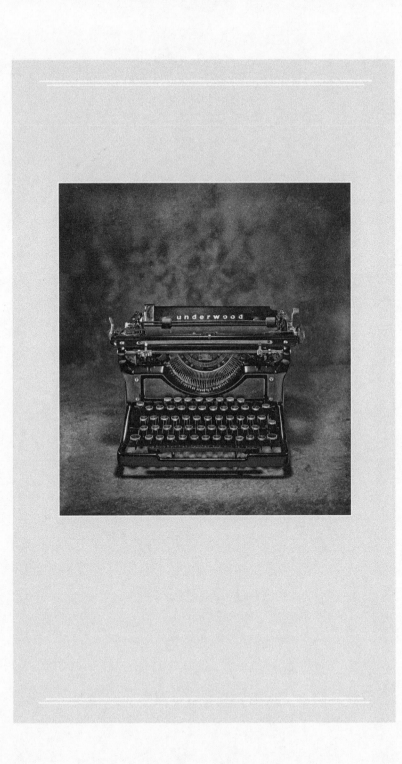

The Past Is Important to Us

———————

Because his plane was getting a new designer interior installed, J.J. Cox was hitching a ride to New York on Bert Allenberry's WhisperJet ViewLiner.

"I thought you were a smart man, Bert!" J.J. was yelling at his friend.

They'd known each other since they were twenty-year-old college kids, drivers for FedEx, full of moxie and spunk—their two heads bursting with ideas. They pooled their paychecks to rent a windowless garage on the outskirts of Salina, Kansas, which became their live-in workshop. After three and a half years of working 120-hour weeks, they'd come up with a prototype of the Shuffle-Access Digital Valve-Relay. They might as well have invented fire. Thirty years and $756 billion later, J.J. was just **now** learning that Bert had paid

$6 million a pop to some outfit called Chrono-metric Adventures for—get this—**time travel vacations**. No, no, no!

Cindee, the fourth and youngest ever Mrs. Allenberry, was clearing the lunch china herself. She was well practiced at the chore, since she had been the flight attendant on the plane just a year ago. She had to work fast as there were but minutes before landing. Two problems with the View-Liner: speed and vertigo. The flights from Salina to New York City took only sixty-four minutes, barely enough time to lick your fingers clean of BBQ ribs. The transparent floor and ultrawide windows made for a nail-biter of a flight, especially if you were afraid of heights.

"I thought they had dosed us with some narcotic," Cindee called out from the plane's galley. "You wake up with a terrible headache and the room looks all different. Then you conk right back out and sleep for hours."

J.J. could not believe what he was hearing. "Let's figure out this scam. You go into a room, you fall asleep and wake up **when?**"

"Nineteen thirty-nine," Bert chirped.

"Of course you do." J.J. smirked. "But then you pass out, wake up **again** in 1939."

"Right there in the City. In a hotel on Eighth Avenue." Bert was looking down through the fuselage. Pennsylvania was becoming New Jersey. "Room 1114."

"And you spend the day sitting in a hotel room?" J.J. wanted to slap his own head, as well as some sense into that of his friend and partner.

"Everything looks real," Cindee continued as she returned to her seat to buckle up for landing. "You can touch things. You can eat and drink. And smell. The men wear stinky hair oil and the women use too much makeup and everyone smokes. And their teeth! Crooked and stained."

"Roasted coffee is in the air." Bert was smiling. "From a factory in New Jersey."

"You woke up in 1939," J.J. said. "And smelled the coffee."

"Then Cindee took me to the World's Fair," Bert said. "For my birthday. We had VIP passes."

"It was a surprise." Cindee shot her husband a smile and took his hand in hers. "The Big Six-Oh only comes once."

J.J. had a question. "Why not go back in time to see the signing of the Declaration of Independence or Jesus on the cross?"

"You can only go to 1939," Bert explained. "June 8, 1939. Chronometric Adventures has a franchise in Cleveland. You can go to 1927 and see Babe Ruth hit a home run, but I'm not a baseball fan."

"Babe Ruth. In Cleveland." J.J. nearly spit. "Jesus on the cross."

"He's gone back four times without me," Cindee said. "I'd had enough of everyone thinking we were father and daughter."

"I'm going again tomorrow." Bert smiled at the thought.

J.J. was laughing now. "Thirty-six million dollars! Bert, for half that I'll arrange for you to meet Adam and Eve in the Garden of Eden and do the naked limbo. You'll just have to trust me on how I make it happen."

"My husband would **live** in 1939," Cindee said. "But he can only stay twenty-two hours."

"Why only twenty-two hours?" J.J. asked.

Bert told him why. "Wavelength in the Time-Space Continuum is finite. You can ride the echo only so long."

"They provide this money made of paper and old-fashioned coins," Cindee said. "I bought a tiny, gold-plated space needle and globe."

"The Trylon and Perisphere," Bert corrected her.

"Right. Yeah. But when we woke up it had turned into dried-out putty."

"That's the Molecular Singularity." Bert was not buckling his seat belt for landing. He owned the plane. Screw the FAA.

"Why not go back and change history?" J.J. wanted to know. "Why don't you kill Hitler?"

"Hitler wasn't at the World's Fair that day." The WhisperJet began to slow, the ground rising up to meet them. The articulating engines were tilting minutely, soon to allow a vertical landing on the roof of 909 Fifth Avenue. "Besides, it wouldn't matter."

"Why the hell not?"

"Singular Dimensional Tangents," Bert said, looking down at Central Park, which hadn't really changed all that much since 1939. "There's an infinite number of tangents, but we all exist in just one."

J.J. glanced at Cindee. She shrugged her shoulders—what could she do with the old guy?

"He likes seeing what the future was going to look like. But, we're **living** in the future. You'd think that would spoil everything," she said.

——

Twelve minutes later, J.J. was zipping along the HoverLine in his Floater, headed to his private island in the sound. Bert and Cindee had taken their private elevator from the landing pad on the roof and were settling into their apartment on floors 97 to 102. Cindee immediately changed into a new outfit from one of her closets. They were going to Kick Adler-Johnson's twenty-fifth birthday party and a private hologram performance of the Rolling Stones. Bert could not stand Kick Adler-Johnson though he respected her husband, Nick, who had made a fortune buying up air and water rights around the world. Besides, the actual Stones had played the company Christmas party in 2019, when he was married to L'Audrey, wife number three. He wanted to stay home, but Cindee wouldn't allow that.

Bert wished he could go through time right then, forward to the morning, then back to 1939, to the Fair that was filled with so many promises of the world as it could have been.

———

On that first birthday visit, Cindee felt ridiculous in the old-style clothes. Bert, though, was in heaven in a double-breasted suit made to measure by the tailors of Chronometric Adventures. He marveled at every little detail, every second of the twenty-two hours they spent in 1939. How small New York City seemed! The buildings were not tall **at all,** so the sky was much more open, the sidewalks had space for everyone, and the automobiles and taxis were **huge** and **so roomy**. The cabdriver **wore a tie** and complained of the traffic out to Flushing Meadows, but if **that** were a traffic jam, Bert would take it.

The World's Fair featured the tall Trylon and the huge orb called the Perisphere, both one-of-a-kind architectural marvels that were bleach white and brilliant against the open blue sky. The Avenues of Patriots and Pioneers were meant to be taken seriously and—get this—**Courts** were dedicated to Railroads and Ships, celebrating technologies that required engines the size of his WhisperJet. There was a Giant Underwood Typewriter, an Aquacade Show, and Electro, the Mechanical Man—he walked and counted numbers on his steel fingers! Chronometric Adventures supplied a pair of VIP passes so Bert and Cindee never had to wait in line.

The fairgrounds were kept spotless. A light breeze wiggled the flags and pennants. The hot dogs cost five cents. Fairgoers were dressed to the nines, and some women even wore gloves. Hats were on most men's heads. Bert wanted to see all of the World of Tomorrow, but Cindee was uncomfortable in her ugly shoes and wouldn't eat hot dogs. They left around three in the afternoon, bound for drinks and dinner at the Hotel Astor in Times Square. Cindee was tipsy, tired, and sick of all the cigarette smoke by the time the two of them were back in room 1114 for Progression, the trip forward in time.

Two weeks later, Cindee loaded the Whisper-Jet with her pack of girlfriends and flew to a spa in Morocco, allowing Bert another twenty-two hours of 1939. He ordered morning coffee for just himself from Percy, the room service waiter. He had breakfast alone in the coffee shop in the Hotel Astor, the gorgeous place smack on Times Square. He had the same cabbie with the tie. Alone, he covered areas of the Fair he had missed, like the Town of Tomorrow and the Electrified Farm; he had lunch in the Heinz Dome, surveyed the Temple of Religion, and celebrated the workers' paradise that was the Union of Soviet Socialist Republics. He listened to the conversations around him, studied the enthusiasms of the fairgoers, noting the lack of foul language and the bright colors of the clothing—not a black-on-black outfit to be seen. Fair employees seemed proud to work in their various uniforms. And it was true; a lot of people smoked.

It was on that second visit, without Cindee, when he spotted a petite, lovely woman in a green dress. She was sitting on a bench by the Lagoon of Nations, overseen by the massive sculptures of the Four Freedoms. She showed a modest amount of leg over brown shoes with straps. She carried a small purse and wore a hat with a white bud of a flower on it, more of a cap, really. She was engaged in an animated conversation with a young girl, dressed more for Sunday school than a day at the Fair.

The two of them were laughing, talking with their hands, whispering secrets to each other like they were the best of pals on the best of days in the best of places—they were the spirit of the Fair in feminine form.

Bert couldn't take his eyes off them, watching as they left the bench, heading arm in arm toward the Eastman Kodak Building. He thought to follow them, to see more of the Fair through their eyes. But his watch showed nearly 5:00 p.m., meaning there were little more than two of his twenty-two hours remaining. Reluctantly, he turned for the taxi stand that stood outside the North Entrance of the Corona Gate.

Another tie-clad taxi driver drove him back to Manhattan.

"Ain't the World Fair something?" the cabbie asked.

"It is," Bert replied.

"You see the Futurama? The trip to 1960?"

"I did not." Bert, born in 1966, chuckled to himself.

"Oh, you gotta see the Futurama," the cabbie said. "It's in the GM Building. It's a long line, but worth it."

Bert wondered if the lovely woman in the green dress had seen the Futurama. And if so, what she thought of 1960.

———

Although the human body takes a terrific beating by traveling back and forth in time, the Chronometric Adventures Medical Team gave Bert the go-ahead for a third trip. The World's Fair was too vast to see on just two visits, he explained to Cindee, which was true. What he didn't tell her was that, on his return to Flushing Meadows in 1939, he'd spend the day looking for the lady in the green dress.

She was not in any of the buildings dedicated to the great humanitarian works of U.S. Steel, Westinghouse, or General Electric. She was not somewhere in the Plaza of Light, the Avenue of Labor, the Court of Peace, or Continental Avenue. She was nowhere Bert had searched. So, a few minutes before 5:00 p.m., he headed to the Lagoon of Nations, and, sure enough, the woman in the green dress was there, her little friend in tow, on that bench under one of the Four Freedoms.

He sat on a bench close enough to hear them

compare notes on the marvels of the Fair, their local accents turning New York into **Noo Yawk.** They simply could not decide what to do next, before the evening came and the Fountains of Light would put on a show of technical, colorful wonder.

Bert was trying to summon the courage to speak to them when they rose up and hurried off to Eastman Kodak arm in arm, chatting and giggling. He watched them as they walked away, admiring the feminine carriage of the woman in the green dress, her hair bobbing against the back of her neck. He thought about following them, but the time was getting late and he had to return to room 1114.

For weeks, for every other minute, Bert thought of the woman in the green dress—of the way she talked with her hands and of her bobbing hair. He wanted to learn her name, to know her, if only for an extra hour or so of 1939. When Cindee announced she was joining Kick Adler-Johnson on a horseback ride through Cuba, he booked another exam with the Chronometric Adventures Medical Team.

———

He was on the bench by the Lagoon of Nations at 4:45, and yes, right on the tick of the singularity clockwork, the woman in the green dress and her young friend sat down and began their conversation. Bert guessed she was probably in her mid-thirties, though the fashions of the times made everyone look older by today's judgments. She was heavier than Cindee, than most modern-day women, as the 1939 diet was not very calorie conscious and exercise, then, was the stuff of athletes and laborers. The woman had an actual figure; the curves did her service.

He'd planned on what to say in this first conversation with a woman he had wanted to meet for over eight decades. "Excuse me," Bert said. "Do you ladies know if the Futurama is running today?"

"It is, but the line is very long," said the woman in the green dress. "We spent all afternoon in the Amusements Area. What a time we had!"

"Have you rode the Parachute, mister?" The girl could not have been more delightfully enthusiastic.

"I haven't," Bert confessed. "Should I?"

"It's not for the weakhearted," the woman said.

"You go up and up and up," the girl said, waving her hands. "You think you are going to come floating down slow and soft. But you don't. You land **ka-joink!**"

"It's true." The woman and the girl traded laughs.

"Have you seen the Futurama?" Bert asked.

"We didn't want to wait through that long line," the woman said.

"Well," Bert said, reaching into the pocket of his double-breasted suit. "I have a couple of special passes I'm not going to use."

Bert handed over the same two heavy cards Chronometric Adventures had supplied for his first trip with Cindee, the tickets embossed with the Trylon and Perisphere and the letters **VIP**. "If you show these to the attendants at the bottom of the ramp—I mean, the **Helicline**—they take you in via a secret passage."

"Oh, that's so nice of you," the woman said. "But we are definitely not VIPs."

"Believe me, neither am I," Bert said. "I have to get back to the city. Please use them."

"Can we, Aunt Carmen?" the girl asked, begged actually.

Carmen. Carmen was the name of the woman in the green dress. Carmen. The name fit her perfectly.

"I feel like a sneaky pete," Carmen said, pausing. "But let's! Thank you so much."

"Yes, thanks!" her niece said. "My name is Virginia and this is my aunt Carmen. Who are you?"

"Bert Allenberry."

"Well, thank you, Mr. Allenberry," Virginia

said. "We owe our Future to you!" Arm in arm, the women headed down Constitution Mall toward the GM Building, home of the Futurama. Bert watched them go, feeling grand, happy he had returned to 1939.

For months, he daydreamed of the lovely Carmen, the sneaky pete. Though his body was in the office in Salina, the board meeting in Tokyo, on the boat off Mykonos—his mind was in Flushing Meadows, on a bench under the Four Freedoms on a day in early June of 1939. When a shareholders' meeting demanded his presence in **Noo Yawk,** he made time for another $6 million visit to room 1114.

———

The events played out as before. He offered Carmen and Virginia the VIP passes, and off they went, owing their future to him. Bert, though, wanted just a bit more time with Carmen—not long, just another half hour or so—so he stationed himself at the exit of Futurama. He waved to them as they came out.

"How was it?" he called to them.

"Mr. Allenberry!" Carmen said. "I thought you had to leave."

"Oh, I'm the boss, so I decided to change the rules."

"You're the boss?" Virginia asked. "Of what?"

"Of all the people I get to boss around."

"Since you are now in the presence of a couple of VIPs," Carmen said with a laugh, "may I treat you to some pie?"

"I happen to love pie."

"Let's go to Borden's!" Virginia piped. "We can see Elsie the Cow."

The three of them sat together with ten-cents-a-slice pie, cut into perfectly measured wedges. Carmen and Bert had nickel-a-cup coffees. Virginia had a glass of milk and talked about what marvels the year 1960 would bring, according to Futurama's predictions.

"I hope I don't still live in the Bronx in 1960," she said. Virginia's family lived in an apartment on the Parkway with her mother (Carmen's sister) and father, who was a butcher. She was in the fifth grade, belonged to the Radio Club, and wanted to be a teacher when she grew up, if she could afford college. Carmen shared a fourth-floor walk-up on East Thirty-Eighth Street with two room-mates who worked as secretaries at an insurance company. She was the bookkeeper in a handbag factory downtown. All of them agreed that the World's Fair of 1939 was even better in real life than in the newsreels.

"Is your wife in New York, Mr. Allenberry?"

Bert wondered how Carmen knew he was married, then realized he was wearing the wedding ring provided by Chronometric Adventures. He'd put it on by habit.

"Ah, no," he said. "Cindee is with friends. In Cuba."

"That's where Mom and Dad went on their honeymoon," Virginia said. "I came along not long after!"

"Virginia!" Carmen could not believe her niece. "Be proper!"

"It's true!" Virginia said. She had eaten all her pie filling, saving the crust for last.

"Are you married, Carmen?" Bert asked. "I'm sorry, I don't even know your last name."

"Perry," she said. "Carmen Perry. So rude of me. And, no. I'm not married."

Bert knew that already, as no ring rode her left hand.

"Mama says if you don't find a man soon, there'll be none left for you!" Virginia said. "You're almost **twenty-seven!**"

"You **hush**," Carmen hissed, reaching over with her fork to stab the best piece of crust, then popping it into her mouth.

"You dirty rat!" Virginia laughed.

Dabbing her lips with a napkin, Carmen smiled at Bert. "It's true. I'm the last hen in the barnyard."

Carmen was only twenty-six? Bert could have sworn she was older.

After the pie, they looked at Elsie the Cow, then toured the Academy of Sports. After watching films of trick water-skiers, Bert looked at his vintage wristwatch. It was almost 6:00 p.m.

"I really do have to leave now."

"It's a shame you can't stay to see the fountains in the light show," Carmen said. "It's so lovely, they say."

"And there's fireworks every single night," Virginia piped up. "Like it's the Fourth of July all summer long."

"Virginia and I have a spot picked out to watch." Carmen's eyes were on Bert. "Are you sure you can't stay?"

"I wish I could." Bert truly wished he could. Carmen was as lovely a woman as he had ever seen. Her lips were not too thin, her smile was firm and mischievous, and her eyes were hazel, emerald green, and tinted brown.

"Thank you for a great time!" Virginia said. "We were VIPs!"

"Yes, thank you, Mr. Allenberry." Carmen offered her hand. "You've been very kind and a lot of fun."

Bert took Carmen's hand, her left hand, the hand with no wedding ring. "I've had a grand day."

In the cab on the drive back into Manhattan, Bert could almost smell Carmen's perfume—vanilla-scented lilac.

———

After one too many encores by the holographic Rolling Stones, Kick Adler-Johnson's birthday party had gone until four in the morning. Cindee was now asleep in bed, with the door closed and the blackout shades tightened down. Bert, though, was up at eight, showered and dressed, with a coffee in his hand. He had a breakfast of Mixed-Juice and an In-One protein roll, then ordered a Solo-Car as he rode the elevator down to the street level.

A moment after confirming his destination as Chronometric Adventures, the car began to drive itself down Fifth Avenue at an algorithmically safe seventeen miles per hour. It crossed town on Fifty-Second, bypassing the Times Square Dome, then made three left turns before stopping on Eighth Avenue between West Forty-Fourth and West Forty-Fifth Streets.

Bert exited the car at the building that had been, in reverse order, the Milford Plaza, the Royal Manhattan Hotel, and, in 1939, the Hotel Lincoln. Most of the structure was now a service area for the Dome, which it bordered, as well as offices related to the Times Square Authority.

Chronometric Adventures was located on floors 9 through 13 of the building, not by choice or convenience, but because of historical flukes and miracles of science. Enough of the building retained the exact architectural lines of its hotel days, and one room in particular, 1114, had miraculously escaped every remodel and renovation since the place opened in 1928. With its dimensions unchanged, the room possessed the Volume Authenticity needed to echo—with pinpoint accuracy—a ripple in the Time-Space Continuum, an arc intersecting with June 8, 1939. The massive pipes, cables, and Plasma-Grids needed for Time Travel had been retrofitted to the exterior of what had been the Hotel Lincoln, above, below, and leading into room 1114; the equipment was filled with about a million of the Shuffle-Access Digital Valve-Relays invented by Bert Allenberry.

He took the lift up to the ninth floor, hearing a feminine voice announce "Chronometric Adventures" just before the door opened. The company's motto—**The Past Is Important to Us**—was inscribed on the wall, and, under it, Howard Frye was waiting.

"Mr. Allenberry. Good to see you again." Howard had been the facilitator of every one of Bert's adventures. "I trust you are well?"

"Dandy. You?"

"Just over a cold. My son brought it home from school."

"One advantage of not having kids," Bert said. Cindee had not once said anything about wanting a child, L'Audrey before her would have made as horrible a mother as she did a mate, Mary-Lynn very much wanted to conceive but when a doctor told her that Bert's low sperm count made the biology highly unlikely, she looked to other men for satisfaction. She had remarried and quickly popped out two girls and a boy. His first marriage, to Barb, produced a baby girl. But the divorce was so filled with rancor and enmity that the only contacts Bert had with his daughter—once she turned eighteen—were occasional dinners in London, where she lived far too comfortably thanks to his support checks.

"Shall we get you to Pre-Ad?" Howard asked.

"Time's a-wasting."

"Funny, but time is actually a-plenty." Howard chuckled.

In the Pre-Adventure room, Bert was rechecked by the Medical Team. His fluids were sampled and scanned, his heart registered, and the twelve other physical properties that are affected by Progression/Reprogression were tested. He was given the five injections that would bolster his body on the molecular level and the antinausea meds to ease those initial moments of 1939. He removed his clothes as well as his rings, watch, and the thin gold chain he wore around his neck. No items from today could survive the trip to yesterday, as their molecules could irreconcilably screw up the process. Once naked, he put on a robe with the Chronometric Adventures logo and sat through the pro-forma legal warnings.

First there was the video—slick and snappy—warning of dangers and explaining the protocols. Then came the reading material, which repeated—word for word—what had just been said. Bert already knew a person could die during Reprogression, though no one ever had; an adventurer had options for experiences—one could spend the day doing anything he or she wished—but none when it came to certain key procedures. With his thumbprint, Bert acknowledged—once again—that he understood and agreed to it all. Then Howard came into the Pre-Ad room with the large shake-like drink that would protect his digestive tract from pesky germs, circa 1939.

"Bring on the shoe leather, Howard," Bert said, toasting his glass at him.

"By now you should be able to recite this to me," said Howard, clearing his throat. As Bert sipped the blueberry-flavored liquid, Howard put into simple terms the conditions Bert had already agreed to. "You have voluntarily chosen to have Chronometric Adventures provide physical time Reprogression to this very location on June 8, 1939, for a period of no more and no less than twenty-two hours as measured by standard recognized time. From the same Volume, at 7:00 p.m. of June 8, 1939, you progress back to this place on this very day. You understand that, don't you?"

Bert nodded. "Yep."

"Chronometric Adventures in no way claims your holiday in the past is free of risk. Your adventure is governed by the same laws of physics, rules, and behavior as we know to be common."

"I fall down, I break a leg. I get punched in the nose, it's broken."

"Indeed. You will be unsupervised during those twenty-two hours. We suggest you adhere to the Agenda we have prepared with you. Another day at the World's Fair, yes?"

"You should go yourself, Howard."

Howard laughed. "Being African American, 1939 New York doesn't hold the same wonder for me."

"I get that," Bert said. On his trips back in time almost every black face he saw belonged to a porter or a janitor. Though there were black families at the Fair, taking in the same exhibits, dressed for the occasion, they were looking for promises of a future different from his.

"Should you change plans—like seeing a show or loafing in the park—there is no risk as long as you adhere to the protocols for Progression."

"I'm going back to Flushing Meadows. Maybe next time I'll loaf in the park." Bert thought of spending a day with Carmen in Central Park and wondered how he could pull that off. Virginia could ride the carousel! They could take in the zoo as it originally looked!

"Ah, yes. **Next time**." Howard called up Bert's file on his pad. "Mr. Allenberry, I'm afraid you have reached your limit for Reprogression at this C.A. franchise."

"What?" Bert still had a third of his shake to finish.

"Your numbers from the Pre-Ad exam were a bit off from your last trip with us," Howard said. "You are showing elevated levels of Trillium in your blood and lowered measurements of cellular fluidity."

Bert didn't like the sound of that.

"Everyone's **constitution** is different, Mr. Allenberry. In fact, some of our clients have been allowed only two or three of our packages. Six is going to max you out."

"Why?"

"Molecular dynamics, Mr. Allenberry. The round trip to 1939 is a very long haul for your tissues, your body proteins, your marrow density, and your nerve endings. We can't run the risk of wearing you out. It's hypothetically possible a seventh, or even an eighth adventure to the World's Fair would be safe for you, but our insurance model disallows that. That's the bad news."

Bert was thinking of Carmen, of Virginia, of the three of them eating pie and visiting Elsie the Cow. He would do those things with them just one more time. Bad news, indeed.

"The good news," Howard chirped, "is that your Chronometric Adventures don't have to end in 1939 New York. There's Nashville in 1961. You could go to the Grand Ole Opry. We have a franchise opening in Gunnison, Colorado—a beautiful cabin in 1979. Not much goes on there, but the views are terrific."

Bert had stopped drinking. He was thinking of Carmen, of her vanilla-lilac scent and her hazel eyes.

"I am sorry, Mr. Allenberry, that's the way it is. The past is important to us, but your long life is more so."

"In that case, I'm going to need something else to take back with me," Bert said.

———

Bert felt the compression suit tighten as all the atoms of room 1114, including his, were jigged up by the mechanics of Chronometric Adventures. He had learned not to panic during Reprogression but still was not used to how **cold** it got, so cold that he lost all focus, all equilibrium. He knew he was lying on what would become a bed in 1939, but everything was tumbling. He fought to stay awake, alert, to see the actual process of the room reverting in time, but, as before, he passed right out.

When he felt a pounding headache, he knew he was in 1939 once again. The headaches were brutal but mercifully brief. Bert fought his way out of his compression suit—like a scuba diver's, one size too small—and sat naked on the edge of the bed, biding his time until his cranium no longer felt the crash of ball-peen hammers.

As before, the double-breasted suit was hanging in the open closet with shoes and socks on the floor. On a thin wire hanger was a button shirt and tie. Undergarments were in a basket on a chair. On the nightstand were the watch, a wedding band, a signet ring, and the wallet that contained his ID and other items that were accurate for the period and made out of pre–World War II materials. There was cash, a total of fifty dollars in the funny-looking paper currency that was once legal tender. There were heavy coins as well—a half dollar imprinted with a lady holding wheat looking toward the setting sun and ten-cent pieces, called dimes, with the head of the god Mercury. Nickels were worth five cents, and single pennies had real value in 1939.

He collected the compression suit and locked it in the vintage suitcase on the luggage stand, hiding it until he'd put it back on for Progression. Then he slipped on the vintage watch, already keeping time at three minutes after 9:00 p.m. He put the signet ring on his right hand, but remembered to leave the gold wedding band where it lay.

He saw the envelope on the desk, which would have his VIP passes for the Fair—he had ordered **three** for this, his last trip to 1939.

The window onto Eighth Avenue was open just a crack, allowing evening air to come into a room that had yet to know air-conditioning along with the sounds of traffic from Times Square. Bert wanted to get up, to get dressed and go out into the night, to walk down to East Thirty-Eighth Street, where Carmen lived in an apartment, but his body ached so. Damn the physics! He felt tired, just as before. He lay back on the bed and fell back to sleep, just as before.

He woke up when dim light was coming

through the window and the city was quiet. He felt normal, like he'd taken a Green Tab and slept a healthy ten hours. His watch read ten minutes to seven. It was the morning of June 8, 1939, and he had all of twelve hours to find Carmen and Virginia. He lifted the heavy telephone receiver, pressed the only button on the phone, and was connected to the hotel operator. Once more, he asked for room service. After the same five minutes, a uniformed waiter named Percy was at his door with a tray holding a silver pot of coffee, a pitcher of real cream, cubes of sugar, a glass of water, and the morning edition of the New York **Daily Mirror**. On five previous mornings, Bert had tipped the waiter a dime, prompting a polite response of "I thank you, Mr. Allenby." This morning, Bert palmed Percy the half-dollar coin, and the man's eyed went wide. "Oh, Mr. Allenby, ain't you **flush!**"

Real cream makes coffee a thick, heavenly pleasure. Bert enjoyed the second cup as the water for his shower heated up—with the plumbing of 1939, this took a few minutes. After his scrub, he dressed. He had been taught how to knot his tie, which he thought was a silly thing to wear, but he loved the double-breasted suit that had been tailored for him nearly a century later. The fabrics were from the period, the socks did not have much elastic in them, and the shoes were like gunboats, wide and heavy, but comfortable.

Riding down in the elevator, Bert again smelled the operator's hair tonic. He didn't think it was all that stinky.

"Lobby, sir," the elevator operator said as he opened the meshed grate.

Bert was now familiar with all the smells of the Hotel Lincoln, and he liked them—the cigar smoke mixing with the wool carpets, the flowers being arranged by the black housekeepers, the florid perfume of the well-dressed ladies heading out for their day in Manhattan. Outside on Eighth Avenue, taxis idled and buses headed uptown, spewing fumes of combusted gasoline.

On foot, Bert turned right out of the lobby and right again on West Forty-Fifth Street, inhaling the scent of roasted coffee, wafting on a breeze from the Hudson River, from the Maxwell House Coffee factory in New Jersey, coffee that was good to the last drop.

This morning of June 8, 1939, he'd not take breakfast at the Hotel Astor, with its famous clock and its opulent décor. Instead Bert was going to poke his head into as many nearby coffee shops and cafes as time allowed. Carmen lived only seven blocks away. What if she was nearby, grabbing a quick breakfast before taking the subway to the Bronx to pick up Virginia? Maybe she was sitting in a Broadway diner right now, having coffee and donuts. He could meet her right then and not have to wait all day for that moment on the bench by the Four Freedoms.

He covered Times Square and the side streets, ducking in and out of cafes and peering through the windows of diners, but there was no sign of her. Reluctantly, he gave up, taking a seat at the counter of a place on Seventh, paying twenty-five cents for a breakfast of eggs, sausage, pancakes, juice, and coffee.

Bert was leaving a Mercury dime as a tip. "Ma'am," he said to the uniformed waitress with overpainted lips, "is it possible for me take the subway to the World's Fair?"

"Honey," the waitress said, "it's the best way to go." She swept the dime into her apron pocket and gave Bert directions to the IRT line.

His first ever trip on the subway cost only an Indian head nickel. The car was a jumble of people, who all smelled of **something,** if only the laundry starch of their freshly pressed clothes. No one was staring at a phone or tablet. Most of the riders read the morning papers—some oversize rectangles of newsprint and ink, others the smaller-formatted tabloids. And there were magazines with pages that held more text than pictures. Many people were smoking, even a few men with cigars and two puffing on pipes. Judging from all the guidebooks and flyers, many passengers were, like Bert, making for the World's Fair.

At each stop Bert stepped off the car just long enough to scan the stations for Carmen and Virginia because, who knows? They could be riding the IRT out to Flushing Meadows. If so, Bert could ask them for directions, they would volunteer to guide him along since they were going, too, he could confess that his **three** VIP passes were burning a hole in his pocket and why not let him treat the two ladies to a hassle-free day of no lines, no waiting? And just like that, what had in the past been less than two hours with Carmen would, in the present, become an entire day together.

But Carmen never got on the train.

"Wow! Look at that!" a rider shouted. Out the window were the Trylon and Perisphere—the Fair. Bert could see the huge globe and its attendant tower, bright and white in the morning sky. Everyone on the train gave the landmarks a glance.

The IRT discharged fairgoers at the Bowling Green Gate, where Bert paid seventy-five cents for admission and bought a guidebook for a dime.

It was only 10:30, so unless fate was to intercede there were hours before he would see Carmen again. He took a look at the Home Building Center, admired the sofa beds in Home Furnishings, and found the exhibits in the American Radiator Building just about hilarious. He kept chuckling to himself at the dazzling-in-those-days presentations by RCA, American Telephone & Telegraph, the Communications Building, and the museum-like presentations of the Crosley Radio Corporation.

He joined the line for Democracity, the lesson in social studies that was inside the Perisphere. He was soon talking with the Gammelgards, a family of six including grandparents, who had taken the train all the way from Topeka, Kansas, to spend a week at the fair. This was their very first day, and Pop-Pop Gammelgard said to Bert, "Young man, never have I dreamed the good Lord would allow me to see such a place as this." Bert was happy to be considered a **young man**. His $756 billion afforded him every procedure in the world to look much younger than his sixty-one years.

He told the Kansans he had friends in Salina, which prompted an invitation for dinner at the Gammelgards', should Bert ever find himself in Topeka.

All morning he checked out every woman dressed in green, hoping to find Carmen. He toured every building in the Court of Power, the Plaza of Light, and along the Avenue of Labor, where uniformed ladies working for Swift & Co. demonstrated the slicing and packaging of fresh bacon. At noon, he blew two nickels on hot dogs at Childs and compared the cut of his double-breasted suit to the fashions-to-come, according to the prophets of Men's Apparel. He then walked all the way to the Amusements Area, heading for the tall iron tower that was the parachute drop. The Amusements were the Fair's most popular attractions, and the carnival crowd was thick and jumbled. Bert circled the area again and again, stopping at the parachute tower repeatedly, expecting to find Carmen and Virginia as they rose up, up, up, and came down **ka-joink**. But they were never there. So he started one last, slow walk around the area and back toward the main fairgrounds.

Then he saw her! Not Carmen at first, but Virginia! He was crossing the bridge by the Amphitheater, where the Aquacade performed, when a multicar tram passed him, Virginia sitting on the rail and, yes, Carmen beside her! They had been among the amusement rides after all, and were now en route to the Plaza of Light. Bert checked his wristwatch. If he could catch up with that tram, he'd meet Carmen nearly an hour early! He ran.

He kept sight of the tram all along the Avenue of Labor, but lost them at the Schaefer Center on Rainbow Avenue. He just couldn't keep up. The tram continued, passing the Court of States, then stopping at Constitution Mall to empty and take on new passengers. They had to be nearby! Sweating in that double-breasted suit, Bert checked Beech-Nut, Jewish Palestine, the YMCA, the Temple of Religion, and the Works Progress Administration, but no joy. Resigned to the singularity of the Time-Space Continuum, Bert was pivoting toward the lagoon benches when she appeared right in front of him.

Carmen was coming out of Brazil, holding Virginia's hand. They were laughing. Good Lord, the woman laughed so much and her smile was so adorable. He almost called out her name but remembered they had yet to meet, so instead he fell in behind them by a few yards, following them across the walkway over the man-made river that fed the Lagoon of Nations. He didn't trail them into Great Britain but headed for the bench. A few minutes later, there she was again, with Virginia. Right on time.

"Excuse me," Bert immediately said, just as Carmen and Virginia were sitting down. "Do you ladies know if the Futurama is running today?"

"It is, but the line is very long. We spent all afternoon in the Amusements Area. What a time we had!"

"Have you rode the Parachute, mister?"

"I haven't. Should I?"

"It's not for the weakhearted."

"You go up and up and up. You think you are going to come floating down slow and soft. But you don't. You land **ka-joink**!"

"It's true."

"Have you seen the Futurama?"

"We didn't want to wait through that long line."

"I certainly don't want to miss it." Bert reached into the breast pocket of his suit. "And I have these special passes."

Bert showed them the three heavy cards embossed with the Trylon and Perisphere and the letters **VIP**. "I'm told these will get us into the Futurama via a secret passage. No waiting. I have three. And I'm alone. Would you like to join me?"

"Oh, that's so nice of you. But we are definitely not VIPs."

"Believe me, neither am I. Not sure why I even have these."

"Can we go, Aunt Carmen?"

"I feel like a sneaky pete. But let's! Thank you so much."

"Yes. Thanks! My name is Virginia and this is my aunt Carmen. Who are you?"

"Bert Allenberry."

"Well, thank you, Mr. Allenberry. We'll see the Future with you!"

The three chatted as they walked the length of Constitution Mall, below the huge statue of George Washington, and around the Trylon and Perisphere. Virginia told of all they had seen of the Fair in that day, most of it spent on the rides in the Amusement Area.

"Have you seen Electro, the Mechanical Man?" Bert asked. "He can add up numbers on his metal hands."

The General Motors Building was next to that of the Ford Motor Company. Ford showed fairgoers how their automobiles were built, then let them drive a car along a dipsy doodle of a road around the building. GM took its visitors into the future, first by ascending a long ramp, one so modern they called it a Helicline, to a cleft in the architecture so majestic it looked like a gateway into the Promised Land. The line of people waiting to see Futurama looked to number in the millions.

But, flashing their VIP cards at a pretty girl in a GM uniform, Bert, Carmen, and Virginia were taken to a door on the ground level.

"I hope you aren't tired," the girl said. "We have a few flights to climb."

The machinery of the Futurama bumped and whirred around them. They could hear music coming through the walls along with the murmur of a narration.

"You'll notice the soundtrack matches exactly what you are seeing," the girl explained. "GM is truly proud of the engineering that went into the Futurama. It's absolutely modern."

"Are we going to be driving a **car**?" Virginia asked.

"You'll find out!" The girl opened a door revealing the starting point of the ride—sunlight and people were streaming in through the opening. "Enjoy your stay," the girl said.

There were no automobiles, but rather a long train of wheeled, sofa-like carts lined end to end, each enclosed in a shell. Passengers were climbing into the shells, which never stopped moving as the cars passed through the opening of a tunnel.

The three intrepid voyagers climbed into one, Virginia first, then Carmen, followed by Bert. Before they knew it they were in darkness. Music played and a narrator welcomed them to America, as it would be in the year 1960. The voice was so clear it was like the announcer was in the car with them.

A city appeared before them—a world in miniature that stretched to the horizon. The sky-scrapers in the center stood like trophies, some connected to each other by sky bridges. The narrator explained that in just a few decades American cities would be planned and built to the specifics of perfection. Streets would be clear and ordered. Highways would flow with modern automobiles—GM cars, each of them—with traffic that never cluttered or jammed. The sky would be filled with aircraft carrying goods and passengers to terminals as conveniently placed as filling stations. The countryside would be scattered with farms, homes, and power stations, supplying 1960 with all the food, space, and electricity the American people would need.

The houses and towers and cars and trains and planes were filled with a happy, invisible populace that had tamed the wild chaos of the past; they'd figured out not only how to build the future but how to live in it side by side, in peace.

Virginia was riveted to her seat as the future rolled by. Carmen smiled at her and looked at Bert. She leaned toward him and whispered, "She'll live there and likes what she sees."

The words landed on Bert like so many soft kisses. The narration had paused, leaving only the swelling strings of violins and cellos from the musical score. He smelled Carmen's perfume, the soft whiff of lilac mixed with vanilla. Her lips stayed close to his cheek.

"Do you think it will all happen?" Carmen asked quietly. "Just like this?"

Finding her ear surrounded by the dark curl of

her black hair, Bert whispered back, "If it does, it will be wonderful."

When they exited, the afternoon shadows had grown longer. As they crossed the Bridge of Wheels over the Grand Central Parkway, Virginia announced that she would be thirty years old in 1960. "I wish I could jump in a time machine right now and go there!"

Bert checked his watch—it was 5:56 p.m. In the past, he had been in a taxi by now, on his way back to room 1114. By 7:00 he had undressed, removed all the items that had been provided for his adventure, like the rings and the watch, had squeezed back into his compression suit, and was lying on the precisely placed bed for Progression out of 1939. He **should** be leaving right now; the taxi stand was just outside the gate on the other side of Chrysler Motors. Instead, he asked Carmen when the Fountains of Light show was to start.

"Not until dark," she said. "Hey, since you are now in the presence of a couple of VIPs, may I treat you to some pie?"

"I happen to love pie."

"Let's go to Borden's!" Virginia said. "We can see Elsie the Cow."

Over pie and coffee, he relearned about Carmen and her niece—of the Radio Club and the roommates on East Thirty-Eighth Street. Everything was just as it had been. Then the past took a turn.

"Do you have anyone special in your life, Mr. Allenberry?"

Bert looked into Carmen's eyes. Framed now in the décor of Borden's Food Court, they'd turned an even deeper shade of green.

"She means are you married!" Virginia teased.

"Virginia! I'm sorry, Mr. Allenberry. I don't mean to be forward, but I see you have no wedding ring and I just thought, well, a fellow like you **must** have someone special."

"I've thought so, many times," Bert said, wistfully. "I'm forever looking, I guess."

"You bachelors are so lucky. You can wait and wait for the right girl to come along and nobody says **boo**." She rattled off the names of movie stars and athletes who had yet to marry, names Bert did not recognize. "But us ladies? If we wait too long we become old maids."

"Mama says if you don't find a man soon, there'll be none left for you!" Virginia giggled. "You're almost **twenty-seven**!"

"You **hush**," Carmen hissed, reaching over with her fork to stab the best piece of crust, then popping it into her mouth.

"You dirty rat!" Virginia laughed.

Dabbing her lips with a napkin, Carmen smiled at Bert. "It's true. I'm the last hen in the barnyard."

"How old are you, Mr. Allenberry?" Virginia asked. "I'm guessing you're like Mr. Lowenstein, my school principal. He's almost forty. Are you forty yet?"

"Young lady, I am going to throw you into the Lagoon of Nations! Mr. Allenberry, I'm sorry. My niece has yet to learn the practice of tact. Maybe by 1960."

Bert laughed. "I'm like your aunt Carmen. The last rooster in the barnyard."

They all laughed at that. Carmen reached over and took his wrist. "Aren't we a pair?" she said.

Bert should have excused himself right then. Six p.m. had passed. If a cab was available, he could be in room 1114 just in time for Progression. But this was his last day ever with Carmen. He would never see the woman in the green dress again.

Now, Bert Allenberry **was** a smart man, many say a genius. His invention of the Shuffle-Access Digital Valve-Relay had changed the world and garnered him the rapt attention of audiences at conferences full of movers and shakers—in Davos, Vienna, Abu Dhabi, and Ketchum, Idaho. He had teams of lawyers obeying his dictates, researchers and developers turning his ideas of whimsy into realities. He had more money than the GNP of most nations of the world, including those where he owned factories. He had donated to very good causes and had his name on buildings he had never even bothered to visit. He had everything a man—a very rich man—was supposed to have, need, or want.

Except for time, of course.

Chronometric Adventures said he had twenty-two hours of June 8, 1939, to do whatever he wanted. But now, what he wanted was to **stay awhile.** There must be some wiggle room, right? After all, Progression, or was it Reprogression—he was never sure—could not begin until his body, all his atoms and molecules, were in place in room 1114 of the Hotel Lincoln on Eighth Avenue. He understood why Chronometric Adventures demanded such terms—to cover their asses! Why did he **have** to be in that tight compression suit and on that bed according to the tick of the clock? Was he Cinderella at the Ball? Why couldn't he saunter into the room at, say, midnight, then slip into that rubber suit and then **whoosh** away? What was the big deal?

"Have you seen the Time Capsule?" he asked Virginia.

"I read about it in school. It's buried for the next five thousand years."

"They have what's in it on display in Westinghouse. Electro the robot, too. Do you know what television is? You just have to see television." Bert was rising from the table. "Shall we go to Westing-house?"

"Let's!" Carmen's eyes were smiling again.

The Time Capsule was loaded with silly stuff—Mickey Mouse comics and cigarettes and whole sets of books printed on microfilm.

Though the Time Capsule and Electro were impressive, television was what had Virginia over the moon. She could see her aunt and Mr. Allen-berry on a small screen, in black and white, almost like they were stars in a movie, but their images were in miniature, projecting from a screen in a cabinet no bigger than the radio at home. In fact, they were in another **room**, standing in front of a camera, one unlike any she had ever seen, and they were also in front of her. The vision was thrilling. When they switched places, Virginia waved and spoke into the microphone: "This is me, on the television saying hello from right **here** and you can see me right **there!**"

"Look at you!" Carmen said. "You look so pretty! So grown up! Oh, Bert!" She turned to him. "This should be impossible, but here it is!"

Bert was looking not at Virginia on the screen but at Carmen. He was thrilled that he was no longer Mr. Allenberry.

Checking his watch, Bert saw that it was 7:06. The deadline had passed, the twenty-two hours were up, and, lo and behold, there was wiggle room!

They visited the DuPont, Carrier, and Petroleum Industry Buildings, none of which had the socko exhibits to match television. The Glass Building, the American Tobacco exhibit, and Continental Baking were just time killers; the longer they lingered in them the sooner came darkness and the light show.

After watching films of water-skiers in the Academy of Sports, he bought cups of ice cream, which they ate with little wooden spoons.

"Here's our spot for the show!" Virginia claimed a bench for the three of them. In the growing indigo of the evening, they could see all the way from the Lagoon to giant George Washington, silhouetted against the Perisphere, surveying the great nation he had sired. As night fell, the buildings of the Fair became so many tracings of brightly lit lines on deepening black. The skyscrapers of Manhattan lit up the horizon. The illuminated fairground trees looked to be glowing from within, from their own inner light.

Bert Allenberry wanted this night to last forever, for all time. He wanted to sit beside Carmen at the Lagoon of Nations, listening to the murmur of the Fair, with her scent of lilac and vanilla stirring the warm air of 1939.

When Virginia collected their ice cream cups and took them to a trash bin, Bert and Carmen were alone for the first time ever. He reached for her hand.

"Carmen," he said. "This has been a perfect day." Carmen was looking at him. Oh, those hazel eyes. "Not because of Futurama. Or television."

"Elsie the Cow?" Carmen said, her breath catching as she smiled.

"Would you allow me to give you and Virginia a ride home when the Fair closes?"

"Oh, I couldn't do that. My sister lives too deep in the Bronx."

"We'll take a taxi. Then I can drop you off at your place. On East Thirty-Eighth Street."

"That would be very kind of you, Bert," Carmen said.

Bert wanted to hold Carmen in his arms, to kiss her, maybe in the back of a taxi on East Thirty-Eighth Street. Or, in room 1114. Better yet, on the one hundredth floor of his building at 909 Fifth Avenue.

"I'm glad I came to the Fair today." Bert smiled. "So I could meet you."

"I'm glad, too," Carmen whispered. Her hand never left his.

Music began to play from speakers hidden around the Lagoon of Nations. Virginia ran back to the bench just as the fountains shot water into the sky, lights turning the geysers into columns of liquid color. Every patron of the Fair stopped to watch. Projections turned the Perisphere into a luminescent ball of clouds.

"Wow!" Virginia loved it.

"Beautiful," Carmen said.

The first fireworks broke into the sky, bursting into cascading comets, fading to smoke.

That's when Bert felt a ball-peen hammer strike his forehead. His eyes went painfully dry and scratched terribly. His nose and ears started to run with blood. His legs went numb, and his lower back seemed to separate from his hips. A hot, searing pain shot through his chest as the molecules that made up his lungs began to separate. He had the sensation that he was falling.

The last words he heard were Virginia yelling, "Mr. Allenberry!" The last thing he saw was the fear in Carmen's hazel eyes.

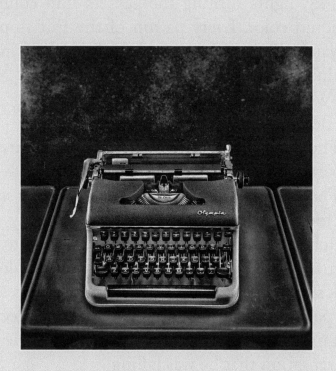

Stay with Us

MUSIC: "Mama Said Knock You Out" by LL Cool J

FADE IN

EXT: LAS VEGAS. MORNING

We know this place—the Strip. The casinos. The fountains. But wait . . . there is a new, huge, luxurious hotel on the skyline.

OLYMPUS.

Bigger than all the others. If you are a Big Roller, you frolic and gamble with the gods at OLYMPUS.

CLOSE ON: EYES OF FRANCIS XAVIER RUSTAN

A.K.A.: F.X.R. Green eyes, flecked with gold, that dance with delight at all they see.

CLOSE ON: COMPUTER SCREENS

Left screen: DETAILED ARCHITECTURAL PLANS, of a vast SOLAR ENERGY COLLECTION FIELD

Middle screen: Google Earth IMAGES of unsettled, bare parcels of land, USGS MAPS, topography CHARTS, and environmental GRAPHS

Right screen: FLOATING IMAGES. A guy catching a marlin, a guy hang gliding, a guy rock climbing, a guy white-water rafting. Steve McQueen in BULLITT. The guy is always F.X.R.

Except for Steve McQueen.

A NEWS TICKER scrolls along the bottom of this screen. Windows pop up with ALERTS and MESSAGES and NOW PLAYING, which switches from LL Cool J to . . .

MUSIC: "Mambo Italiano" by Dean Martin

A TEXT BOX pops up:

MERCURY: **Boss? Breakfast as usual?**

CALLER ID shows us MS. MERCURY—Jet-black hair cut short. Slashes of red lipstick.

F.X.R. replies with **clicks** of his keyboard.
F.X.R.: **Called it in. Nicholas is bringing it up.**
MERCURY: **Who?** F.X.R.: **New guy.**

CUT TO:

INT. SERVICE ELEVATOR—SAME

MS. MERCURY is a stunning specimen, as intimidating as a supermodel. Six feet tall, rail thin, Pilates-shaped physique. Dressed in black on black. She is a woman not to be messed with in any shape or form.

She has read the text, and screams!

MS. MERCURY

What **new guy**!?

She has been the aide-de-camp for F.X.R. over the last 12 years—a job she lives and breathes every minute of every day.

‖ 357 ‖

That a "new guy" is bringing her boss his breakfast is a fact that should never have escaped her!

She is tapping away on a gizmo on her wrist, a large WATCH/COMPUTER— getting MEMOS, TEXTS, SCHEDULES—and finally a series of EMPLOYEE PHOTOS. She swipes the screen until she finds . . .

NICHOLAS PAPAMAPALOS—19 years old. A look of confusion in his eyes, like a kid starting his very first job ever, which he is.

The elevator doors open and there he is— NICHOLAS PAPAMAPALOS, in the uniform of a room service waiter at Olympus, pushing a table of covered dishes.

> MS. MERCURY (CONT'D)
> (smiling way too much)
> Nicky my boy!
> **Nicky is confused. Why does**
> **this tall lady know his name?**
> **He enters the elevator.**

> NICHOLAS
> I'm new here.

MS. MERCURY
You sure are! Look at you in your too-big
uniform, with your breakfast order for
F.X.R. all ready!

NICHOLAS
Am I in trouble?

MS. MERCURY
Not yet, kiddo.

NICHOLAS
How do you know I'm taking this to Mr.
Rustan?
**Ms. Mercury presses the
button for the 101st floor.
The doors close and the
elevator slowly rises.**

MS. MERCURY
Because I know everything that happens
at Olympus, Nick-chick. Do you
know why?

NICHOLAS
No. I'm new here.

MS. MERCURY
Let me tell you a little about myself.
(then)

You know what I was doing until three a.m. this morning? Seeing to it that Francis X. Rustan's collection of one hundred and thirty-two antique motorcycles were moved into a new climate-controlled warehouse, where they will be kept in perfect running order on the off chance that he chooses to someday take one out for a spin. The last time he did that was May of 2013. That he has yet to inspect the new storage facilities for his collection of antique player pianos or the vintage Burma-Shave signs he's purchased over the years did not deter me from having two dozen men put motorcycles in protective wrapping and gingerly place them in a high-tech garage the size and approximate cost of Bruce Wayne's Batcave.

(then)

F.X.R. is a very rich man who pretends to be all-knowing and all-seeing when it comes to his vast empire. Accent on, line under, italicize **pretends.** Here's something none of his millions of admirers, acolytes, influence peddlers,

and brownnosers understand about El
Jefe—he couldn't make his own lunch
given a kaiser roll, cold cuts, and a jar of
mayonnaise. His head is in the clouds
because that brain of his is so damn full
of the knuckleheaded schemes that pay
off so well. So, we are here—you and
I—to make the life he leads possible. I to
work twenty-two-hour days at his beck
and call. You to prep his meals and taste-
test them for poison. I'm kidding. About
the poison. Or am I?
   **Ding! They are on the 101st
   floor.**

INT. SERVICE HALL, 101ST FLOOR—SAME It's
a long hall!

                    MS. MERCURY
               (still smiling)
Tell me you have his breakfast order
perfect or I'll cripple you.

                    NICHOLAS
I had it all set. The seven-grain organic
granola, sliced mango and pineapple,
tomato juice and cinnamon cafe au lait.
But then . . .

MS. MERCURY
(smile? Vanished!)
But then?

NICHOLAS
Half hour ago he messaged the kitchen.

MS. MERCURY
Show me the message!
**Nicholas shows her his
Watch/Computer:**

**FXR: Stove Team —Flag on play—Me want
griddle cakes!**

MS. MERCURY (CONT'D)
Griddle cakes! GRIDDLE CAKES? No no
no!
**She lifts a cover! There, on
a plate: griddle cakes. Also
known as pancakes.**

MS. MERCURY (CONT'D)
Jiminy Expletive! Those are griddle cakes!

NICHOLAS
With boysenberry syrup.
**Ms. Mercury is now beside
herself with worry.**

‖ 362 ‖

MS. MERCURY

Oh, Nicky—Nicky. This is not a good
sign. My day may have just been ruined,
and I tell you this—if I'm going down
today I am taking you with me.

NICHOLAS

Because of griddle cakes? I didn't do
anything! I'm new here!

MS. MERCURY

The Boss only orders cakes from the
griddle when he's antsy with ideas. I'll
have to arrange an expedition to the
fjords of Iceland for thirty of F.X.R.'s
closest friends so he can paddle a
kayak in open water. Or have a zip line
assembled over the gorges of the rain
forest in Uganda so anyone can look
down and see chimpanzees in the wild
go by. Or make sure every employee of
Olympus is shackled to . . .
        (the Watch/Computer)
. . . one of these things. And I've actually
had to make real those very orders.
Griddle cakes mean I'm getting a work
assignment that wouldn't make sense to
hamsters. **Griddle cakes** have just ruined
my already miserable day.

NICHOLAS
Why do you do this job?

MS. MERCURY
I have no answer to that question other
than my big honker of a paycheck.
**They are at the door of the
only hotel room on the 101st
floor.**

MS. MERCURY (CONT'D)
Set up by the fake waterfall. Straighten
your name tag. And smile. He likes
employees who look like they love their
jobs.
**She pauses. Takes a breath
and changes her demeanor
to a sunny smile. Her ability
to transform this way is
frightening.
She knocks . . . and enters.**

INT. PENTHOUSE—DAY

A snazzy place, complete with a fake waterfall,
state-of-the-art exercise equipment, wall-size
video screen in front of a row of vintage movie-
theater chairs. The windows look out on most of
Las Vegas.

MS. MERCURY
(happy as could be)
I have griddle cakes for the big boss man!
**F.X.R. rises from his computer
workstation.**

F.X.R.
That was fast.

MS. MERCURY
You always say that!
**Nicholas sets up the room
service table.**

F.X.R.
You Nicholas?
(reading the name tag)
Looks like it. Welcome aboard. What
happened to O'Shay?

MS. MERCURY
O'Shay's wife had that baby, remember?
And yes, I already sent over a new crib
and a cold-water humidifier, along with
two full-time nurses.
F.X.R. sits for his griddle cakes.

F.X.R.
Look at these beauties. If they were made
in a pan, they're pancakes. A griddle, and

they are griddle cakes. Were these made
in a pan or on a griddle, Nico?

NICHOLAS
I didn't actually see, sir. I'm new here.

F.X.R.
Sir? Around here I'm plain old F.X.
        (then)
I say they're griddle cakes.
        (he pours the berry syrup)
Ms. Mercury. I don't know what was
on the docket for today but cancel
everything.

MS. MERCURY
Last time you said that you had me
tramping through Mississippi so you
could buy up every kenaf farm in the
Delta.

F.X.R.
Think I nailed down the place for the
Solar Pipeline Facility.

MS. MERCURY
Wow. No kidding. Super.
        **She sighs and plops herself
        down on the couch. She starts**

**swiping around the Internet
on her Watch/Computer.
(to herself)**
Gonna be a long day . . .
**F.X.R. picks up his plate and
walks to the computers,
pulls up images, and points
with his fork dripping with
boysenberry.**

F.X.R.
Shepperton Dry Creek ain't nothing
much now. Flat, wide. Dusty. But, a
miracle of Mother Nature that gets more
sunshine than Taylor Swift gets Facebook
likes.

MS. MERCURY
**(Ms. Mercury is "LIKING"
a post on Taylor Swift's
Facebook page)**
That's a lot.

F.X.R.
Old Route 88 cuts close to Shepperton
Dry Creek.

MS. MERCURY
Does it? **I don't know anything.**

F.X.R.

Someone enterprising is going to start
buying up the land along that stretch of
highway for the influx of traffic it's gonna
bring.

MS. MERCURY
(bored, examining nails)
Uh-huh.

F.X.R.
So, let's get goin'.

MS. MERCURY
Goin' where?

F.X.R.
Along old Route 88. It'll be fun! Just
like that trip we took in Costa Rica on
the Pan-American Highway to collect
spiders.

MS. MERCURY
Yeah. That was a blast. I was bitten.

F.X.R.
You healed.

MS. MERCURY
Make Nick go with you today.

F.X.R.

I can't boss Nick around. He's in the
union.
     (then)
You are in the union, right?

NICHOLAS

I am, sir. Er, F.X.

MS. MERCURY

Why can't you get married and make
your wife do this stuff?

F.X.R.

I don't need a wife. I have you, Ms.
Mercury. Wives don't put up with guys
like me.

MS. MERCURY

But I have to? I've got too many things
to do right here to keep your empire
afloat.

F.X.R.

A road trip will do us both good.
     She throws up her hands.

MS. MERCURY

You see, Nicholas! You and your griddle
cakes!

NICHOLAS
What did I do?

F.X.R.
What did Nick do?

MS. MERCURY
One of these days I'm gonna quit this
job and do something dignified, like
professional water skiing . . .
   (typing on her Watch/Computer)
I'll get the jet ready.

F.X.R.
The big jet and the little jet. You take the
little one and scrounge up some ground
transpo. I'll come in the big jet after I've
done my workout.

MS. MERCURY
Whatever you wish, O Titan of Industry.
Which fantasy automobile do you want
to add to the warehouse? A Monza?
Surfer Woodie?

F.X.R.
Let's keep a low profile to blend in with
the locals. The economy bypassed that
part of the nation.
   (pulls out a wad of cash)

Get me whatever car eight hundred
dollars can purchase.

MS. MERCURY
Eight hundred dollars? For a car? It'll be
a hunk of junk!
F.X.R. pulls out a few more bills.

F.X.R.
Make it eight fifty.
(pulls a twenty)
Nick? For you.
Nicholas takes the money.

NICHOLAS
Thank you, Mister F.X.

CUT TO:

EXT. AIRFIELD, SOMEWHERE IN THE MIDDLE
OF NOWHERE—DAY

A single landing strip and a weathered Field
Business Office. Not many aircraft land at this
place. But look here . . .

A Big Jet is taxiing up beside a parked Little Jet.
Both planes have the Olympus logo painted on
the sides.

Ms. Mercury—still in her black on black—
sits behind the wheel of a 1970s-era Buick
convertible with the top down.

The stairs of the Big Jet pop open, and there is
F.X.R. in clothes he thinks the common people
wear—a fruity-looking western shirt with too
much piping tucked into an old pair of Jordache
designer jeans, a belt with a huge Marlboro
cigarettes belt buckle, and flame-red cowboy
boots.

He wears a too-perfectly-broken-in John Deere
cap and has a straw cowboy hat in his hand.

> MS. MERCURY
> Hey, Duke, or Bo, or whoever you are. Is
> my boss in that plane?

> F.X.R.
> **(re: his costume)**
> Pretty good, huh? Authenticity is the key.

> MS. MERCURY
> Glad some of the casino showgirls let you
> raid their dressing room.

> F.X.R.
> **(re: the car)**
> How's she running?

MS. MERCURY
I've burned half a tank of gas and a pint
of oil just driving from the lot. Good
news is, I bargained down to seven
hundred bucks.

F.X.R.
Put the change in petty cash. Here.
  (the cowboy hat)
Blend in!
  He plops the hat on her head.

F.X.R. (CONT'D)
  (laughing)
Don't we look great?

MS. MERCURY
All that fortune and your idea of fun is
dressing up like a poor mortal with no
fashion sense. I can arrange this to be
permanent. Just give me all your money
and you'll live happily ever after.
  **F.X.R. runs around to the
  passenger seat, trying to hop
  in over the door. He lands in
  a heap on the front seat, one
  foot hooked on the door.**

MS. MERCURY (CONT'D)
Gangway for adventure!

**She hits the gas and the car
spins out and away, spewing
dust and gravel.**

MUSIC: "I've Been Everywhere" by Hank Snow

EXT. HIGHWAY 88—LATER
**The Buick chugs along down
the highway. F.X.R. smiles
into the wind.**

F.X.R.
I should get out of that penthouse more
often!

MS. MERCURY
Two weeks ago you were boogie boarding
on the Great Barrier Reef!

F.X.R.
To see America. Don't see enough of my
native land. Open road. Big sky. Asphalt
ribbon with nothing but a dotted line
and the horizon. I love this country! God
help me, but I do love it so!
    (then)
It's good for the soul to come down
from the mountaintop sometimes, Ms.
Mercury. Otherwise, all you see are the

tops of mountains. I should put that in a memo to all the employees.

MS. MERCURY
Do that. It would inspire us all.
(then)
So, where are we going, cochise?

Sending a message from his Watch to hers . . .
F.X.R.
Here. A little town called Phrygia.
(he tries three different pronunciations)
Population 102.

WATCH: **Photos, facts, information about Phrygia . . .**

F.X.R. (CONT'D)
Formerly a major stop on Route 88 that once billed itself as America's Hospitality Capital. Let's see how hospitable they are to the likes of us.

MS. MERCURY
Before you buy up every square inch and acre.
(studying her Watch)

Oh, hell. This drive will take us hours!
I'm gonna fry!

EXT. A HUGE SIGN—Faded, ancient, with
broken neon tubes and peeling paint that says
MOTEL OLYMPUS . . .

Still barely visible are the large figures of a
man and woman, both waving to nonexistent
traffic, calling out in sun-bleached letters **"Stay
with us!"**

MUSIC: **"Que Te Vaya Bonito"** on an accordion

**SUBTITLES IN ENGLISH OF THE SPANISH
LYRICS**

"I don't know if your absence will kill me

even if my chest is made of steel . . ."

CUT TO:

EXT. MOTEL OLYMPUS, PHRYGIA—DAY—
SAME

Nothing at all like its namesake in Las Vegas . . .
Nothing at all.

Like the sign, the Motel Olympus has seen better days. The best that can be said of it? It's clean.

The MUSIC is coming from JESUS HILDALGO, who plays the final bars of a song so beautiful it even sounds great on an accordion.

SUBTITLES: **"But no one will call me a coward**

Without knowing how much I love her . . ."

An old couple—PHIL and BEA (yes, that's them on the sign)—applaud as Jesus packs away his instrument and loads it into his old pickup truck.

> PHIL
> Talent like I never seen!

> BEA
> Every time you play I find myself all
> **misty**. You have a gift, Jesus.

> JESUS
> You make me feel so good, Mr. Phil and
> Mrs. Bea. You have always made me feel
> I was at home.

> BEA
> That's because you have been, Jesus.
> You've been at our home.

PHIL

Good luck there in Chesterton. I hear
they get benefits galore at that windshield
factory.

JESUS

Thank you. I will come back to see you
many times. I promise I will.

BEA

Bring us a windshield you made yourself.
Jesus climbs in, and the
pickup truck pulls out of
the motel lot, honking. Phil
and Bea watch the truck
disappear down the road.
They are quiet for a moment.

PHIL

There goes our only guest. One less bed
to make.

BEA

Lord, am I going to miss him playing
that 'cordine.

PHIL

Sixty-two less dollars a week. Why would
anyone want to leave this little spot of
paradise to live in a podunk burg like
Chesterton . . .

BEA

Oh, stop serving crab apples. Do some
weeding.

**Phil sizes up the woman he
married. The woman he still
finds so very beautiful . . .**

PHIL

Don't treat me like some hired hand.
(then)
Unless you wearing that pretty dress
means you want to play Seduce the
Hired Hand.

BEA

You go out there with the weedwacker
and flex your rippling muscles, maybe I'll
get all heated up.

PHIL

Tell you what, woman. Give me twenty
minutes to clear the south forty, then
meet me in room 10. I just might be
naked in the shower.

BEA

It's a date.
**A Buick convertible is
coming down the road, its
turn signal blinking.**

BEA (CONT'D)
Hold on. Looks like we have guests.

PHIL
Rats.
(shouting)
Come back in an hour, folks!
**The car pulls in to the motel.
Hey, it's none other than
F.X.R. and Ms. Mercury! The
top is still down.
He is smiling. She looks
like hell after driving three
hours in a convertible with
the top down. They pull
right up to Phil and Bea.**

F.X.R.
Howdy!

PHIL
Howdy-do?

BEA
Howdy-do to you.

MS. MERCURY
How-diddly-dee-dooty-do.

F.X.R.
(all "folksy")

As you can see, we happen to be weary
travelers who have been on the road too
long.

                    MS. MERCURY
With no sunblock.

                    F.X.R.
We seek a respite from our journey. You
know—some real hospitality.

                    BEA
How about trying a motel of some kind?

                    F.X.R.
Know any good motels around?

                    BEA
Well, let's think here. Motels. You need a
motel . . .

                    PHIL
Best motel in the world is right here
on the outskirts of Phrygia. Called the
Olympic or the Olympian or something.
        F.X.R. looks at the faded sign.

                    F.X.R.
Motel Olympus!

                    PHIL
That's the one.

F.X.R.
Ms. Mercury! Motel Olympus! This is
fate!
>Ms. Mercury wants out of the
>car and into a shower ASAP.

MS. MERCURY
It must be. This parking lot screams
destiny.

BEA
Welcome. I'm Bea. He's Phil. Stay
with us!
>**These two adorable old folks
>immediately freeze in the
>positions of the sign behind
>them, complete with waving
>arms.
>F.X.R. and Ms. Mercury
>share a look. Phil and Bea
>have not moved. They are still
>frozen in their "sign" position.
>They remain so. For a beat.
>Then another.
>And another.**

MS. MERCURY
So, do you have a vacancy?

BEA
(breaking her pose)
Nothing but.

CUT TO:

INT. MOTEL OFFICE—SAME

CLOSE ON:
A faded photo from fifty years before—young
Phil and Bea, in that same pose. Obviously
the model for the sign back when it was
constructed.
  The office is clean and cozy. F.X.R. inspects the
photo as Bea prepares the paperwork.

BEA
If it seems like you have the place to
yourself, you do.

F.X.R.
Business slow, is it?

BEA
Ever since Eisenhower built the
interstates.

F.X.R.
That how long you've owned this place?

BEA

Not quite. But Phil and I have been here
since Phrygia was a three-star stop with
the Autoclub.
**She hands him a registration
card and a cheap
ballpoint pen.**

EXT. MOTEL OLYMPUS—SAME

**Ms. Mercury is parking the
car. The engine is making
lots of horrible noises. Phil
comes up.**

PHIL

I think the squirrels are dying.

MS. MERCURY

Three or four quarts of oil and the
gnashing sound disappears.
**Smoke starts coming from
under the hood.**

PHIL

The woods are on fire!
(then)
Shut it down, honey.
**Did he just call Ms. Mercury
"honey"?**

                    MS. MERCURY
Okay, lamb chop.
          **She shuts down the
          engine just as something
          EXPLODES. The motor
          stops, but the after-chug
          makes the car seem alive.**

                    PHIL
This thing has a life of its own. Pop the
hood!

                    MS. MERCURY
How exactly does one pop that?
          **She finds a lever and pulls.
          The hood goes up, emitting a
          column of smoke.**

INT. MOTEL OFFICE—DAY
          **F.X.R. sees the smoke as Bea
          inspects the registration card
          he's filled out.**

                    BEA
F.X.R?
                    F.X.R.
Present!
                    BEA
No credit card, huh?

F.X.R.

Lord no. Had one once. For a department store in Flint, Michigan. Ran up a tab, then had to split town.
He never did any such thing.

BEA

We've seen some of that.
(then)
I'll need cash. In advance, 'cause I don't know you.

F.X.R.

How much?

BEA

Two rooms'll be thirty-eight fifty.
As he pulls out his western-style wallet, a prop he picked out himself.

F.X.R.
(worried)
Oooohhh . . .

BEA

Or, one room with double beds—twenty-two fifty.

F.X.R.
(digging around in his wallet)
That much, eh?

BEA
Single room, double bed, sixteen fifty.

F.X.R.
Turns out, I've only got . . . twelve
dollars . . . and some change.

BEA
Well . . . we'll give you the only-guests-
in-the-motel special, then.

EXT. MOTEL OLYMPUS—DAY
**Ms. Mercury leans over the
hood of the car with Phil,
who is monkeying around
with a wrench.**

MS. MERCURY
What do I know about cars? I just put
gas in it and go.

PHIL
You'd think it'd be that easy, wouldn't it?
(he pulls out the oil pump)
You know what this is?
**She looks at the part like it is
a dead rat.**

MS. MERCURY
A dead rat?

PHIL
This is a De-Hypoxified Fusion
Accelerator with Calcitrant Oxyspoilers.

MS. MERCURY
Really?

PHIL
I can get you another. Just gotta make a
call to Tommy Boyer. He'll run a rebuilt
one out here soon as he can.

MS. MERCURY
Fine. Great.

PHIL
I can put it in for you so you'll be on
your way with the dawn.

MS. MERCURY
At dawn I'll be in bed for another three
hours, but you go ahead.
   A shout is heard.

F.X.R. (O.C.)
Ms. Mercury!
      **Heads swivel. F.X.R is with
      Bea as she unlocks the door
      to one of the rooms.**

F.X.R. (CONT'D)
Come and see our accommodations.

INT. MOTEL ROOM—DAY
**Bea and Phil stand and watch
as F.X.R. tests out the bed
while Ms. Mercury inspects
the bathroom.**

F.X.R.
I hate to be a pest, but I have a bad
disc from a fall I took chopping trees in
Alberta.
**Ms. Mercury shoots him a
look. He never did any such
thing.**

F.X.R. (CONT'D)
This mattress will kill me before it gets
me to sleep.

BEA
(thinking)
Doesn't room three have a newer
mattress?

PHIL
Only a few months old. I'll change it,
pronto.

F.X.R.
(feeling the sheets)
And these, um, "sheets"? Way too
scratchy. I have a skin condition.

BEA
I can break open a fresh set.

F.X.R.
Will they be washed? Nothing is worse
than brand-new sheets.

BEA
Not even heart disease. I'll soften them
up for you.

PHIL
(concerned)
Better try the pillows. Too firm won't be
any good for that back of yours.

F.X.R.
Too firm and I can't move my neck in the
morning.
(he tries a pillow, grabs his neck)
Ouch! No way!

BEA
We sleep with some good down models.
We'll put fresh cases on them and let you
have them for the night.

BEA
When you do, let the hot water run. It
takes a while.

F.X.R.
Okay. Last item. How does a soul get
nourishment around here?

PHIL
Used to be a cafe right across the
road. Truman's, it was called. Great
pie. Even better pot roast. Closed in
1991.

BEA
Fast-food places over in Chesterton.
Thirty-six miles as the crow flies.

PHIL
I'd rather eat crow than fast food in
Chesterton.

MS. MERCURY
Just as well. We're stuck here. The car
blew its oxyspoiler.

PHIL
(remembering, and bolting)
I gotta call Tommy Boyer!
As he leaves . . .

MS. MERCURY
Any chance of room service?

BEA
If you don't mind getting your hands a
little dirty.

CUT TO:

EXT. BACK OF MOTEL—LATER

A mini-farm. Complete with henhouse and
garden. Beautifully kept. Bea is expertly
inspecting vegetables while Ms. Mercury tries to
get tomatoes off a vine.

MS. MERCURY
(tossing into a basket)
Okay. Tomatoes. Radishes. Those
long green things. And half of my
fingernails.

BEA
Wouldn't avocados be perfect? I've got to
plant some avocado trees.

MS. MERCURY
They grow on trees?

BEA
Yes. But you need two. One male tree
and one female tree. Otherwise no
avocados.

MS. MERCURY
The trees . . . have sex?

BEA
Once a week. Just like that old man
and me.
          **Bea LAUGHS. Even the
          chickens SQUAWK in jest.**

MS. MERCURY
That is way too much information . . .

CUT TO:

EXT. POOL AREA—DUSK
          **Phil has been preparing
          an old barbecue, where a
          scrawny chicken rotates on
          a spit. The pool, empty of
          water . . .**

F.X.R.
So you never had kids?

PHIL
(shakes his head)
Couldn't. Didn't mind though. Back in
the old days this place was swarming
with kids all the time. That's 'cause of
this swim pool. A dozen motels along
Eighty-eight before the interstate cut
us off. Only three had swim pools. I
put up signs every twenty miles, saying,
'Mount Olympus—Swim Pool.' Guess
where the kids demanded to stay?

F.X.R.
With Phil and Bea.

PHIL
You ever work in the hospitality
business?

F.X.R.
Not legitimately.
Phil gives him a look.

PHIL
It's a line of work you can't learn. Has
to come natural. You have to like people
and trust 'em. And lie a little when those
with crazy eyes ask if there's a vacancy.
No shame in that. Wisdom.

F.X.R.
You must like the motel business.

PHIL
I like this motel. Could use a bit more
business.

MUSIC: "Last Date" by Floyd Cramer

CUT TO:

EXT. LANDSCAPE—SUNSET

At the very moment the sun blinks out, gone,
beyond the horizon.

CUT TO:

EXT. MOTEL OLYMPUS—THE WHOLE
PLACE—NIGHT

The sign is not lit up itself, but has only a cheap
garden light shining up on it.

Down by the pool we see that a picnic dinner
has been enjoyed by the two innkeepers and their
guests.

PHIL
Tell me something. How long you kids
been together?

MS. MERCURY
What?

PHIL
You two. You an item?

BEA
Phil, whose business is that?

MS. MERCURY
(her eyes go wide!)
Are we an item? An item? **Item?**

PHIL
A man and a woman drive up. In a car
together. Check in together. Have a room
together. It's only happened about a
million times . . .
Ms. Mercury rolls her eyes.
Then she shakes her head.
Then she laughs to herself.

MS. MERCURY
(pointing to F.X.R.)
This man could no sooner be my half of
an "item" than I could fart toast.

BEA
Oh, I'm gonna steal that.

F.X.R.
As Ms. Mercury says, we have an
employer-employee relationship that is
proper in every way.

MS. MERCURY
If he isn't sleeping on the couch, and he
isn't because he's never slept on a couch, I
sure as hell am!

PHIL
Okay.
    (then)
You a gay lesbian, Ms. Mercury?

MS. MERCURY
No, I'm not that fashionable. I'm just
single.

BEA
No man in your life?

MS. MERCURY
Look . . . Let me explain this aspect of
my life to two relative strangers, as nice
as you are.
    (then)

A man would complicate my life in
the extreme. I need a man right now
like your chicken coop needs a satellite
dish. I am unattached, connected to no
one. The day will come when I chuck
it all and bid my boss adieu, and go
for the mate, the kids, the hand-made
Halloween costumes, all of it. Until then,
I'm happily solo, working for this guy . . .
    (F.X.R.—**who nods**)
Who drives me nuts but can take a joke.
I'm making good bank and I see the
world, from Tasmania to this lovely inn.
I. Have no room. For a boyfriend.
    Things are silent for a beat.

BEA

Then there's my answer.
    And another beat. The
    quiet is all-encompassing,
    beautiful.

F.X.R.

Listen to that.

MS. MERCURY

To what? I don't hear anything.

F.X.R.

You're not listening.

MS. MERCURY
I sure as hell am.

BEA
The quiet. He means listen to the quiet.

MS. MERCURY
Oh.
    (she does)
I am really trying here . . . but I don't
hear anything.

F.X.R.
The only time I feel like this quiet makes
me feel is . . .
    (whenever it is he keeps it to
    himself)
And it never lasts.

PHIL
It does around here.

BEA
I've come to marvel in its totality. No
matter the problems or worries, there's
solace in the quiet of the night.
    Phil looks at his wife. F.X.R.
    also looks at Bea. Ms.
    Mercury looks out into the
    night.

MS. MERCURY

Oh. I hear it now. Nothing. You mean
the sound of nothing.
(she listens)
Ooh. Aah.
A distant CAR HORN honks.
Headlights appear, and a
panel truck pulls into the
motel lot.

F.X.R.

So much for that.

BEA

That's Tommy Boyer.

PHIL

With that part for Bachelorette Number
One's car.
(to Ms. Mercury)
Since you're not fashionable, you might
like Tommy.

MS. MERCURY
(more eye rolling)
Gosh, let me fix my hair . . .

PHIL
(calling)
Tommy!

‖ 402 ‖

STAY WITH US

**From out of a truck comes
TOMMY BOYER. He is the
most gorgeous male creature
on the planet Earth.**

MS. MERCURY
That's Tommy Boyer?
(she is transfixed)
My lord . . .
She immediately **starts
primping her hair.**

MS. MERCURY (CONT'D)
Oh my. My my my . . .

BEA
He loves to cook.

MS. MERCURY
(licking her hair into place)
Are. You. Shitting. Me?
**The great Tommy Boyer
approaches. He carries an
engine part.**

TOMMY BOYER
Evening, Bea. Folks.

BEA
You eat, Tommy?

TOMMY BOYER

I did, thanks. You call for an old GM
fuel pump, Phil?

PHIL

Yep. For this little lady right here.
    Everyone can see that Ms.
    Mercury is smitten with Tommy.

TOMMY BOYER

Hi.

MS. MERCURY
    (giddy)
Howdy-oo-doody-doo!

TOMMY BOYER

Car problems, huh?

MS. MERCURY

Yes indeedy. Terrible that pesky little car
problems with of mine.

TOMMY BOYER

That it over there? The Buick.

MS. MERCURY

Is it a Buick? Yes. Our sad, bad broken
Buick . . .

TOMMY BOYER

Let's see if we can't get 'er running.

MS. MERCURY
Okeydokey. I'll come pop the hood . . .
(whispers to Bea)
I keep talking like a six-year-old.
Help me.

BEA
Tommy divorced three years ago. Has a
little girl. Gave up smoking last summer.
Reads a lot.

MS. MERCURY
Got it. Thanks.
**Off she goes with Tommy
Boyer.**

PHIL
Once again, the Motel Olympus works
its magic spell.

BEA
(rising)
I'm going to clean up. You men waste
time like you always do when women
start cleaning up.

PHIL
Okay.
(then to F.X.R.)
Care to patrol the perimeter?

CUT TO:

EXT. MOTEL OLYMPUS—EDGE OF
PROPERTY—NIGHT
**Out on the perimeter of the
motel property, Phil and
F.X.R. walk.**

PHIL
(pointing)
I was hoping to do something with
those ten acres over there, but nothing
ever came of it. I once almost put in a
snake hut.

F.X.R.
A snake hut?

PHIL
Yeah. We'd have signs out on Eighty-
eight—"Visit the Snake Hut: 140 miles."
"Snake Hut: 62 miles. Air-Conditioned!"
But then Bea pointed out that I knew
very little about raising snakes. So, we
just made do with the motel.

F.X.R.
It's a lovely motel. An hospitable little
place. I love the name.

PHIL
Can't stay here 24/7 without going
nuts. One day a week, each of us gets
a solo trip to Chesterton to go to the
bank, do some shopping. Use the wi-fi
at Theo's Coffee Hutch. Connect to
the outside world a couple of hours a
week.

F.X.R.
(wistful)
That's the way to do it.
**(recovers his "folksy"
personality)**
If I ever get one of those laptop computer
pads, I'll try that.
Phil eyes F.X.R. as they walk.

PHIL
What middle name starts with X? Other
than Xavier?
(then)
Francis Xavier Rustan.
**F.X.R. stops. Knows he's been
busted.**
Bea fingered you, when you signed the
register. F.X.R. You ever heard the phrase
'nom-dee-plume'?

F.X.R.
(no longer "folksy")
I'm sorry I was dishonest with you.

PHIL
You weren't. Other than being a rich and
famous man in a poor man's car.
(then)
You on some incognito vacation lark?

F.X.R.
Well, no.

PHIL
You going to sue us over the name, like
Olympus is a trademark you own?

F.X.R.
I don't operate that way.

PHIL
You're one of the few.

F.X.R.
I'm looking for land and sunshine.

PHIL
Lotta both around here. The land will
cost you. The sun is free.
(then, pointing)

We own from over there to over there.
We ain't going to be around much
longer, according to both the doctors and
common sense. We would like to close
out our days someplace as nice as what
we've had here.

> F.X.R.
> So, should I make you an offer?

> PHIL
> **(stopping him with a hand)**
> You talk business with Bea. She's my
> boss.
> **(then)**
> I'm going to head back for a cup of
> Ovaltine.
> **F.X.R. watches the old
> man go.**

CUT TO:

EXT. MOTEL OLYMPUS, PARKING LOT—
NIGHT

The hood is up on the Buick. Ms. Mercury is
holding the light for Tommy Boyer, passing him
tools.

MS. MERCURY
So, the metric tools are **different** from
standard tools?

TOMMY BOYER
Them's the facts.
    (then)
Okay. Try to start 'er up.
    She hops behind the wheel.

MS. MERCURY
Okay! Startin' me up!
    **She turns the key. The Buick
    roars into life!**

MS. MERCURY (CONT'D)
Hot damn! You must have read a lot of
books on car fixing!
    F.X.R. walks up.
Boss! Tommy Boyer and me are going to
take the car out . . . for a test drive.

TOMMY BOYER
We are?

MS. MERCURY
Gotta see how it handles a long stretch of
Eighty-eight! We'll be gone for a while.
So don't wait up. Not that you would.

Wait up. For me to come back. From test
driving the car . . .
    (finally, to Tommy)
Wanna take shotgun?
    Tommy gets in the car and
    buckles his seat belt. Ms.
    Mercury hits the RADIO
    on and then gears into
    REVERSE. She and Tommy
    peel out into the night.

MUSIC: "We've Only Just Begun" by the
Carpenters

INT. MOTEL OFFICE—NIGHT

TYPING is heard. F.X.R. enters to find Bea at a
desk pecking on a typewriter. An Olympia.

    F.X.R.
It true you have Ovaltine?

    BEA
The hot plate.
    F.X.R. finds a pan of milk, a
    cup, a jar, and makes himself
    a hot malty beverage.

BEA (CONT'D)
I'm gouging you a little on the facilities,
knowing you'll tear everything down
anyway.

You planning on getting all the land
around here?

F.X.R.
If I can.

BEA
Then we'll be your first purchase. Kind
of an honor for us.

**He looks at the photograph
of Bea and Phil, the original
source for the dead sign out
front.**

F.X.R.
How old were you when this was taken?

**She sees him looking at that
photo.**

BEA
I was nineteen. Phil was twenty-three.
Our honeymoon. In Greece. An island so
warm, so quiet we didn't want to leave.
Had to, of course. He went into the Air
Force. I finished school. Came driving up

old Eighty-eight and saw a place to sink
all our savings into. Worked out pretty
well.

**She pulls the paper from the
machine and hands it to him.**
Your lawyers will put their fingerprints
all over this, but it's the basics—take it or
leave it.

He doesn't even look at it.

F.X.R.

Ever go back to Greece? On vacation?

BEA

We're moteliers. Every day is a vacation.

CUT TO:

EXT. MOTEL OLYMPUS, PHRYGIA—PARKING
LOT—LATER

F.X.R. folds a typed piece of paper, tucks it into
his breast pocket as he walks back to his room.
Behind him, the lights go off in the office, and
the dim spotlight goes out on the old sign.

He pauses in the quiet night . . .

FADE OUT.

MUSIC: "Mi Reina y Mi Tesoro"

SUBTITLES: "Now I know

That I truly love her . . ."

FADE IN

EXT. MOTEL OLYMPUS, PHRYGIA—EARLY
EVENING

The sun is well down as the light of day fades to
blue.

SUBTITLES: "I will work hard

To conquer her heart . . ."

A PARTY is going on. LIGHTS strung across the
parking lot bring a magic to the growing night.

Jesus Hildalgo is there with his BAND playing to
COUPLES dancing. As he sings about his queen
and loving her with all his heart, his extended
family is there, with KIDS splashing in the newly
filled swimming pool.

STAY WITH US

Tommy Boyer is there with his little DAUGHTER and her PALS playing JUMP ROPE with a very different looking Ms. Mercury, who now sports jeans and a halter top.

WORKMEN swarm around trucks, storing away tools, finally quitting work for the day.

Nicholas, the room service waiter, puts the finishing touches on a superb dinner that looks like something served on the lido deck of the Love Boat.

LOCALS from as far away as Chesterton have come around for the big party, having brought their own lawn chairs.

F.X.R. is dressed in a fine, yet casual suit. He is talking over plans on a blueprint with a HALF DOZEN ARCHITECTS.

In two chairs, dual places of honor, sit Phil and Bea, who both have **To Tell the Truth**–style blindfolds over their eyes.

> BEA
> Oh, I've missed that man and his 'cordine!

PHIL
From the way things sound, we're gonna
see a circus when we take these things off.
As Bea sways to the
Mexican melody, a Foreman,
COLLINS, comes over and
whispers something to F.X.R.,
who then smartly dismisses
the architects.

F.X.R.
Ms. Mercury! We're ready.

MS. MERCURY
(turning that jump rope)
Who is Ms. Mercury?
F.X.R.
Oh. Sorry. Old habit.
(tries again)
Diane! We're ready!

MS. MERCURY
Okay, F.X.! Be right there!
(to Tommy's daughter)
Come on, Lizzie. Let's go see the show!
Jesus concludes his music
with a flourish. There is
applause for the band.
F.X.R. goes to Phil and Bea.

F.X.R.
You guys peek? Tell the truth.

PHIL
No!

BEA
You aren't lining up a firing squad,
are you?

F.X.R.
Diane, is it dark enough?

MS. MERCURY
I say yes.

F.X.R.
Okay. Collins!
**Collins is at the main power
switch.**

COLLINS
Shutting down!
**Collins shuts OFF all the
lights in the motel lot. The
place is dark now.**

F.X.R.
Okay. You may remove your blindfolds.
They do. All is dark.

PHIL
Hell, I can't see a thing.

BEA
Where am I supposed to look?

PHIL
Where's the bloody circus?

F.X.R.
(a shout)
Let there be light!
> Collins throws another
> switch. The parking lot,
> and all the people in it,
> are suddenly bathed in . . .
> shades of red, blue, and
> golden neon light.
> Ms. Mercury's face
> sees something so very
> beautiful. Tommy Boyer
> is with her, holding his
> daughter.

TOMMY BOYER
Wow . . .
> The guests, every one of
> them glowing, look up in awe
> into the sky.

MS. MERCURY
Oh, lord! What a heavenly light!

CLOSE ON: Phil and Bea, the lights playing across their faces like a magic show in the heavens, are silent . . .

THE SIGN

Big Phil and Big Bea, illuminated in colors brilliant and bold, greet the world like twin giants in the nighttime sky. "Stay with us!" they say, arms raised, bright, hospitable, young.

The sign is beautiful. Truly beautiful.
> **Bea reaches out and takes her husband's hand. They look into each other's eyes.**

> BEA
> It's like we'll live here forever . . .
> **F.X.R. hears this. He looks up at the sign. The colors play on his face, too.**

> CUT TO:

EXT. MOTEL OLYMPUS—THE WHOLE PLACE—SAME

The sign dominates the vision of the Motel Olympus.

And then . . .

The landscape slowly TRANSFORMS into that of a . . .

BUSTLING CROSSROADS.

The empty desert becomes filled with neatly ordered buildings, each an architectural gem.

The OLYMPUS SOLAR ENERGY COLLECTION FIELD has been built, stretching far into the distance.

Phrygia has grown into a lovely small city . . .

Around that landmark of a sign . . .

Around Bea and Phil, who will, for generations, bid all who pass by to **Stay with us**.

FADE TO BLACK.

Go See Costas

Ibrahim had been true to his word. For the price of one bottle of Johnnie Walker Red Label, he had provided Assan with two, most certainly stolen but that didn't matter to either of them. In those days, American liquor was more valuable than gold, even more valuable than American cigarettes.

With both bottles clanking in his knapsack, Assan, dressed in his nearly new blue pin-striped suit, searched the many tavernas of the port city of Piraeus, looking for the chief of the **Berengaria**. It was known that the chief savored the taste and effects of Johnnie Walker Red Label. It was also known that the **Berengaria** was taking cargo to America.

Assan found the chief at the Taverna Antholis, trying to enjoy his morning coffee. "I don't need another fireman," he told Assan.

"But I know ships. I speak many languages. I am good with my hands. And I never brag." Assan smiled at his little joke. The chief did not. "Ask anyone on the **Despotiko**."

The chief waved to the waiter boy for another coffee.

"You are not Greek," he said to Assan.

"Bulgarian," Assan told him.

"What is this accent of yours?" During the war, the chief had done a lot of business with Bulgarians, but this one talked in an odd cadence.

"I'm from the mountains."

"A Pomak?"

"Is that a bad thing?"

The chief shook his head. "No. Pomaks are quiet and tough. The war was hard on the Pomaks."

"The war was hard on everyone," Assan said.

The boy brought the chief his other coffee. "How long have you been on the **Despotiko**?" the chief asked.

"Six months, now."

"You want me to hire you so you can jump ship in America." The chief was no idiot.

"I want you to hire me because you have the oil fuel. A fireman checks the bubble in the tube is all. He doesn't shovel the coal. Too long with a shovel and it becomes all a man knows."

The chief lit a cigarette without offering one to Assan. "I don't need another fireman."

Assan reached into the knapsack between his feet, pulled out a bottle of Johnnie Walker Red Label in each fist, and set them on the table beside the chief's morning coffee. "Here. I am tired of carrying these around."

———

Three days out, some of the crew began giving the chief troubles. The Cypriot steward had a bad leg and didn't clean up after meals fast enough. The seaman Sorianos was a liar, saying he had checked the scuppers when he had not checked the scuppers. Iasson Kalimeris's wife had left him—again—so his hot head was even faster to flare. Every conversation with him turned into an argument, even over dominoes. Assan, though, caused no worries. He was never idle with a smoke in his lips, but was always wiping down valves or taking a wire brush to the rust. He played cards and dominoes quietly. And perhaps best of all he stayed away from the eyes of the captain. The captain noticed everything, the chief knew. But he did not notice Assan.

Past Gibraltar the ship met the heavy seas of the Atlantic. At sea, the chief rose early every morning, to wander the **Berengaria**, looking for possible headaches. This day, as usual, he climbed up to the bridge for the coffee that was always there, then worked his way down. He found all was well until he came to the fuel station and heard Bulgarian being spoken.

Assan was on his knees, rubbing the legs of a man leaning on the bulkhead, a man black with oily grime, his damp clothes sticking to his skin.

"I can walk now, let me stretch," said the filthy man, taking wobbly steps back and forth on the steel deck. He, too, spoke Bulgarian. "Ah. Feels good." The man drank deep from a bottle of water, then wolfed down a thick slice of bread from a wrapped bandanna.

"We are in the ocean now," Assan said.

"I could feel it. The ship, rocking." The man finished the bread and drank more water. "How much longer?"

"Ten days, maybe."

"I hope it's less."

"You better go back in," said Assan. "Here, your can."

Assan handed him an empty tin that once held biscuits, taking from the filthy man a can that was once for coffee but was now, the chief could smell, filled with sewage. Assan covered the tin with the bandanna and then handed over a corked bottle of water, and the filthy man crawled back into a hole, a narrow gap in the decking from where a plate had been lifted. With some struggle the filthy man squeezed through and was gone. Assan used a bar to lift and slide the steel plate back into place, like a puzzle piece.

———

The chief did not report what he saw to the captain. Instead he went back to his cabin and looked at the Johnnie Walker Red Label, two bottles, one for Assan, the other for his friend hiding in the half meter of space between the steel decking. On ships heading to America stowaways were not uncommon, and life was easier if eyes saw nothing and questions were not asked. Of course, sometimes a full coffin was off-loaded as a result.

Ah, the world was a mess. But it seemed a little less messy after a drink from the first open bottle. If someone else discovered the filthy man crawling around in the black space between decks, there would be hell to pay, plus all the paperwork for the captain. It was up to Assan. If the captain never found out, well, he would never find out.

———

Two storms at sea slowed down the **Berengaria**, then the ship had to wait two days at anchor until a harbor pilot finally came out in the little boat, climbed up the pilot ladder, and made his way to the bridge to guide the ship into the port. It was night by the time she was tied up at the dock, one ship of so many. The chief saw Assan at the rail, looking at the skyline of a city in the distance.

"That is Philadelphia, Pennsylvania. America."

"Where is Chee-ca-go?" asked the Bulgarian.

"Farther from Philadelphia than Cairo is from Athens."

"So far? Son of a gun."

"Philadelphia looks like paradise, eh? But when we dock in New York, New York, you will see a real American city."

Assan lit a smoke, offering one to the chief.

"Better cigarettes in America." The chief smoked, eyeing the Bulgarian, who had caused no problems for him. Not a single one. "Tomorrow they search the ship."

"Who?"

"American big shots. They search the ship, high and low, looking for stowaways. Communists."

At the mention of Communists, Assan spit over the rail.

"They count heads," the chief continued. "If the numbers don't match up, it's trouble. If they find nothing, we off-load and then go to New

York, New York. I will take you for a shave there. Better than the Turks can shave."

Assan said nothing for a moment. "If there are Communists on this ship I hope they find them," he said, spitting over the rail again.

———

Assan lay in his rack faking sleep as other crewmen came and went. At 4:00 a.m. he dressed quietly and slipped into the passageway, checking around each corner to make sure he was not seen. He made his way to the fuel station and used the iron bar to lift one plate of the steel decking and slide it open.

"It's now," Assan said.

Ibrahim crawled up from below, his elbows and knees rubbed raw and bleeding from living in the low, dark space between the deck and the ship's inner hull. How long had he been down there? Eighteen days? Twenty? Did it matter? "Let me get my can," Ibrahim whispered in a croak.

"Leave it. We go. Now."

"A second, please, Assan. My legs."

Assan massaged Ibrahim's legs for as long as he dared, then helped his friend to stand. Ibrahim had been on his feet only a few minutes each day. His back ached horribly and his knees were actually shaking.

"We have to go," Assan said. "Follow me by two meters. We wait at every corner. If you hear me speak to someone, hide where you can."

Ibrahim nodded, taking small steps, following.

A ladder led to a hatch that led to a room that led to another hatch and another passageway and another ladder. At the top of it, another passageway and one more ladder, though this was more like a stairway. Assan pulled on a heavy steel door that opened inward and halted. Ibrahim smelled fresh air for the first time in twenty-one days, that's how long it had been since the **Berengaria** had left Piraeus with Ibrahim hiding under the steel decking.

"It's okay," Assan whispered.

Ibrahim stepped through the doorway and was finally outside, the night a blessing, as his eyes tried to adjust. The air was warm, the air of summertime. They were at the portside rail, facing away from the dock, the water twelve meters below. Hours earlier, the ship's Pomak fireman had tied a rope, anonymous as any on deck, to the lowest rung of the rail. "Climb down this. Swim around to the dock and find a way up."

"I hope I can still swim," Ibrahim said. He was laughing like it was a funny joke.

"There are bushes nearby. Hide in them until I come tomorrow."

"What if there are dogs?"

"Make friends with them." That made Ibrahim laugh again as he swung over the rail, the rope in his hands.

———

The chief was with the captain on the starboard wing of the pilothouse taking their morning coffee. The longshoremen had off-loaded most of the cargo, and the docks were busy with trucks and cranes and workers.

"We'll go to the Waldorf Hotel," the captain said just as the chief saw Assan walking down the gangway and off the ship, with his knapsack that once held bottles of Johnnie Walker Red Label. He was carrying, too, a parcel under his arm. Crewmen returned to the ship with parcels, filled with goods they could buy only in America, under their arms. But here Assan was leaving with one.

"Big steaks, like this." The captain held up his fingers showing the thickness of what his steak would be. "The Waldorf Astoria Hotel. They have the steaks."

"That's a good place," the chief said as Assan disappeared into some bushes.

———

Assan found no sign of Ibrahim and was worried that American big shots had searched the bushes for Communists and uncounted heads with no papers. Not wanting to call out, he howled like a dog. He heard a dog howl back, but it was Ibrahim, who came out of the bushes, stripped to the waist and carrying his grease-caked shoes.

"Who's a big dog?" he asked, smiling.

"Were you all right through the night?"

"I made a bed of reeds," Ibrahim said. "Soft. And the night never got a chill."

Assan opened the parcel, showing some clothes and soap and food and a shaving kit. There was also a folded newspaper bound in twine. Inside was Ibrahim's share of the drachmas the two had saved from all the odd jobs they had worked in Greece. Ibrahim pocketed the bills without counting. "How much will a train cost to get to Chee-ca-go, Assan?"

"How much from Athens to Cairo? Find a money changer at the train station."

After Ibrahim had eaten and washed, Assan sat him down on a rock and took the razor to his face, shaving his friend, as there was no mirror for him to do it himself.

———

From the bridge wing, the chief searched the bushes through a pair of glasses. In a gap between waving branches, he saw Assan shaving the face of a man he could not recognize. A problem had left the ship without bothering the captain. No need for a coffin, either. Assan was one smart Pomak.

As Ibrahim ran a comb through his wet hair, Assan tried to clean his friend's shoes. "The best I can do," he said, handing them over.

Ibrahim reached into his pocket and pulled out a single drachma and slapped it into Assan's hand. "Here. A perfect shine on perfect shoes." Assan took a bow and both men laughed.

They walked together to the end of the dock-yards, able to mingle with others coming and going. They saw huge cars, trucks the size of houses grinding gears and pulling big loads, and more ships, some much larger and newer than the **Berengaria,** others rusted buckets. They saw men eating rolls with sausages in them at a kiosk with a sign Assan could spell out—he had been learn-ing the American letters—H O T D O G S. Both Bulgarians were hungry but neither had American money. At the end of the dockyards there was a gate with a guard in an office, but every American walked past without so much as a pause.

"Assan. I will see you in Chee-ca-go one day," Ibrahim said. Then in English he said, "Tenk choo berry mich."

"All I did was carry your shit away," Assan said, taking one cigarette, then giving the pack to Ibrahim. He smoked it while watching his friend walk to the gate, pass the guard with only a nod, and disappear down the road toward the skyline of Philadelphia.

———

Returning to the ship, Assan kept busy all morning, not getting to the galley until the first meal was nearly over and only a few of the crew were around. He collected what bread, vegetables, and soup was still available and sat at a table. The Cypriot with the limp brought him a coffee from the galley.

"America for the first time?" he asked Assan.

"Yeah."

"America is the top, I tell you. New York, New York, has anything you want. Wait until you see."

"The big shots. When do they come on board?" Assan asked.

"What big shots?"

"The Americans who search the ship. Looking for Reds. Making big trouble."

"The fuck you talking about?"

"They make sure our heads match. The chief told me. Big shots come and search the whole ship."

"Search for what?" The Cypriot went back to the galley for a coffee for himself.

"They check our papers, right? Line us up and check our papers?" Assan had lined up so many times to have his papers checked, it made sense that he'd do the same in America.

"The captain takes care of that shit." The Cypriot downed half of his coffee. "Hey, I know a whorehouse in New York City. Bring money tomorrow and I'll get us laid."

———

Back in his village, Assan had seen black-and-white movies flickering on a white wall. Sometimes the movies were American, with cowboys on horses shooting pistols that threw out long plumes of smoke. He liked best a newsreel that showed factories and construction sites and a new building rising to the sky in a city called Chicago; Chicago had many tall buildings and streets jammed with black sedans.

But New York, New York, looked like a city with no end, a city that threw a haze into the night sky, making the low clouds golden and the water shimmer like colored smoke. A hot wind blew as the ship moved slowly up the wide river, the city passing like a brilliant jeweled curtain; a solid mass of a million lighted windows, bright towers shining like castles, and twin lights of cars, so many cars, buzzing every which way like insects. Assan stood at the rail, the wind rippling his clothes, his mouth open, and his eyes wide.

"Son of a gun," he said to New York, New York.

———

In the morning, the chief found him at the fuel station. "Assan, put on that striped suit of yours. I want a shave."

"I have duties, here."

"I say you don't, and I'm the chief. Let's go. And leave your money here so you don't get pick-pocketed on your first day."

Cars flew down the streets, many of them colored yellow with words printed on their sides, screeching to stops at corners as people got out and different people got in. Lights in boxes mounted on poles flashed red then green then orange again and again. Signs were everywhere, attached to poles, walls, and in windows; so many that Assan stopped trying to make out the letters. Rich-looking Americans walked fast. Americans who didn't look rich hurried, too. Three black men, with muscles ripping at their sweat-stained shirts, were moving a large wooden crate up a stairway into a building. There was shouting and music and engines and radio voices coming from every-where.

A young man rode a two-wheeled motor bicycle, roaring by so fast, almost hitting Assan and the chief as they crossed a broad street. Assan had seen a newsreel with policemen on big motored bicycles, but that young man was not a cop. Could anyone ride such a thing in America?

They passed a kiosk selling papers, candy, drinks, cigarettes, magazines, combs, pens, and lighters. Two minutes later they passed another, selling the same goods. It turned out the kiosks were everywhere. A river of moving cars, people, crowded buses, trucks, and even horses pulling wagons flowed along streets that stretched to the edge of sight.

The chief walked fast. "In New York, New York, you have to walk like you are late for an important meeting or thieves mark you." They crossed street after street and rounded many corners. Assan had draped his blue pin-striped jacket over his arm. He was sweating and dizzy, his head too full of America.

The chief stopped at a corner. "Let me see. Where are we?"

"You don't know?"

"I'm just thinking of the best way to go from here." The chief looked around and saw something that made him laugh. "Will you look at that?"

Assan tilted his head and looked, too, up at a window on an upper floor of a building. He saw a flag in the window, posted like a sign—the blue and white flag of Greece with the cross for the church and the stripes for the sea and sky. A man in shirtsleeves and a loosened tie stood in the window, shouting into a telephone and waving a cigar.

"We Greeks are everywhere, no?" The chief laughed again, then held up the palm of his hand. "Look. New York, New York, is a simple city to learn. It is shaped like your hand. The numbered avenues are long and run from your fingertips to your wrist. The numbered streets run across the palm. Broadway is the lifeline and curves the length around. The two middle fingers are the Central Park."

Assan studied his own palm.

"Now those signs"—the chief pointed to two signs forming an X on a post—"tell us we are at Twenty-Sixth Street and Seventh Avenue. That puts us about right here, see?" The chief pointed to the map of his hand. "Twenty-Sixth and Seventh. Understand?"

"Like my hand. Son of a gun." Assan felt as though he understood. They continued walking up the shaded side of Seventh Avenue, then turned a corner. The chief stopped at steps that led into a basement barbershop.

"Here's the place," he said and stepped down to the door.

The place was for men only, not unlike barber-shops in the old country. Everyone looked over at the chief and Assan when they came in. A radio was playing, not music, but a man talking and talking over the sounds of a crowd in the background. Sometimes the crowd would roar or applaud. The shelves were lined with bottles of different-colored liquids. Cigarettes were smoked, so many that two standing ashtrays were overflowing with butts.

The chief spoke English to the older barber—there was another, younger barber, the son perhaps—then took a seat off to the side. Assan sat next to him, listening to the English and looking at the magazines with pictures of crooks with guns and women in tight skirts. Three Americans waited as well, until one of them took a place with the other barber, sitting in a big, comfortable chair made of leather and steel. After a customer paid and said something that made the men all laugh, he walked out the door and up the steps to the street. When another customer was done, he said something funny, too, gave the barber some coins, and was gone.

The chief took a seat in the big leather barber chair and spoke, pointing to Assan like he was explaining something. The barber looked at Assan and said "Yoo bet-cha." He draped a white cloth over the chief, pinned it tight behind his neck, then gave the chief a shave. Three times with the hot towel, the lather, and the razor, as close a shave as the Turks give a man in Constantinople. Then he trimmed the chief's hair, shaving around his ears and the back of his neck with the lather and razor. The men laughed and told stories, the chief using so much English he must be fluent, thought Assan. The Americans laughed and looked at Assan, as if he were in on the jokes.

When the chief was clean and smelled of spicy cologne, he paid the barber with paper money, said something in English, and pointed at Assan. The barber said "Yoo bet-cha" again and waved Assan into his chair.

As the barber draped his cloth around Assan, the chief spoke in Greek.

"A free shave. I paid already. And this is for you." The chief handed Assan a wad of folded paper money. American money. "A smart man like you will do well in America. Good luck." The last Assan saw of the chief was his shoes, climbing the steps back up to the street.

———

Assan walked, feeling his smooth face and smelling the cologne, as the late summer night fell on New York, New York, and the lights took on new warmth. He saw so many amazing things: a window filled with dozens of roasting chickens rotating on mechanical spits, a man selling windup toy cars on a box with a wooden rail nailed to the top to keep the toys from rolling off, and a restaurant with one wall all glass, where inside Americans sat at tables and on stools at a long counter. Waitresses swung around, carrying platters of complete meals and small dishes of cakes and pastries. Assan passed a long stairway that led down below the street, fenced in with decorated iron and crowded with people going up and others going down, all in a hurry and none of them easy marks for pocket pickers.

The buildings stopped and the sky opened up, and on the other side of a busy street there were thick trees. Assan figured he must be at his middle fingers, at the Central Park. He did not know how to cross the broad street but followed with others when they walked. By a low rounded wall a man with a cart was selling H O T D O G S, and Assan was suddenly very, very hungry. He pulled out the paper money the chief had given him, finding a bill with the number 1 on it. He handed the money to the man, who kept asking him questions that Assan had no answer for. The only word he could make out was Coca-Cola, the sum total of his English, really.

The man handed over a sausage sandwich that

was dripping with sauces of red and yellow and stringy, wet onions and a bottle of the Coca-Cola. Then the man gave Assan a fistful of coins of three different sizes, which he pocketed with his free hand. Assan sat on a bench and ate a most delicious meal. With half the Coca-Cola left, he went back to the man. He held out the coins, the man took one of the thinnest, and made another richly burdened sausage sandwich.

The sun had gone down and the sky was dark and the lampposts were shining as Assan walked along the paths of the beautiful park, finishing the Coca-Cola. Assan saw fountains and statues. He saw men and women as couples, holding hands and laughing. A rich lady walked a tiny dog, the funniest dog Assan had ever seen. He almost howled at it as a joke, but Assan thought maybe the rich lady would complain to a cop, and the last thing he wanted was a cop asking for his papers.

At a side entrance to the park, a gate in a wall, Assan came to where the city began again. It was late now, and people were crossing the street, heading into the park with blankets and pillows. Assan could see these people were not like the rich lady with her dog, but families of white and black and brown people with giggling kids and men and women who looked tired from a day's work. Assan suddenly felt so very tired, too. He followed a family back into the park, coming to a big field of grass, where others were laying out blankets and bedding to sleep outdoors in the hot, humid night. Some were already asleep. Others hushed their kids and made sleeping spots near the trees on the border of the field.

Assan found a spot with soft grass. He removed his shoes and used his jacket as a pillow. He fell asleep to the sounds of distant traffic and quiet conversations between husbands and wives.

———

Assan washed his face in a public restroom in a stone building. Flicking his fingers, he brushed his pants and suit jacket and shook out his nice shirt, then put his clothes back on, wondering where he would walk today.

That was when he thought of the man who had been shouting into a telephone, the man who made the chief laugh, the man in the window with the Greek flag. Where was that again? He looked at the palm of his hand, at the map there, and remembered the chief saying Twenty-Sixth Street and Seventh Avenue, and Assan knew he could find it again.

No one was in the window at Twenty-Sixth and Seventh when Assan looked up, but the Greek flag was there. Assan found an entryway nearby that had a small sign with another small Greek flag on it and words in Greek: THE HELLENIC INTERNATIONAL SOCIETY. Assan went through the door and up the stairs.

The day was already hot and the office was sweltering, even with the door ajar and the windows cracked open. Assan heard music playing—a slow tune with a voice repeating words. **Ay . . . ay . . . ay . . . space . . . es . . . es . . . es . . . space.** A **clacking** typewriter noise came with each word. **Dee . . . clack . . . dee . . . clack . . . dee . . . clack.** At the office door, Assan saw only a messy desk and some easy chairs.

Eff . . . clack . . . eff . . . clack . . . eff . . . clack . . . space . . . thunk. Assan stepped inside. A girl was in the small inner office, sitting in front of a small green typewriter on a tiny table. She was concentrating on the fingers of her left hand, pressing the keys that matched the instructions on the record. Assan stayed quiet, not wanting to disturb the typing lesson.

"**Tikanis.**"

Assan turned. The man who had been yelling into the telephone yesterday was walking in, carrying a small paper bag. "Who are you?" the man asked in Greek.

"Assan Chepik."

"Not Greek?"

"No, Bulgarian. But I come from Greece. I saw the flag."

The man pulled a cardboard cup filled with what smelled like coffee from the paper bag, along with a round cake with a hole in the middle. "You did not tell me you were coming today, Assan, or I would have brought you breakfast!" The man laughed out loud. "Dorothy! We need another coffee for Assan, here."

Ell . . . ell . . . ell . . . space. "I just started a lesson!"

"Pick up the needle. When Bulgarians are hungry they get nutsy." The man turned to Assan. "Dorothy will get you a coffee. At least it's what they say is coffee here."

Assan sipped a hot drink, mostly milk and sugar with something of a coffee taste. Dorothy was back at her typewriter, **clacking** along with the record. **You . . . you . . . you . . . space . . . eye . . . eye . . . eye . . . space.** Demetri Bakas, which was the man's name, asked questions of Assan. Assan told of his job on the **Berengaria** and that just yesterday he had left the ship, but said nothing of Ibrahim hiding between the decking or getting off in the city called Philadelphia.

Assan also said nothing of the four years since

the war ended, nothing about all his attempts at crossing the border between Bulgaria and Greece. He did not tell of the early morning when his brother made the mistake of starting a fire to heat some water. They were in the mountains, had slept between two rocks, and were planning to move along quickly, but Assan had some coffee in his pocket. His brother wanted just one cup, for energy he said, but he really wanted the taste of hot coffee on a cold morning. The Communist bounty hunters had been trailing after them and saw the smoke from the fire. Assan had been taking a shit on the other side of a copse of trees. Unseen, he watched his brother put up a fight and a Communist shoot him in the head. He didn't tell Demetri about the man he'd had to kill, either. Assan was drinking from a stream that ran alongside a path when a local man almost stumbled upon him. The man wore a Party pin on his threadbare jacket, and the look in his eyes said all Assan needed to know. The man was running back to whatever village was nearby to report seeing a traitor making for the border, but Assan chased him down, hit him with a rock, then threw his body down into a gully. And Assan was silent about the time he finally arrived in Athens and made a friend who told him to go to a certain house where refugees like him lived together. When Assan went to the house, he was beaten up, thrown into an unmarked truck, and taken back across the border into Bulgaria, handcuffed to others who had fallen for the traitor's trick. Assan said nothing of the Communist captain who chained him to a chair, then yelled questions at him and, not liking the answers, used his fists and then special tools as he yelled the questions again and again. Assan said nothing of the camp, of the prisoners he saw shot in the camp, of the prisoners he saw hanged in the camp.

He said nothing of the girl he met after his release, of their short romance, or of how hungry they always were. He didn't say her name was Nadezhda or tell of her becoming pregnant, or of their marriage just months before a boy was born, his son, named Petar. He said nothing about his young wife struggling during the birth and the midwife not knowing how to stop the bleeding. Without his mother's milk, the boy lived only a month. Demetri did not hear of Assan's son, Petar.

Assan said nothing of his arrest for stealing empty bottles, even though he had not stolen any empty bottles. His name was on a list, so he was again sent to prison. Assan said nothing of his fourth attempt at escape, his arrest, his year in the work camp, of meeting Ibrahim there and the night the train came by and separated them from the guards on the other side of the track and how they threw down their shovels and jumped into the river. He said nothing of the farmer who found them miles away, wet and freezing, who could have turned them in to the Party official in the village, but instead gave them hot food as their uniforms dried. He gave them some money, too—twenty levs each.

Assan and Ibrahim bought tickets for the bus to the mountains near the border with Greece. When the police came on board to check papers, they had none. But their prison uniforms happened to be the same as the ones for privates in the army, just with no patches or insignia. When Assan told the cop that they were reporting to the Army Hospital because they were carriers of typhus, the cop's eyes went huge at the word **typhus** and he nearly ran off the bus.

They crossed the border high in the mountains. In Athens they earned drachmas with picks and shovels, with their hands and their backs for most of that year until Assan got the fireman job on the **Despotiko,** shoveling coal into the boiler as the ferry made its way between Piraeus and the many Hellenic islands.

Assan said nothing of all that, but only of being

a fireman on the **Berengaria** with the oil bubble in the tube, and now here he was in America having jumped ship.

Demetri knew there was much more to Assan's story but didn't care. "Do you know what I can do for you, out of this office?"

"Teach me to type?" Dorothy was now pecking out **Cap . . . thunk . . . Cue . . . clack . . . space . . . thunk . . . Cap . . . thunk . . . Double-You . . . clack . . . space . . . thunk.**

Demetri laughed loudly. "We have good people who will help us help you. It will take time. But let me tell you right now, if you get into any problem with the law—any problem with the police—everything becomes trouble. Understand?"

"Sure. Of course."

"Okay. Now. You are going to learn to speak English. Here is an address of a free school. It meets nights. Just walk in, sign up, and pay attention."

Assan took the address.

"You have anything of value you can sell? Anything gold or fancy from the old country?"

"Nothing. I left everything on the ship."

"My old man did the same thing. In 1910." Demetri pulled a cigar from his jacket pocket. "Come back in a few days and we'll have some spare clothes for you. Dorothy! Size up Assan for a couple pairs of pants. Some shirts, too!"

"When I'm done!" Dorothy never looked away from her keyboard. **Cap. Tee. Space. Cap. Gee. Space. Thunk-clack-thunk-clack . . .**

"You have any lines on a job, Assan?" Demetri lit his cigar in a ball of fire that came from a huge match.

Assan had no lines on a job.

"Go here. It's downtown." Demetri wrote something on another piece of paper and handed it to Assan. "Ask for Costas."

"Costas. Okay." Assan was leaving the office just as the typing record stopped and Dorothy turned it over for lesson two.

———

The address was very low on Assan's palm, down where streets had no numbers and went every which way. He spent most of the day tramping the odd-shaped blocks, going round and round and passing the same points more than once. He finally found the place, a little restaurant, with a sign that said OLYMPIC GRILL surrounded by a Greek key border. There were all of four little tables connected to the wall with leather benches and eight of the pole stools at a counter. Every seat was taken and the cafe was hot. A woman was behind the counter, too busy to look at Assan until he stood in one place a bit too long. She barked at him in Greek: "Wait outside for a seat, fool!"

"I am here to see Costas," Assan said.

"What?" the woman shouted.

"I am here to see Costas!" Assan shouted back.

"Honey!" the woman hollered, turning her back on Assan. "Some fool is asking for you!"

Costas was a short man with a brush for a mustache. He had no time to speak to Assan but did anyway.

"What do you want?"

"Are you Costas?" Assan asked.

"What do you want?"

"A job," Assan said with a laugh.

"Oh, Jesus," Costas said, turning away.

"Demetri Bakas sent me to see you."

"Who?" Costas was clearing dishes and taking money from a customer.

"Demetri Bakas. He told me you would have a job for me."

Costa stopped what he was doing and looked Assan in the eye; he was so short he had to lean back to glare at the Bulgarian.

"Get the fuck out of here!" The customers who spoke Greek looked up from their meals. The ones who only spoke American kept on eating. "And don't come back!"

Assan turned and got the fuck out of there.

———

The walk back to the two middle fingers of the Central Park took a very long time. The air was so hot and thick—Assan's shirt became wet against his back and didn't dry. He walked and walked along one avenue, until bright flashing lights shone down on a place where nine streets seemed to collide in a storm of people, buses, yellow cars, and even soldiers on horses, or maybe they were cops. Assan had never been in the middle of so many people, with everyone going everywhere.

In a huge cafeteria, he spent coins on another sausage H O T D O G and a paper cup filled with sweet juice, ice cold, and as delicious as any drink he'd ever had—even Coca-Cola. He stood as he ate, like most of the people in the place, though he wanted to take off his shoes more than any-thing in the world. Across the triangle of streets and humanity, he recognized what was a cinema, with a chain of lights chasing each other around and around. Assan saw the price—forty-five cents. That was four of the smallest coins in his pocket and a larger, thicker coin that had a humpbacked cow printed on one side. Assan suddenly wanted to sit in a nice seat, take off his shoes, and see a movie. He hoped it would be about Chicago.

The cinema was like a cathedral, with uniformed men and women directing a stream of people to seats, chattering couples, and young men in groups, everyone talking loud and barking in laughter. The columns were like those in the Parthenon in Athens, modern angels were etched in gold on the wall, and a deep red curtain stood thirty meters tall.

Assan took off his shoes just as the curtain opened and a short movie appeared on a screen as big as the hull of the **Berengaria**. Music played as fancy words flipped and spun on the screen, appearing and disappearing so fast Assan couldn't sound out a single letter. The movie showed ladies dancing and men arguing. Then another short movie played, with more music and flying words. This movie had boxers in it and skies full of airplanes. A third short movie showed a very serious woman saying very serious things, then weeping, then running down a street calling out a name, then that movie was over. A moment later the screen burst into vivid colors as a funny-looking man dressed like a cowboy, but not a real cowboy, and a gorgeous woman with black hair and the reddest of lips sang songs and said things that made the cathedral echo with laughter. Despite that, Assan soon fell asleep hard and deep.

The next day there was no one at the Hellenic Society. The whole city seemed quiet, with fewer people coming up out of the stairways that led to tunnels and many of the buildings empty. Assan found the address for the English lessons, a building on Forty-Third Street, but there was no one around the place to speak English with.

When Assan returned to the park, though, it seemed like all the buildings surrounding the two middle fingers had emptied into the trees, the paths, the playgrounds, and the broad green fields. Kids and families were everywhere—in a zoo, in rowboats, sliding around on shoes with wheels attached, at a concert of music, with dogs playing, and kids throwing, catching, and kicking all kinds of balls. Assan liked the dogs the most and watched them for the longest time.

When clouds darkened the sky late in the afternoon, the families packed up, the games of ball stopped, and the park emptied. Rain came soon after, so Assan found a covered archway and ended up spending the night there, sharing the spot with a few other men who slept on boxes and covered themselves with only their jackets. None of them spoke any of the languages Assan knew. None of the others seemed happy at all, but Assan had been stuck in the rain before and was not at all miserable. He had hidden under bridges, been in wet clothes, walked for days, even run from men in the old country who had the same faces of misery as these guys. This? This was nothing.

In the morning, Assan woke with a cough in his throat.

―――

"These pants should fit you." Dorothy was speaking Greek. "The boots, too. Try them on in the lavatory in the hall."

"What is the lavatory?" Assan had never heard that word.

"The toilet. The men's room."

The pants fit well enough. The used boots not only fit his small feet but were already broken in. Dorothy gave him stockings, a few different shirts, two pairs of heavy pants—all felt good after so many days in his blue pin-striped suit, which Dorothy took from him for cleaning.

"What happened to that Bulgarian guy who was here Friday?" Demetri walked in with a bag of round cakes with holes in the middle and more sweet American coffee. "Assan? You look like you live in Jersey!"

Dorothy sat down at her typewriter again and put on another record. Music played in a faster tempo—**Cap tee aitch eee space cue you eye see kay space**—as Dorothy clattered at the keys.

"Did you see Costas?" Demetri asked.

Assan sipped his coffee and bit into a round cake, which hurt his throat but tasted good. "Yeah. He told me to get the fuck out." Assan glanced through the door to Dorothy, who luckily did not hear his foul language.

"Hah! Costas must not have liked the way you looked. But now, you look like a guy from Hoboken, like Sinatra on a weekend." Assan had no idea what that meant. "Costas owes me, so you go back and tell him I sent you. You did tell him I sent you, right?"

"He didn't care who sent me."

"Tell him I sent you."

———

Assan again walked all the way downtown, arriving at the Olympic Grill when only half its seats were occupied. Costas sat on the stool farthest away from the door, reading a newspaper with a cup of coffee in front of him, so short he swung his legs back and forth, like a little boy. Assan approached, waiting for Costas to look up from his paper. But he didn't.

"Demetri says you will give me a job."

Costas kept reading. "Huh?" he said, writing a word on an open tablet with a pencil. There were many words on the page.

"Demetri Bakas. He sent me to see you."

Costas didn't move, but managed to change his focus from the newspaper and the list of words to Assan.

"What the hell? What is this?"

"Demetri Bakas. Said to see you for a job. Because you owe him."

Costas turned back to his reading and writing. "I owe Demetri Bakas shit. Order something or get out of here."

"He said to see you for a job."

Costas was off the stool with fire in his dark eyes. "Where are you from?" he shouted.

"Bulgaria, but I come from Athens."

"Go back to Athens! I can do nothing for you! You know where I was when you were jerking off in your shit-filled barn in Bulgaria? I was here! I was in America. And you know what I was doing? Getting my ass kicked for even thinking about this restaurant!"

"But Demetri said to go see Costas. So, I came."

"He can kiss my ass and you can go piss in a hat! I feed cops here! They'll crack your head open if I ask. Come back again and it's the cops for you!"

Assan hurried out of the diner. What else could he do? He didn't want trouble with any cops.

———

The day was as hot as ever. The roar of cars and buses was as loud as a storm wind. The chatter of so many people who all had jobs and money in their pockets and few worries clogged Assan's ears. His throat was burning and his legs felt like bags of sand.

He was heading to Forty-Third Street and the English lessons, but stopped in a tiny, triangular patch of grass and trees as a wave of ache came over him. A new pain in his head knocked and knocked, right above his eyes. At a drinking fountain he cupped his hand to collect enough water to slurp but the fire in his throat would not go out. He saw two men sharing a bench in the shade, a bench large enough for four, and he wanted to sit down very quickly. Then a violent, invisible punch to his stomach bent him in two and sickness came out of his insides.

A man was asking him questions he could not understand as another led him by the shoulder to the shade of the bench and someone, a lady maybe, gave him a kerchief to wipe his mouth. Someone handed him a bottle of warm soda water, which Assan used to rinse and spit out. Someone yelled at him for doing that, but Assan said nothing. He leaned his head back on the bench and closed his eyes.

————

He thought he slept for a few minutes, but when he opened his eyes the shadows were longer and different people were in the tiny park. Americans who ignored a napping man on a bench.

Assan reached into his pocket. His American paper money was gone. Some coins remained, that was all. Just as the Chief had warned, he had stopped moving and a thief had pocket-picked him. His head ached as he sat for a very long time.

As the afternoon became early evening, he didn't want to walk all the way up to the Central Park, but a cop came around and eyed him. So, he got moving. An hour or so later he was asleep under a park tree, his head on his rolled-up pair of extra pants.

————

There were other people in Demetri's office, all wearing suits and carrying leather cases filled with papers. None of them were Greeks. Demetri was standing in the window, yelling into the telephone, in English, as he had the first day Assan saw this place. Two of the men in suits laughed at something Demetri said, others lit cigarettes. One man blew smoke rings. Assan could hear Dorothy typing, **clack clack clack** without the aid of the record playing music.

"Hold on," Demetri said, seeing Assan, cupping his hand around the telephone. "Dorothy has your suit. Dorothy!"

Every eye in the office looked at Assan, his rumpled clothes, the growth of his beard, seeing another of the poor, ignorant bastards that were forever showing up in Demetri's office. Dorothy came out with the suit on a wire hanger; the jacket and pants were crisp and fresh, his shirt folded into a square like a tablecloth. Assan took his clothes and backed out of the office, nodding his thanks. The eyes and faces of the men in the office had him feeling small, like in the old country when soldiers searched him, roughed him up, and checked his papers longer than necessary, like when the guards made him stand and answer questions over and over, or like when he and the other prisoners in the camps were lined up for the roll calls that took hours.

As he descended the steps to the street, he heard a burst of laughter from the men and Dorothy taking back up her typing: **clack-clack clack. Clack.**

As Costas was counting out his supply of change in the cash register, a man in a clean blue-striped suit took a stool at the counter. The lunch rush would be picking up soon, the regulars would come and go until after 3:00 p.m., and Costas would need to make change for paper money. After that, Costas would have time to read the paper and find his list of new words. English was not a hard language to learn as long as you studied the newspaper every day and had a lot of American customers to listen to talk and talk and talk.

His wife was wiping down the tables, so it was Costas who asked the man in the clean and pressed blue pin-striped suit, "What can I bring ya, pal?"

Assan laid his few coins on the counter, the last of the money in his pocket. "A coffee, please. American coffee, sweet, with milk."

Costas recognized Assan and flushed with anger. "You some kind of joker?"

"I make no jokes."

"Demetri send you back here? Again?"

"No. I just came for a coffee."

"Bullshit you came for just a coffee!" Costas was so angry he slammed a mug down so hard in front of the coffee urn he cracked it. "Nico!" he yelled.

A boy, as short as Costas, popped out from the kitchen. "Huh?"

"More coffee mugs!"

Nico carried out a tray of heavy mugs for the American coffee. There was no way the boy was not Costas's son. The only differences between them were twenty years and ten kilos.

Costas almost tossed the hot coffee into Assan's lap. "That's a nickel!" he said, taking one of the thick coins off the counter, the one with the humpbacked cow. Assan poured milk and sugar into the mug and stirred slowly.

"You walk into my place and think that because you made it to America a job is waiting for you." Costas was leaning on the counter, so short his eyes were equal with Assan's. "You go cry to that Corfu bastard and he says, 'Go see Costas,' and I'm supposed to pay you to work for me?"

Assan sipped his coffee.

"What the hell is your name?"

"Assan."

"Assan? Not even Greek and here for a job!"

"Today I'm here for coffee."

Costas was rocking on his heels, like a man so angry he could leap across the counter and start a fight. "I'm supposed to be so rich I must have jobs for anyone, eh? 'Costas is a big shot! He has his own restaurant! He does so much business he has jobs coming out of his ass! You can come to America and work for him!' Bullshit!"

Assan's mug was almost emptied. "Can I have another, please?"

"No! No more coffee for you!" Costas stared Assan in his eyes for a long moment. "Bulgarian, huh?"

"That's right." Assan had finished the coffee, setting the mug on the counter.

"Okay then," Costas said. "Now take off that nice jacket and hang it on a hook in the back. Nico will teach you how to scrub the pots."

Our Town Today with Hank Fiset

YOUR EVANGELISTA, ESPERANZA

CUPPA JOE, PAL? Addicted to the stuff! Coffee, that is. I'm a newsman, you see, and the newsroom that doesn't run on coffee puts out a lousy paper, I'll bet. The pots here at the **Tri-Cities Daily News/Herald** are filled to the brim, even as most of the staff head out for the ubiquitous high-end spots, the ones with baristas and flavor shots for six bucks a throw. A tour of the caffeine parlors in our three conjoined metropolises will prove that good wake-'em-up is roasted, brewed, pressure-steamed, and poured in damn fine style. Try Amy's Drive-Thru, a converted taco stand on the Miracle Mile. She'll pop your eyes wide with a triple-bang espresso with a hot-pepper stirrer. . . . The Corker & Smythe Coffee Shop in the old Kahle Mercantile Building on Triumph Square just recently offered takeout, and reluctantly at that. Better to sit at the counter and sip that **nectar d'noir** out of those deep porcelain mugs. . . . Kaffee Boss has three stores—one at Wadsworth and Sequoia—serving the locals in leather-sleeved mason jars. Whatever you do, don't ask for milk or creamer. They are coffee purists and make a point of telling you why. Java-Va-Voom on Second Boulevard at North Payne in East Corning has something no other coffee place can match—a unique sound. There is the **whissh** of the frother, the chitter-chatter of the staff and customers, and music, soft, in the background, like the musical score of a movie playing next door. Occasionally, there is also the **click-clack** made by a typist, but in no ordinary sense of the word.

* * *

ESPERANZA CRUZ-BUSTERMENTE, born and raised in nearby Orangeville, is an Account Adviser for a local bank, though, to many people, that is her **second** job. Many folks know her as an **evangelista**, a typist who uses her words-per-minute skills for other people. In Old Mexico, educated nuns served their flocks by typing important documents— applications, receipts, official papers, tax records, sometimes even love letters for the illiterate and those who lacked access to the once-technological marvel that is a typewriter. Esperanza's parents, like many others, learned touch typing from the **evangelistas,** then made a living by typing the messages, missives, and memoranda needed by the public. No one got rich, but sentences got stamped into paper.

* * *

ESPERANZA HAS A table at a Java-Va-Voom, where, with her large drip-with-soy, she works from a stack of blank, naked pages at the ready beside her typewriter. She's been using the place for a while now. For those unfamiliar with the sound and rhythm of a typewriter in use, Esperanza's **clacking** took some getting used to. "There were complaints at first," Esperanza told me. "I'd be typing away and get asked why I wasn't working on a laptop, which is quieter and easier. Once, two policemen walked in and I thought, Have they called the cops on me? Turns out, they were just coming in for lattes."

* * *

WHY GO ANALOG? "My email was hacked," Esperanza told me. By who? "The Russians? The NSC? Fake Nigerian princes? Who knows? My data was stolen. My life was such a mess for months." These days she uses the Internet sparingly and has an old-style flip phone, with which she can text but which she prefers to use the old-style way—by getting and receiving actual telephone calls. She never has to ask for the wi-fi password. And as for Facebook, Snapchat, Instagram, et al.? "Gave them up," she says, almost bragging. "When the hack happened and I went off social media, my day gained, like, six hours! I spent so long checking my phone every few minutes. Never mind how much time I wasted playing SnoKon, catching colored balls of ice in a little triangle cup for points." The only negative? "My friends had to be taught how to get ahold of me." What is written, exactly, on that typewriter of hers? "Lots! I have a big family. Birthdays, the nieces and nephews get a letter and a five- or ten-dollar bill. I write memos for work that I either copy or rewrite and email at the office. And here . . ." She held up a page filled with the neatest, most perfectly formatted document you could ask for. "This is my grocery list."

* * *

OTHER CUSTOMERS SEEK Esperanza for her Little Nun services. "The kids are fascinated by my typewriter. I let them peck out their name as Mom waits for her order. Older ones type out raps and poems." Grown-ups seek her services, too. "No one has typewriters anymore, none that work. But typewritten letters are special. Some folks come with letters they've composed on a computer they want me to type out for them and make one of a kind. Before Valentine's or Mother's Day, I could sit here for hours and type notes for folks lined up around the block. If I charged, I'd be as rich as a good florist." For such personal service Esperanza may accept a free coffee. Regular in the mornings. Decaf in the afternoon.

* * *

"**THIS ONE FELLOW** was waiting for his coffee and started telling me about an old typewriter he had thrown out. He wished he still had it. He was going to ask his girlfriend to marry him. If he did so in a typed letter, it and the moment would last forever. What could I do but roll in a new sheet and let him dictate? I was his Steno-of-Love. We did six different drafts." What did he say to pop the question? I asked. "None of your business." Did the girlfriend say yes? "I have no idea. He read over the letter a dozen times to make sure the words fit the occasion. Then he left with it and a vanilla-shot cappuccino and has not been seen since."

* * *

HER PORTABLE TYPE-WRITER allows Esperanza to take her keyboard services anywhere, but Java-Va-Voom is her faux Plaza

Centrale. "This place puts up with me and gets my mind churning. I like having people around," she said. "And, some of them have come to need me." Oh, more than you may know, **Evangelista** Esperanza!

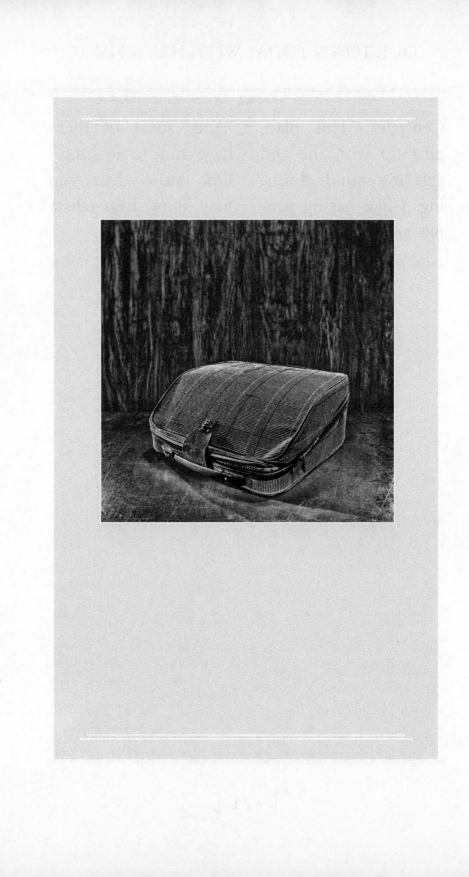

Steve Wong Is Perfect

— ◆ —

Because videos go around the world in nano-seconds, little pigs are celebrated for saving little lambs from drowning. No, wait. That video was an Internet hoax. What Steve Wong did was real, it happened, in front of witnesses, even, so he went viral.

We went bowling one night, you see, and Steve truly was the alley-ooper who threw or rolled—who **bowled**—an impossible number of strikes, so he deserves the reverence of all who bowl for fun and profit. Still, if you had not been there to eye-ball Steve's run, you might think Anna, MDash, and I had faked it all.

Steve's accomplishments were not falsified, nor were they a fluke. He'd been the captain of the Freshman Bowling Team at St. Anthony Coun-try Day High School, winning trophies at Young Bowler Tournaments at the Surfside Lanes. He even had a perfect game—twelve consecutive strikes for a score of 300—when he was only thirteen years old. His name was in the paper and he was given a lot of free swag from the Surfside.

When MDash hit the Year-One anniversary of his becoming a U.S. citizen, we celebrated by taking him bowling. We convinced him that it was a great American Tradition, that immigrants from Vietnam, Chile, et al. went bowling after a year of citizenship and that he should, too. He bought it. Steve Wong brought his professional-quality glove for his rolling hand as well as his custom-made bowling shoes! We wore crummy rentals with mismatched laces that were kept in dank cubbies behind the front desk while he wore one-of-a-kind yellow and brown bowling slippers, STEVE and WONG written across the toes, with three Xs on each heel—XXX—representing the final frame of that perfect game of years before. The shoes came in a matching bag in the same hideous two-tone brown-yellow. We kept rubbing them, hoping to summon a genie as if they were magic lamps. When our beers arrived, I hollered, "My wish came true!"

MDash had never bowled in his native sub-Saharan village, so we got him his own lane and had the staff pull up the kiddie rails, the things that help little kids keep their balls out of the gutter. With his ball ricocheting from bumper to bumper, he always hit some pins for a high score of 58. My top game was 138—respectable as hell, what with all the Rolling Rocks I'd chugged. Anna, bless her, focused so much on her mechanics that she beat my high by six pins—a 144. Flushed with the thrill of victory over me, she was giddy, wrapping up MDash in her taut-as-coiled-rope arms and calling him "our American friend."

But the surprise of the night was Steve Wong and his alley prowess. His three games—236, 243, and a final high of 269—made moot our competitive loop. He was so good we grew fatigued marveling at the splits he turned into spares. At one point he rolled eleven straight strikes over two games. I threatened to steal that glove of his and burn it.

"Next time I'll bring my own ball," he told us. "I couldn't find it."

"But you keep those ugly shoes where you can grab them in a jiffy?"

We bowled again the next week, the four of us. Steve found his ball with my help. I picked him up from his too-big house in Oxnard and went through the garage and three closets. His bowling ball bag—that lovely yellow and brown leather—was behind an old, beat-up plaid typewriter case on the highest shelf in what had been his sister's closet, next to a box that held about a hundred old Barbie dolls with vacant smiles and impossibly trim waists. The ball was also that odd color combination, like a sphere of fake puke from a novelty store. The Chinese character for lightning was stamped within the trinity of finger holes. When we got to the Ventura Bowling Complex, he put the ball in a machine that turned out to be a bowling ball polisher. And he fitted Anna with her own glove, one with a lot of wrist support.

MDash was still on the bumpered lane beside our alley—his four games topped out with a high of 87. My first game was a 126, then I stopped caring because, well, we had bowled the week before and to my sensibility four games of bowling in one year is a fine total. Anna? Possessed! Again! She changed balls three times in the first game before going back to the rack for her original choice. With that special glove of hers, her concentration on her stride and on her release point, and constantly drying her palm with the little fan above the ball return, the woman flirted with 200 all night, finally topping out at 201. She was in such a good mood she took swigs from my beer.

And Steve Wong? With those three fingers of his slotted into the precision-fitted holes in that shiny orb, he put on a show of shows. His years

of experience appeared in the grace of his foot-
work, the arc of his swing, the release of his ball
hand sweeping upward to the projected computer
scoreboard. He had the balance of a dancer, his
cantilevered foot splayed behind his left shoe, his
right toe tapping the hardwood in a triple-X kiss
of brown and yellow. He never bowled less that
270 that night, finishing with a score of . . . 300.

That's right. The computer flashed PERFECT
GAME PERFECT GAME PERFECT GAME as the
manager rang an old ship's bell behind his desk.
Other patrons—who take bowling seriously—
came around and shook Steve's hand and slapped
his back and paid for every Rolling Rock I ordered,
proving that yes indeed, his were magic shoes.

We played again a couple of days later—at
MDash's demand. He'd been dreaming about the
game. "Sleeping, I can see the black ball, curving
to the 1 pin, to knock down all of them, but they
don't smash like I want. I want to smash them all
down!" Breaking 100 was now a Vision Quest
for him. On what would be only his third trip
to the lanes, he eschewed the kiddie bumpers and
promptly rolled five gutter balls in a row.

"Welcome to the varsity squad," I told him
before missing the 9 and 10 pins by a foot. Score
me an open-frame 8. Anna picked up a spare by

nicking the 7 pin so was already beating me. Last up, Steve Wong rolled a strike.

A flash flood begins with a drop of rain on stone. A forest fire tells with just a whiff of distant smoke. A perfect game of bowling is a possibility only when an X is recorded in the little box in the corner of frame number 1, the first of twelve in a row. Steve Wong racked up nine straight strikes, so in the tenth and final frame of our first game that night—MDash posted a 33, and I had a 118, Anna a 147—a gang had gathered around our lane, about thirty people (by frame 6 the other games had quit to watch what might be Steve Wong's second perfect game in a row—an oddity and marvel as rare as twin rainbows).

He opened the tenth with a strike. The crowd crowed and Anna screamed out, "Atta baby!" A hush fell, Steve strolled and swiped, and all ten pins fell again, his eleventh strike of the game with one more needed for perfection redux. It would be a bad joke to say, "You could hear a pin drop," but you could. Dead silence met Steve's final roll. When PERFECT GAME PERFECT GAME PERFECT GAME honked on the computer scoreboard, you'd have thought it was New Year's Eve on the same night the Brooklyn Bridge opened, Neil Armstrong walked on the moon, and Saddam Hussein was dragged from his spider hole. Wong-mania was in full force, and we didn't get out of the place until exactly three in the morning—3:00. Get it?

Had we bothered with a second game that night, you might not be reading this. Steve could have bowled a 220 and then played pinball. But Fate is a kooky dame. Four nights later, bowling for free as a prize for his twenty-four consecutive "tens-at-one-blow," we returned for a goofy night of watching MDash try for something other than an open-gutter 33. But Steve Wong altered the tenor of the evening by rolling Chinese **Lightning** for a strike. He then rolled another. And, well, holy cow, as they say at bowling alleys on the subcontinent of India.

Steve rolled strike after strike, talked less and less, and entered a Concentration Zone that blocked out the rest of existence. He said nothing, never sat down, and never looked at what was happening behind him. People were texting their bowl mates to get down to the lanes on the PDQ. Free pizza was delivered. Smart-phone cameras came out in force, and a family of six showed up, the little kids in their pajamas, pulled out of bed because a sitter could not be found and Mom and Dad did not want to miss another perfect game. Steve Wong had yet to bowl anything other than a big black X for his third game in a row. In an atmosphere of utter wonder and magic, he kept right on smacking down thirty-point frames for his fourth, fifth, and—wait for it—sixth game. In a row.

We were openmouthed and hoarse from screaming, the three of us, huddled around the little desk between lanes 7 and 8, surrounded by a crowd of 140 and then some. I had stopped bowling. Anna began pacing instead of playing in the fifth frame of game 2, not wanting to somehow mar the alley and screw up Steve's run. Only MDash kept rolling, two gutter balls to every one that found the stack.

Huzzahs rose and fell from lofty levels to silences thick with stilled lungs. Anna's "Atta baby" became the common cheer not just for each of Steve's strikes but, charitably, for MDash's knockdowns as well. When the seventy-second consecutive strike for S. Wong was computed as his sixth perfect game in a row, the man-in-full stood at the foul line rubbing his eyes, his back to the berserk crowd, which screamed and stamped and pounded bottles of beer and cups of soda. None of us had ever been present for that kind of achievement— trivial to some, as what is bowling but a game? But come on! Six perfect **anythings** are a permanent memory.

Check out the Internet for videos of the evening and you'll see Steve stone-faced as strangers and pals celebrate him like a congressman-elect. Look at the comments: about 90 percent of the Anonymous Horde call it a hoax, but never mind them. The next day Steve was fielding calls from media outlets that wanted comments, photos, and appearances on camera. He went on the local news, the four channels shooting him individually on lane 7 as he stood stiffly, the embodiment of on-camera discomfort. You actually roll all those perfect games? How's that feel, rolling all those perfect games? What were you thinking? You ever think you'd roll so many strikes? Yes. Good. Trying to get another. Nope.

Each camera crew asked him to finish the interview with a roll down the alley. He obliged with four strikes, on camera, on cue. The string continued. The capper was a call from ESPN for an appearance on a show called **Alley Nation**. They'd pay him seventeen hundred bucks for just showing up, and if he rolled **another** perfect game, he'd get one of those six-foot-tall checks for $100,000.

You'd think such a heady few days would be fun, with an invite to be on TV and all. But Steve comes from a long line of quiet, humble Wongs. He clammed up. MDash saw him at work at Home Depot, standing stock-still in Power Tools, supposedly racking saber saw blades, but all he was doing was staring at two different blades in their clamshell packaging like the labels were written in a foreign language. He woke up at night with the dry heaves. When we picked him up in my VW Bus to drive to the ESPN gig, he almost forgot the bags with his monogrammed shoes and Chinese **Lightning**.

The show was going to be at Crowne Lanes in Fountain Valley—a long drive, so we stopped at an In-N-Out burger before hitting the freeway. In the drive-thru lane, Steve finally confessed what had been bothering him. He did not want to bowl on TV.

"You against the idea of getting free money?" I asked him. "The closest I've ever been to a hundred K was a Powerball ticket with two numbers right."

"Bowling should be fun," Steve said. "Laughs in an informal social contract. We roll when our turn comes up and no one cares about the score."

MDash wanted him to take his winnings in silver dollars.

Steve continued as we crawled through the line. In-N-Out is always busy. "I stopped competitive bowling at St. Anthony Country Day when it became a letter sport. You had to file an application and sign score sheets. Keep up an average. It wasn't fun anymore. It was stressful then. It's stressful now."

"Look at me, Stevie baby," Anna said, reaching around the seat and grabbing his face in her hands. "Relax! There is nothing you can't do on a day like today!"

"On what waiting room poster did you read that?"

"I'm just saying, turn this day into fun with a capital F. Today, Steve Wong, you are going to go on TV and you are going to have fun. Fun fun fun fun."

"I don't think so," Steve said. "Nope, nope, nope, nope."

Crowne Lanes had been a site for PBA tournaments. There were grandstand-style seats and ESPN banners, lights for the TV, and multiple cameras. When Steve saw the seats filled with avid bowling fans, he let out a cussword, rare for Steve Wong.

An exhausted woman with a headset and a clipboard found us.

"Which one of you is Steve Wong?" MDash and I raised our hands. "Okay. You'll be on lane 4 after the game between Shaker Al Hassan and Kim Terrell-Kearny. The winner of that plays the winner of the Kyung Shin Park–Jason Belmonte game for the final. Nothing's expected of you until then."

Steve went out to the parking lot to pace with

Anna on his heels, talking about how **fun** it must be to work at ESPN. MDash and I grabbed sodas and sat in a VIP section to see Kyung Shin Park beat Jason Belmonte by 12 in what was a damn fine exhibition of the hardwood game of tenpin. In the second game, MDash rooted hard for Shaker Al Hassan—he knew a lot of Al Hassans before coming to the USA—but Kim Terrell-Kearny (who was a woman pro, by the way) nipped him 272–269. While the cameras were being rolled over to lane 4 and the crew started tweaking the lights, the crowd milled about and Anna came looking for us.

"Steve is throwing up in the parking lot," she told us. "Between the TV trucks."

"Nerves?" I wondered.

"Are you an idiot?" she asked.

MDash left us to get a selfie with Shaker Al Hassan.

I found Steve sitting outside on a low wall by the entrance, his head in his hands like he was fighting a fever and might **chook** again.

"Wong-o," I said, squeezing his shoulder. "Here's what you are going to do today. You roll Chinese **Lightning** a couple of times. You go home seventeen hundred bucks to the better. Easy. Breezy."

"Can't do that, man." Steve raised up his head, eyes to the horizon across the parking lot. "Everyone expects god damn perfection. Drive me home right now."

I sat with him on the low wall. "Let me ask you a question. Is this bowling alley not like every bowling alley on the planet, with the foul line and the arrows in the wood? Are there ten pins down at the other end of the lane? Will your ball come back to you magically via an underground slot?"

"Oh, I see. You are giving me a pep talk."

"Answer my insightful questions."

"Yes. True. Golly, jeepers, I see that you are right. Everything will be hunky-dory now that you have talked some sense into me." Steve was speaking in a monotone. "I'm special and I can do anything I set my mind to and dreams do come true if I just carpe diem."

"Atta baby," I said. We did not move for a couple of minutes. The exhausted woman in the headset came yelling for us that it was **post time** for Steve Wong.

He ran his fingers through his jet-black hair, and then rose up, letting loose with a string of very un-Wong expletives. Good thing his parents weren't around.

———

When Steve put on those ugly bowling shoes, a ripple of "hey . . . that's that **guy** . . ." went through the crowd. His Internet legend had preceded him. When the tape was rolling and he was introduced by the host of **Alley Nation,** the place echoed with applause. Even the pro bowlers looked over at lane 4.

"Steve Wong," the host intoned. "Six perfect games in succession. Seventy-two strikes in a row. But questions linger as to whether your incredible streak has been the creation of clever editing and computer special effects. What is your reaction to such allegations?" The host stuck the microphone up to Steve's lips.

"Makes sense, what with the Web being the Web." Steve's eyes darted from the host to the crowd to us to the floor and back to the host—all so fast it looked like he was having an attention-induced seizure.

"Have you ever thought you'd reach such a level of technique and form that so many closed frames would be in your game?"

"I just bowl for fun."

"The official record for straight strikes is held by Tommy Gollick at forty-seven, but here you claim to have rolled twenty-four consecutive Turkeys. Many in the bowling world wonder if such a string is even possible."

I turned to a fellow next to me who, with his bowling shirt emblazoned with a Crowne Lanes logo, must have been a citizen of Alley Nation. "What does he mean by **Turkeys?**" I asked him.

"Three strikes in a row, dipshit. And no way in hell did that punk roll twenty-plus of 'em." He then yelled **"Hoax!"** at the top of his lungs.

"As you may hear, Steve Wong, there are some who doubt not just your claim but also the word of the manager of your home alley, the Ventura Party, Billiards, and Bowling Complex."

Steve looked the crowd over, probably seeing only the glaring eyes of unbelievers. "Like I said. I bowl for fun."

"Well, as I always say, the proof of any bowler is in the crash of pins, so, Steve Wong, step up to the line and show us what game you brought with you today. And remember, folks, a great time is waiting for you and your family at your nearby Bowling Alley and Fun Center. Take up bowling and get on a roll."

Steve walked to the ball return, strapping on his glove as the three of us hooted and hollered "Atta baby." Some in the crowd catcalled. Steve heaved a sigh so deep and soulful we could see his shoulders sag, and we were perched far away in the upper row. He turned his back to us all and sighed again. By the time he took Chinese **Lightning** into his hands and placed his fingers into the ball's custom-drilled holes, we who knew

Steve Wong could tell this about him—he was not having fun.

And yet, his movements were still a vision of grace, his release of the ball smooth and effortless, the flick of his hand applying the same spin we had seen so many times, his fingers reaching for the ceiling in one hand waving free, the toes on his right foot tap-tapping on the hardwood akimbo to his left shoe, XXX flashing from his heels.

Rumble. Smash. Strike. Cries of "Lucky!" echoed throughout Crowne Lanes. Steve, his back to the world, cooled his hand waiting for Chinese **Lightning** to appear from below. With ball in hand, he assumed the pose and did it again. Rumble. Smash. Strike number 2.

Then came strikes number 3 through 6, netting a score of 120 in the fourth frame. Steve had turned the crowd decidedly in his favor, but I doubt he noticed. He didn't so much as glance our way.

Shaker Al Hassan was asked what he thought of Steve's form. "Unworldly magnificent!" he said on camera to all citizens of Alley Nation.

Strikes 7, 8, and 9 had all four professionals weighing in on Steve's balance, his mechanics, his cool-under-pressure command, in what Kyung Shin Park called "the Tunnel" and Jason Belmonte knew as the "Line of Fate." Kim Terrell-Kearny said the PBA had a place for a competitor as poised as Steve Wong.

When ten X-ed frames were superimposed on the TV monitors, the host became flabbergasted—actually saying, "I am flabbergasted by the performance of this fine young example to bowlers everywhere!" The crowd was on its feet shouting encouragements equal to those for the gladiators of Ancient Rome. Steve's eleventh roll was a surreal moment in time, a dream ballet, a free fall out of the sky that hit the perfect pocket between the 1 and 3 pins and **kablooey** went all eight of the rest of them.

With one last strike needed for a perfect game, $100,000, and ESPN immortality, Steve soft-shoed to the ball return without any tell of emotion—no expectation, no anxiety, no fear. No fun, either. As far as I could tell from the back of his head, his face must have looked like an open-eyed death mask.

As he held his ball before his heart in preparation for his windup, something more encompassing than silence fell on Crowne Lanes—a void of sound, like the room had been vacuum-pumped of atmosphere, robbing sound waves of their purchase. Anna's fingers were digging into MDash's and my arms, the words **atta baby** forming mutely on her lips.

The exact moment of the beginning of Steve's twelfth and final roll was imperceptible, like the slow liftoff of a rocket to the moon, so heavy a thing that nothing moves despite the ignition of boosters and all the flames and fury. The nanosecond Chinese **Lightning** hit the hardwood a roar exploded so loud you'd have thought every member of Alley Nation was on the cusp of simultaneous orgasm with the love of his or her life. A SABRE jet engine is not as loud as the roof-busting blare that grew and grew as that brown and yellow orb spun along its arc. Just inches from the impact of ball on pin, Crowne Lanes was engulfed in a wall of sound.

The smash of ball in the pocket just between pins 1 and 3 happened in some other place, a clap of thunder a hundred miles away. We all saw the flash of white, like the smile of a giant with perfect teeth suddenly busted, all ten pins scattering and clattering until what was left was empty space and dead soldiers—ten of them.

Steve stood at the foul line surveying the emptiness at the other end of the alley as upright pins appeared on automatic reset. As the host was yelling into his headset, "Steve Wong is perfect!" our friend knelt on one knee, appearing to thank God-as-he-knew-God for such a triumph.

Instead, he was unlacing his left shoe—STEVE. He took it off and set its toe on the foul line. He did the same to WONG on the right, neatly setting his custom-made bowling footware so that XXX showed on TV.

In stocking feet, he padded to the ball return and took up that which had already been delivered. Carrying Chinese **Lightning** in two hands like it was nothing more than a paving stone, he set it on top of his shoes in a gesture that Anna, MDash, and I knew to mean, "I will bowl no more. Forever."

As he tossed his bowling glove into the crowd—setting off a melee for the memorabilia hounds—Kim Terrell-Kearny ran up and kissed his cheek in an embrace, while the other pros offered handshakes and head rubs.

By the time we made our way through the adoring bowlers—all of them now fans—Anna was weeping. She threw her arms around Steve Wong and sobbed so deeply I was worried she would pass out. MDash kept saying something in his native language, a superlative, I am sure. I toasted Steve with a beer I had found in a cooler by one of TV cameras, then grabbed his stack of bowling gear and stuffed it all in his bowling bag.

Only the three of us heard him say, "I'm glad that's over."

None of us went bowling again for the next few months, though not by plan. I had a dime-size growth on my leg that went all raised up and spooky on me, so I scheduled outpatient surgery to have it removed, sliced away, potato-peeled off. Nothing serious. MDash got a new job, walking away from his career possibilities at Home Depot for a position at Target, his new workplace separated from his former job by a vast, shared parking lot. He walked to the other store, changed his polo shirt, and never looked back. Anna took fly-fishing lessons at a place run by the Parks Department—at the Stanley P. Swett Municipal Casting Ponds, a place no one had ever heard of or could find without Google Maps. She tried to get me to sign up along with her, but I look on fly-fishing as a companion sport to luge racing—never will I do either one.

Steve Wong's life settled down. He figured out how many ESPN dollars would go to taxes and planned accordingly. He went back to work, had to take selfies with customers for a while, and told MDash that leaving Home Depot for Target was like emigrating from his sub-Saharan home country to North Korea (such is the competitive rhetoric of Home Depot management). One thing Steve never did talk about was bowling.

But one night, there we were, bowling for free,

the regulars at the lanes sidling up to Steve for bumps with the fist that had rolled those perfect games. Steve and I arrived first. I had picked him up, but he came out of his house empty-handed!

"You dope!" I said as he climbed into the shotgun seat of the VW Bus.

"What?"

"Go back inside and get your stuff. Your shoes and your bag and Chinese **Lightning**."

"Okay," he said, after a long pause.

By the time Anna arrived, then MDash, I had finished a Rolling Rock and Steve was pumping quarters into a video motocross game. We carried his equipment down to our assigned lane, changed into our rental shoes, and picked out our bowling balls, Anna considering every single one, I think. When we called to Steve that we were ready to begin, he was still racing on the machine and just waved blindly for us to start without him. We ended up playing two games, just the three of us. Anna won both, I lost them, and MDash was crowing about being a Silver Medalist over me.

Steve came down to our lane and watched the last frames of that second game. We were debating whether or not to go again, since it was getting late and it was a Thursday night. I wanted to go home, MDash wanted to beat Anna for the Gold, and she wanted to crush all our dreams for the third straight time in one evening. Steve didn't care what we did, saying he would sit out the next line and maybe have a beer or two.

"You aren't going to bowl with us?" Anna was incredulous. "When did you get so stuck-up?"

"C'mon, Steve," MDash pleaded. "You and bowling mean America to me."

"Put your shoes on," I told him. "Or you are walking home."

Steve sat there for a moment, then called us a bunch of jerks and took off his street shoes to change into his ugly bowling footwear.

I rolled first, hitting a paltry four on my first ball, then missing the remaining pins by millimeters. MDash nearly died laughing. His first ball left three standing, which he then clobbered to pick up the spare.

"Tonight," he hissed at Anna, "you are going to die!"

"Bit heavy with the taunts," she told him. "No one dies bowling unless a tornado is involved." She then knocked down nine of the pins and expertly closed the frame on her second ball—she and MDash were tied.

Then came Steve Wong, sighing as he took his custom ball out of its custom bag, the spherical tool of his legendary alley work. I may exaggerate by saying the bowlers in the place stopped what they were doing to watch a master at work, that the whole joint suddenly went silent, wondering if, somehow, **Lightning** would strike again and start another chain reaction of perfect games, proving that Steve Wong was the true God of Turkeys. I think it was mostly in my head.

He stood still on the lane, holding the ball once again to his heart, his eyes locked on the faraway wedge of ten white pins. Then he began his swing and step-step-stepped to the lip of the foul line and released **Lightning,** lifting his bowling hand up to the sky. His right toe tapped the floor behind his left heel, the total of six Xs displayed for all to see. His ball curved and spun down the long lines of the shiny hardwood, headed for that pocket between the 1 and 3 pins, looking to be a strike for sure.

Acknowledgments

Many thanks to Anne Stringfield, Steve Martin, Esther Newberg, and Peter Gethers—the four in-laws of these married words.

Special credit to E. A. Hanks for her blue pencil and sharp, honest eyes.

Plus, a tip of the cap and a buck apiece to Gail Collins and Deborah Triesman.

And thanks to all those at Penguin Random House who examined, admired, improved, and made presentable these stories.

A NOTE ABOUT THE AUTHOR

Tom Hanks has been an actor, screenwriter, director, and, through Playtone, a producer. His writing has appeared in **The New York Times, Vanity Fair,** and **The New Yorker.** This is his first collection of fiction.